Also by James Scott Bell

Try Dying

Try Darkness

Available from Center Street wherever books are sold.

TRY FEAR

JAMES SCOTT BELL

CENTER STREET

NEW YORK   BOSTON   NASHVILLE

Center Street
Hachette Book Group
237 Park Avenue
New York, NY 10017

Visit our Web site at www.centerstreet.com.

Center Street is a division of Hachette Book Group, Inc.
The Center Street name and logo are trademarks of Hachette Book Group, Inc.

Printed in the United States of America

First Edition: July 2009
10 9 8 7 6 5 4 3 2 1

Library of Congress Cataloging-in-Publication Data
Bell, James Scott.
  Try fear / James Scott Bell.—1st ed.
    p. cm.
  ISBN 978-1-59995-686-2
  1. Buchanan, Ty (Fictitious character)—Fiction. 2. Los Angeles (Calif.)—Fiction.
I. Title.

PS3552.E5158T794   2009
813'.54—dc22

2008050885

My memories of growing up in L.A. come to me mostly in black and white. I see myself as a kid stepping through an episode of *Perry Mason*. That's because my dad was an L.A. criminal lawyer, and I remember downtown as being made up of white, sun-bleached buildings, hot in the summer sun. When I first rode Angels Flight with Dad—I was six, and Dad was involved with a grassroots movement to save the venerable L.A. landmark, a movement that was ultimately successful—it was to the top of the Bunker Hill from *Criss Cross*, the Burt Lancaster noir classic (a black-and-white film, of course). And when I recall first seeing my dad in court, it was in the days of the fedora, which TV shows never depicted in living color.

There were a few things about Dad that remain "black and white," in symbolic terms, too. Dad did not tolerate racism. He had played baseball at UCLA with Jackie Robinson, was even his roommate on road trips, and as a defender of poor clients brooked no color barriers when it came to justice. He taught me to think the same way, and made me want to become a trial lawyer like him. So I did. And even got to work with him, as his office mate, in the last few years of his life.

And so this book is dedicated to a great L.A. lawyer and a great man—my dad, Arthur S. Bell, Jr.

ACKNOWLEDGMENTS

The author is greatly indebted to the following for their exceedingly valuable help in the preparation of this book and series: Cindy Bell, Christina Boys, Manuel Muñoz, Leah Tracosas, Karen Thompson, Al Menaster, Gina Laughney, Rene Gutteridge, Ellen Tarver, Michael J. Kennedy, Sgt. Mike Sayre, LAPD, Capt. Tom Brascia, LAPD, and Special Agent Michael Yoder, FBI.

Fear at my heart, as at a cup,
My lifeblood seemed to sip.

—Coleridge

1

THE COPS NABBED Santa Claus at the corner of Hollywood and Gower. He was driving a silver Camaro and wearing a purple G-string and a red Santa hat. And nothing else on that warm December night.

According to his driver's license his name was Carl Richess, a thirty-three-year-old from West Hollywood.

But he insisted he was the one, the only, Santa Claus. He said he could prove it, too. He pointed repeatedly to his hat.

The police officer who initiated the stop—for not wearing a seat belt—mentioned the Santa hat in his report, and the G-string. Also the open, nearly empty bottle of Jose Cuervo Gold on the seat next to the jolly elf.

After noting red eyes, slurred speech, and the odor of an alcoholic beverage, the officer ordered Richess out of his car for field sobriety tests.

Richess protested that he was late, that his reindeer needed to be fed. He said this even as he was failing the heel-to-toe and lateral gaze nystagmus tests.

He loudly screamed the same thing at Hollywood station, where they had him blow into the Intoximeter a couple of times. And again when they cuffed him to a metal rod on one of the wooden benches outside the holding tank. He was still muttering about reindeer when they booked him into the jail and stuck the six-foot-five, 280-pound would-be Kringle in a cell. They gave him some old clothes to cover himself.

They took his hat, let him keep the G-string.

Three others shared the community cell with St. Nick—two gangbangers and a Korean street performer who'd been fire-eating in front of the Pantages Theater. I found out later he set a well-dressed woman's hair on fire, which is against several city ordinances.

About the time Father Christmas was being cuffed and stuffed—copspeak for arrested and jailed—I was nursing a Gandhi Latte at the Ultimate Sip. The Sip is an honest coffee establishment owned and operated by one Barton C. "Pick" McNitt, a former philosophy professor at Cal State Northridge who went crazy and now pushes caffeine and raises butterflies for funeral ceremonies.

He makes up drinks that have philosophical significance. He is serious about this. He came up with the Gandhi Latte because his style of foam, he believes, encourages nonviolence in those who drink it.

This has yet to be proven scientifically.

Pick also waxes loud on any subject he deems appropriate for the betterment, or castigation, of mankind. He does not believe in God. Father Robert Jackson, who everybody calls Father Bob, does. In the middle I sometimes sit, watching a philosophical Wimbledon.

But on this particular night there was no match, so I was wrestling with the *Dialogues of Plato*. That's one thing to do if you're trying to recalibrate your life and figure out what, if anything, it means. At that moment it was a tie between *not much* and *something just out of reach*. Which is why I was digging hard into the dialogue called *Phaedrus*.

And then I got a call from Father Bob.

"There's a fellow in jail in Hollywood," he said. "He needs a lawyer."

"Anyone in jail in Hollywood needs a lawyer," I said.

"I mean it. His mother called me, very upset."

"What's he in for?"

"He told his mother he sort of got arrested for drunk driving and telling the police he was Santa Claus."

I cleared my throat. "My dear Father, it is illegal to drive drunk, but not to say you are Santa Claus."

"He was dressed in a Santa hat and, I guess, a G-string. That's what he told his mother, anyway."

I put the *Dialogues* down on the table. "Are you sure it's a lawyer he needs?"

"His mother says he's been under a lot of strain lately."

"Does he have money to pay a lawyer?"

"His mother does."

"I'm reading Plato."

"She was in tears."

"I would be, too, if my son got busted in a G-string."

"Ty, will you go?"

"To see Santa Claus?" I said. "By golly, who wouldn't?"

2

LAPD's HOLLYWOOD STATION is a squat brick building on Wilcox, south of Sunset, across the street from the appropriately named SOS Bail Bonds. I got there a little before ten and parked in front. It was a Wednesday night, quiet in Hollywood. Tomorrow the club scene would start in earnest and fill the weekend.

At the front desk I put my card down and told the desk officer I was there to pick up Richess.

He laughed. "Santa?"

"He'd be the one," I said.

"Biggest Santa I've ever seen," the officer said. He had short black hair and a pointed chin. His name plate said HOWSER.

"Can we cite him out?" I said, meaning Richess wouldn't have to post bond. I knew the decision would depend on his previous record, and what he said or did since they popped him.

Howser said, "I'll be back." He got up and went into the inner office, leaving me with a kid, maybe eighteen, who was sitting by the vending machine, head in hands.

I looked around. On the wall, facing the desk, were some framed portraits. I had no idea who they were. A couple of them looked 1950s vintage. Severe hair. Serious looks. Jack Webb types. It was Webb and *Dragnet* that made the LAPD famous. So I've been told. I never saw *Dragnet*. I grew up on Thomas Magnum.

When I was twelve I almost ran away to Hawaii. I was going to work until I was eighteen, then get a private investigator license. My mom put the kibosh on that. My dad had died a couple years earlier and she wasn't about to let me even think something stupid.

But she did buy me some Hawaiian shirts. I wore them all summer, tucked into jeans. Little Magnum.

Howser came back and said I was in luck. "If you call it luck."

"Meaning?"

"I'm authorized to tell you his reading, on both tests, was point one-eight. Sound's like a fun one to handle, huh?"

"Fun's why I went into law," I said. "How dull would it be if my clients blew oh-threes."

"He'll be out. Have a seat." Howser went back to his computer monitor.

I sat on one of the black metal bench seats and waited. A middle-aged woman in a faded pink sweatshirt came in the front doors and used the QuickDraw. They put ATMs in a lot of the stations so people can get money without fear of being robbed on the street.

Now if they could only put in a machine where criminal defense lawyers could withdraw a little respect.

A couple of plainclothes detectives came in. I could tell because they went right through the door marked "Detectives." I am very sharp that way.

Through it all the kid by the vending machine just sat there, looking at nothing in particular. Probably waiting for someone to pick him up. I wondered who it would be. Did he have a father, one who was actually around? Or one who liked to take out his own frustrations on the kid's skin?

Did he have a mother who cared about him? Or did she like to get high while her kid went out and did whatever the hell he wanted?

Part of me wanted to talk to him. Wanted to say, *Look, if your parents are around, and they're halfway decent, don't do this to them. It's not worth it. Don't—*

The door next to the front desk opened and an officer came out with Carl Richess. I could tell it was him because he was holding his Santa hat. At least they were letting him keep the ill-fitting clothes that now covered him.

Ill fitting because Richess was huge. He had a head like a mastiff. Jowly, in keeping with his girth. Furrows in his forehead deep enough to hold loose change.

"My mom call you?" he asked after I introduced myself. His breath could have peeled paint.

"She called her priest, who called me," I said. "Don't say anything else."

I signed him out and got him to my car.

3

"WHAT ABOUT MY car?" Richess said as we headed for the freeway.

"You'll have to get it out of impound," I said.

"What'll happen to me? Will I go to jail?"

"You been convicted before?"

"Never."

"Arrested?"

"No."

"Okay, if you plead out, for a first offense, no jail time," I said. "You'll have your license suspended. Three years probation, DUI school. Fine, penalty, assessments. Standard package."

"I don't wanna plead."

"Not many of us do."

"We can fight it."

I smiled. "Yes, we can fight it, but I have to tell you, you go to trial and lose, you'll get slammed by the judge. You'll do the max."

"Then don't lose."

"Santa Claus, my jolly friend, you blew a one-eight."

"So?"

"So that's over twice the limit. Contesting a first deuce with a reading that high is a bad idea, unless you can find some obvious error. Like the machine was dropped in the toilet before the test. Or a rogue police officer poured a whole bottle of Cuervo down your throat, started your car, and sent you down the highway, and somebody captured it all on digital."

Richess was silent. I hoped his brain was soaking up what I said. I wanted him to be disabused of any fantasies concerning his situation. A little straight talk up front saves a lot of grumbling down the line.

"Don't mind my asking," I said, "what were you doing in a G-string and Santa hat?"

"What's that matter?"

"Just like to have all the facts, put it that way."

He grunted. It sounded like a dog holding in a belch. "I was just being crazy. I was at a party and got crazy."

"That's one word for it."

Carl burped, hiccupped, and groaned.

"What do you do when you're not doing Santa?"

"Concrete," he said. "So can you do anything for me or not?"

"I'll check out everything I can. When we go in for the arraignment, you'll dress in a suit and tie, and you'll act sorry for what you've done, and we'll see what the best deal we can make is."

Santa sighed. "No," he said. "No deals."

"At least hear their offer."

"No. We fight. We prove the machine was wrong."

"We?"

"Can you?"

"Carl, a toaster could have told them you were drunk. Machine error might work on the threshold, but not on a one-eight."

"I don't care. I want to fight. I want somebody to fight for me. You're getting paid, aren't you?"

"Not yet."

"You don't want to rep me, I'll find somebody else."

"Frosty the Snowman's free," I said.

Carl Richess said nothing. A couple of minutes later he started snoring. He sounded like a leaf blower.

4

IT WAS A modest, two-bedroom home on Corbin Avenue in the part of the Valley called Winnetka. I pulled into the driveway next to a blue Civic that looked like it had seen a lot of miles.

I got out and went around and opened Carl's door. I shook him awake. He snorted and sat up. "Wussgoinon?" he said.

"Don't worry," I said. "You haven't missed it."

"Huh? Missed what?"

"Christmas Eve. Come on." I grabbed his arm and hauled him out. We went toward the front door. A light was on in the window. The door opened before we got there. A large woman, backlit, stood in the doorway.

"Carl," she said, distress in her voice.

"Hi, Mom," Carl said, like he was ten years old and had been caught picking the neighbor's flowers.

She put her arm around him and walked him inside. She looked back at me. "Please come in. I'm Kate."

I went in, closed the door, and waited as Kate took Carl toward a bedroom. I stayed by the door and looked around. The place seemed too small for the Richess family. This was more Mickey Rooney size.

But it had a warmth to it. Tidy, simple, and, I could imagine, full of laughter at one time. Before drunk driving charges. There was a wall with some family pictures, a few black and white that hearkened back to the forties or so. I could see a brick fireplace in the living room and a sandstone hearth.

Kate came back alone. "He just fell asleep in his old room," she said. "Was he very drunk?"

"Yes," I said.

"Please, come sit a moment."

Kate Richess looked in her late fifties. She had short brown hair with gray streaks, and wore a voluminous, orange-flowered muumuu above blue slippers. Her face had a kind of dignity. Immediately I thought she was a straight shooter, and one who expected you to be the same. In that way she reminded me of my own mom.

She had me sit in a recliner in her living room. I saw a couple of framed photos on the mantel. One was of a large kid in a football uniform. I assumed it was Carl. There was another one of a woman in a numbered jersey of blue and white.

She saw me looking at it. "I was on the Roller Derby circuit for a while," she said.

"No kidding," I said. "My mom used to watch that in Florida."

"She a fan?"

"Was. She passed away."

"I'm sorry. How long's it been?"

"I was fifteen," I said.

"That's hard," she said. Her eyes were sympathetic, inviting me to talk about it if I wanted to. That we had come to this level of intimacy so quickly told me a lot about Kate Richess. She was the kind of woman who opened her arms to the world, and sometimes got slapped for it. But would do it again if she thought you were hurting.

What she didn't know, and what I barely knew at the time, was that I was incapable of talking about my mom's death. That event was hidden away behind a locked door in a dark corner of my mind.

My dad's death was different. That was vivid to me. Maybe because I didn't see it, and my imagination took over. He died in the line of duty as a Miami cop. I was ten and remember all the details from the finding out, to the screaming into my pillow until I wore out and fell asleep, to the fear of the unknown, the wondering how I'd ever get along in life without him.

All those things I could see and hear, usually without willing it. Anything could set the visuals in motion. A black-and-white driving by. A cop movie trailer. Anything about cops, in fact. Or frightened boys, or funeral processions through city streets. Anything like that and then there they'd be—the pictures of Dad leaving my mom and me, spilled out all over my brain's landscape like a batch of color photos dropped from a plane.

Not so with Mom's death. All I had there were fuzzy images of hospital rooms and IVs and neighbors paying visits. And that's all I ever wanted to see.

It doesn't take a psych to know it was a defense, that at fifteen I wanted to push it all aside. I never talked about my mom dying to anybody. The family I went to live with after—my friend Vincent's—wasn't the warm, open kind, so it never came up.

Now, for some reason, with Kate I felt the key in the lock of that closed door starting to turn. I heard a click, and stopped it right there by saying, "I'm impressed. Roller Derby's not for wimps."

She smiled.

"Ever miss it?" I said.

"Sometimes I hear the sound of skates in my head. But then I remember

I have two blown-out knees and my right shoulder will never work like it used to. Still, I was one great blocker in my time."

"If you ever want to go down to Hi-Fi, catch a match, let me know." Hi-Fi is Filipinotown, northwest of downtown Los Angeles. A warehouse down there has become the center of a resurgent Roller Derby circuit in L.A.

"I don't know," Kate said. "The girls are a little different these days. Names like Eva Destruction and Broadzilla and Tara Armov. They're more into hurting each other than good theater."

"A little more punk than back in the day?"

"Not to say that in my prime I couldn't have taken one of these little wisps out. That was always fun. But fun doesn't last, and you get old." She sighed. "I gave it up when I got pregnant with Carl. He needed me because I'm all he has. Me and his brother. His father was not exactly present. He left for good when Carl was seven."

I said nothing. If she wanted to go on, she could.

"Donald was a big man," she said, "but not in the character department. He was a wrestler who never quite made it. And a drunk. Carl is like him in that way. He can't handle alcohol."

"That's the way it is for some."

"Can you help him at all?"

"I'll do what I can, Mrs. Richess, I—"

"Kate, please."

I nodded. "But I have to be up front. His breath test came out really high, and that's almost always the whole thing. If he pleads no contest, he'll get the standard first offense package."

"Will he have to go to jail?"

"No. But he told me he wants to go to trial. I have to do what he wants, but you need to be aware that if he loses at trial, the judge'll get a little mad. He'll think we're making him work for no good reason, clogging the system. They toss people in the can after all that."

She shook her head. "You know, Carl just never seems to get a break. Ever since he got out of the navy. He was going to get married, but when she left him, he kind of went into a spin. That's when he really started drinking a lot."

"Has he tried AA?"

"It didn't take." She looked at the window without looking out of it.

"Tell you what," I said. "Let me take a look at everything and see what's there, and I'll let you know."

She turned back, relief on her face. "That would be wonderful."

"Done."

"How much do I owe you?"

"You're one of Father Bob's parishioners?"

"I go to mass up at St. Monica's."

St. Monica's is the little Benedictine community in the Santa Susana Mountains where I get to stay, for the time being, in a trailer. The one next to Father Bob's.

"I know they're trying to raise money for their homeless shelter," I said. "Why don't you give a donation and we'll call it square?"

"Are you sure?"

"They're treating me nice up there. I offer some legal services for them. It all works out."

"I can't tell you how much that means to me," she said. She reached out her hand and I took it. It was delicate. So unlike what I would have associated with a Roller Derby queen. It reminded me of my mother's touch. Mom was a smallish woman, but fought like a tigress if she thought I was in need.

"It means a lot to me, too," I said.

And that was how I came to represent Santa Claus a little before Christmas.

5

SATURDAY MORNING MEANT my usual game of one-on-one with Sister Mary Veritas.

The sparky nun who had once run the hardwood of Oklahoma high school gyms likes to shoot hoop on the court in the back section of St. Monica's. It's right outside my trailer.

If I'm not up and ready by 7 a.m. on Saturday morning, she dribbles around and throws the ball against the board, until I get the message.

There was also something going on beneath the surface. In both of us.

Sister Mary had told me a while back that she didn't want me to leave St. Monica's. I ran after her and turned her around in an alcove and almost kissed her.

"Will I go to hell for this?" I said.

There was a second where it looked like she wanted to cross the line too, forget her vows, and in that second I felt sick.

We'd looked at the ground at the same time. Sister Mary muttered something about being late, and walked off.

I let her go that time. We hadn't spoken about the moment since. But there was always a little thread pulled taut between us. And I was afraid if there was one more tug the whole thing could unravel, in a way that was bad for both of us.

As usual, Sister Mary was in her sweats, with an OSU top (the orange and black of Oklahoma State, not the black and orange of Oregon State), and a pair of well-worn Converse All Stars.

And elbows of fury.

Even though I'm six-three and Sister Mary a little over five and a half feet, you don't want to get on her wrong side. Especially when playing hoop.

You don't often think of sisters of the Benedictine order pounding you in the paint or bodying you out of bounds. The Benedictines follow the Rule of St. Benedict, which is supposedly known for hospitality. They are compelled to receive guests as "Christ himself."

Which is not a feature of Sister Mary's game. Unless elbowing for Jesus is some form of acceptable piety.

Today, her game was extra intense. Her flashing blue eyes were concentrated, twin lasers. Even her short, chestnut-colored hair had attitude this day.

She really wanted to win this one, more than usual.

I played ball in college and know my way around the court. I'm deadly from twenty, and dangerous from downtown. Even have a spin move or two, and that after arthroscopic surgery on the left knee.

This morning, though, I could not get near the basket.

Sister Mary hipped me every time I got close.

At first, I laughed.

But then she started with the elbows and I got a little miffed.

"You trying to make the Olympic team or something?" I said.

"Bring it," she said.

Bring it?

I tried, but I was off. Every time I put up a shot, I had this terrier nun in my face.

It was, in its way, admirable. If she had been a litigator, I would have approved. I would have wanted her in court with me. I would have gladly let her cross-examine any hostile witness.

I staged a comeback and tied the score 10–10. "Are you sure you have the holy calling?" I said.

"You sure you want to keep playing?"

"*You* bring it."

And she did. She backed me into the paint, the way Charles Barkley used to do it.

Then she tried a little Magic Johnson hook, and I blocked it.

That brought a cry of frustration from Sister Mary.

I got the ball. She was snorting like a bull. I guess I was the cape.

I stayed outside. At the freethrow line I faked right, crossed over, stopped, and put up a fadeaway. It was beautiful. Nothing but net.

11–10.

As per the rules of one-on-one, I got the rock again. I took the ball to the top of the key and let Sister Mary check it. She dropped it back to me.

And got in a crouch. Her lips were tight. Her eyes were beams of blue flame. I thought, if she's this tough against sin, the Church is going to be perfect in a couple of years.

Boom, I gave her my best move, a stop and go, and was on my way to the hoop. It would be one for the highlight film. I went up.

And she undercut me.

Sister Mary Veritas, Catholic nun, speaker of Latin, gentle little lamb of the flowers of St. Monica's, went low bridge.

I landed on the asphalt. Hard. Little sparklers went off behind my eyes. I couldn't believe what just happened.

As I lay there, looking up at the sky, I said, "What was that?"

"Charge," she said.

"What?"

"You lowered your shoulder."

"What are you talking about?" My right arm was starting to throb.

"You fouled me," she said.

"*I'm* the one on the ground!"

"Oscar nominated."

Now I was hacked off. I scrambled to my feet. I'd started taking Brazilian Jiu-Jitsu at a studio in Canoga Park, and was thinking about practicing a hip throw on this overexuberant nun. Instead I said, "What is up with you today?"

"What is up with *you?*"

"You mean what is *down* with me, don't you?"

"It's my ball."

"How can it be your ball when you almost broke my neck?"

"You want to play or not?"

"Not until we review the Geneva Convention."

"Just forget it," she said. She broke into a jog and headed off toward her quarters.

6

I SAT ON the edge of the court in some grass and weeds and looked at the sky. At least, in the immortal words of Randy Newman, it looked like another perfect day.

When the sky is clear in L.A., when the sun shines in the winter, there's no better place on earth.

That's what I said.

See, it's days like this that bring out the envy in other cities. When we're tossing Frisbees on the beach in the winter, sub-zero curmudgeons dip their pens in bile and write things like Truman Capote once did—"It's redundant to die in L.A."

Or the wag who, no doubt with frostbitten digits, typed, "What's the difference between L.A. and yogurt? Answer: Yogurt has an active culture."

Will Rogers called it Cuckoo Land. H. L. Mencken dubbed it Moronia.

I call it home.

Even though I've been beat up and beat down here. That doesn't matter, because you can get beat up and beat down anywhere. That's the great thing about America.

But if it has to happen, it might as well happen in L.A. You can douse yourself in the Pacific or snowboard down a mountain.

You can regain your soul.

Which is not something I used to think about much. But I have been lately. Jacqueline thought about the soul and I want to think she lives on, somewhere.

That's why I'm reading Plato. I'd dipped in a little philosophy in college. It was kind of a goof then. Now it seemed to me maybe those Greeks had a window on something.

Father Bob came out of his trailer, the only other one on the grounds, and joined me. He's the only priest I know, the only black priest I've ever met, the only one I've ever heard of who can play jazz drums. He was sent to St. Monica's as a sort of exile, having been falsely accused of sexual abuse. I helped him clear his name, but the archdiocese wanted this sleeping dog to lie. Father Bob saw it as God's plan. I didn't.

"Game over so soon?" he said.

"What, were you watching us or something?"

"Just listening." He sat next to me. He was in jeans and a black T-shirt. He looked like a Beat poet. He pulled some grass and played with the blades. "You playing a little rough?"

"Me? That little nun of yours went all Spanish Inquisition on me."

He tossed the grass in the air. "You need to cut her a little extra slack."

"Maybe she needs to stop throwing elbows." I was half joking, half not.

"Lighten up."

"Hey, I'm fine."

"You sure?"

I just looked at him. He obviously wanted to say something to me, so I waited for him to say it.

After another grass toss, he said, "I want you to consider something your friend Plato said. About love."

"You're bringing Plato into this?"

"You've been reading him, haven't you?"

I nodded.

"Not all love is the same," Father Bob said. "There is the love that the body longs for, which can also be called lust. There is the love for another human being in a deep and meaningful way. And there is the love of knowledge and wisdom."

"What about the love of good pastrami?" I said.

"Plato did not include that, though he well could have. What I'm getting at is that the love of wisdom is the highest and best, because it directs the others. In dealing with Sister Mary, I ask you to be wise."

"All right, you've tiptoed around this long enough. What's wrong?"

"Sister Mary is quite vulnerable right now. She has an agile mind and creative spirit, as you well know."

"And sharp elbows."

"Be that as it may, she is under the all-seeing eye of Sister Hildegarde, and that is not a pleasant place to be."

"You're telling me." Sister Hildegarde is the head nun of this little community, and she runs the place like Castro's sister.

"I fear she is going to be driven from the community," Father Bob said. "That she will be found to be 'recalcitrant.' It's a black mark for a nun."

"Then we'll take it to the archdiocese, like I did with you. We'll fight."

Father Bob shook his head. "It is much more than that. It strikes directly at her calling. This is what she may be questioning. And you, my legal friend, complicate matters."

"How?"

"You know how."

I paused before answering. "You think I'm going to put a move on her?"

"Didn't you once?"

"I showed wisdom and restraint," I said. "The very thing you're telling me to do now."

"And you must continue to do so."

"I wouldn't have it any other way."

"Then you are wise," he said. "That's all I'm looking for." He stood up. "And now I'll get ready to head down to the Sip with you."

He went back to his trailer. A man comfortable in his own skin. Something I was not. Did he really have a bead on the truth? Or was it all just a happy illusion?

And is there anything wrong with that? If an illusion gets you through the day, big deal. If it puts an ice pack on the groin kicks of life, why not?

I tried to argue myself into believing that, but something about illusion bothers me. I always want to know the truth.

They say the truth shall set you free. But sometimes it just elbows you in the chops.

7

LATER THAT MORNING, Father Bob and I entered the Ultimate Sip.

Pick McNitt's place is in a strip mall on Rinaldi. Pick spent some time in a sanitarium, where Father Bob first visited with him by walking into the wrong room.

They argued then and have been friends ever since.

I pay Pick a little chunk each month for the use of the Sip as an office. And for a P.O. box in the little franchise Pick owns next door.

"Well there they are!" Pick shouted as we walked in. "The two most misguided men in the city and county of Los Angeles and perhaps in the whole of civilization."

He was spoiling for a debate, as usual. He was wearing his standard Hawaiian shirt, double X. With his bald head and full white beard, he could have been a Santa too. The Christmas spirit was getting a real going over with Pick and Carl Richess as reps.

"Two specials," Father Bob said.

Pick said, "There is no greater business than knowing thyself, as the divine Socrates said."

"Didn't Socrates commit suicide by drinking your coffee?" Father Bob winked at me as he took an Arturo Fuente cigar from his shirt pocket. He doesn't wear the collar on the street.

Pick himself smokes a pipe. Inside. He is on a one-man resistance effort against L.A. County smoking ordinances.

The Sip is adorned with scads of framed political cartoons Pick has drawn over the years. He did an especially wicked Nixon, but his Bill and Hillary Clinton make me crack up every time.

Pick delivered two Gandhi Lattes to our table. He sat, putting down his own cup of joe. He slid it toward us.

"Smell that," he said. "It's Joan of Arc."

"Joan of Arc?" Father Bob said.

"French roast," Pick said. He took out his pipe and packed it from a leather pouch. As he lit up he said, "Anything more on the death of God?"

And so it began once again. Wimbledon. I leaned back in my chair and listened.

"Greatly exaggerated," Father Bob said.

"It's in all the papers," Pick said. "Just look at the evil out there."

"The acts of evil men prove only the existence of evil, it doesn't—"

"Then God cannot be good," Pick said.

"At least now you admit God exists."

"I admit no such thing."

"Of course you do," Father Bob said with a glint in his eye. "You are arguing that the existence of evil isn't compatible with a good God. Okay, then it may be a bad God, but there is a God. We can argue about his character, but not his existence."

Pick blew a plume of smoke my way. I fought it off with my hands and a few coughs.

"I'm with Bertrand Russell," Pick said. "If I face God after death I will tell him, 'Sir, you did not give us enough evidence!' "

"To which he will reply," Father Bob said, " 'You chose to ignore the evidence you had.' "

"And then what? God sends me to hell for that? For eternity? Because I didn't see enough evidence?"

"It is not good to ignore evidence. Any decent lawyer will tell you that." Father Bob smiled at me.

"When you find a decent lawyer," Pick said, "send him over."

"Aren't all the lawyers in hell?" I asked. "Isn't that the old joke, where is God going to find a lawyer?"

"Better to reign in hell," Pick said, "than serve in heaven."

Father Bob took a puff on his cigar. "When he starts quoting Milton, I usually take my nap."

The door opened and a skinny, ponytailed guy of about thirty walked in. He wore a white T-shirt with a sprig of cannabis on it. "I'm looking for the lawyer," he said.

I offer free legal advice on Saturdays, for the benefit of the poor St. Monica's sends my way. But word has gotten out, and all sorts of wonderful clients seep in throughout the day.

Pick McNitt has taken to calling me Forrest Gump. Because, he says, I never know what I'm going to get.

Boy howdy.

8

I TOOK MY place at the table in the far corner, by the magazine rack. Pick, who is the only receptionist I have, told Mr. Ponytail to ride on over.

"My name's Only," he said.

"Only what?"

"Just Only."

"Only the Lonely?"

"Right on," he said, and laughed. Sort of a snort laugh. As he sat I caught a whiff of the Mary Jane.

"This is free legal advice?" he said.

"The Sisters of St. Monica's are raising funds for their homeless shelter," I said.

"St. Monica's?"

"Up in the hills. Donate on the way out. Whatever you can."

"Cool."

"How can I help you?"

"I got fired from the phone store, man," Only said.

"And?"

"And what?"

"Do you have an employment contract?"

"Contract?"

"I didn't think so. How about an employee's handbook?"

He shook his head.

"Were you given any verbal assurances, letters, e-mails, anything that would give you the impression you couldn't be fired except for good cause?"

"No, man."

"You're what's called an At Will employee, Mr. Only."

"Just Only, remember?"

"I may have some trouble with that, but listen. An At Will employee means they can fire you anytime, without cause."

"But—"

"And you can walk, whenever you want."

"I—"

"Unless they did something like harass you, or discriminate against you."

"That's it!" Only said, sticking his finger in the air.

"That's what?"

"Discrimination, man! That's what I been trying to tell you."

He was excited. I was not. I sighed. "Okay, and how did they discriminate against you?"

"I'm part of a minority."

"Are you gay or a woman?"

He blinked.

"Are you black or Hispanic?"

"No, but—"

"Jew or Muslim?"

"No."

"Quaker? Amish? *American Idol* loser?"

"I'm an American, period, and I demand my rights. I got a doctor's prescription."

"Medical marijuana," I said.

He smiled. "How'd you know?"

"Wild, wild guess."

"Right. And my doctor—"

"What's your condition?"

"I'm fine, man."

"I mean, that you smoke for?"

"Oh. Back pain."

"How'd you get a bad back?" I said.

"Skateboarding. I was bustin' an insane acid drop and had to bail."

I just looked at him, wondering why I went into law.

"Off my friend's roof," Only explained. "Caught a little air there."

"Let me see if I've got this straight," I said. "You skateboarded off your friend's roof and fell and hurt your back?"

"Yeah."

"And for that, you have a doctor's prescription to suck ganja for the pain."

"Right."

"Is this a great country or what?"

"Exactly," he said. "So I smoke a little at lunch. Not at work, lunch. The manager confronts me. I show him my prescription. But they fire me anyway. That's not right. They can't do that."

"But they can."

"How?"

"The California Supreme Court says they can." Now we were on my turf. I know squat about skateboarding and I've been off hemp since college. But California law is my meat. "Even though medical marijuana is legal here, and even if you only use it off work, and even though it doesn't even affect your job performance, an employer can still show you the door. Even if you're not an At Will employee."

"I can't believe that! What's happening to our country?"

"You got me, Only. It's not like the old days, is it?"

"No way. When Clinton was president, he understood. Even though he didn't inhale, he knew what the score was. So what do I do?"

"Smoke less, work more," I said. "And don't skateboard off any more roofs."

He frowned. Then smiled. Then frowned. Then smiled again. Like Stan Laurel.

"That's really good advice, man. Thanks."

It's nice when you can change a person's life for the better.

9

MY NEXT "CLIENT" was a woman—short, round, and fortyish—who wanted to sue her insurance company for bad faith. She had driven her Prius into her neighbor's garage door. The front end of her car was turned into an accordion. She put in a claim.

Which the insurance company refused to pay.

"Maybe I'm missing something," I said. "But didn't you drive your car into the door?"

"By accident, yeah."

"You were the cause of the damage," I said.

"No," she said. "The garage door caused the damage."

I spent the next ten minutes trying to explain the rules of causality to her. She did not get it. Or refused to. She said I was a hack and she was going to sue the company herself and then maybe me for malpractice.

I wished her well.

She cursed at me.

This is now my life in the law. Drunk Santa Clauses. Toking telephone store employees. People who drive cars into garage doors that are not their own, then want money for it.

In many ways, it's a lot more interesting than the white collars I used to rep at one of the biggest firms in L.A., Gunther, McDonough & Longyear. Most of those clients were of a piece. You don't get as much diversity in corporate America as you do at the Ultimate Sip.

Of course, you don't get much money at the Sip, but I was in a whole reassessment mood about that. I'd sold my real estate before the southern California land bust of '07, and the funds were sitting in some CDs, breathing along.

It was kind of nice for a change not to be thinking about money.

10

WHEN WE GOT back to St. Monica's, I thought the rest of my day would be like one of those old ranchero deals. That was L.A., originally. Rancheros and hammocks in the shade and everything moving to the rhythm of a slow burro.

Not to be. Pulling into the lot, I saw a knot of nuns outside the office.

"Not good," Father Bob said as we got out of my car. He has a sense of these things, especially after getting hit with that false accusation of child molesting during the pedophile priest scandals. He's sort of a walking Catholic radar system.

As we approached, we got looks. Wide eyed. Sister Perpetua, the oldest nun in the community, motioned us over.

"The devil is behind it all," she whispered.

She looked seriously spooked.

The office door opened, and there stood Sister Hildegarde. She does not wear the habit. She favors off-the-Walmart-rack specials. Her short, graying hair is dead straight and parted in the middle.

"Come in," she said.

Sister Mary was sitting in the office, her face devoid of color.

"What's going on?" Father Bob said.

Sister Hildegarde shut the door. "I'll tell you what's going on. There has been an incursion. An e-mail." She motioned to the monitor on the desk. This was the computer Sister Mary usually handled.

On the screen was an e-mail, sent to St. Monica's:

> Mary, Mary, quite contrary.
> I will do to you what you deserve.
> Don't fear God.
> Fear the one you don't know.
> I can't wait to get to know you better.

I looked at Sister Mary. Her eyes were more frightened than I'd ever seen them.

"Who would do this?" Sister Hildegarde said.

"A punk," I said. "It's cyberstalking. The address is no doubt fake, but we need to get the cops on it."

Father Bob said, "Wouldn't this be an FBI matter?"

"The feds leave this to the states. They haven't got the manpower, unless they think it's terrorist related."

"Is it a felony, then?"

I said, "It's a wobbler. Means it can be charged as a misdemeanor or felony, depending on how bad it gets."

"How bad is that?" Sister Hildegarde asked.

I looked at her and said nothing. But my clenched jaw was a dead giveaway.

"I think all of us need to catch a collective breath," Sister Hildegarde said. "I've just been saying to Sister Mary, a retreat is in order. She'll be going to Louisville for a time of self-assessment."

That sounded ominous. Father Bob nodded slowly, but not in an agreement way. It was an I-get-what's-going-on-here nod.

I got it a half second later. This was a way for Sister Hildegarde to put a black mark on Sister Mary.

"Let's get the cops up here and file a report," I said.

And hoped that would be the end of it. Some jerk had sent a single e-mail, and wouldn't be heard from again.

Yeah, that's what I hoped, all the time knowing hope is for kids on Christmas. It's not a thing the rest of us can lean on. You try to and you fall hard.

Like getting dumped on the asphalt in a pickup game of hoop. You can get seriously hurt that way.

11

I SPENT CHRISTMAS Day with Fran Dwyer—who was to have been my mother-in-law—and the little charge, Kylie, she has taken in. Being with them brought up all sorts of memories, and pictures.

I never got a Christmas with Jacqueline Dwyer as my wife. Even though

I could see her here, decorating the tree. Unwrapping presents. Shadows of what might have been.

As Kylie opened the present I got for her, *McElligot's Pool* by Dr. Seuss, I got a jolt of joy for the first time in months. But joy is a plaything in the hands of chance. It gets tossed around, maybe you catch it for a while, but if you get too attached, it ends up getting lost or broken.

So I didn't grab too hard for joy as it passed by. I just kept wishing it for Kylie and Fran. Kylie hadn't known much hope growing up. Didn't know her father, and her mother was dead.

And Fran was still devastated by Jacqueline's death.

But somehow, these two had found each other, and it was a good thing. It would fight back the loneliness. I thought about that, and thought maybe I was losing that fight. I had wanted Jacqueline in my life more than anything else in the world. There was a faint, shuddering fear creeping up in me that I'd never be able to replace that void. Not fully, anyway.

Kylie loved the book. She made me read it to her three times, sitting on my lap, her arm around my neck. The little house in Reseda filled up with the smell of Fran's cooking, and that was Christmas, a pleasant one in L.A.

12

IN THE MIDDLE of January the rains came.

I don't like L.A. in the rain. It seems out of sorts, like a dog in a sweater. It wants to roam free, but the wet puts the kibosh on everything. Beaches go deserted, tires skid on freeways, and at country clubs around the city retired vice presidents sit inside and suck gin-and-tonics and complain about their wives.

The rains turned foul. Mud started sliding in Malibu. A couple hillside homes became ground-level houses. A large dollop of wet earth and rock tumbled across the Coast Highway, blocking access for days.

It was not a fit season for man nor beast, so I spent a lot of time in my trailer, reading my buddy Plato and occasionally looking out at the wet basketball court. It looked sad, abandoned. And Sister Mary was in Louis-ville, doing Sister Hidlegarde's peculiar penance.

A friendly detective named Fronterotta, out of the Devonshire Division, was looking into the cyberstalking e-mail to Sister Mary. Which meant, if the tone of his voice was any indication, we had a better chance winning the lottery than finding the guy.

I continued to dispense legal advice in the corner of the Ultimate Sip. I advised several people to start small-claims actions. I argued one woman out of filing suit against the government for invasion of her brain and got her to a hospital instead.

I had one guy come in and describe himself as an "exotic talent coordi-nator." A little delving and I found out he just didn't like the word "pimp." He thought that was beneath him. I told him the law didn't care what he called himself, he still couldn't peddle flesh.

He wondered if he was protected by the Equal Protection Clause of the United States Constitution.

Um, no.

Then a stripper came to see me. She was upset about her working condi-tions. I told her she could call herself a "disrobing technician" and quit.

Only, the toking ex-employee, came back to see me. Said he got a new job that never required him to pee in a cup. I asked him what the job was. A psychic hotline, he said. He had come to thank me. And offered me a blunt. I told him no, I don't take medicine away from the sick.

"It's a gift, man!" he said.

"The greatest gift," I said, "would be knowing that you're back in full, vigorous bloom."

He looked at me and frowned. Then said if I ever needed some help with an investigation, to give him a call. He might be able to predict what moves I should make. Or, if he couldn't do it, he could ask some of his psychic friends.

I told him to get off the Jane and try fresh juices.

He said, "Something's going to happen to you, I have a real feeling about that."

"You'll go far, my friend," I said.

13

THE RAINS LET up toward the end of the month. And on a sunny Tuesday in January, I had an actual court appearance. Nothing like going to court to clear out the existential toxins. You could concentrate on the venom of the justice system for a while.

Even with a client like Carl "Santa Claus" Richess. Not exactly a name to inspire fear, like Sammy "the Bull" Gravano.

But it was all I had, and I was glad. I needed to get back in the game.

The Hollywood branch of the Los Angeles Superior Court sits in a sand-colored building on Hollywood Boulevard, east of Gower, bracketed by a tattoo parlor on one side and a meeting hall of the Salvation Army on the other.

What a town this is. You can get tagged, convicted, and saved, all in the same day, without walking more than a block.

I parked in the front lot and went through security and into Department 77, the only courtroom on the first floor. It was half filled with people waiting to be arraigned, or waiting with family members waiting to be arraigned, or people who, in the future, would no doubt be arraigned.

And some lawyers.

Carl Richess was waiting for me inside. He stood up, filling about half the courtroom. The other half was filled up with two more of the Richess family—Kate and a guy almost as big as Carl. Carl introduced him as his brother, Eric.

"Moral support," Eric said. He was dressed in blue jeans and a denim shirt with the sleeves rolled up. I could see the family resemblance, though Carl looked a bit more like his mother. Still, I couldn't help thinking of Tweedledum and Tweedledee. Put the brothers in striped shirts and beanie hats, and you'd think you were at Disneyland.

Carl wore a brown sport coat over black slacks, and a red-and-green-striped tie. It was funny and pitiful at the same time. He was trying to look respectful, and no doubt this was the best he had in his closet. Probably something off the Big and Tall rack at Sears.

I respected his effort. He looked like he needed effort on his behalf, too. Like Kate had said. He was holding a Dodgers baseball cap in his hands. "My lucky hat," he said.

Terrific. I was in a blue suit, also an off-the-rack job, and didn't feel lucky at all.

"I know you said we didn't have to come," Kate said. "But we've always stuck together, no matter what."

"That's right," Eric said.

"You da man," Carl said to me.

"I am da man, oh, yes," I said. "Only it's not going to be very exciting."

"Can't you get them to just throw it out?" Kate said.

"The case?"

She nodded.

"I'm afraid not," I said. "Not at this stage."

"What's going to happen?"

"First thing," I said, "I talk to the deputy city attorney."

"Is he reasonable?" Kate said.

"I'm not even sure it's a he, Mrs. Richess."

"You da man anyway," Carl said.

I felt so much better.

14

THE DCA WAS not a man. She was a blonde, late-twenties. Dressed to impress, but without shouting about it. Noticeable but understated jewelry. Makeup to accentuate very clear positives.

I knew this look. It was Harvard or Yale. Maybe Georgetown. The kind who thinks they own the whole courtroom because they know so much more than you do. Maybe have designs on being a judge someday.

But right now, she was a newish prosecutor doing everything she could to show she's not going to be pushed around. She was standing at the counsel table, looking through a stack of files.

I approached. She didn't look up.

"I'm da man," I said.

She whipped around. "Excuse me?"

"My name's Buchanan," I said.

"What's your client's name?" She had an angular face that suggested early Katharine Hepburn. Cheekbones and all that. In perfect proportions.

"Innocent," I said. "That's his name."

"Hilarious."

"Just a little arraignment humor."

"Name."

"Richess."

She riffled through the files on the table, pulled one out, opened it. "Oh my," she said.

"If that's about the G-string, I want you to know it has nothing to do—"

"He blew a one-eight."

"Those darn machines never work right."

She didn't smile but her emerald eyes did a little dance. "This is a standard," she said. Meaning the bottom-line deal they offer with a first offense.

"That's what I wanted to talk to you about," I said.

"Nothing to talk about. Not with a one-eight."

"See, we're going to plead not guilty and take this down the road."

"The offer won't change," she said. "You should know that."

"I figured."

"Then let's clear this thing now."

I said, "My client, see, he has this odd notion that he has the right to confront and cross-examine the witnesses against him and—"

"Please." She tossed the file on the table like it was an overdue bill. "Is that really what you're going to do?"

"Yeah, but I just wanted to tell you, it's nothing personal."

"I bet you can read the relief in my face," she said.

"Remember Rodney King? Can't we all just get along?"

She didn't answer.

"Do I have to go to the office to find out your name?" I said.

She stuck out her hand. "Kimberly Pincus," she said, "and if we go to trial on this, I'm going to eat your lunch and take your milk money."

I smiled. "I think you really mean that."

"Oh I do, Mr. . . . . what was it again?"

"Cochran. Johnnie."

"Sorry, Johnnie's not with us anymore. But not even he could do anything with this case. Don't make this harder on yourself than—wait a second." She turned and faced me fully. "You're the guy who was up for murdering that reporter."

"Guilty. I mean, yes, but not guilty."

Now she smiled. "You used to be a big-time litigator somewhere, didn't you?"

"That's the rumor."

"What are you doing down here in the trenches, dealing deuces?"

"I'm not dealing, remember?"

"Your rep is good, as I recall. Are you a gambler, Mr. Buchanan?"

"I played regular poker through law school. Didn't pay my tuition, but bought me some pretty nice meals."

"The stakes are higher here. And the odds favor the house."

"But going to trial is fun," I said. "And you need to be put through your paces every now and then."

She took a long, hard look at me. The corner of her mouth went up slightly.

"We're not racehorses," she said.

That's when the judge decided to enter.

"The flag is up," I said, and walked to the first row of the gallery before Kimberly Pincus could say another word.

15

THE JUDGE WAS Sharon Solomon, late forties, African American. She had reading glasses on her nose and a red and blue scarf around her neck. Tall and regal. We all stood as she took the bench, and court was called to order by the clerk.

Judge Solomon began dispatching cases with relentless efficiency. I watched her closely, trying to get a read. One of the best skills a lawyer can have is judge reading. Figure out what annoys them, where their hot buttons are.

And then, depending on the circumstances, hit or don't hit those buttons.

I could tell after the first few arraignments that Judge Solomon liked lawyers who were prepared, who could cite authority on the spot, and who didn't try to dance around the obvious.

Not like the poor, balding sap who tried to get his client out O.R., and when the judge said no, said, "You have to, Your Honor." And Judge Solomon said, "Why do I have to?" And the sap said, "Because you just do."

At which point the bailiff, clerk, and Ms. Kimberly Pincus issued synchronized sighs. Then Judge Solomon said, "Don't you ever come in my courtroom and tell me what I can and cannot do unless you have a case, a page number, and a host of angels by your side, do you understand me?"

The sap opened his mouth, closed it, opened it again, and said, "Yes, Your Honor."

A good time was had by all, then my case was called.

"Good morning, Your Honor," I said. "Tyler Buchanan on behalf of Mr. Richess, who is present in court. We will waive a reading of the complaint and statement of rights and enter a plea of not guilty. We will not waive time."

Judge Solomon looked at me over her glasses. "You want to set this for trial?"

"Yes," I said.

"Have you read the arrest report?"

"Yes."

"Have you talked to Ms. Pincus?"

"Yes, Your Honor. She said she was going to eat my lunch."

The judge looked at the DCA. "Ms. Pincus, did you tell Mr. Buchanan you were going to eat his lunch?"

"Yes, I did," Kimberly Pincus said.

"Then what will Mr. Buchanan eat?"

"Crow," Ms. Pincus said.

She was quick. And she said it with a glimmer. I had to respect that. Talking smack with a little style never hurt a trial lawyer.

"We shall convene the meal on the twenty-sixth, if that's all right with counsel," Judge Solomon said.

"Works for me," I said.

"I'll be here," Ms. Pincus said.

"Who's bringing dessert?" I said.

Judge Solomon smiled, which I took as a minor victory. But then she said, "I can assure you, Mr. Buchanan, I will be the one cooking the goose."

I decided to give her the last line.

16

"WHAT DID SHE mean?" Kate Richess asked me in the parking lot. "About cooking goose?"

I looked at Carl. He would indeed be stuffed and basted if we lost at trial. Which seemed to be highly likely.

"She's just trying to scare us," Eric said.

"Us?" Carl said.

Eric put his hand on his brother's shoulder.

The sky was dark and spitting drops.

"Maybe you should be scared," Kate said to Carl.

"I'm tired of dancing like a monkey," Carl said. He put his Dodgers cap on defiantly.

Eric Richess said, "People want to push us around. Maybe we don't want to be pushed."

"You're not accused of anything," I said.

"Yeah, but if I was, I'd fight it out."

"You guys like to fight," I said.

"That's what Mom gave us," Carl said, putting his arm around her shoulders. "It's in the genes."

17

AFTER CARL AND Kate went off to their car, Eric said he wanted to talk to me.

"I don't know how much you know about Carl," he said.

"I know he's heading for a possible jail sentence."

"Do you really think so?"

"It's a maybe. The judge has that option, and there's really not all that much I can do. I've advised him to take the plea deal."

"You don't know us," Eric said. "We're kind of a stubborn breed. If you let the world push you around, you'll never get anywhere."

"The law is a pretty hard pusher."

"You've got to understand something else," Eric said.

"I'm listening."

"Carl has never really fit in. Did my mom tell you about his almost getting married?"

"She said that when the girl left, he started drinking a lot."

"She doesn't really know why the girl left," Eric said.

"He beat her up?"

"Nothing like that. Carl is gay."

I said nothing.

"It hasn't exactly worked out for him," Eric said. "That's why he drinks. I mean, I think because his love life hasn't exactly worked out. He's really kind of lonely."

"Are you sure Carl wants you to be telling me all this?"

"I'm telling you because he won't tell you himself, and it may help explain some things, and why he drinks so much, and gets depressed."

"Eric, your brother's sexual preference is not relevant to the drunk driving charge. And the law doesn't care why he drinks. There's no sympathy factor in a DUI. It's merciless."

"That completely bites," he said.

"There's no question he was over the limit. Unless I can find a way to beat the machine, there's no reason to go into who he was drinking with or why. This is a very limited set of facts we have here."

"I'm just trying to get you to see," Eric said. "Carl always seems to come up on the short end. I thought getting him this job in Hollywood would help."

"What job?"

"That big office-building project, between Cahuenga and Ivar, south of Sunset."

"What's your line of work?" I said.

"Electrician," he said. "Major industrial. I'm the sub on that, and Carl freelances in cement, from pour to finish. So I hooked him up with another sub. He liked it that we'd be together on this thing, even though not at the same time. But I just wish he wouldn't drink so much. Beat this rap, will you?"

I wondered when the last time was that somebody actually used the phrase *beat this rap.*

"Believe me, I'll do my best," I said.

"Thanks," Eric said. "That's all I'm asking." He turned and walked toward his car.

I checked my watch. Almost eleven-thirty. I was in Hollywood, so I drove down the boulevard to Musso & Frank. I found a meter in front, fed it, went in, and sat at the counter. And ordered liver and onions.

That's what I said.

My mom used to make liver and onions, and I always liked it. With ketchup. The old waiter—there is no other kind at Musso's—gave me a plate of sourdough bread and a dish with butter pats. He asked if I needed anything else.

"Ketchup," I said. "For the liver."

He leaned over, and with a slight Hungarian accent said, "Don't tell the chef." Then added, conspiratorially, "I like it that way, too."

18

A COUPLE OF weeks went by. I thought about Sister Mary in the wilds of Kentucky. I thought about Kimberly Pincus in the wilds of L.A. courtrooms.

And on the Friday before Carl's pre-trial hearing I was at the Sip, thinking about the laws of the State of California. When it comes to DUI, they are like the jaws of death. I had my laptop and was looking at the vehicle code. For something, anything, that I could argue on behalf of Carl Richess.

It was while I was lost in this vast desert of legal sanctions that Pick suddenly appeared at my table and said, "The canary is dead."

I looked up. "Excuse me?"

"The canary! In the coal mine. You know about that?"

"Sure," I said. "I grew up in a coal mining family. From West Virginia. The strike of 'ninety-four was—"

"Shut up! I mean the *canary has died*. In our civic life! The poison gas is unleashed. Did you see this?" He slapped the front page of the *Los Angeles Daily News* on the table. I looked at it.

The headline said that our mayor was suspected of having an affair with a local radio reporter. It was something everybody knew anyway. But denial is not just a river in Egypt. It's the syntax and currency of every politician who gets his hand stuck in the cookie jar.

"So?" I said. "Political scandal is nothing new."

"Not that! This!" He pointed to a story below the fold. It said that a wiener stand, Big Duke's, one that had been a Valley institution for forty years, was closing down. Lost lease.

"That's the tragedy?" I said.

"Look around you. Do you have eyes? Do you have any sense of history? What do you see, just outside these doors? Coffee Bean & Tea Leaf! Quiznos! Chipottel!"

"I think you mean Chipotle."

"What is that? What's a cheap outlay anyway?"

"It's a type of jalapeño chile, dried—"

"That's not the point! It's the death of individuality, that's the point! When I grew up out here, there were mom-and-pops all over the Valley. You knew the people who ran the stores. They didn't hire the latest high school dropouts to stand behind a computerized cash register pushing buttons that add and subtract for them. You had to do your own adding and subtracting. It made you human. There is no humanity left, none. The canary is dead, and we're next."

With that he turned around and billowed back behind the coffee bar. I went back to my legal research. And it occurred to me Pick and I were more closely related than I thought.

He did not have a corporate headquarters to help him. Or to answer to. And I was trying to defend clients without the resources of a big law firm behind me.

But I didn't want one. Because canaries died in law firms, too.

Once, when I was a new associate at Gunther, McDonough, I was in the kitchenette in our office getting a drink of water. One of the partners wandered in.

It was strange, because he was the kind of man who never wandered anywhere. He was the quintessential go-getter, a creature of constant motion. Exactly the kind of high-powered lawyer who makes it big in the kind of high-powered law firm I'd joined. He made many hundreds of thousands of dollars every year. I wanted to be him.

He was not wearing a tie. But he always wore a tie. He was always, in fact, impeccably dressed.

No tie, and the first three buttons of his shirt were undone.

He looked at me, and looked sick.

"Are you all right, Mr. Henry?" I said.

His look changed not one bit. "How long have you worked here?" he said.

"About six months."

He laughed. Which jolted me, because he never laughed. "You know how many years I've been here?"

"No."

"Twenty-two. Twenty-two years I been coming in, day after day."

And then his eyes grew dark, as if gazing over the desolation that is lost youth. "Why am I doing this? I should be on my boat. I should be out on my boat."

Before I could say anything else he turned and walked away.

I finished my water and threw away the cup. As I walked out of the kitchenette to return to my office, I looked down the long hallway.

Mr. Henry was there, ambling slowly toward the other end of the building. I watched him. Every so often he would reach out and tap the wall with his hand.

One month later he was dead.

19

MONDAY MORNING I drove to the Hollywood courthouse.

Carl and his mom and brother were waiting for me outside Department 77. The three of them took up an entire bench, with Mom in the middle. Parts of Carl and Eric drooped off the ends of the bench.

They stood up as one to greet me.

Carl was dressed in the same tie and coat he had on at the arraignment. He had his lucky Dodgers hat on. Fine. We could use any luck that was hanging around.

"Do I have to take the stand or anything?" Carl said.

"No," I said. "I'm just going to argue some law to the judge."

"What law?"

"The Constitution of the United States."

"That covers drunk driving?"

"Stupid," Eric said. "All them founding fathers were drunk. Of course it covers it."

"Thanks for the history lesson," I said. "Let's just go in and have a seat and we'll see what happens."

"I got confidence in you," Carl said.

20

KIMBERLY PINCUS WAS dressed in a fire engine red suit with a white blouse. Her hair and makeup were perfect, of course. Her demeanor less than collegial.

"This is a waste of time," she told me as I joined her at the counsel table. "Why are you doing this?"

"It's the system we got, Kim."

"It's Kimberly, and you can call me Ms. Pincus, and I can't possibly see any point to this except showing off for your client."

"I'm stunned," I said. "You are an officer of the court. We all get to have our day, even those who are accused of misdemeanors."

"You don't really believe that, do you?"

"Ms. Pincus, I'm shocked. Shocked."

The judge entered the courtroom.

"You're going to get shocked right out on your ear," Ms. Pincus said.

21

I THOUGHT SHE might be right, because Judge Solomon did not seem in a cheery mood. She called the case and said, "So are you really going to press your 1538.5?" She was referring to the penal code section dealing with motions to suppress evidence.

"Yes, Your Honor," I said. "It was a warrantless stop. As such, it is presumptively invalid. The burden of proof passes to Ms. Pincus. She must present evidence that justifies an exception to the warrant requirement."

"Ms. Pincus, do you agree?"

"I agree only that this is a waste of time, Your Honor," she said.

"Then all you have to do is provide a justification for the stop, Ms. Pincus, and you can have your precious time back."

It sounded to me like Solomon was a little put out with the prosecutor. For whatever reason. Which gave me the slightest bit of hope.

"Call your witness," the judge said to Kimberly Pincus.

Patrol Officer John Caldwell of the LAPD took the stand and was sworn. He was a P-2, had been on patrol for three years. He looked young and still idealistic. That usually fades for a cop by year five or six.

That said, he was the kind of officer who would look extra hard for a stop if the conditions were right. And that pre-Christmas night on Hollywood Boulevard, they were. You don't often get a six-foot-five Santa driving your beat.

The key part of the testimony came when Ms. Pincus asked, "And what did you observe?"

"The defendant, driving a Camaro, without his seat belt on."

"Anything else?"

"He was wearing what appeared to be a Santa Claus hat, and no shirt."

"And what did you do next?"

"I dropped behind him, and my partner activated the lights and we pulled him over just past Gower. I approached. The driver-side window was rolled down. I observed the defendant in the car and detected an alcoholic-beverage smell. I shined my flashlight in the car and saw an open bottle on the passenger side. When I asked the defendant if he had had anything to drink, he answered no, but his speech was slurred and his eyes were watery. That's when I ordered him out of the car for the field sobriety tests."

Kimberly Pincus turned to the judge. "As the only issue is reasonable suspicion to stop, Your Honor, that concludes my direct examination."

"You may cross," Judge Solomon said to me.

I almost didn't hear her, as I was flipping fast through my copy of the vehicle code.

"Mr. Buchanan?" the judge said.

"If I may have just a moment, Your Honor."

"Oh sure," she said. "We don't have anything else to do today."

"Thank you," I said, riffling. "Just one sec—"

And then I found it.

22

"OFFICER CALDWELL," I said, "you stated that you observed the defendant driving without a seat belt, is that correct?"

"That's right," the officer said.

"You did not see any erratic driving, isn't that true?"

"That's correct."

"In other words, you didn't suspect that Mr. Richess might be driving under the influence, did you?"

"Not at the time of the stop, no."

"In fact, it wasn't until you had pulled him over and approached the car, and looked in the window, that you developed a suspicion of DUI, correct?"

"Correct. That's the way it usually happens."

"By the way, it is not illegal to drive without a shirt on, is it?"

"No."

"Or wearing a Santa hat?"

Caldwell smiled. "Not that I know of."

"So the only reason for the stop was for violation of the vehicle code, specifically the seat belt law."

"Right."

"Tell me, Officer Caldwell, how you could determine Mr. Richess wasn't wearing a seat belt."

"It was pretty easy," he said. "The defendant is rather large, and without a shirt on, I could see there was no strap going across his body."

"No shoulder strap?"

"That's right."

"And that's when you decided to drop behind Mr. Richess and stop him."

"Yes."

"Thank you, Officer Caldwell. You've been most helpful this morning."

The officer frowned, as if confused. I looked over at Kimberly Pincus. Her face was impassive.

"Do you have another witness?" Judge Solomon asked.

"None, Your Honor," said Pincus.

"Mr. Buchanan?"

"No witnesses, Your Honor. I'm ready to argue the motion."

"Well that's nice," Judge Solomon said. "I like it when someone is actually ready."

What I heard the judge saying was that Ms. Kimberly Pincus had not been ready on some previous occasion. The judge was rubbing it in.

This was my moment.

23

KIMBERLY PINCUS SAID, "Your Honor, it is manifestly clear that Officer Caldwell observed a vehicle code violation. He therefore had probable cause to effect a stop. No warrant required in this instance, of course. So all the evidence observed subsequent to the stop is admissible. Maybe Mr. Buchanan will want to talk about settling now."

"Excuse me, Your Honor," I said. "But doesn't Ms. Pincus know that I get to make an oral argument, too?"

"She was rather jumping the gun," Judge Solomon said. "Isn't that right, Ms. Pincus?"

The CDA said nothing. But I thought I saw steam rising. It was kind of cute.

"All right, Mr. Buchanan," said the judge. "You have my attention. I'm curious to hear what you have on your plate. As I recall, Ms. Pincus said she would be eating your lunch."

"With all the trimmings," I said. "We are a nation of laws, Your Honor, and as such we believe that the laws passed by legislatures have meaning. The meaning is in the text itself. Where the text is clear and unambiguous, that is what we follow. If the legislature sees a need to change the text, they will. But we don't do that on the trial level."

"Thank you for the civics lesson, Mr. Buchanan," Judge Solomon said. "Is this going anywhere?"

"Good question," Kimberly Pincus said.

"I'll handle the argument, Ms. Pincus, thank you very much," the judge said. "Mr. Buchanan?"

"I quote, Your Honor, from the vehicle code, the exact text of the seat belt law: 'A person may not operate a motor vehicle on a highway unless that person and all passengers sixteen years of age or over are properly re-strained by a safety belt.' I emphasize the last word, Your Honor. *Belt.*"

Judge Solomon peered over her glasses. "Yes?"

"Nowhere in the statute is the term *belt* defined by the legislature, thus leaving it to common sense and common understanding. A belt is a strap placed across one's lap, keeping one's rear end in contact with a seat."

Kimberly Pincus, sharp little tack that she was, stood up. "Your Honor," she said. "I see where this is going. This is crazy, and—"

"Ms. Pincus," the judge said, "please sit down and do not speak again unless you have a valid objection. I want to hear Mr. Buchanan out. This is nothing if not creative."

"Does Your Honor have a dictionary handy?" I said.

"Right here," Judge Solomon said. She took a volume and opened it up. Turned the pages.

Each page seemed to be a stake to the heart of Kimberly Pincus.

The judge stopped, then read. " 'Belt. A flexible band, as of leather or cloth, worn around the waist to support clothing, secure tools or weapons, or serve as decoration.' "

"Around the waist," I said.

"Interesting," Judge Solomon said.

"I object," Kimberly Pincus said.

"Overruled," said the judge.

"But you haven't heard—"

"Overruled, Ms. Pincus. Continue, Mr. Buchanan."

I wanted this to last forever. I flipped a few pages in the vehicle code and said, "I can well understand the frustration of the prosecution, but allow me to turn to another section of the vehicle code, Section 27314.5(a)(1). Here the legislature prescribes a warning for used-car dealers which reads as follows. 'Warning. While use of all seat belts reduces the chance of ejection, failure to install and use shoulder harnesses with lap belts can result in serious or fatal injuries.' What this shows, Your Honor, is that the legislature distinguishes between *belts* and shoulder *harnesses*. In other words, they knew exactly what they were doing when they wrote seat *belts*."

"Fascinating," Judge Solomon said with a smile.

"Officer Caldwell said he saw no shoulder strap on my client, and that's why he stopped him. But there was no probable cause to stop Mr. Richess, because he could very well have been in compliance with the seat belt law by wearing a lap belt. In other words, there was no crime committed in the officer's presence. No crime, illegal stop. Everything Officer Caldwell observed afterward was fruit of the poisonous tree."

I love that phrase. It comes from an old Supreme Court case. It basically means if an illegal action by the cop leads to the incriminating evidence, that evidence is tainted. And therefore cannot be considered in court.

"Well done, Mr. Buchanan," Judge Solomon said.

"May I respond now?" Ms. Pincus said.

"You may."

"This is ridiculous. The term *belt* obviously has several different meanings."

"Do you have a dictionary, Ms. Pincus?"

"No."

"Then you are making a claim without a citation."

Seam. Bursting. "Your Honor, please! At the very least, the term is ambiguous."

"If I may?" I said.

"Yes, Mr. Buchanan?" the judge said.

"I have already shown that the legislature was very careful in choosing its terms. But even if we were to concede Ms. Pincus's point, that the term is ambiguous, the Keeler case controls. It held that when a statute is susceptible to two reasonable constructions, it *shall be* construed favorably to the *defendant*."

You could have cut the silence with Kimberly Pincus's tongue. Ms. Pincus herself was speechless. She shook her head disbelievingly, like a teenager who's just been told she can't drive the car tonight.

"Give me just a moment," Judge Solomon said. She took off her glasses and scratched her chin with one of the stems.

She was thinking about it. She was really thinking about it.

I wanted to dance.

Once, I had danced on a fancy conference table in a fancy law office, because I was hacked off at the stuffed sausage of a lawyer sitting across from me. That almost cost me my license, but it was worth it.

But I stayed seated. The dancing would come later. And it would come, because Judge Solomon, bless her heart, said the following.

"In the matter of the People of the State of California versus Carl Richess, I am going to grant the 1538.5 motion. The warrantless stop of the car was not justified, for the reasons so ably given by counsel. Therefore, all of the observations subsequent to the stop are fruit of the poisonous tree. The observations, the field sobriety tests, and the breath test results are suppressed. Do the People wish to proceed?"

A stunned Kimberly Pincus slowly stood up. "In view of the court's holding, we have no evidence with which to proceed."

"Then the complaint is dismissed," Judge Solomon said. "In time for lunch," she added, winking at me.

24

CARL RICHESS THREW his arms around me and squeezed. I was a mouse to his python.

"Drinks are on me," Carl said.

I pushed him away. "Don't go there, Carl. You dodged a bullet. You need to get to AA."

"What's that supposed to mean? Mom, what've you been saying?"

"Honey," Kate said, wiping away tears, "we just want you to get better."

"I'm *fine*."

"Brother," Eric said, "you got a disease."

"Will you all just shut up?" Carl put on his Dodgers cap, turned for the door, and stormed out, leaving a comet tail of denial behind him.

When he was out the door, Eric said, "That didn't go so well."

Kate was still crying, though for a different reason now. I put my hand on her shoulder. "One step at a time," I said. "He'll realize he's been given another chance. I'll call him in a couple of days and talk to him."

"Thank you," Kate said. Eric took her arm and led her out the door.

I turned around and saw Kimberly Pincus. She walked over to me. Her eyes were electric.

"Don't Tase me, bro," I said.

She put her hands on her hips. "I guess you're pleased with yourself."

"Like a diva with a divorce settlement," I said.

"I cannot believe Judge Solomon went for it."

"It's the law, Ms. Pincus."

"That was one of the most outrageous arguments I've ever heard in a court of law."

"Thanks."

"Do you really enjoy putting drunks back on the street?" She gave me the steel gaze.

I gave her the same right back. "Is this going to be one of those criminal-defense-lawyers-get-criminals-off-on-technicalities conversations?"

"Shouldn't it be?"

"The legislature makes laws. You and the cops have to follow. So follow."

"But *seat belt*? That's the very definition of technicality."

"If you ignore what the law actually says, pretty soon doors get kicked in. You want to change things, go to the legislature. But in court, don't tell me how to do my job."

"You know what?" she said. "I can respect that, believe it or not."

"It's such a pleasant day, Ms. Pincus, how about I believe it?"

She smiled. "Done. Let's have a drink."

25

YOU DON'T ARGUE with Kimberly Pincus without a judge on the bench.

We met at the Snortin' Boar, a Hollywood reclamation project. It had been one of the hot places in the forties, a nightclub that was a favorite of directors and stars. The Andrews Sisters sang here. Lawrence Tierney got in a famous fight with Dana Andrews in 1955. Both were so drunk they couldn't remember it the next day.

The place went under in 1964 and was, for a time in the seventies, a head shop. In 1995 it was an independent pizza place that almost burned down.

A couple of film-fan businessmen bought the place and restored it a few years ago. They brought back the vaulted ceiling and dark wood interior, and dim lighting. And comfortable booths, which is where I sat with the deputy city attorney.

A waiter came by and Kimberly ordered a Grey Goose martini, dirty. I opted for a beer.

"And so," she said, "where do you come from?"

"Grew up in Florida. You?"

"New Jersey."

"Law school?"

"Harvard."

"I knew it," I said.

"What do you mean, you knew it?"

"You give off a Harvard vibe."

"What kind of vibe do you give off?"

"UCLA. Of the people."

She laughed. "Uh-huh. Or maybe you're just as ruthless as the rest of us."

"Me?"

"You'll do anything to win."

"Well, I won't kill baby seals."

"Do you think I would?" she said.

"I refuse to answer on the grounds it may incriminate me," I said.

She put her chin in her hand and leaned on the table. "You fascinate me. What are you doing taking on misdemeanor deuces? You were with—who was it?"

"Gunther, McDonough."

"Right. You're a fortieth-floor guy. What's this all about?"

"The law is the law. Even for people like Carl Richess."

"But life's so hard for a solo."

"Yes, but I have all the fruitcake I can eat."

"Excuse me?"

"St. Monica's is known for its fruitcake. Not that I'd recommend it."

"What is St. Monica's?"

"It's where I'm living right now. It's a Benedictine community. It's a long story."

"You're Catholic?" she said.

"No, cynic."

"I don't believe you."

"That makes you a cynic, too."

Our drinks arrived. Kimberly lifted her glass. "Let's drink to a healthy dose of cynicism, enough to keep us sane." We clinked and drank.

"So what was it like?" she said.

"What was what like?"

"Being on the other side. Being accused of murder. What was it like to be in jail?"

"Not something you ever want to be in, Ms. Pincus."

"Call me Kimberly, Ty."

"You know they got viruses down there at the men's jail they don't even have names for yet. They put five people in a cell built for two. I got off easy, being a K-1, high risk. I had my own cell. The rest of the place, you know what it looks like? Remember in *The Matrix*? When Neo wakes up and sees that dark place housing all the human bodies? That's what it's like, only worse, because you're not in suspended animation."

"And of course most people deserve to be there."

"They deserve to be housed like people, not dry goods."

"Don't do the crime if you can't do the time."

I motioned with my thumb. "I can ask the waiter to bring over some milk of human kindness, if you want."

"I don't want," she said. "What good is kindness in a criminal courtroom?"

She was starting to remind myself of me, whenever I get into a philosophical tangle with Father Bob or Pick McNitt.

"Are you really as cutthroat as you pretend to be?" I said.

"I can't stand to lose. You beat me. I want to eat your heart."

"Say what?"

"You know, the way the Mayans would eat the hearts of their enemies."

"I'm using mine right now, if that's okay."

"Then how about something else?" she said. "You were one of the best trial lawyers in the city."

"Was?"

"That was your rep. Now I think it must be justified. I can learn from you."

"You want trial lawyer lessons?"

"Just between friends."

"I thought we were enemies. You know, eating my heart and all."

"I'm over that," she said. "I think we're going to be good friends." She lingered over a sip of her drink. And smiled as she did.

26

"ALL RIGHT," I said later, over fried mozzarella, "I'll tell you the best piece of advice I ever got about being a trial lawyer. Be yourself."

"That's it?" Kimberly said.

"It's more than you think. Or, actually, less. See, I saw you posing a lot in court."

She stiffened. For a second I thought she was going to take a bite out of her martini glass. But she came back to earth and said, "You think so?"

"And the judge thought so, too. That's probably why she was so hard on you. You're pushy."

"Am I going to need another martini?"

"No. But you can come off as arrogant."

"You're just all compliments today, aren't you?"

"If you were to be yourself, you'd have any jury eating out of your hand. See, the greatest actor of all time was Spencer Tracy."

"Yeah?"

"You know his work?"

"Not really."

I did. Jacqueline and I used to watch old movies together. A lot. "Tracy was the best. Bogart said he was. Because you couldn't see the wheels turning. And somebody asked Tracy what his secret was, and all he said was, be yourself and listen to the other actor. But lawyers want to get up in court and put on a show. If you really want to win, don't make it about Kimberly Pincus. Make it about justice. Make it about the People. Make it about— why am I telling you all this? I'm giving away the store."

"I want to keep shopping," she said. "I really want to keep shopping. What about dinner?"

"Are you asking me out?" I said.

"Boy, you really *are* good. How about it?"

"Aren't things moving a little fast?" I said. "I mean, I wouldn't want you to think I was easy."

She laughed. Like she didn't believe me.

Personally, I didn't know what to believe.

She reached into her purse and pulled out a red Bicycle deck of cards.

"You said you were a gambler, remember?" She slipped the deck out.

I had no idea where this was going. But I was both amused and interested.

She gave the deck an overhand shuffle then plopped it on the table. "Cut a card," she said.

I ran my thumb halfway down the deck. I turned the cards over at that point, showing the jack of spades.

"Not bad," she said. "Now shuffle the cards and put them down."

I did a pretty smooth riffle-shuffle on the table. I pressed the cards together and pulled my hands back.

Kimberly looked me in the eye as she reached for the cards. She cut and held a card up for me to see. Queen of diamonds.

Then she looked at the card for the first time, as if she knew it would be a queen, king, or ace. Her smile was full of self-satisfaction. "The lesson is you shouldn't gamble with me, right?"

"I don't know," I said. "Let's study this a little further."

I picked up the cards and did a one-handed cut. Her eyes widened in appreciation.

Here is what she didn't know. I had a friend in law school who was a member of the Magic Castle, a private Hollywood nightclub housed in a Victorian mansion on Franklin. We would go and hang out there a lot, and I got interested in magic.

He introduced me to the world champion magician. Johnny "Ace" Palmer was the first close-up magician to win the award. Nice guy, too. When he found out I was interested in learning some tricks, he told me to go get a book called *The Royal Road to Card Magic*, and concentrate on learning a few techniques.

After I did, and spent a few weeks working on them, Johnny gave me a little coaching in the bar area of the Castle. That was the equivalent of Astaire helping a janitor learn a two-step. But I did learn.

I had Kimberly shuffle the cards. I took the deck from her. "Well, let's see what the top card is."

I turned the card over. Two of clubs. I turned it face down and placed it on the table. "That will be my card. That two of clubs. Remember that. Now let's take a look at the next card."

I turned that card over, and it was the six of hearts. I turned it face down and placed it on the table in front of Kimberly. "That's your card, the six of hearts. Put your finger on it."

She did.

"Now, you saw me put the two of clubs in front of me, and the six of hearts in front of you, and you even have your finger on it. Let's compare."

I picked my card up from the table and turned it over. Of course, it was the six of hearts.

The look on her face was priceless. She turned over her card. Two of clubs.

"How did you do that?" she said.

"Very well," I said.

"No, come on."

"I'm afraid the magician's code precludes me from sharing the secret. But the point is, I'm magic, and magic beats gambling every time."

"I think I like you," she said.

27

ON FRIDAY, THE skies above L.A. were still dark. And bad things were happening.

I should have read the signs.

The night before, the cops were involved in a shoot-out in Northeast L.A., with the notorious Cypress Assassins gang.

It was like something out of Tombstone.

There was a drive-by, with some gangbangers in a car mowing down a forty-year-old *veterano* on Drew Street. He was holding a two-year-old girl's hand at the time.

The girl survived. He didn't.

Some bystanders who knew the guy saw this, and took out guns and fired at the car.

Everybody is packing heat in this part of town, apparently.

A twenty-two-year-old 'banger stumbled out of the car and returned fire with an AK-47. He killed two before getting back in the car and taking off.

The cops arrived about three minutes later. One black-and-white after another. SWAT arrived, and ten blocks of city was cordoned off.

They found the car, a white Nissan sedan, near Washington Irving Middle School. The driver again got out, this time with two others who were also armed, and the gun battle started.

When it was all over, ten minutes later, three Assassins and one cop were dead.

This sort of thing happens here and puts death in the air. It hangs there, like a mushroom cloud, and you think about diving for cover.

It seemed to put Pick McNitt in one of his moods. Father Bob and I were at the Sip when Pick said, "You know what I hate more than anything in the world? People who use *begs the question* when they mean *asks the question*. That's not what it means! It's a logical fallacy. To *beg the question* means you have *avoided* the question. I hate that!"

"You hate that more than anything in the world?" Father Bob said.

"At this moment in time, yes. You can only hate in the present moment. And I'll tell you something else I hate. When the morning shows say 'Good morning.' "

"Excuse me?"

"Yes! Stupid! Three thousand people die in a tsunami in the Philippines, and Meredith Vieira goes to the reporter on the scene and says, 'She's covering the terrible tragedy there. Good morning, Ann.' And the reporter goes, 'Good morning, Meredith. Yes, bodies littered everywhere in the aftermath . . .' Just get to the story! It's not a *good morning!* I hate that."

"You are on a hate binge today," Father Bob said.

"If you don't hate something you're not alive."

"God hates, too."

Pick looked stunned.

" 'Do not swear falsely, the Lord says. This I hate.' Book of Zechariah."

I said, "That means he hates half the witnesses who testify in court."

"And all congressmen," Pick said.

"Not so fast," Father Bob said. "He loves the sinner. It's the sin he hates."

"Fantasy," Pick said.

"How do you even know what *hate* is?" Father Bob said. "You must have love to have hate. You must know what love is to know what hate is. You must have good to know evil."

"I do know all these things."

"But how?"

"Because I sense 'em," Pick said. "The way I can tell yellow from blue. I can't prove to you yellow exists—we have to see it together. So love and justice are the same. We see 'em, and distinguish 'em from hate and injustice."

"What's there to tell us our senses are correct?"

"Experience," said Pick. "We've all figured out a way to get along with each other."

"Tell that to the gangs," I said. "They're killing cops and each other."

"It's the way of all flesh," Pick said. "There is nothing to save us."

"Love saves," Father Bob said.

Pick flicked his hand, as if batting away a fly.

Father Bob said, " 'The mind has a thousand eyes, and the heart but one. Yet the light of a whole life dies when love is done.' "

Pick just looked at Father Bob, who seems to pull these things out of thin air. You can argue with philosophy, but poetry is another matter.

Then Pick said, " 'I strove with none, for none was worth my strife. Nature I loved and, next to nature, art. I warmed both hands before the fire of life. It sinks, and I am ready to depart.' "

I was afraid Pick was dangerously close to one of his episodes. Every now and then he went off like a cherry bomb. It would take days to put the pieces back together.

So I said, "Let me contribute a thought."

They both looked at me. Incredulously, I might add.

I said, " 'I do not eat green eggs and ham. I do not like them, Sam-I-am.' "

They said nothing.

Then Father Bob started laughing. Pick scowled but at least didn't launch.

Then my phone played "Potato Head Blues." I answered.

"Help." The voice was barely a whisper.

"Who is it?" I said.

"Oh God, help."

"Kate?"

"Carl's dead. Oh, dear God, help me."

28

CARL'S APARTMENT WAS on Havenhurst in West Hollywood. The building was Spanish revival style. A throwback to the 1920s, when movies couldn't talk and the cops were as crooked as an English waiter's teeth.

The LAPD is a whole lot more professional now, so I was not surprised by the efficient police presence on the ground floor. I told a uniform I was the family lawyer and showed him my Bar card. He told me I could go in.

Kate was sitting in a wingback chair in the foyer. Slumped. Eric was on his knees, his arm around her.

"Oh Ty!" she said when she saw me. I went to her and took her hand.

"They wanted to ask Mom questions," Eric said, "but she said she wanted to talk to you first."

"Is there someone in charge here?" I asked.

"A detective," Eric said. "He's in the apartment. 102."

Kate said, "I don't know what to do, Ty."

"Give me a minute." I walked down the hall and found 102, which was yellow-taped. Another uniformed officer met me there. I told him who I was. He went inside and a moment later a plainclothes came out to the hall-way. He had dark curly hair and a Roman nose. About my height. Brown, intelligent eyes. Mid-fifties.

He shook my hand. "My name's Zebker. You're the family lawyer?"

"Yes," I said.

"How well do you know the mother?"

"Not very. I was retained to help Carl in a DUI."

"Is she strong? Emotionally?"

"Why?"

"There are some details about the death that are not very pleasant. It might be better coming from you. I can give the generic. It'll all come out in the news sooner or later."

"All right. What was it?"

"A nine-millimeter in the mouth. Ugly."

"Suicide?"

"Maybe."

"Was there a note or anything?"

"I have to reserve that information for now."

"Come on, Detective."

"We'll follow procedure here. Right now my concern is for the mother. She's pretty upset."

"There will be an autopsy, right?"

"Yes."

"All right," I said. "Let me talk to her. And I might talk to a few of the residents."

"Now hold on," Zebker said. "We're conducting an investigation."

"So am I."

"What does that mean?"

"I want to know what happened."

"You'll find out when we tell you."

"Why don't we just cooperate?"

Zebker looked down the hallway, where a few people were milling around. "I don't want you plodding through my crime scene."

"Detective," I said. "I don't plod. I used to plod. I gave it up."

He didn't smile.

"And as you know," I said, "you cannot prevent me from questioning anybody I want to question, unless you're holding them as a material witness."

"Where did you learn that?"

"It's the law."

"Listen to me carefully. You try to question anybody before I do, I'm going to arrest you. That clear?"

"Detective Zebker—"

"That's it. Now please go talk to the mother and take her home. I'll be in touch about the autopsy."

"How about I take a look inside?"

For a moment I thought Zebker was going to yellow-tape my mouth.

I left before he could.

29

I HAD TO tell Kate. I was glad Eric was there, to hold her up.

"There's no other way to say this," I said. "It looks like Carl killed himself."

A shudder ran down her body. Like electric ripples. Then she convulsed into tears.

"Take her home," I told Eric. "If you have a sedative, give it to her. I'll come by later and tell you what I can find out."

"Why why why?" Kate said, through sobs.

Good question. She deserved an answer.

30

AFTER ERIC TOOK Kate home, I hung around outside the apartment building.

Zebker did not want me sniffing for witnesses. But what if I just sidled up to one? Any law against sidling?

What would a judge say?

The First Amendment certainly preserves the right of people to peaceably sidle.

I watched the small crowd on the sidewalk. The people were a typical L.A. knot. Different kinds, shades, and attitudes. A short woman with black hair, wearing a blouse with jungle foliage print, was talking to a guy who looked Filipino. He wore glasses with black frames.

"Was the meat a little gamey last night?" the woman said.

The guy shrugged. "You do what you got to do."

"But it should have been fine."

"Did you cook it slow?" I said.

They both looked at me.

"Sorry, couldn't help overhearing," I said. "Slow cooking, that's best for . . . what was it?"

"Duck," the woman said.

"Now I love a good duck," I said.

"You live around here?"

"No. I'm friends with the family of the guy who died."

"Then it's true?" the man in glasses said. "Was it the big guy?"

"You knew him?"

"Well yeah, to look at. Say hi to. That's all."

"Nice guy, was he?"

"I guess," he said. "What happened?"

"Maybe suicide."

"Oh man." He shook his head.

The woman looked stunned. "Bummer," she said. "I was afraid something like this might happen."

"Oh yeah?" I said.

She nodded. "There's a whole Stephen King vibe going on around here. You can feel it."

"You can," Glasses said.

"Stephen King?" I said.

"Like in that movie with John Cusack," the woman said.

"*1408*," said Glasses. "The haunted-room one."

"No, it wasn't haunted," the woman said. "It was evil. The room itself was evil. I almost felt like telling him—was his name Carl?—not to go back in the room."

I looked at her. "When did you feel like telling him that?"

"Tonight, in the garage. He was going in. I was going out."

"What time was that?"

"I don't know, maybe seven or so."

"Think about it," I said.

She looked up at the sky and blinked a couple of times. "I got to Pearl's a little before seven. I remember that because she always watches *Jeopardy* and it wasn't on yet."

"He doesn't know who Pearl is," Glasses said.

"Oh yeah," the woman said. "She's a friend, lives about fifteen minutes away. So I probably saw him about six-thirty or so. That help?"

I said, "Did he look upset to you, anything like that?"

"No. He was coming back from the store, I guess."

"How could you tell?"

"He had a bag with him. I think it was BevMo. Everybody knows he's a boozer."

"How do they know that?" I said.

"More than a few nights, out by the pool, he stumbled around and made a lot of noise."

"Thanks," I said. It looked like the typical, sad scenario. There are a million variations but it's all the same theme. A descent into loneliness, as his brother Eric had suggested. A slide greased by liquor or drugs or both. You look at your life and it's not what you ever thought it would be. You look at the future and you only see fog or darkness, but not another person to share it with.

Enough of that and you figure, why stick around?

I knew the feeling. It had poured over me after Jacqueline died. No man is an island, the poet said, but there are lots of stray rocks on barren hillsides.

Somebody tapped me on the shoulder.

31

HE WAS WELL dressed, professional looking. Mitt Romney hair. Blue dress shirt with creases that could cut lunch meat. Red tie, loosened.

"Excuse me," he said. "Are you working on this matter?"

I said, "And you are?"

"I knew Carl. I'm Morgan Barstler. You?"

"Family lawyer," I said. "Ty Buchanan."

"Oh, you were representing him, right?"

"Did he tell you that?"

He nodded. "Carl told me what a great guy you are, great lawyer."

"Great may be pushing it," I said. "How well did you know Carl?"

"Very well."

"Can you tell me about it?"

He looked down and put his hands in his pockets. "Why? What good?"

"I'm looking out for his mom. I'd like to find out why this happened."

"And how exactly *did* it happen?"

"The police say he shot himself."

Barstler's eyes started to tear up. He was going to say something, then stopped himself.

"Not here," he said.

32

WE WENT TO a bar on Melrose. Cool, contemporary interior with a palm-tree-and-teak motif. Barstler was shaky and ordered scotch rocks. I had an amber ale called Goliath, a local brew.

"Carl and I were together about a year," Barstler said. "It didn't last, but we stayed friends."

"How long ago was it you were together?" I said.

"It's been about three years now."

"And you've stayed pretty much in contact since?"

"Oh yeah. We spoke all the time. On the phone. Met for movies, dinner sometimes. Saw each other at parties. E-mailed each other."

"What is it you do, Morgan?"

"Real exciting. Accountant."

"Nothing wrong with that."

"Wish I'd gone into law. I think it'd be a lot more fun." He looked into his glass. "I can't believe he's dead."

"Any reason you can think of why he'd want to commit suicide?"

Barstler shook his head.

"He was an alcoholic," I said.

"Yeah. Why we broke up. He couldn't handle it, and I couldn't handle *that*."

"He have a long-term relationship after you?"

"Nothing that lasted. One was pretty bad."

"In what way?"

"He was with an actor named Tim for a while, but Tim was hooking up with this other guy, a real jerk who hangs on the boulevard pretending to be somebody. But he's just mean. Carl had some nasty fights with him."

"With Tim?"

"And this other guy."

"You know Tim's last name?"

"I think it was Larchmont."

"And he's an actor?"

Barstler nodded. "He was studying at the Stella Adler school, as I recall."

"And this other guy's name?"

"Oh, he's ripe. He calls himself the Reverend Son Young Moon, if you can believe it."

I blinked a couple of times. "Hasn't that name been taken?"

"It's not the same as that other guy. It's *Son*, as in Son of God. And Young, as in young. Takes some stones to call yourself the Son of God, doesn't it?"

"Where do I find this guy?"

"He's hard to miss. Retro punk Mohawk up to here." Barstler held his hand about twelve inches over his head. "He hangs out across from the big brick Scientology center, right near the Stella Adler Theatre. He runs his own street scene on the sidewalk. Talking to people, handing stuff out."

"What kind of stuff?"

Barstler shrugged.

"Is this guy capable of killing somebody?" I said.

"What are you saying? That Carl didn't kill himself?"

"I'm not saying anything. Just trying to get all the information."

"Well, I think anybody's capable of anything, under the right circumstances. Or wrong circumstances. Whatever."

His face drifted to a sad place again.

I said, "The night Carl was arrested for DUI, he said he'd gotten crazy at a party. Were you at that party?"

"Matter of fact, I was."

"Anything you can tell me about it?"

Barstler sighed. "Christmas party. A mixed bag. An actor friend gave it. About twenty, twenty-five people."

"Was Tim or this Sonny Moon there?"

"Tim was there early, but he left. I don't know if he had a fight with Carl or not. All I know is Carl was out of it and just drinking like crazy. I tried to stop him but he told me to . . . well, he told me off. I got mad and avoided him. At some point he was parading around in a Santa hat and not much else. I went outside after that, spent some time talking to other friends. When I went back in the house he was gone."

"Did Carl get into it with anybody else?"

"I didn't see it. People were pretty ripped and laughing."

I gave him my card. "If something comes to you and you want to tell me about it, give me a call, huh?"

"How's Kate doing?" he said.

"Shook up, of course."

"Tell her I said hi. I always liked her."

33

THE NEXT DAY I drove down to Hollywood and parked in front of the Scientology building, just east of Highland. I looked across the street but didn't see anybody who matched the description Barstler gave me. I put in a Duke Ellington CD and watched the passersby.

It was like being in a pod in some space movie. I was observing another planet.

Hollywood has changed a little since that day in 1887 when a land speculator named Dixon decided this spot would be a good place to build homes. It was mostly Chinese fruit growers back then, leasing the land. Life was slow and productive.

Now it was fast and pointed in no particular direction. Years ago the city planners thought a glitzy new center at the corner of Hollywood and Highland would spread renewal up and down. The street is cleaner, but the stretch from the Pantages to the El Capitan Theatre still seems to be rife with smoke shops, tattoo parlors, clothing stores, tourist traps, eateries, and tagger practice. On weekends the club scene springs to life, but that's largely hidden in the day.

Yet Hollywood represents nothing if not hope. And huge industrial cranes in the skyline signaled major projects ahead. An influx of business, some that might even stay, despite the tax burden.

The one constant is the street scene, the crazy mix of those who hang out on the brass stars of the Walk of Fame. Many of them runaways. They say maybe four hundred kids live on the streets of Hollywood at any given time. They scour the alleys at night, trading sex for a fix, or paying with what they make panhandling.

If they're lucky, somebody at one of the teen drop-in centers gives them just the right break, the right word, maybe the right kick in the pants. And they get out of the life.

Most aren't so lucky.

The con has always been a big part of the Hollywood scene. And phony religionists run some of the biggest. Any nimrod can set himself up as providing the way, the truth, and the life, and start collecting donations.

Just spout some high-sounding claptrap in L.A. and it's a sure bet more than one person will start handing you the green.

Ellington was taking the A Train and I was wondering what sort of religion I'd set up if I were a conman, when I saw a Mohawk across the street.

34

THE HAIR WAS only part of the giveaway. The acolytes around him were another. Five or six young women stood around in a traveling ad hoc circle, flyers in their hands. A guy in a large-brimmed hat worked a guitar behind them.

The circus came to a stop in front of the white brick building next to the Hollywood Wax Museum. Here they set up shop.

I got out of my car and crossed the street at Highland. Then I walked down toward the new breed of moonies.

One of the girls handed me a flyer. It was full color, double sided. On the front was a headline: *The CIA's Plan to Brainwash All American Citizens.* There was a drawing of man's head in the middle of the page, with half his skull removed so you could see his brain.

Several little men in suits were standing on the brain with mops, scrubbing. Text wrapped around the picture. I didn't read it.

"Thanks," I said, putting the paper in my back pocket.

"We take donations," she said. She was maybe eighteen and had that runaway look.

"I want to talk to the reverend," I said.

"Are you a cop? Because we—"

"No, just another pilgrim."

"Pilgrim?"

"You know, like Thanksgiving."

She didn't know. Her face was a blank. I walked past her and came up behind the Mohawk, who was talking to another girl. She looked at me and Mohawk turned around.

"Reverend Son Young Moon?" I said.

"That's me, brother." He smiled.

"Crazy name," I said.

"Not if you're the second coming."

"Of Jesus?"

"What do you mean by *Jesus*?" he said. "Do you think Jesus is some person dropping out of the sky, or is he a universal spirit?"

"You tell me," I said.

"We are the Universal Worldwide Church."

"Sort of redundant, isn't it?" I said.

"What is?"

"If it's the universal church, that includes the world already."

He just looked at me.

"So do you have any celebrity clients," I said, "like your competitors across the street?"

"Sure. But I can't tell you."

"Uh-huh. Confidential, right?"

He nodded. He looked like a peacock nipping at water.

"So I guess you're not all that credible with the tourists yet. You need a celebrity."

His ragtag acolytes were crowding in. Like this was going to be a show.

"Are you familiar with the Demiurge?" Sonny Moon asked with a smirk, as if I wouldn't have a clue.

"Sure," I said. "It's a term I believe first used by Plato. Later, by Plotinus. Right?"

That set him back a little. "Very good, but that's not the only place. The Gnostics identified the Demiurge as the Yaweh of the Old Testament. They thought he was evil, because the world he created was evil. Now, if you were to make a movie about the Demiurge, who would you have play him? Christopher Walken, of course. No question about it. Chris Walken looks evil, but in fact he is good."

I said, "People actually pay you for this?"

One of his disciples, a girl with a railroad spike through her lower lip, said something in what sounded like a clicking African dialect. Then I realized it was a tongue stud clacking on her teeth. Anyway, what she said sounded like an insult. I think she was suggesting I try rectal-cranial inversion.

"Far be it from me to criticize the free exercise of religion," I said. "But maybe a little truth in advertising would help."

"What do you mean by that?" a woman with a hawkish nose said.

I said, "Why do you think gas stations are advertised in the Yellow Pages under service stations?"

They all looked at me like I had issued a Zen koan. Maybe I had.

"Because," I said, "our commerce depends on the benign lie. If you drink the right beer, you'll get the right chicks. If you take our pill, all your problems will be solved. And the idea is to get the money to flow to the top. And the Rev here is the top of this particular chain."

"Man," he said, "did you come down here just to take me on? You don't look the part."

"I'm always interested in what people think," I said. "Especially if they've set up a business."

"Not business. Religion."

"Oh right. So it's tax free."

He smiled. His little friends laughed. Like he was the cleverest thing on earth.

"I'm also interested in where you were on the night of January thirtieth," I said.

"Why would you be interested in that?"

"Because somebody died."

"That's news? People die all the time."

"Carl Richess only died once."

The Rev didn't change expression. "Is that someone you know?" he said.

"I was going to ask you the same thing."

He shook his head.

"He's somebody you'd remember," I said, "because you had some fights with him, when he was with Tim."

The Rev's eyebrows twitched. His plume shuddered a little. "Who are you?"

"Somebody who is in search of all truth. Now, why don't you tell me where you were on January thirtieth?"

"I don't got to tell you nothin'."

"Suddenly you're talking street?"

Railroad Spike Girl said, "He don't got to tell you nothin'."

"World without end, amen," I said. "Only maybe the cops would like a word with you."

"Look, man, what do you want from me? So I knew Carl, why should I tell you about it? You come to my house and practice deception. That's the evil in you. I can get it out if you want me to."

"I can get it out all on my own," I said.

"I haven't seen Carl in months, okay? I have no idea why he'd want to kill himself."

"Did I mention he killed himself?"

He didn't so much as blink. "I can't waste any more of my time," he said.

"You know what I think, Reverend? I think you're a hack. I think making up a religion and taking people's money from them is what small-minded hacks like you do because you can't do anything else."

This time there was a little twitch around his cheekbone.

Then a very large dude in a T-shirt without sleeves shouldered his way to me. He was my height but beefier. He had one arm that was tat sleeved, and a face like a can of knuckles. He looked older than the rest, maybe mid-thirties. And it was like he came out of nowhere, or some doorway, because I hadn't seen him before.

"You better get outta here," he said. He smelled funny. His hair was black and slick and gave off some sort of perfume. A sweet smell. Sick sweet over knuckles. A stomach turner.

I waited for Moon to call him off, the way a homeowner directs Fido back into the house. But he didn't say anything.

"You hear me?" Knuckle Face said.

"Is this a religion of peace?" I said.

The guy started to reach for me with his right hand. So I gave him the *oay ubi shime*. The jujitsu thumb grip. Old but reliable. I caught his thumb in the webbing of my right hand and bent it back, and down he went. He was on his knees in half a second. And screaming out.

The Rev said, "Let him go!"

"Call him off," I said.

Instead the Rev, the man of enlightenment, the punk preacher, kicked me in the shin.

I let the big guy go and grabbed a handful of the punk's hair. That made it easy to manipulate his head. Like riding a horse with a handful of mane.

I jerked his head down. He retaliated by hitting my knee with his nose.

Blood spurted from the holy proboscis. He dropped to the sidewalk.

His followers cackled and cheeped and gathered around their fallen master.

Then I heard one blast of a siren. A black-and-white pulled up. Good. Let the law settle this one. The law was just. The law was fair.

35

"WHAT ARE YOU arresting *me* for?" I said as one of the patrol officers cuffed me.

"In the car, please, sir," he said. "Watch your head."

"Why don't you clean up the street?"

The officer helped me into the back of his car.

At Wilcox station they marched me in, past a wooden bench to which a skinny old man was shackled. He smelled like he was sitting out a drunk.

The arresting patrol officer put his gun in a locker, then had me buzzed in to meet the jailer.

They took my property, scanned my prints, then stuck me in a cell with two other guys.

One of them was a white kid, sitting on the end of a bed. He had his head in his hands.

The other guy was in his early twenties, black, wearing a blue hoodie. He sat on a top bunk, dangling his legs. He studied me as they clanked the cell door shut.

"What you doin' here, man?" he said, smiling.

"Good question," I said.

"DUI?"

"No."

"Why they puttin' you in a cell?"

"Violence."

"You?" He said it almost mockingly. "You beat on some guy?"

"Yeah."

"Cool. What for?"

"Bad religion."

My cell mate frowned. "What you talkin' about?"

"Some dweeb out on the boulevard," I said. "Taking people's money."

"Oh yeah. Got it. Whatta you do, man?"

"I'm a lawyer."

This seemed to please him. I got a clue from the laughter that lasted almost a minute. The guy with his head in his hands finally looked over at me, like I was a new exhibit at the zoo.

The laughing guy said, "Man, I wish a couple of my lawyers'd get thrown in here."

"That's nice," I said. "What are you here for?"

"Ice," he said.

"How much?"

"Couple of rocks."

"Man, that stuff'll kill you," I said.

"So?"

"So you want to be dead?"

He shrugged. "Gonna be someday."

"Why rush it?"

"Why not? We just doin' time. You, me, him." He jerked his thumb at our silent cell mate.

"So why don't you do something with the time?" I said. "Besides get high."

"Like what, man?"

"Find stuff out."

"What are you talkin' about?"

The quiet one broke in with, "Yeah, what? We're in jail, dude."

"That's the best time," I said. "Ever hear of Boethius?"

They both shook their heads.

"He was a guy who had a pretty thing going with a king. He was like the king's philosopher."

"This a fairy story?" the Ice Man said.

"No, man, it's true. This was a real guy and a real king, back in the Roman days. You know about the Roman days?"

"Nah."

"People in togas and all that."

"Okay."

"So this guy Boethius is smart and all that, and then he has some people who get envious of him, and they diss him to the king behind his back. They tell the king he's a traitor, and the king buys it and throws him into jail."

"See?" Ice Man said, slapping his thighs. "You can't win."

"But you can," I said. "In jail, with nothing, this guy Boethius has to think. And what he figures out is that *what* you think about your circumstances is the main thing. Do you like being in here?"

"You crazy?"

"See, that's only you reflecting on your desire to be out. And desire frustrated is where unhappiness comes from."

"Do *you* like being in here?" he said.

"Right now, at this very moment, saying these words to you, I don't mind it at all."

The quiet guy said, "Dude's wack."

"No, man," Ice said. "He look like he's wack?"

"He in here," Quiet said. "Like us."

"No," I said and pointed to my head. "I'm in here."

They looked at me.

"How 'bout those Dodgers?" I said.

That's when the jailer came back for me.

36

ZEBKER WAS WAITING for me outside the jail. "Imagine my surprise," he said.

"You're cutting me loose?"

"I want to know what you were doing beating on some street people."

"It was a simple religious disagreement," I said.

"Religious?"

"I object to any religion being represented by a rooster."

Zebker shook his head.

"The Reverend Son Young Moon," I said. "It's what he calls himself. He's got this giant comb on the top of his head. He should be called Son of Foghorn Leghorn."

"What are you talking about?"

"He's a guru wannabe, up on the boulevard. He was in a love triangle with Carl Richess."

Zebker paused. Nodded. "Thanks," he said.

"Always happy to help out the police," I said. "Unless I'm cross-examining."

"I'll remember that," he said. "Need a ride to your car?"

"You'll naturally fix the parking ticket that's attached to it by now."

He just smiled.

37

IN HIS CROWN Vic, on the way up to Hollywood Boulevard, Zebker said, "You a Dodger fan?"

"Yeah," I said.

"Me too. Lifelong. Went to my first game in 1965, with my dad. I remember walking into the stadium, seeing the green field. Don Drysdale was pitching. He looked about ten feet tall."

"I started following them in '88, the year of the—"

"Kirk Gibson home run," Zebker said. "Yeah, that warmed my heart. After that the Dodger fortunes went down, but you know how many times I went to see O'Malley, or Lasorda, to get in their faces?"

I shook my head.

"Goose egg. Didn't interfere. Because it's not my place to interfere with the Dodger professionals, am I right?"

I saw where this was going. "Detective, I have a job to do. I'm not trying to get in your way, but I have to make my own way at the same time."

"Tell you what," Zebker said. "Fill me in on how you found this guy, this Moon guy, and why you were talking to him."

"I talked to somebody at Carl's apartment," I said. "A guy named Morgan Barstler. He used to be with Carl."

"Carl was gay?"

"Yep."

"What'd this guy Barstler say?"

"I asked him if he knew any reason Carl would want to kill himself, and he couldn't think of any. Carl did have a drinking problem and didn't have a partner, so who knows?"

"And your connection with Carl Richess was a DUI?"

"Yes."

"What was the dispo on that?"

"Dismissed. On a one-eight BAC, I might add."

"How'd you manage that?"

"Brilliance," I said.

"Wish I hadn't asked," Zebker said.

He did drop me at my car. It did have a parking ticket. And he did say, "Them's the breaks," before he left me there.

I drove to Highland, took a right. Up near the Hollywood Bowl, just before the freeway, somebody had spray-painted the wall with *Jesus Saves From Hell.* But another enterprising prophet had added to the words in the same black paint, but with slightly different lettering.

It now read *Jesus Saves From Hello Dolly!*
Not a bad thing to be saved from, I thought.

38

BACK AT ST. Monica's I was almost to my trailer when I saw Sister Mary.

She was coming out of the chapel with two other nuns. She stopped when she saw me, then came over.

"You're back," I said.

"Good call," she said. Her face reflected a kind of repose I hadn't seen in her recently. "It was a good trip. Good people. And I visited a holy place. Do you know about Thomas Merton?"

"Heard of him," I said. "A monk, wasn't he?"

"A Trappist," she said. "The holy ground is the corner of Fourth and Walnut in Louisville, where Merton had a famous revelation. There's a plaque there on the spot."

"What revelation was that?"

"He was standing there, in the center of the shopping district, and he said he was overwhelmed with the realization that he loved all the people around him. That he belonged to them, and they to him. And they could never be alien to each other, even though they were total strangers. He said it was like waking up from a dream of separateness."

It seemed to me there were tears forming in her eyes.

"Have you ever felt that way?" she said.

"Not since I started going to court," I said.

Her blue eyes flashed, like colored glass glinting in the sun. "His joy came from being a member of a race in which God himself became incarnate. As I was standing there, I looked around and got that feeling, too."

She was obviously moved, and maybe a little embarrassed, because I wasn't catching the feeling. I think she wanted me to. An uncomfortable moment passed between us.

"So when we play ball," I said, "Can I expect a softer, gentler Sister Mary?"

She smiled and I knew my comment had relieved the tension. "Not if you're going to the hoop."

"So look, I . . ." I kicked at some grass like a shy little kid. "I wonder if you think we can still work together."

She paused, then said, "I don't know."

"I value your input."

She nodded.

"And I want you to know," I said, "I can act appropriately."

"Can you?"

"If I don't, feel free to slap me."

"Sometimes I want to slap you anyway." She smiled, then added, "But don't worry. I can handle myself appropriately, too."

A little voice inside told me to say no. This wasn't a good idea. That everything would get jumbled if I worked with Sister Mary too closely. *Think about it*, the voice said.

But I didn't want to think about it. I didn't want to analyze anything. She was back and I wanted her to help me.

"Deal," I said.

39

ON TUESDAY I drove to the coroner's office on Mission Road and picked up the autopsy report on Carl Richess.

It was dated February 3, and signed by a deputy medical examiner named Lyle Schneuder. Hollywood Division Detectives Zebker and Stevenson were listed as witnesses.

I scanned the summary.

AUTOPSY:

The body is that of an adult Caucasian male, consistent with the age of 33 years. The normocephalic head is covered with brown hair. Eyes are brown. There is a tattoo on the left upper quadrant of the chest. See attached diagram.

FINDINGS:
Entry gunshot wound of mouth (posterior pharynx) with exit of mid-occipital skull:
    A. Disruption of sphenoid body, base of skull and occipital and parietal bones of skull.
    B. Aspiration of blood.

Evidence of gunshot injury is found in the base of skull and posterior palate. There is a pyramidal shaped defect of the palate beginning 2/3 of the distance between the alveolare and the posterior edge of the bony palate. A perforating defect is found through the sphenoid body which is internally beveled. The track is traced from anterior to posterior, inferior to superior through the regions occupied by the rostral pons, posterior corpus callosum and cerebellar vermis as well as the medial occipital lobes of the brain, impacting the skull in the upper occipital area at the juncture of the sagittal and lamboid structures.

Toxicological Test Results
BLOOD	ETHANOL	POS	00.09
URINE	ETHANOL	POS	00.08
BLOOD	AMPHETAMINE	NEG	
BLOOD	COCAINE ETS	NEG	
BLOOD	CANNABISNOIDS ETS	NEG	

Gunshot Residue Kit Results
The chemical elements Barium, Antimony and Lead are elements of virtually all primer mixes. Trace amounts of Antimony were found on the anterior of decedent's right hand. See attached.

What it all added up to was strong evidence that Carl had shot himself. The traces of ethanol, even accounting for time lapse, indicated he'd been drinking heavily just before he died.

I drove to Kate's house to deliver the news personally.

40

"I KNEW HE was upset about something," Kate said. We were sitting in her living room. She'd made some coffee and it tasted good. "I could tell."

"Do you have any idea what it could be?"

"He was lonely. Is that enough to make somebody kill himself?"

"I think it can be." I remembered how I felt in the weeks after Jacqueline died. Like I wanted to step in front of the bus. Just to make the pain stop.

"But he had his work. He got a break and got out of that DUI. I just don't understand."

She teared up. I sat with her in silence.

"If there's anything you need, Kate, call me. Help with funeral arrangements or paper work, or if you just want to talk. Okay?"

"Thank you, Ty." She took a labored breath, then said, "Why do you do this?"

"Do what?"

"These little cases. I know you used to be with a big law firm and all."

I thought about it. "You probably smashed more than a few skaters in your Derby days, am I right?"

She smiled. "Oh yes. I was the enforcer."

"Well, that was sort of what I did at my old firm. My job was to lay out the opposition in any way I could. I played all the legal games. And then one day it didn't seem worth it anymore. I'm sort of rethinking what the law is supposed to be about. For me, at least."

She put her hand on mine. "I think that's a wonderful thing, Ty. A very wonderful thing."

It felt nice, her saying that. As comforting as warm biscuits, the kind my mom used to make from scratch.

My cell sang out.

"Go ahead and answer," Kate said. "I'll top off your coffee."

I flipped the phone open.

"Ty, it's Kimberly. I just heard about Carl Richess."

"How?"

"There was an autopsy. Somebody thought I should know, Richess being my dismissed deuce and all. I'm sorry."

"Thank you. I'm here with his mother now."

"You're amazing," she said.

"Not."

"Come see me. I want to talk to you."

"When?"

"Are you almost done there?"

"You mean now?" I said.

"Meet me at the Snortin' Boar at seven."

"I—"

"See you there."

She hung up.

Kate came back in with the coffeepot. "Everything okay?"

"I think so," I said. "That was our friend, the deputy city attorney."

"From Carl's case?"

"The very same."

"But why?"

"It's a social call."

Kate sat back with her cup of coffee. "She's quite beautiful," she said.

"I noticed."

"And you're quite handsome."

"Let's not get carried away," I said.

41

MAYBE I WANTED to get carried away. Maybe it was time.

Kimberly was already in a booth at the Snort when I got there. She had a martini in front of her and a copy of the city's main legal paper, the *Daily Journal*, in her hand.

"Did you see this?" she said, as I slid in across from her. She put the *Journal* in front of me. She pointed at the story on the left side. *The Top Twenty Women Litigators in California*, the headline said.

"No," I said. "Where's your picture?"

"I'm not in there," she said. "But that's something I'm going to remedy."

"From the city attorney's office?"

"No way. These are all firm people. Some big, some small. And civil. All civil."

"So why you doing criminal?"

"Get my trial work in," she said. "I figured this was the best place for me to get experience. We filter over a hundred thousand misdemeanors a year, you know."

"Which is why you and I will never run out of things to do," I said. A waiter came by and I ordered a Sierra Nevada. The place was starting to fill up. The TV above the bar had the Laker game on.

But I had no interest in anything but the woman across from me. Because Kimberly Pincus was, quite simply, stunning. She was dressed to the nines plus change, but it seemed effortless, completely natural. She'd always look one shade better than any other woman in any room she entered. Courtroom, boardroom, or any other kind.

"I want to thank you," she said.

"For?"

"Today, I had the great pleasure of making a defense lawyer stammer. And you made that possible."

"Little old me?"

"Because of that ruling you got out of Judge Solomon, I did a little extra research on a 1538.5 that was being run. I didn't want to be caught looking unprepped, like what you did to me."

"My job. Nothing personal."

"So I found a case on point that absolutely destroyed the other side. It's not even in the official reports yet, just the advance sheets. The guy didn't know what hit him. Judge Solomon was very pleased to lay this fellow out."

"You're talking about one of my brothers," I said. "I might get the impression you didn't like us."

"There are exceptions," she said, smiling. I started falling into that smile.

The waiter saved me, bringing my beer, then said he'd check back with us. Like he knew we needed to be alone or something.

"Dinner is on me, by the way," Kimberly said.

"Are you trying to charm me?" I said.

"Absolutely. How'm I doing?"

"I believe you're doing fine."

42

KIMBERLY SAID, "I really was sorry to hear about your client."

"You never know what's going on inside people, do you?"

"Maybe not."

"Which leads to my question," I said. "What's going on inside Kimberly Pincus?"

"You really want to know?"

"Absolutely," I said. "It's my only protection."

"There's not much to tell," she said, running a finger along the rim of her martini glass. "New Jersey, privilege, all the best schooling. Maybe that's why I feel a need to prove myself."

"Need?"

"My dad was a Chicago Bears fan. Remember Dick Butkus?"

"Sure, I know about Butkus."

"My dad used to tell me a story about him, and why he was so great. He said that Dick Butkus used to dream about hitting a quarterback so hard his head would fly off. Butkus wanted to see a quarterback's head rolling along the field. That's what Butkus lived for." She looked down into her drink, as if it held the memory. "That's how my dad raised us, me and my two sisters. Three girls, but he made sure we always finished first or feel like we'd . . ."

Her voice trailed off. Her eyes stayed down. "Anyway, I go to court, I feel a little like Butkus." She raised her head and looked at me. "Strange?"

"I think I understand completely," I said.

"I think you do. I think you're exactly the same way when you walk in a courtroom."

"Nah, I'm as gentle as a kitten."

"Yeah, right." She took a sip of her drink and said, "Why don't we finish these and go to my place?"

"Your place?"

"I'll whip something up for us to eat. If I didn't go into law I was going to go to culinary school."

"Things are moving pretty fast here."

"This is L.A.," she said. "If I wanted slow I'd be DA in South Dakota."

43

KIMBERLY'S DOWNTOWN LOFT had a corner view, with the Disney Concert Hall on one side, and on the other the Music Center and Los Angeles Superior Court. Culture and clash, high art and high stakes, all within walking distance.

The interior of the loft was as perfect as Kimberly seemed to be. Nothing out of place. I looked for one errant pillow, a mislaid magazine. What I found was immaculate interior design—cool urban and tastefully eclectic.

Eye catching on the crème-colored walls were a series of framed black-and-white photographs of New York City.

Kimberly handed me a glass of white wine as I perused the photos.

"Looks like a 1950s theme," I said.

She nodded. "I love New York in that period. You know, Madison Avenue, Plaza Hotel, Ayn Rand."

"Ayn Rand? *Atlas Shrugged*?"

"Read it?"

"Got halfway through and decided life was too short."

"I'll let you borrow my copy."

"Is it hardcover?"

"Yes."

I shook my head. "It'd tip over my trailer."

"Trailer?"

"Kind of a long story."

"We've got nothing but time," she said, then went to the kitchen. And proceeded to cook up something Thai as we chatted about law and trial work and our recent pasts.

I told her about Jacqueline and the sisters of St. Monica's and my time away from the trajectory of the ambitious lawyer. She told me about Aaron, who she was going to marry only three years ago, a big-time litigator in San Diego. But he had cut it off, another woman it was, and she hadn't been serious since. Work was work, easy to get lost in, but in some ways it made her who she was, and isn't that like you, too, Ty? Isn't that the rush that makes you feel alive, when you stand in front of a jury and hear them give you a *guilty*? And no, Kimberly, I like *not guilty* a whole lot better, let's agree to disagree and this is about the best meal I've had in Los Angeles.

After dinner we sipped a brandy and sat on the sofa and listened to Charlie Parker.

Kimberly Pincus slipped her arm around my shoulder.

I don't remember who made the first move. Maybe it was a tie. But a soft, warm kiss followed. Naturally, she did it well.

My body was a box of fireworks.

If I'd been the Ty Buchanan of college days, or law school, or the first heady years of high-stakes litigation at Gunther, McDonough—had I been that Buchanan, this would have been no contest. That Buchanan would have taken hammer and tongs and gone at Kimberly Pincus with the abandon they call reckless.

But I was not him. Not anymore. Not after Jacqueline. That's just the way it was, not that I was some paragon of manly virtue. Old Buchanan was on the bench, yelling to get back in the game. Down, boy, down.

"What's wrong?" Kimberly whispered, her breath caressing my lips.

"Too fast," I said. "Even for L.A."

"Stay." She kissed me again. Sparklers started going off.

I pulled back. "If I was a jury, I'd give you the verdict."

She smiled.

"I need more time to deliberate," I said.

She brushed her lips over mine.

"You don't know anything about me," I said. "About my past as a serial killer and game show host—"

"We can talk about that over breakfast."

I stood. I was a roman candle. A spinner. A Tasmanian devil. "I don't know any smooth way to do this."

Kimberly stood. "Do what?"

"Slip out the door."

"Did you enjoy tonight?"

"Oh yes."

"It doesn't have to end." She draped her arms around my neck.

"Think of what we'll have to look forward to."

She kissed me again. Fireworks again. The whole box at once. I was overwhelmed by colors and the oohing and ahhing of the crowd. Last time anything close to this happened, it was with a reporter too soon after Jacqueline's death. And it didn't end well for either of us.

I came up for air and made my mouth say, "Good night, Kimberly."

"Let's do this again soon," she said.

I managed to get to the elevator without passing out. As I got on, I thought about falling, as in somebody cutting the cable and down I'd go. And then I'd look up from the smashed wreckage, unable to move, and I'd see Kimberly Pincus way up on the top floor, holding a pair of heavy-duty cable cutters.

And all the time, lying there, I'd think, Let's take that ride again.

44

FATHER BOB WAS sitting outside his trailer, smoking a cigar, when I got back to St. Monica's.

"Out late?" he said.

"Yes, Mother," I said.

"Cigar?"

"Don't mind if I do."

He snipped an Arturo Fuente for me, then offered a light. I sat on the other canvas chair. We smoked in silence for a moment.

"Ty, there's been another e-mail," Father Bob said.

I paused with the Fuente halfway to my mouth.

"It came in an hour ago. She had me look at it. We're the only ones who know. I'd rather not have Sister Hildegarde, shall we say, upset."

"What'd this one say?"

"It's not so much what it said, but what it showed." He tilted his head back and looked at the sky. "Why do people still not see the depravity of man?"

"What was it?" I said, no longer interested in cigars or theology.

"There was an attached drawing, showing a vile act on a nun. Along with some doggerel. 'A young nun from Nantucket' and so on. Foul."

"Same e-mail address?"

"Yes. Oh, and the nun in the drawing, it looks like her. Like Sister Mary. Almost as if someone worked off her picture."

My thumb indented the cigar against my first two fingers. I threw it on the ground. "Where is she?"

"She's praying. For him."

"For the *guy*?"

"That's what we do," he said.

"That's not what I do." I took out my phone.

Jonathan Blake Blumberg did not give his private number to just anyone. B-2, as he is known in the entrepreneurial business world, is a friend of mine. It happened when I helped him with a divorce problem. He took a liking to me, which is a good thing, because he's very handy to have around. He produces prototypes and gadgets in a never-ending stream, some of which I get to play with.

You can have your Steve Jobs or your Bill Gates. B-2 is like them, only cooler.

"How you doing, Ty?" Even his voice sounded like it worked out.

I told him what was going on with the e-mails. B-2 has a team of R&D geeks who were writing computer code in their playpens. He told me to forward the messages to him and he'd get somebody on it.

After the call I left Father Bob and went to the chapel. Where I found Sister Mary kneeling behind a pew.

I slipped into it.

She looked up, crossed herself, and said, "Do you know?"

"Father Bob told me. How you holding up?"

"I can't imagine why this is happening. It's awful. It's . . ."

I wanted to pull her to me and hold her. But the veil was between us and I'd promised to act appropriately. I let my hate for the stalker take over. What I wanted to do to him should not be mentioned anywhere near a church.

"Maybe down at the homeless shelter," I said. "Somebody who took a liking to you."

"That could be any number of people."

"I'm getting B-2 on it, I want you to know. He can do more than the police. If this guy can be found, he'll find him."

"I don't know."

"What do you mean you don't know?"

"Keep your voice down, please," she said. "He is someone who needs help, he—"

"Now don't start in with that Thomas Merton stuff, okay? I can't—"

"Stuff? It's not *stuff*. It's what makes us human."

"When it comes to humanity," I said, "I'm more of a law-of-club-and-fang guy."

"What?"

"From *Call of the Wild*. Jack London. If I was standing on a street corner in Louisville, or anywhere else, that's what I'd see. Everybody out for himself, and ready to take away what's yours. That's my revelation." And had been ever since I'd been beat up looking for Jacqueline's killers.

Sister Mary looked at her hands. I felt like a jerk.

"Can you hold up?" I said.

She nodded. "As long as it's just e-mail, but . . ."

I waited. She looked at me in the dim light of the chapel. Half her face was in shadow. "We both know it's not going to end at e-mails, don't we?"

45

PROBABLY NOT.

Which was no doubt why I had trouble sleeping. Thinking of that scum out there, laughing. And then wondering about Merton and how Sister Mary could buy into it and why couldn't I? Or did I even want to? And in all of that the memory of Thai food and wine and the smell of Kimberly's hair.

And what did Plato ever have to say about Thai food and soft kisses in the night? The old fart.

I finally drifted off looking at a fingernail of moon outside the small window in my trailer bedroom.

It felt like I got ten minutes' worth. A little after three my phone jolted me awake.

It was Kate Richess.

"They've arrested Eric," she said. "I don't know what to do."

"Arrested Eric? What for?"

No answer. I could hear her labored breath.

"Kate, what was he arrested for?"

"For . . . killing his brother."

I didn't say anything. My thoughts weren't exactly jelling.

"What can we do?" Kate said.

"Where is he?"

"Jail, downtown. He asked me to call you. I'm sorry I woke you. I just can't sleep, I can't do anything. . . ."

"I'll go see him tomorrow."

"Don't let this happen, Ty. I can't lose my other son."

I wish I could have waved a magic wand for her. But this wasn't sounding good at all. Brother killing brother, that was the oldest crime on the books. Cain killed Abel. After that, Cain was a goner. Convicted and sentenced. The boy never had a chance.

Lawyers hadn't been invented yet.

46

IN THE EARLY afternoon I drove downtown with Sister Mary.

The Twin Towers Correctional Facility is on Bauchet Street, across from the Men's Central Jail. A newer and more secure housing than Central, it is usually reserved for the more troublesome inmates, like heavy gangbangers, or those with severe medical needs.

They call the design of the place "panoptic," which basically means they can always see you. You can't always see them.

Creepy.

We entered the lobby and walked past the long row of cement benches, where the public waits to be called up for visitations. Sister Mary sat on one of the benches and took out a book.

I went to the front window and gave them my attorney slip, which had Eric's name and booking number on it, and my Bar card and driver's license. I signed in, and the large deputy with arms like logs said, "Fourth floor."

I walked through the security scanner—they don't allow any electronics or cell phones—bringing only my briefcase. Then I walked down the long corridor, alone but not alone.

There are cameras everywhere and hidden glass through which you can be observed. Even though I didn't see another human body, I knew I was being watched. The institutional yellow walls, sort of early vomit, felt even more constrictive than normal.

There's an antiseptic feeling to the place, no personality. You would think an inmate would prefer to be housed here, where you might only have one other cell mate, as opposed to four or five at Men's Central. But the inmates actually like the camaraderie, if you can call it that, at Central. Here it's like being housed in a Soviet prison.

Or a refrigerator. The air conditioning is always amped up. They could store meat as well as inmates. And some of the deputy sheriffs, who run the place, don't really care to know the difference.

At the end of the corridor I came to the elevators, got in, and went up to the fourth floor. I turned right and went through the heavy metal doors and toward the attorney booth at the end. I walked by the bank of phones where the public talks to their inmates on the other side of the Plexiglas. You can see through the glass into the day room, where blue-clad inmates wander or sit, some looking at nothing, some playing cards. Some thinking, no doubt, about who they are going to hurt when they get out.

Across from the phone bank I punched the intercom button and announced my presence. Then I went into the open attorney booth, which is about twice the size of a phone booth, and sat down on my side of the Plexiglas.

There are no handsets in the attorney booth. A little microphone picks up everything on each side. On the inmates' side there is a round bolt, the "doughnut," in the middle of the table, to which they are shackled.

On the shelf in front of me some goober had left an empty Skittles bag and Juicy Fruit wrapper. This could have come from a slob attorney or even a member of the public. They leave the door of the attorney room open, and sometimes a person ducks in for a look.

The deputies don't seem to care about that, and it shows.

A minute or two later, Eric, dressed in jail blues, was brought in by a deputy.

47

ERIC'S EYES WERE bleary, like he'd been crying.

"You okay?" I said.

"Do I look okay?" he said. "What is going on?"

"You tell me."

"They're saying I killed my own brother! Get me out of here!"

"Keep your voice low. Just talk to me, and answer my questions directly. And don't lie, okay?"

"Why should I lie? Oh God . . ." He put his head down and into his cuffed hands.

"Easy," I said.

"I can't believe this is happening. Mom . . ." He looked up. "Where's Mom?"

"She's at home, resting. I told her I'd come see her after this."

Down went his head again.

"Eric, we need to talk about this. And I mentioned lying because almost all people in custody think they can do themselves some good if they cook the truth a little. You can't. Are we clear on that?"

He looked at me and nodded.

"Did they ask you any questions?" I said.

"They asked me about a fight I had with Carl."

"You had a fight with Carl?"

"Yeah."

"When?"

"I don't know, a couple of nights before he shot himself."

"Can you be a little more precise, please? When *exactly* was this fight?"

He thought a moment. "Okay, maybe it was the night before."

I closed my eyes. "Think before you answer, okay?"

"Sorry."

"Having a fight the night before your brother is shot is a pretty significant detail, don't you think?"

"It's just a coincidence. We had fights before. Brothers have fights."

"Did they ask you any other questions?"

"I stopped them and said I wanted a lawyer. Then I called my mom."

"That was your first good move," I said. "Tell me about this fight. Where'd it happen?"

"In a bar."

"Did it get physical?"

"Almost. Mostly it was just yelling."

"What bar was this?"

"A place in West Hollywood."

"What's the name of the place?"

"I can't remember."

"You said that a little too fast," I said. "You start throwing out *I can't remembers* like that, no jury is going to believe you. Or your lawyer, either."

"I mean I can't remember," he said. "It was a funny-sounding name. I didn't want us to go there, but Carl wouldn't take no for an answer."

"All right, we'll get the name later. What was the fight about?"

"It was about his drinking. And what it was doing to Mom. And about the people he was hanging with."

"What people?"

"He was involved with some actor, a snot-faced kid. Arrogant. I didn't like him. I can't remember his name."

"Anybody else?"

Eric looked at the ceiling. "There was that real conservative guy, Mr. Perfect Hair."

"Morgan Barstler?"

"I think that may have been his name."

"Anyone else?"

Eric shook his head. "That was it. But mainly it was about getting him to AA, and he needed to go, and how Mom was so worried about him all the time."

"Where were you when your brother was killed?"

He started to open his mouth. Stopped. Looked down.

"What is it?" I said.

"It's kind of hard for me to say."

"You have to say."

"I was sort of with someone."

"Okay. Give me the who and the where."

"It's complicated," he said.

"Let's try to sort it out," I said.

"I'm married."

"That's what's complicated?"

"My wife, see, she's not the most understanding, know what I mean?"

"Are you trying to tell me that you were with another woman when Carl was killed?"

"You're pretty good at sorting things out."

"Who's the woman?"

"But my wife—"

"I'm not a marriage counselor, Eric. I'm a lawyer. My job is to represent you to the best of my ability, but I can't do that if you don't give up the very evidence that may lead to your acquittal. If you were with another woman, I want to know who she is, now."

"That's just the thing," Eric said.

"Don't tell me she was a pro."

"How'd you know that?"

"Oh, I just thought of the absolute worst thing for you to tell me, that's all."

"But it's true."

"So your alibi witness is a hooker?"

"Is that bad?"

"It's very bad," I said.

"She's not really a hooker," Eric said. "More of an escort."

"Ah, now that's a relief."

"But it's *true*."

"So is the fact that it's very bad. A provider of sexual services is not exactly a great witness to put on the stand."

"I don't even know if I can find her again," he said.

"Boy, this just keeps getting better and better."

"I'm telling you the absolute truth!"

"How long were you with her?"

"A couple hours."

"And what time was this?"

"Like nine or so."

"Where?"

"Long Beach."

Which is a good long drive from West Hollywood. "Did you use an escort service?"

"Kind of."

"What does *that* mean?"

"I used a guy a bartender told me about."

"You have the guy's name?"

Eric looked at me hard. "You're the man. I didn't do this thing. You can get me off, can't you?"

"I'm not representing you yet. There's a conflict here. I repped your brother."

"So?"

"You're going to have to tell a judge that you want me to be your lawyer, and you don't care about any conflict."

"I don't. I know you're good. I want you."

"Then you have two choices. You can help me find this alibi witness you have, or you can start planning what you're going to do with twenty-five to life."

He thought about it. His forehead pinched. He looked at the table. Took a deep breath. Then he said, "Okay, Turk Bacon. That's the guy."

"He's the one between you and Miss Long Beach?"

"Yeah," Eric said.

"Now you're being straight with me. That's a good start. How do I find this Turk Bacon? I don't imagine he's listed in the white pages."

"The bartender at a place called Addie Qs. Her name's Tosca."

"All right. Next time I see you is at the arraignment." I started to get up. "By the way, has your wife been to see you?"

"No."

"She has to be told," I said. "You want me to be the bearer of the news?"

"Maybe you better," he said. "She might reach through this glass and kill me if I told her. Oh man, I messed up big time."

I didn't argue with him.

48

WHEN I GOT back to reception, Sister Mary was sitting next to a Hispanic woman. It looked like she was comforting her.

She was, in other words, doing her thing, just as I'd been doing mine. I chatted with a deputy sheriff until she was finished.

As we drove toward the freeway I said, "So you want to talk about Sister Hildegarde now?"

"What? Why?"

"She's trying to muscle you out."

Sister Mary looked straight ahead. "You don't know the first thing about what we do."

She was right, and I reminded myself again not to get involved in the workings of a religious community whose religion I did not share. Then I ignored the reminder.

"I know this," I said. "You and Sister Hildegarde are like Oscar and Felix."

"You're calling us the Odd Couple?"

"Only it's not neatness you argue about, it's nun stuff."

"Nun stuff?"

"Theological term," I said. "But you've talked about it before. You want to go back to when nuns were nuns. When they brushed their teeth with Brillo. Sister Hildegarde is more, what's the word, progressive? She likes politics. You like to pray. You two are bound to clash."

"That's always part of community life," she said. "It's why God puts us together. To learn how to humble ourselves."

"There's a difference between humility and doormats," I said.

"And between lawyers and nuns," she said. "Speaking of which, what did your client say?"

I pulled onto the 101, heading toward Hollywood. "It's what he didn't say that bothers me."

"Is he guilty?"

"Not for me to say."

"Can't you tell if he's guilty or not?"

"Not my job," I said.

"Don't you even want to know?"

"No."

"Why in heaven's name not?"

"Leave heaven out of it," I said. "I got enough trouble on earth. And the answer is, I don't want to know. I want to know the evidence. Unless I think a plea deal and allocution is best, I want to be free to do my job. Can you work under those conditions?"

"Yes, Mr. Buchanan, I believe I can."

"Good. Let's get a drink."

"Excuse me?"

49

WE KILLED A little time in Hollywood first. Went to a bookstore. Browsed.

Sister Mary picked up a copy of *Conjectures of a Guilty Bystander* by Merton.

I found a book called *Never Plead Guilty*, about a lawyer named Jake Ehrlich. According to the back of the book, Ehrlich was a legendary criminal lawyer back in the mid-twentieth century.

A quick scan told me this was a guy who loved to fight it out in court. And he was apparently pretty good—if gaining acquittals for almost all his clients accused of murder is pretty good.

"Here," I said, when I met up with her at the front of the store. "My book versus your book. Your guy pleads guilty, my guy says never."

"Never confess?" she said. "Did you notice I'm Catholic?"

"So that's it. I knew there was something about you. The clothes. The beads. You're a nun, aren't you?"

"And you're a failed comedian, am I right?"

"Looks like I need that drink. Let's go."

50

AROUND FOUR-THIRTY WE drove to Addie Qs. It was at the eastern mouth of the Sunset Strip, just past Crescent Heights. Upscale, catering to professionals.

A number of whom were at the bar for what the sign said was happy hour.

We sat at the end of the bar. The conversation got very quiet as we did. Heads craned our way.

One middle-aged joker said, way too loudly, "Hey, a nun and a parrot walk into a bar . . ."

A healthy knot of the people cracked up.

"What about the Irishman?" Sister Mary said.

The guy slapped the bar top. "That's a good one! Have a drink on me, Sister."

The bartender was tall, buff, Asian. She was dressed in the color of night. Her hair was long and black. She came over with an expressionless look and a scent of gardenia, and asked what we'd have. Sister Mary ordered a Coke. I did the same.

"Tosca?" I said.

The bartender blinked. She had long, curling black lashes over exotic, ebony eyes. She could have been the star in one of those Hong Kong woman-who-kicks-male-tail-with-bad-lip-syncing movies.

"I'm asking for a friend," I said.

She scooped ice into a couple of glasses and put them on the rubber collar of the bar. She grabbed the soda gun and started filling the glasses with Coke. "What friend would that be?"

"Eric Richess," I said.

She shook her head. "I don't think I know him." She put two red cocktail napkins on the bar, then the glasses on the napkins.

"How about Turk Bacon?" I said.

She stiffened like drywall. "Who are you? And who is she?"

"My name's Buchanan. And this is Sister Mary Veritas of the Benedictine order. I'm a lawyer, she's a nun. If you put us together, you get a perfectly balanced human being."

Tosca just looked at me.

"I'm here," I said, "because Eric Richess is accused of murder and I'm representing him. And we need to find the lady he was with on the night of the killing."

"So what does that have to do with me?" Tosca said.

"You can put me in touch with the said Mr. Bacon," I said.

She shook her head. "Don't know him."

"Is this the part where we slip you a twenty?" Sister Mary asked.

I looked at her. She was looking at the bartender, hard.

"Excuse me?" Tosca said.

"Because you clearly do know Mr. Bacon," Sister Mary said. "If you want us to grease your palm, just say so."

For a second, Tosca the Bartender looked like someone had thrown a drink in her face. Then: "We reserve the right to refuse service to anyone. And I'm refusing to serve you anymore. You can leave now."

"You're refusing to serve a nun?" I said.

"That's what I'm doing," Tosca said.

"You've heard of anti-discrimination laws, haven't you?"

"Hey, we can—"

"And the free exercise of religion that is guaranteed under the Constitution?"

"I didn't say anything—"

"I'm pretty sure I can convince a court that kicking a nun out of a bar is discriminatory."

"And I'm not even drunk," Sister Mary said.

"Yet," I said.

Sister Mary gave me a kick under the bar.

Tosca narrowed her eyes, blinking those big lashes a couple of times.

I was aware that people were calling to her, but she wasn't moving. A former extra from *The Sopranos* came over and stood next to Tosca. He was ample in girth, had black hair, and wore a fine black suit and gold tie.

"There a problem?" he said, with a smile. He did a double take on Sister Mary.

"We'd like to finish our drinks," I said.

"They're asking questions," Tosca said. "They're not here to drink."

The suit looked at the bar top. "Are those not drinks?"

"Strictly for show," Tosca said.

"We have other customers," the guy said to Tosca. She shot us a couple of glares and headed for the other side of the bar.

The *Sopranos* extra said, "You two enjoy yourselves. But let us run our business, huh?"

51

"I'M NOT DRUNK *yet?*" Sister Mary said.

"Nice touch, wasn't it?" I said. We were on the freeway heading back to St. Monica's.

"Oh yeah. Very smooth and respectful."

"You ever been drunk?"

"I beg your pardon?"

"Just asking."

"Rather personal question," she said.

"If we're going to be working together, I need to know if my partner's a lush."

"You're really on a roll today."

"In a courtroom, I'd object to your answer as non-responsive."

"You're in a car, pal. Drive."

I shut up. Talking to a nun about alcohol consumption is probably not a wise thing, especially if she has elbows.

But then, just before I got on the 118 west, she said, "Once."

"Oh yeah?"

"With my friend Julie James. We were thirteen. We went to a movie. *Toy Story*. And we had a bottle of Boone's Farm Strawberry Hill."

"You're kidding."

"No."

"You got drunk on Boone's Farm wine while watching *Toy Story?*"

"I remember about half the movie," she said. "Then I remember thinking the world was a whirligig and I got very, very sick. Right there in the theater."

"A very touching story," I said. "Are you sure you're off the sauce now?"

"I can't remember the last bar fight I was in," she said. "So I must be fine."

I smiled. "I'm trying to picture you doing that, and I'm having trouble."

"Why?"

"Because, well, you're Sister Mary Veritas."

"And *veritas* is Latin for *truth*, so there you go." She put her head back on the seat. "Truth is, I did some things in high school I'm not proud of."

"Cool. Like what?"

"Please drop me at the homeless shelter," she said. "Sister Hildegarde wanted me to pick up some fruitcake tins."

"Sure. Getting back to high school—"

"Just drive, can't you?"

52

THE SHELTER RUN by St. Monica's and a couple of churches is off Van Nuys Boulevard near Hansen Dam Park. It's a converted apartment complex with a wrought-iron gate and a big parking lot in the middle. I pulled in and parked and Sister Mary told me to wait and not get into any trouble, and I said, Thank you, Sister, and put my head back and looked out my rearview mirror.

I was wondering if among those wandering around like lost souls on a ghost ship was the guy sending Sister Mary e-mails. I tried to read faces, see if anybody was homing in on Sister Mary as she walked.

Turns out, several people were. Men, women, and children. They were gathering around her as if she were some sort of event, or a visiting celebrity.

But I could tell from their expressions, and hers, that she was the opposite of the glitterati. She was relating to each person on a completely equal basis. She did not pick and choose, she did not assume any air of superiority or intrinsic goodness.

She just was *there*, for them. She made each one feel important. Several obviously knew her, and were happy in their greeting. Sister Mary seemed happy, too.

It hit me, those words she had quoted from Merton. His revelation in Louisville. Sister Mary was living it, right here. These people were part of her, and she of them, and she loved them all.

I wondered if I would ever feel that way about anything. Or anybody. Or if I wanted the risk.

Somebody slapped the roof of my car and said, "Dude!"

I turned to the driver's-side window and saw my old friend Only, the toking psychic. He was bent over to look in the car, smiling. "What are you doing here, man?" he said.

"Driving a nun around," I said. "What are *you* doing here?"

He looked at the ground. "I got fired again."

"From the psychic hotline?"

He nodded sheepishly.

"It wasn't for smoking on the job, was it?" I said.

He shook his head. "I got mad at a guy on the phone. He was all ripping me because I wouldn't tell him what stocks to pick. He started calling me names, man. So I told him a plague of boils was gonna grow on his butt. So he complained."

"For that little thing?"

"So now I'm out on the street."

"You'll get another shot," I said. "You toning down the weed?"

"I can't afford it, man. My back hurts and I gotta get a job."

"You will," I said. "They'll help you out here."

"Never thought I'd be living near nuns," he said.

"You and me both," I said.

53

AFTER DROPPING SISTER Mary off at St. Monica's, I called Kate and told her I'd seen Eric, and that he'd be arraigned tomorrow, and that it would be short and Eric would just plead not guilty. She didn't need to be there.

I asked her for Eric's wife's number and said I needed to speak to her.

"Just be aware," Kate said, "that she's . . . excitable."

Whatever that meant.

I called the number and a woman with a slight southern accent picked up.

"Is this Fayette Richess?" I said.

"Who is this?"

"Ty Buchanan, Eric's lawyer. I wonder if we could talk."

"What do you need?"

"Can I come to where you are? I'd like to talk face-to-face if I may."

"Why?"

"Just to fill you in on a few things."

"You can fill me in now, can't you?"

"There's some information I'd rather not relate over the phone. It's about the case."

"I figured it was about the case, why else would you be calling me? And no, it's not convenient to talk just now. I have a life I can't put on hold because Eric's been arrested."

"Mrs. Richess, if I could—"

"I don't go by Richess. My last name is Scarborough."

"I'll make a note of it."

Long pause. Then: "All right, fine, you want to talk to me, I'll give you twenty minutes."

She told me where she lived and I got there in half an hour.

54

IT WAS A townhouse complex in the Warner Center area of Woodland Hills. Eric's unit was on the second floor.

Nicely done up, and I wouldn't have guessed that. Eric didn't seem the type for a place like this. He was a sports-bar guy. The way the home was decorated had the unmistakable woman's touch.

Fayette Scarborough was the woman.

She was about thirty, with wheat-colored hair and gray eyes. The eyes were big and round. Owlish, which is probably why I felt like a field mouse. She didn't smile or offer any pleasantries. It was like she was daring me to talk.

So I didn't. I looked the place over until she said, "So is he guilty?"

"The prosecution thinks he is."

"That doesn't answer my question."

"I can't help but observe, Ms. Scarborough, that you don't seem all that broken up about Eric being in the clink."

"I don't think he killed his brother, if that helps. I don't think he's that low."

"Do you think he's somewhat low?"

"I don't like the way you're talking to me."

"That doesn't answer my question."

Frost crackled out of those wide eyes. "What exactly are you here for? What was so important?"

"Let's sit down."

"I don't want to. Just tell me."

"All right. Eric was with another woman when Carl died."

She took a long breath. "Who is she?"

"A prostitute, apparently."

"Well, that's just wonderful." She turned and faced the french doors that looked out on the balcony and had a view of Warner Center Park.

I said, "I'm sorry there wasn't an easier way to tell you."

"Oh, it's not your fault. And it's not surprising. I knew what I was getting into when I married him."

"So why'd you marry him?"

She turned on me. "Are you married?"

"No."

"Ever been?"

"No."

"Gay?"

"It's been nice chatting with you."

"It's all right to be gay."

"Ms. Scarborough, my sexual orientation has got exactly nothing to do with anything."

"I'm asking, because you don't seem to understand what goes into being married these days. It's all a crap shoot. It's not like fifty years ago, when you got married and you stayed faithful and you had two and a half kids. It's not that way anymore. Men have no qualms about going out about town, as the saying used to be."

"Adultery's always been around," I said.

"But it used to be frowned upon, even if one was indulging in it."

"Why did you marry Eric, if you don't mind my asking?"

"Now you may sit," she said. I parked myself on a white sofa while she took a soft leather recliner.

"I thought I was in love," she said. "I should have listened to my parents. They didn't think Eric was up to their standards."

"Their standards?"

"It's called breeding by some, class by others. But it exists. My parents believe I married down. Eric was different than these metrosexuals my parents wanted to fix me up with. Maybe part of it was I wanted to stick it to my parents, if you know what I mean."

"Not a good way to start a marriage, though."

"But I worked at it. I did all the heavy lifting. I can't say Eric did the same."

"Why didn't you divorce him?"

"I'm stubborn, I guess. I wanted to make it work. I don't want a divorce hanging over me. It's like a failure. And Scarboroughs are not into failure."

She sat back and closed her eyes. Maybe Scarboroughs weren't into failure, but they could get discouraged.

"Again, I'm sorry," I said. "But I guess I want to know if you're going to be with Eric or against him."

"If I thought there was any hope for us, maybe I'd be more open to it. I'm not going to cause any problems, if that's what you're worried about."

"How about bailing him out after he's arraigned?"

"Maybe."

"Maybe?"

"In jail he can't get into any more trouble, can he?"

"I don't want to get all Dr. Phil on you, Ms. Scarborough, but I would think it's better to work things out face-to-face, instead of through Plexiglas."

"What you think isn't any concern of mine. Is that all?"

"Can you think of anyone who might have wanted Carl dead?"

"Oh, who knows? I don't know anything about his life. I never talked to him. He wasn't particularly pleasant toward me."

What a surprise, I thought.

"All the same," I said, "think about bailing Eric out. I don't think his mother should have to do it."

"Why not? She's the mother hen. That's what she likes."

"You make it sound like a bad thing."

"She overdoes it."

"She's a mother," I said. "With one son dead and another in jail. She deserves some slack."

Fayette Scarborough just stared at me as if I were a burn mark in her rug. "I think we're through here," she said.

I was more than happy to get out of that love nest.

I put a jazz station on in the car as I drove back to St. Monica's, taking Topanga all the way, trying to sort through what Fayette would mean to the trial, if anything. The marital-trouble angle would support Eric's story about being with another woman, but wouldn't do anything to establish time or place for an alibi.

Besides, the jury probably wouldn't like her, and you don't want them disliking your wits. Bad for the overall case.

I thought about Eric's marriage. Why had it gone sour? Was it inevitable?

I wondered what I'd be like right now if everything had gone according to plan, and I'd married Jacqueline. I'd still be at Gunther, McDonough pulling down hefty bucks. I'd be a different person, too.

So who was I now? Somebody who'd gotten knocked around by some bad people. I knew I was not going to let that happen again. I would strike first and ask questions later. I liked my head in one piece.

Would I keep it that way up at St. Monica's?

Something told me I wasn't going to last up there much longer.

55

THURSDAY MORNING, ERIC Richess was arraigned in Division 30, the felony arraignment court, fifth floor of the Foltz Building downtown. Sister Mary and I arrived at 8:35 and I showed her around the place.

It used to be called the Criminal Courts Building, or CCB, and many of the lawyers who practice down here still call it that. The city had renamed it for Clara Shortridge Foltz, the first woman admitted to the practice of law in California.

I wondered what Clara would have thought of Kimberly Pincus.

Then we went up to Division 30 for the festivities.

Kate Richess was waiting on a wood bench outside the courtroom. She looked like the rest of the multi-cultured family members scattered around the hall. Tense. Uncertain. Half suspecting the wheels of justice to be more like the Jaws of Life—cutting, crushing, grinding.

She stood and greeted us each with an embrace. Sister Mary took her by the arm and sat down with her. It looked like they were going to pray.

So I went inside to wait.

I knew the courtroom well. I had been arraigned myself here once. I knew what it was like to be stuck in the box where Eric now sat in his prison jumper.

They knew me here, too. The same commissioner was on the bench. Commissioner K, as he was known. Kenneth Khachatoorian. He still looked like he should be playing second clarinet in the high school band.

Kate and Sister Mary came in and sat in the back row. I nodded at them and waited as the arraignment calendar meandered along.

When K finally called Eric's case and I stated my appearance, he smiled. "Well, well, well," he said. "If it isn't the celebrity."

Of course, when he said that, all the other activity stopped at the DA and PD tables, where the churning of files was going on.

"Nice to see you again, Commissioner," I said. "Under better circumstances."

"How right you are. You're doing criminal now?"

"Yes, Your Honor."

"I guess you can relate to your clients, huh?"

Some chuckles from the DA side.

"Right you are," I said. "Speaking of which, my client is right over there, Mr. Eric Richess. We waive a reading of the complaint and statement of rights. Ready to plead."

Commissioner K looked at Eric, who was standing in the box. "Mr. Richess, has your lawyer explained the charges against you?"

"Yeah," Eric said.

"Do you understand your constitutional rights?"

"I think so."

"Did your lawyer explain them to you?"

"I think so."

I winced. Commissioner K winced, too. We were like synchronized swimmers.

"Let's not think so, shall we?" Commissioner K said. "You are presumed to be innocent until proven guilty beyond a reasonable doubt. Do you understand that?"

"Yeah."

"You have the right to a speedy trial. You have the right to a preliminary hearing ten court days from now. If you are held to answer, any information must be filed within fifteen days, and a trial sixty days after it is so filed, unless you agree to waive time. Do you understand those rights?"

"Sure."

"Are you ready to enter a plea?"

"Yeah."

"You're charged with violation of Penal Code Section 187, one count of murder. How do you plead?"

"Not guilty," Eric said.

"All right, let's set this for preliminary hearing."

I looked at the arraignment deputy for the DA's office. He was looking at his PDA.

"We are not going to waive time," I said, and watched the DDA's face go into spasm.

"Well then," Commissioner K said, "since I just told your client about his rights, we've got ten court days. Bail is five hundred thousand."

Outside the courtroom, I explained the bail situation to Kate. There was no way she was going to be able to come up with fifty grand, the amount of a bond. I told her I'd front her the money, but she refused. Said she'd come up with it if she could. I told her she didn't have to, but she insisted, saying it was a matter of principle with her. She hugged me and I hugged her back. I wanted to win for this woman more than any other case I'd ever handled.

56

WHEN WE GOT back to St. Monica's, Sister Hildegarde was shuffling outside the office, as if she was waiting for us.

"Top of the day to you, Sister," I said.

She did not crack a smile. Her face was like a concrete overpass. "You may report to the kitchen," Sister Hildegarde said to Sister Mary. Dutifully, Sister Mary nodded and went off without a word. I had to admire her for that. I would have snapped off a few one-liners.

I don't think I'd make a good nun.

"Mr. Buchanan," Sister Hildegarde said, "I fear you are distracting Sister Mary from her duties."

"Actually, she's been helping me pursue justice, and I—"

"Please, Mr. Buchanan."

"You have one of the best examples of Christian charity in Sister Mary," I said. "And you—"

"We have had this discussion before, Mr. Buchanan. You are not of our faith. You cannot possibly understand what goes on here."

"I don't know if I agree with you. Fairness is fairness no matter where you are. And character is character. I've seen enough religion to know that it doesn't always translate into someone's daily life. Sister Mary's does. You should be glad she's part of this place."

"I am glad for every member of the community, Mr. Buchanan."

"Would that include me?"

"And I'm glad that you brought that up. I've been wanting to talk to you again about how long you plan on staying."

"I sort of hope I've been an asset here. You might call me the legal arm of St. Monica's. Here you have the fruitcake arm, the prayer arm, the ministry-to-the-poor arm, and me, the arm of the law."

"I appreciate your helping those in our parish. But I also have to be concerned for what happens within these walls. It is what I have been given charge of. I would ask that you'd consider setting a goal for when you might leave us. Will you think about that, Mr. Buchanan?"

This was her joint, as it were. I didn't need to be a jerk. "Yes I will, Sister. Thanks for your hospitality."

She gave me a quick nod and headed back toward her office.

I headed back to my trailer, which I was sort of getting to like.

I told myself not to get to like this place, or anybody in it, too much. I sensed that I was setting myself up for a fall.

57

I WAS REPRESENTING a man on a charge of murder. It was time to get serious about trial preparation. I ensconced myself in my trailer and started exercising my head.

Lawyers vary in their approach to trial prep. But the best trial lawyer I ever saw—Art Goldstein, who was my mentor at Gunther, McDonough— showed me how to do it his way. I have never varied from it.

"You start with the closing argument," Art said. "A trial is a story. Doesn't matter if it's murder or shoplifting, insider trading or a dispute about the back fence with your neighbor. The jury wants to know what the story is, and your closing argument is the story. Everything you do up to that point is material for the story. You need to know where you're going before you can get there."

I opened up a new file on my Mac laptop. Back at the firm I had assistants, associates, and various worker bees to do a lot of this work for me. Now it was just me and a computer, and organizing a trial notebook.

The first document I titled *Theory of the Case.* That's basically the core of what Art told me, the theory—or story—of what happened. It has to be logical, understandable, likely, and persuasive. It must be supported by the evidence. This would become my ongoing story document, subject to change as discovery came in and facts were elicited at trial. But the goal is always to keep the story from changing too much. The template was going to be as permanent as possible.

I would take an aggressive approach. Too many lawyers wait for discovery from the other side to determine their opening moves. That's giving too much power to the opponent. I'd start to form up my theory and then go out and look for the facts supporting it.

I opened other documents titled *Opening Statement, Voir Dire, Law & Motions, Witnesses, Jury Instructions, Exhibits, Memoranda,* and *Closing Argument.*

I would go over these documents every day, brainstorming, adding things that were relevant to each area, depending on what my investigation turned up.

In my *Theory of the Case* document I wrote the following:

1. Eric did it.
2. Eric didn't do it.

Under number 1, I put the following subheadings:

   a. With malice aforethought
   b. In the heat of passion
   c. By accident
   d. In self-defense
   e. With mental impairment

Under number 2, I wrote:

   a. Has alibi
   b. No alibi, but misidentified
   c. Carl committed suicide.
   d. Somebody else killed Carl.

Now, with every fact I discovered, I would determine the most likely place it would go. I had to know the prosecution's case as well as my own. At this point I had a minimum of prosecutorial discovery—police reports, the autopsy report, some crime-scene photos, and a few witness statements. I had the distinct feeling they were holding something back, to be revealed at the prelim. For now I had to try to anticipate what they would present at both prelim and trial. "Half of all trial work," Art used to say, "is heading them off at the pass."

I spent about an hour jotting random thoughts and thinking about the case, getting my mind in the right frame for a trial. I guess that's how the old gladiators of Rome would do it, before heading into the arena. They were trial lawyers, all of them. There just wasn't enough legal work to go around, so they went into the Coliseum and beat the caesar salad out of each other.

One thing was odd about the facts as I knew them. How could a big man like Eric get into the apartment building, then Carl's apartment, shoot him, and get out without being seen? That would be a good thing to argue to the jury. Like the dog that didn't bark in the Sherlock Holmes story.

When I looked up from my work I saw it was an orange-sky night. People have this idea L.A. is nothing but a smog blanket with citizens underneath, hacking and wheezing.

The air's actually not as bad as it was fifty years ago, so they tell me. Back then dirt and fog would sit in the bowl they call the Los Angeles basin and it could get so thick you could walk across town on it. Kids, swimming during hot summers, would get out of pools coughing like they were three-pack-a-day smokers.

Sure, there's stuff in the air, but there's one benefit. As if the universe couldn't stand leaving us in the muck without a little compensation. The benefit is how the sun, dropping into the Pacific horizon, gives a bright, burnt-orange hue to the sky. And a deep purple just before night.

On nights like this I think of Jacqueline, and how she loved driving down to Paradise Cove, off Pacific Coast Highway, to catch a sunset.

Once when we did that, sitting on the sand, a blanket around us as the wind blew in cold, I thought it was the happiest moment of my life. A wheelhouse where everything had finally come together for me.

It was all ripped away a few weeks later, when Jacqueline was killed.

I went outside and walked to the parking lot of St. Monica's. I looked down at the Valley, past the 118 Freeway, at the buildings of Warner Center, tall in the oncoming gloom. It's a view people pay millions for and I had it for free.

I sat on the curb and watched dusk become night, aching for Jacqueline and a blanket and a breeze.

58

THE NEXT MORNING I drove into Hollywood to the job site Carl had worked on before he died. Boss Hildegarde had Sister Mary delivering some of St. Monica's signature fruitcakes to victims—I should say customers, but I won't—at locales around the Valley. So I was on my own, which I didn't really want to be. I liked Sister Mary's eyes on the people I questioned.

The dig was, ironically, just a beer can's throw from the Hollywood station where Carl was booked that December evening, and where I got to cool my jets after sparring with Knuckle Face on the boulevard. But I wasn't getting sentimental about it.

The site was also right around the corner from the field office of City Councilmember Jamie MacArthur, the up-and-coming L.A. politico with the square chin of George Clooney and a showstopping wife. This project, everyone in L.A. knew, was MacArthur's baby, because he made sure everyone knew.

I found a place on the street and walked over to the site. It looked like they'd leveled a whole city block for this. A line of concrete trucks was snaking along the street. They were taking turns feeding the beast—the giant snout of the snorkel boom that spat wet concrete for the pad.

A team of rubber-booted workers guided the pour, one with the snout in hand, five others rodding it out with a two-by-four. Another guy was tamping with a handheld, and there were even a couple of workers with trowels. Some things you still had to do with basic tools and muscle. I like that. There's too much comfort in technology these days. A kid can thumb an iPhone, but can he change a tire?

I stood at the entrance of the temporary fence and waited around. Finally, a couple of Hispanic workers, with heavy-duty knee pads and yellow hard hats, came out together, chatting. The larger of the two had a black mustache.

I said, "Hi."

They stopped for a second.

"You guys know Carl Richess?" I said.

They looked at each other, then back at me. The one with the mustache said, "Don't think."

"Big guy." I indicated mountain size with my arms.

The shorter one thought about it, then nodded. "*Sí, con Ezzo.*"

Mustache shrugged. "Maybe with Ezzo."

"Who's Ezzo?"

He turned and pointed down at the pad. I saw a couple of trucks with *Ezzo Cement* on the side.

"Thanks," I said.

They nodded and walked by me. I let myself in through the gate and walked down a dirt path to the large trailer with the sign that said *Dragoni Associates, Inc.* I didn't bother knocking. I went right in and saw a couple of men standing behind a desk, looking down at some papers. One was middle aged and bullish, dressed in a polo shirt and slacks. The other was younger, leaner, and wore a denim shirt over Levi's.

They looked up at the same time.

"Help you?" Polo Shirt said, in that I-don't-really-want-to-help-you-but-I-have-to-say-it tone.

"Are you Mr. Dragoni?" I said.

"I'm Dragoni," he said. "You are?"

"I'm here on behalf of the Richess family," I said. "Carl Richess was part of the cement work, or was supposed to be."

"Oh," Dragoni said. He had prominent teeth in a round head with wispy brown hair on top. The taller one had more hair but smaller teeth. "Yes, we heard about what happened. And they arrested his brother, one of our subcontractors."

"That's right. And I'm representing him."

"I hope he turns out to be innocent."

"He is," I said. "At least that is the presumption under the law."

The Levi's-clad guy grunted. "Lawyer talk," he said.

Dragoni said. "What is it exactly you want?"

"I want to find out as much about Eric and Carl as I can. Since both of them are connected to this project, I thought you might be able to help me out."

"I don't see how. What's done is done."

I said, "Sometimes you don't see it at first, then something comes up that helps you figure out what might have happened."

"They had a connection with our project, sure," Dragoni said. "But from what I understand, they didn't get along with each other."

"Was there anybody else around here who didn't get along with Carl?"

Levi's said, "We build buildings. We don't get involved with personal lives."

"I'm just asking if you may have seen anything, that's all."

"The answer is no," Dragoni said. "Anything else?"

I handed Dragoni one of my cards. "I would appreciate it if you would call me if anything comes to mind."

"Nothing will."

I paused, turned to go. Then I turned back and said, "You are contracted with the city of Los Angeles, is that correct?"

"That's no secret," Levi's said.

"I'm sorry, I didn't get your name." I put out my hand.

Levi's just looked at my hand and said nothing.

I dropped my hand. "And who is your liaison with Councilman MacArthur?"

"That's really all we have to say," Dragoni said. "Thanks for coming by."

"Who's your contact person in the councilman's office?" I said.

Levi's stepped from behind the desk and approached me. "Good-bye."

59

NO MORE PLEASANTRIES exchanged.

I walked out the same way I came in, but headed toward the corner where the cement trucks were coming in and out. I spotted one of the Ezzo trucks as third in line for the boom snout, and walked down the truck ramp. I put myself on the side that kept trucks between me and the mobile office. Just in case anyone was peeking.

When I got to the Ezzo truck I found the driver leaning against the front, arms folded, watching the pour. He was short and Italian looking. I could see him behind a deli counter as easily as driving a truck.

"How you doing?" I said.

He gave me a look like I didn't belong here, which I didn't. But he nodded.

"You a friend of Carl Richess?" I asked.

He unfolded his arms and stood straight. "Who are you?"

"That seems to be the question of the day," I said. I offered my hand. "Ty Buchanan, family lawyer."

He shook my hand tentatively. "What do you want?"

"And your name is?"

He let go of my hand. "I asked what you wanted. I got nothing to say."

"If you don't know what I want, how can you know you have nothing to say?"

"Look, I got work to do."

"How well did you know Carl?"

"I got nothing to say."

But he looked like he could say a lot if he wanted to. "Carl's dead," I said. "And I'm representing his brother, who's being charged. I just want some facts."

"I got nothing, okay?"

"Then do you know anybody at the company I could talk to?"

He shook his head.

"Toss me a bone," I said. "For a guy whose life is on the line."

He looked at his feet. "I'm sorry about Carl, okay? I'm sorry about Eric, but that's the way things break."

I hadn't mentioned Eric's name. But this was a guy who did not want to be pushed, not now. I took out a card and held it out to him.

He didn't take it. "I got nothing for you."

A voice bellowed from in back of the truck. "Nick! Let's go!"

The Italian turned quickly, ducked around to the driver's side, and got in his truck. From the cab he gave me a quick look.

Then I felt whap on my shoulder. A security guard the width of a cement truck said, "You have to leave now, sir. Please don't come back."

60

SINCE I WAS doing so well getting people to talk, I walked the couple of blocks to the field office of Councilmember Jamie MacArthur.

It was functionally governmental, with a reception area. At the front desk a young woman asked how she could help me. I thought about saying, You can tell me who murdered Carl Richess and where to find him, but instead I said, "I don't suppose the councilman is in today."

"Oh, no," she said. "Councilmember MacArthur will be out the rest of this week."

"Cutting ribbons somewhere?"

She said nothing.

"You know, supermarkets and all that?"

She shook her head.

"Maybe I could talk to his aide. I'm a lawyer."

"Lawyer?" she said. "May I ask what this is regarding?"

"Politics. Building projects. Fun."

She said, "Excuse me," got up, and went through a door behind her desk.

I looked at the framed photo of a smiling Jamie MacArthur on the wall. I tried to figure out just how symmetrical his square jaw was. And whether he'd had some work done. Like Stallone. Like just about everybody in this town, at one time or another.

"Hello, I'm Regis Nielsen."

I turned. He was tall and thin, with an almost perfectly round head that seemed too big for his neck. His glasses had black plastic frames.

"Ty Buchanan," I said, offering my hand. "I'm a lawyer. I'm representing a client who used to work on the building project you've got going around the corner."

"It's a major project, all right. Going to be a fine-looking office complex when we're done. Good for Hollywood."

"No doubt. Lots of labor. I imagine you had your hand in setting it up."

"I don't know what you mean by that, but of course the councilmember was heavily involved in bringing this project to the district."

"What I mean is, you probably have the typical labor problems, and we all know what that's like."

"Councilmember MacArthur has always had good relations with the unions. In fact, he has good relations with just about everybody."

I had to bite my tongue. There was a rumor that MacArthur had once had relations with a woman not his wife. Back when he was on the board of the L.A. Unified School District. He'd weathered that, his marriage survived, and now he was framed, on the wall.

"Word is," I said, "that he'd make a great gubernatorial candidate."

Regis smiled in that public-relations way political aides have. "We are dedicated to serving the needs of our constituents. That's all Mr. MacArthur has on his mind right now."

"Reason I'm asking," I said, "is I just want to know what my client's involved with, if he had any dealing with anybody from the job site, or this office. Maybe you have records here on a database and could do a quick search to see if his name comes up."

"Oh, we can't do that, Mr. Buchanan. Unless our records are subject to a subpoena, which we'd fight, our constituents expect that we will not be careless or public with our internal records. You can understand that."

"Sure, and I wouldn't expect anything less from our next governor."

"Then we can count on your support?" His smile looked permanent.

"You never stop, do you?"

"If I did, I wouldn't be doing my job."

"And if I stopped right now, and didn't trouble you a little more, I wouldn't be doing my job either, would I?"

His smile faded. "I don't really see the need," he said.

"People who are getting questioned rarely do. Getting deposed is really such a bother."

"Who said anything about a deposition?"

"I like to cover all the bases."

"Why are you going out of your way to pick a fight with Mr. MacArthur?"

"Maybe because his aide is running too much interference."

Nielsen did not reply.

"Tell you what," I said. "I'll give you a card, and you can let me know if the future governor would like to show his concern for the proper administration of the justice system. Talk to him about it."

He took the card and said, "Thanks for coming in. Have a pen."

He picked up a holder stuffed with ballpoints. I took one. It said *Councilmember Jamie MacArthur* on the side.

"Our tax dollars at work?" I said.

"Privately funded, of course."

"By who?"

"Thanks again for coming by, Mr. Buchanan."

He left without shaking my hand.

I left with a new pen.

61

FROM THERE I drove to Hollywood and Highland, thinking about L.A. politics. The city is, for all intents and purposes, a one-party town. That being the case, every politician looks out for number one.

Jamie MacArthur was no different. It's all stepladder politics. You want to get to the next level. If you can't, you try to stay in your office for as long as possible. You strive to become a beloved local pol.

When I got to the hub of the new Hollywood, I couldn't find a place on the street to park. So I went into the giant parking structure at the Center, then walked back to the Stella Adler Theatre.

I looked for Son of Foghorn Leghorn. Today he wasn't there. Maybe he'd gone up to Alpha Centauri for a confab.

I went into the Adler and up the stairs, which led to a small lobby. A giant black-and-white head shot—Stella herself, I assumed—looked down on me. A woman around twenty-five, with silky hair the color of bricks, was standing there, studying pages. She wore a red sweater, tight as in the Lana Turner legend, and black pants.

She saw me looking at her and put the pages down.

"Hi," I said. "Tim around?"

"Tim Larchmont?" she said.

"Yes."

"He'll be here later. We're in rehearsal." She nodded toward the open door at the top of a little staircase.

"What are you guys doing?" I said.

"An evening of one-acts."

"Which ones?"

"They're new. Three of them."

"Three one-acts?"

"That's right."

"That should add up to a play," I said.

"I suppose." She smiled.

"So how many are you in?" I said.

"Just one."

"What's the title?"

"Nobody Gets Raped in La Jolla."

I paused to see if she was joking. She wasn't. "Catchy."

"You in the industry? You can get comps. You want me to set you up with comps?" She motioned with her hand, toward the corridor. And, no doubt, the ticket office.

"You know," I said, "I might just do that. Plays about La Jolla are my meat. But I want to talk to Tim first."

"Business?"

"Yeah. He was recommended to me by someone."

"Are you an agent?"

"Me? You kidding?"

"Why would I be kidding?"

"Don't you know the old saying?"

"What old saying?"

"You can take all the sincerity in Hollywood and put it into a gnat's navel, and still have room for two caraway seeds and an agent's heart."

She laughed, and that was a good sign. I wanted her to trust me. Actors are always looking for someone to trust.

"Please come and see the show," she said. A guy appeared at the top of the staircase and said, "You're up, Penny."

Penny offered her hand and said, "Really. Come see it." And then she bounded up the stairs. It was the movement of hope, the ascent of a dream. One in a thousand ever makes anything close to lunch money as an actor. I hoped she'd make it.

62

I SAT IN a chair in the lobby and read *L.A. Weekly* for a while. Three guys came in about half an hour later, heading for the stairs.

"Tim?" I said.

One of the guys stopped. He was short and workout thick. Late twenties, I guessed. He wore a black T-shirt and black jeans. "Yeah?" he said.

I stood. "My name's Buchanan. I was Carl's lawyer."

He looked startled. Maybe even shocked. Then regrouped. "I'm really bummed about Carl. He was a good guy."

"Can we talk a minute?"

Tim Larchmont looked at his watch. "I've got ten minutes. Let's go outside."

63

WE WALKED OUT to the boulevard, footing it past some stars on the Walk of Fame. Vivien Leigh, Ray Charles, Lee Strasberg, Stella Adler.

"Good thing Stella's right outside, huh?" I said.

"She was the greatest," Larchmont said. "The real American acting genius, you know."

"Oh yeah?"

"Strasberg gets all the credit, but he ruined more actors than he made."

"No way."

Larchmont nodded. We stopped just short of the corner, on Bessie Love's star. "All that emotional memory, inward-looking junk," Larchmont said. "It just makes for indulgent acting. Stella was about being in the moment, believing it, letting it all happen naturally. That's all acting is. She made Brando, you know."

"I didn't know."

"Took him from a military school dropout and said she'd make him into the best actor in New York, and she did."

"She did that?"

"Yeah. Brando would have been just another pretty boy without her. You like Brando?"

"Early Brando. Not fat Brando, except for *The Godfather*."

"Love Brando. De Niro, too."

"Can we talk about Carl?"

Larchmont looked down. "I can't believe his brother killed him."

"He's not convicted."

"Yet. He hated Carl."

"Hated him?"

"Oh yeah."

"Didn't seem like that to me."

"You haven't been around him that much."

"Why would Eric hate his brother?"

"Because he was gay. Pure and simple."

"You think?"

"I know." He shot me a new look, filled with skepticism. "Why are you asking me all this?"

"I'm representing Eric."

Larchmont's mouth played the chin-drop scene.

"You were at the Christmas party where Carl got drunk and went off in a Santa hat," I said. "You recall that?"

"Who told you? Was it Barstler?"

"Can you just tell me if you were there?"

"He is such a jerk. He hates me."

"Why don't you just tell me what happened?"

"Sure. And there's lots of witnesses, too. Carl was drunk off his butt, is what he was, and I didn't even talk to him. He kept trying to make eye contact with me and I kept not making it. And trying to avoid him."

"Why?"

"I broke up with him and he wasn't happy about it."

"Did you break up with him because of that Sonny Moon guy?"

Larchmont shook his head. "I don't know what you've been told, but it's a crock."

"So you don't know this Moon guy?"

"He's not *Moon guy.* He is a prophet, and he has prophetic powers."

"Telling the future and stuff like that?"

"That's part of it," Larchmont said.

"Why doesn't he bet the ponies?" I said. "He could really bring in the dough."

"He's not into that. He's into helping people."

"How much does it cost?"

"Only what you can give."

"Are you and he together?"

Larchmont turned to me like a little bulldog. "I don't have to answer that."

"Because that could make for bad blood between the Rev and Carl."

"The Son of God would never kill anybody. He is about reconciliation."

"Let me ask you something," I said. "How can you believe that a guy hanging out on Hollywood Boulevard is the Son of God? Wouldn't he have better hair sense?"

Larchmont didn't flinch. "He got me a commercial the first day I met him. He knew I was an actor without me even telling him."

"Tim, if you toss a Mentos at random around here you'll hit an actor. Or a screenwriter."

"But he knew about this call, for Pepsi and—"

"Tim, I'm happy for you. But help me out. Can you think of anybody who might have had a reason to kill Carl?"

"No, man. Carl was big but he wasn't mean, okay? And I have to go to rehearsal."

I gave him a card. "Call me if anything occurs to you."

He took the card and headed back to the theater. I didn't have much. Morgan Barstler provided a couple of names. The Rev, and this actor, and who knew what was up? For all I knew Barstler could have killed Carl.

What I needed was an alternate theory that had some legs, that a judge would allow me to argue. I needed facts, and they weren't coming.

Superman walked by me, pausing for a picture or two with people on the sidewalk. There was only room for one superhero here, so I walked down to Skooby's and ordered a hot dog with kraut, and fries. I sat on one of the sidewalk stools and called B-2 at his office.

He told me there was nothing on the e-mails. Whoever the guy was, he was careful not to leave a trail. I asked him if he could get one of his guys to identify a man named Nick who worked for Ezzo Cement, that I had to track him down, and he said he would.

I ate my dog and listened to swing era music being piped out of one store-front, and acid rock out of another. What happens when swing collides with acid rock in the middle of Hollywood? Maybe it rains Perry Como.

Just as I was about to run my last fry through its ketchup bath my phone bleeped. A private number.

"Mr. Buchanan?" The voice was male, soft and articulate.

"Yep."

"My name is Turk Bacon. I understand you've been looking for me."

I sat up. "As a matter of fact, yes."

"Where are you now?"

"Hollywood."

"Then it should take you about half an hour to get here," he said.

64

THE HUNTINGTON LIBRARY and Botanical Gardens is out in San Marino, named for a Huntington named Henry, a train man who made a fortune in L.A. Had this idea that you could link the city with train and trolley lines. So he did it, and it all worked beautifully. The city was a model of urban transit.

So naturally the oil companies and local politicians on the take choked off the system so everybody would have to drive cars. There is a documentary about this conspiracy, called *Who Framed Roger Rabbit.*

Bacon said he'd be waiting by a painting called *The Long Leg* by Edward Hopper. I asked one of the staff where it was, and got directions.

When I got there I saw a lanky man with silver hair standing in front of the painting. It's a seascape, East Coast, with a lighthouse and three quaint homes on the shore. A sailboat is churning past, leaning with the wind.

I stood next to the man and looked at the painting.

"Everyone prefers *Nighthawks*," the man said. "Do you know *Nighthawks*?"

"Is that the one in the diner?"

"Very good. I'm impressed. Yes, that's the famous one. But this is the Hopper I like. It's hopeful, don't you think?"

"Sure," I said. "Unless the boat is about to capsize."

He looked at me with questioning gray eyes. "Are you Mr. Buchanan?"

"That's me," I said.

"I'm Turk Bacon," he said. He shook my hand. He was dressed in an Italian-cut blue suit and a cerulean silk tie. "Walk with me."

We walked. And ended up in the gardens. The desert section. He stopped at a spike of pointed green leaves, shooting up about thirty feet, like a fuzzy telephone pole.

"*Agave vilmoriniana*," Bacon said. "It's Mexican. It's drought tolerant. A hardy plant for a desolate landscape. But it is also opportunistic. It will seize upon any water it finds and use it to grow faster. And it can bloom in all kinds of soil. It's an all-purpose plant, you see. That's why I like it. That's how I view my own work."

"You bloom where you're planted."

"Something like that. Mostly it's about survival in any environment, and not just surviving, but prospering. I've managed to prosper, sometimes in very forbidding circumstances."

I cleared my throat. "Okay, I've enjoyed the metaphors. Can we do clichés now? Like getting down to brass tacks?"

"You're well educated for a lawyer." He laughed. "I like that. I've dealt with too many legal chuckleheads who are all costs and benefits, no poetry."

"I once memorized 'Casey at the Bat,' " I said. "Does that count?"

"I prefer Robert W. Service myself. 'The Shooting of Dan McGrew' is a particular favorite. About death. Over a woman. Isn't that always the way?"

"Now that you mention it, there's a woman involved in the case I'm defending. One I am trying to find."

"And that concerns me how?"

"I understand you are a dealer of certain services, the escort variety."

"Why am I talking to you, Mr. Buchanan?"

"You can help a man accused of murder. If he was with a woman at the time, he's innocent."

"A rarity among defendants these days."

"So what about it?"

"I'm afraid I can't help you," he said.

"Can't or won't?"

"I am a gardener and a businessman, Mr. Buchanan, and when it comes to flowers—"

"All right," I said. "Let's cut the poetry and posing, okay? I want you to produce the hooker."

"That's an odious term."

"Will you?"

"Your request is crass and unimaginative," he said. "I have no idea who you're talking about, or what you think my connection to all this is."

"Then why'd you drag me all the way out to this place?"

"To introduce you to plant life," he said. "And also to tell you not to disturb me again, or try to interfere with my affairs. I like to keep a low profile, as it were."

"It won't be so low if I subpoena you, will it?"

He didn't flinch. "I found *you*, remember? If I don't wish to be served, I won't be. I am going to wish you luck with your trial, Mr. Buchanan, and tell you, in very polite terms, to lay off. No hard feelings."

He walked away with a *conversation over* finality.

Or maybe it was *case over.*

I was in a foul mood driving away. I wanted to kick a squirrel. Nothing was clicking and I was getting that running-in-mud feeling, like in bad dreams. What else could go wrong now?

Glad you asked.

I was almost to the 118 when I got the call from Father Bob.

"We got another e-mail," he said.

65

I COVERED THE rest of the way as if in a dark tunnel. I was making like an Andretti. It was a wonder I wasn't pulled over by the CHP and slapped in cuffs.

It was road rage, but not leveled at another driver. It was at this e-mail guy, a coward, looking to instill fear from afar.

When I finally got to St. Monica's the sun was just about to drop behind the hills. A few of the Sisters were in the courtyard, including Sister Perpetua. As I approached the office she put her hand out to me. "It's the devil," she said. "He's after Sister Mary."

I patted her wrinkled hand and continued to the office. Father Bob met me outside the door and we went in together.

Sister Mary was in front of the computer, staring at the monitor.

I went to the desk and turned the monitor my way.

> *Mary, Mary,*
> *not OK*
> *just a whore*
> *with hell to pay*
> *someday*

I bit the insides of my cheeks.

She shook her head. "I just wish I knew why."

"Let's find this guy and beat it out of him," I said.

She looked at me reprovingly.

"In love," I said.

"Will the police be able to find him?" Sister Mary said.

"Maybe we can help," I said.

66

JONATHAN BLAKE BLUMBERG works on the top floor of his own building on the west side, with a killer view of Santa Monica and the Pacific Ocean.

He is in his fifties but looks like he could tow a boat with his teeth. When I entered his office the next morning, he jumped up, slapped me on the back, and handed me a one-page printout.

"Nicholas Molina," B-2 said. "Ezzo Cement. You'll find his home address and phone there."

"Wow," I said.

"Now take a look at this." He motioned to his enormous desk, which was packed with prototypes.

His R&D people had come up with a great stun gun that B-2 playfully called the iProd. I'd actually used it to great effect.

Then there was his pepper spray, which I called the iFog, but he called Face Melter. It was not yet legal. Which wouldn't stop either of us from using it if we had to.

Now he picked up an item that was the size and shape of a toilet-paper tube, only capped at both ends and made of some sort of plastic.

"I call this the iFist," he said.

"Okay," I said.

"You remember that Chuck Norris joke? How Chuck Norris doesn't have a chin under his beard, he has another fist?"

"How could I forget it?"

"That's what this is. It's sort of like those cartoons, too. Remember, where the boxing glove shoots out of a box or something, attached to a collapsible extension?"

"Right. It'd always hit Sylvester in the chops."

"That's this baby." He held it like a light saber, pointing it away from us. "You trigger it with a little button, here."

Boom. The iFist split, and the top third shot out about five inches.

"The secret is what we use for the extension," he said. "A new alloy. Flexible but firm, like a good nanny. Only the impact is like being hit by Tyson on his best day."

"Did Tyson have a best day?"

"Good point. Then you just collapse it back in." He pushed it into place with a click. "See?"

"It'll make bar fights a thing of the past."

"Not," he said. "But it might settle 'em faster. You like it?"

"Ahead of its time, as always."

"You got to move fast if you want to catch the lightning." He set the iFist on his desk and picked up a white item the size of a large fountain pen.

"And this," he said, "is the iHear."

"Aren't you going to get sued by Apple?" I said.

"Let 'em. Now, this is sweet." He took up a set of earbuds, plugged them into the iHear. He walked to the door of his office, opened it, motioned me over. He pointed to the open door at the end of the long hallway. I could see some cubicles and a few people moving around.

"Put these in." He handed me the earbuds and I stuck them in my ears.

He clicked the end of the iHear and pointed it at the open door. Immediately I picked up a conversation, as clear as if the people were five feet away. Two male voices.

"... *breaks up with him right there in the theater.*"

"*Cold.*"

"*Yeah it is. Movie wasn't even over.*"

"*I heard it's bad anyway.*"

"*At least watch the movie, then you can dump him.*"

I took the earbuds out. "Wow."

"Wow is right," B-2 said.

"It takes invasion of privacy to a whole new level."

"And what would America be without that? It records everything digitally, too." He tucked the iHear in my pocket. "A gift. Use it at parties. Please and amaze your friends. And have a good time." He closed the door to the office and walked me to a chair. He took a seat behind his desk. "So how's the little Sister?"

"Sistering on."

"You know, there's something about her. She's got something inside that's not cut out for that life. It's got to have expression. It's an energy thing. See?"

"I'm not going to get involved in that," I said.

"Why not?"

"I don't want to get hit by lightning."

"You believe God might do that do you?"

"It would be the ultimate iProd, wouldn't it?"

B-2 laughed. "Just keep your eyes open with her. I think you're in for some surprises."

"Can we talk about the e-mails now?"

"Right." He opened his phone and hit a key, waited, said, "Sid, come on in."

A minute later a T-shirted, curly blond guy with a scraggly beard came in.

"This is Sid Vacuous," B-2 said.

My look said, *Are you serious?*

"He's in a band," B-2 said, "and I don't argue with people what they want to be called. I want to know can they deliver. The kid's our go-to computer guy. So talk to him, Sid."

"Hey, what's up?" Sid said to me, then, "The guy's a gamer. I know it. I can smell it. His e-mails have a pattern. Each one is based on a rhyme."

The last one, the third, had a sexually graphic Dr. Seuss riff.

"I want him," Sid said. "I want to get this guy. I want to shame him."

"You must be a gamer too," I said.

"Oh, you have no idea." Sid smiled proudly.

"Dude's using an IP address routing through some library in Atlanta, only it's a bogus setup because he's spoofing the library's router address, bypassing the need for any type of identification at the front end. So the guy could be anywhere and he's set it up so we can't follow him back. We'll get stuck in Atlanta, and you do not want to get stuck in Atlanta, believe me, all they have is fried food and—"

"Sid, focus," B-2 said.

"Okay, okay," Sid said. "It's just interesting this isn't routed through Romania or something. Tells me the guy's arrogant. That's kind of why I think he's got the gamer thing going on. Anyway, there's something I want to try to get this guy. It'll have to go on your network out at the nun place—what do they call that again?"

"Abbey," I said.

"And if I put in some key words, it can trace the route in real time, alert me, and maybe get us another geographic on this guy. Kind of like a reverse Trojan horse we'll ride back to the scene of the crime. Or not. So can we?"

"We can," I said. "All we have to do is sneak it by Sister Hildegarde."

"Who?"

"Head nun."

"That's nice," Sid said. "That'll be a good sneak."

67

ERIC'S PRELIMINARY HEARING got started on a looming Thursday morning, the kind L.A. seems to offer every now and then as an apology for having great weather. Stratus clouds blanketed downtown like a notice of audit from the IRS.

The courtroom belonged to the Honorable Judge Steven Prakash, one of the younger judges, maybe forty or so. Black hair, dark brown skin, slight M. Night Shyamalan accent.

The deputy DA was Tom Radavich. I knew nothing about him except that he'd been on the first Phil Spector prosecution team for a short time. He was about five-ten, with thinning hair the color of a cowhide briefcase. He wore a plain but crisp gray suit.

Experience has taught me these are the lawyers you really have to watch. There was a guy my old firm tangled with more than once, a defense lawyer for the insurance companies. The guy pulled down a million and a half a year, but when he showed up in court you'd have thought he was a cheese knife salesman from Schenectady.

And juries loved him. They had no idea he was a wealthy lawyer with homes in Beverly Hills, Vail, and Orlando. He was a "man of the people," who just happened to be representing an insurance company.

He cleaned our clocks a couple of times. The third time Pierce McDonough was ready for him, got his own rumpled suit, and beat him to the tune of fifty million in a medical malpractice case.

So even though we shook hands, and he was all smiles, I was not going to get sandbagged by any cornpone.

Kate was sitting in the gallery with Sister Mary. When they brought Eric into the courtroom, in his prison garb, and shackled him to the chair, I caught a glimpse of Kate. She was holding a tissue up to her eyes. Sister Mary patted her gently on the arm.

68

JUDGE PRAKASH GOT us underway at 9:05 a.m.

Just after stating my appearance, I said, "Judge, if I may request that my client not be shackled during the hearing. He's certainly not an escape risk."

Radavich wasted no time shooting to his feet. "Mere statement of counsel is not authority, Your Honor. There is no reason to deviate from procedure in this instance."

"This isn't *Ben-Hur,* Your Honor. Mr. Richess is not a slave to be chained to an oar."

Prakash smiled. "Colorful analogy, Mr. Buchanan. But will the restraints impede your client's ability to participate in the hearing?"

"It impedes his ability to be treated like a man presumed to be innocent."

"I'll be sure to keep that in mind," the judge said. "Let's get on with the hearing."

Radavich started off with an LAPD blue suiter named Baron. He was sworn and gave his name for the record.

"What is your current position, Officer Baron?" Radavich asked.

"I'm a patrol officer–two, working out of Hollywood Division."

"And how long have you been with the department?"

"Four years last month."

"And were you on duty on the night of January thirtieth?"

"Yes, with my partner, Officer Trujillo."

"Please describe what occurred at around ten-thirty."

"We answered a call at ten-thirty-three p.m., a complaint about loud music coming from an apartment. We arrived at the location at ten-forty-five and proceeded to the apartment where the music was coming from."

"The music was still playing?" Radavich said.

"Yes."

"Was it loud?"

"Very loud. Rock music of some kind."

"But you could hear it through the door?"

"Yes. And down the hall. It was obviously a disturbance to the neighbors."

"What happened next?"

"I spoke to the next-door neighbor, who said she had pounded on the walls, and finally the door, but got no response. Which is when she decided to call in a complaint."

"The neighbor?"

"Yes."

"What did you do then?"

"I knocked on the door and announced my presence. I waited approximately ten seconds, then knocked again, and announced again. When there was still no answer, my partner called our supervisor at Hollywood Station to come in."

"You did not attempt to enter the apartment or get a manager to unlock it?"

"Not at that time."

"Why not?"

"There were no exigent circumstances. Loud music alone is not enough. The decision to enter goes to a field sergeant supervisor. Sergeant Leon arrived ten minutes after our call. He then directed the building manager to use a master key to unlock the door."

"Describe for the court what you found when you entered the apartment."

"There was loud music coming from one of the iPod systems, in the front room."

"Can you explain a little more what that looked like?"

"Yes. It was about the size of a toaster oven, with speakers, and there's a place in the center where you put the iPod."

"What did you do next?"

"My partner and I began a sweep of the apartment."

"Did you turn off the iPod?"

"Not at that time. We wanted to keep the element of surprise if anyone was in the apartment who shouldn't be."

"What did you find during your sweep?"

"In the kitchen I found a male Caucasian in a chair at the kitchen table. His head was slumped over the back of the chair. He appeared to have been shot through the mouth. There was blood on the wall behind him, and a gun on the floor by his right hand."

"What did you do next?"

"I checked with my partner and supervisor, who determined there was no one else in the apartment. Then I unplugged the iPod dock from the wall to stop the music. I didn't want to touch anything. My partner called for an ambulance, and Sergeant Leon and I secured the scene and began to canvass for witnesses. I believe Sergeant Leon called for backup and a detective."

"Did you interview anyone at the scene?"

"Yes, I did."

"Who did you interview?"

"May I refer to my report?" Officer Baron asked.

"Certainly."

As he leafed through his pages, I leafed through my Motion Manual, a guide to procedure at prelims, because I knew what was coming. Hearsay. There's a statute allowing hearsay from a qualified officer at a prelim. That's the section I looked up.

"I have it," Baron said. "I first interviewed a Ruth Marion. She lives in the apartment across the hall from the subject, who we had identified as one Carl Richess."

"Can you give us the substance of the—"

"Objection," I said. I stood up, holding open the Motion Manual.

"On what grounds?" the judge said.

"Inadmissible hearsay," I said.

Radavich snorted. Actually snorted. "Your Honor, counsel is perhaps unfamiliar with the code on this point. Officer hearsay is admissible."

Prakash looked at me, as if expecting me to melt into a little ball.

"Your Honor," I said, "I believe Mr. Radavich is referring to Penal Code 872(b)."

"Of course I am," he said.

"Then may I be permitted to take this witness on voir dire?"

"To what possible purpose, Mr. Buchanan?" the judge asked.

"If you'll allow me just two questions?"

He thought a moment, then nodded.

"Officer Baron," I said, "you are a patrol officer–two, correct?"

"Yes."

"And when Mr. Radavich was qualifying you on direct, you stated that you had been with the Los Angeles Police Department for four years?"

"That's right."

"That's two questions, Mr. Buchanan," Judge Prakash said.

"Got me, Judge. Can I have one more?"

Prakash smiled. "I'm in a giving mood."

"Officer Baron, have you ever been told how to testify at a preliminary hearing?"

He answered a bit too fast. "No."

"Never been trained in preliminary hearing testimony?"

"Just normal talking to the prosecutor."

"Officer Baron, have you ever completed a training course certified by the Commission on Peace Officer Standards and Training?"

"Yes, at the Academy I completed numerous POST courses."

"But not one in testifying at preliminary hearings."

"No."

I looked to the judge. "Your Honor, PC 872(b) allows officer hearsay testimony only if the officer has been on the force for *five* years, *or* has completed a POST course specifically dealing with testifying at preliminary hearings. As this officer has only four years' experience, and has not completed the required course, the hearsay testimony is inadmissible."

"No way." Radavich was on his feet. "Judge, he's an officer with an impeccable record."

Prakash tapped at his keyboard, then looked at his computer monitor. "Well, there it is, right there," he said. "Penal Code section 872(b). Mr. Buchanan is absolutely right."

Radavich turned his reddening face my way.

"Scary, isn't it?" I said to him.

Prakash said, "I'm going to exclude all hearsay testimony from this witness, Mr. Radavich. Have you any further questions for him?"

"Not at this time." He was silent as he lowered himself into his chair.

It was my turn to go into cross. The prosecutor only plays a minimal
hand at the prelim. You do what you can with it, hoping to preserve something useful for trial. Now that a major portion of Baron's testimony was
being excluded by the judge, I had only one area to cover.

"Officer, inside the apartment, you did not see anything that would suggest foul play, did you?"

"Yes, I did. The dead man."

The judge smiled at that. I was not in a smiling mood. "The gunshot
could have been self-inflicted, could it not?"

"I was not asking myself those questions."

"Never occurred to you?"

"No."

"That part of your training, not to ask questions?"

"No, sir."

"Then I have no further questions myself."

69

RADAVICH CALLED A forensic expert from the LAPD lab, a Dr. Freeman Jenks. Unkempt, thinning gray hair over birdlike features. Like he
was a giant crane carrying a small nest on his head. I knew exactly why he
was going to testify, so before he was sworn I objected.

"Your Honor," I said, "I would like an offer of proof on the relevance of
this witness."

Judge Prakash nodded. "Mr. Radavich?"

The prosecutor said, "He will be testifying about the blood found on the
murder weapon."

"Seems relevant to me," Judge Prakash said.

Jenks took the oath and stated his name for the record.

The prosecutor asked, "By whom are you employed, sir?"

"I'm a criminalist with the Los Angeles Police Department, Scientific

Investigation Division, working out of the Hertzberg-Davis Center at Cal State L.A."

"How long have you been so employed?"

"Seven years. Previous to that I was with the Los Angeles County Sheriff's Department, for a period of ten years."

Radavich picked up Carl's gun from the counsel table. It had been tagged as an exhibit. "Showing you now the weapon used to kill Carl Richess, can you tell me if you conducted any tests?"

"I did."

"And what did you find?"

Jenks opened up a notebook he'd brought to the stand. "I found a small amount of blood on the barrel of the gun, which I tested, and determined was O positive. This is the blood type of the victim, Carl Richess. I also found a trace amount of blood, a small dot if you will, on the butt of the gun, and the intersection of the slide area."

"And by that, do you mean where the slide, when chambering a round in this semi-automatic pistol, comes back, at that intersection?"

"That's right."

"What was significant to you about that bloodstain?"

"Well, I thought it in an odd spot if the theory is suicide. I particularly wanted to test that, and the test came out O negative."

"What is the defendant's blood type?"

"According to the report, it's O negative."

"What portion of the population is O negative, sir?"

"A little under eight percent."

"Has this sample been tested for DNA?"

"It has, and we are awaiting results."

"Thank you. Nothing further."

I stood and said, "Your Honor, to this point, the prosecution has not made any blood sample available, so that I can have my own expert analyze it. I would ask the court to direct Mr. Radavich to turn over all samples to us before we proceed any further."

Radavich said, "Unfortunately, Your Honor, the sample we submitted for DNA analysis was too small to preserve."

"Then I move that evidence not be admitted," I said.

"On what grounds?" the judge said.

"On the grounds of reciprocity. How can I possibly challenge the validity of the sample?"

"Do you have any law you can cite me?"

I didn't, because there wasn't any. "It's plain fairness," I said. "And moral law transcends opinion."

The judge blinked a couple of times. "What was that?"

"I was just talking about the overall spirit of the law," I said.

Prakash said, "Be that as it may, and it seldom is, the law is that the prosecution may test and if it's used up, that's just the breaks."

"Hardly seems sporting," I said.

"Sporting is not a proper objection," the judge said. "Which means, overruled."

Eric's blood on the gun. Terrific. Wonderful. A jury would love it. They think blood is the be-all and end-all of evidence.

It's called the "CSI effect." With all the TV shows that have a case wrapped up in an hour, because of advanced—and sometimes fictional—forensics, juries are primed to respond to things like blood and DNA evidence.

Prosecutors don't like it, because juries are starting to think that without a slam-dunk match, there's too much reasonable doubt.

But when you have do have a match, the defense has to find a way to limit the relevance.

I had to think of a way to limit this. Not much I could do, but when it was my turn to cross-examine, I asked the good doctor, "There is no way of telling how the sample got there, is there?"

"I believe it was when the gun was fired," Jenks said.

"You don't know that."

"It seems most likely."

"Seems. Believes. You do not *know*, do you?"

"There could be alternate explanations, but I would find them highly unlikely."

I said, "No further questions," and sat down.

70

RADAVICH'S FINAL WITNESS was Detective Lonnie Zebker. In clipped, professional style, Zebker summarized his investigation, questioning of witnesses and, finally, Eric himself.

Establishing, most importantly, that Eric could not prove that he was anywhere else at the time of the shooting.

I asked a few questions, to commit Zebker to a few facts, but made no dents in his story.

Radavich announced he was through, and submitted the matter to the judge.

I made the typical defense argument that there was not enough evidence to bind Eric over for trial. Judge Prakash made the typical ruling— yes there was.

I asked for a reduction in bail, and Prakash denied it.

Another turn of the wheel in the system. When next we met, it would be to pick a jury to decide the fate of Eric Richess.

71

I MET WITH Eric in the lockup, before they shipped him back to Twin Towers.

"You want to tell me about the blood now?" I said. "Or do you want to start by telling me why you didn't tell me about the blood."

"I didn't think anything about it."

"That's quite a detail you didn't think anything about. What happened?"

"It's not like you think," he said.

"Enlighten me, Eric. I really like to be enlightened."

"It's like this, honest. I got nicked on the webbing of my hand." He held up his right hand to show me.

"Nicked by what?"

"The slide. On the gun."

"So you did fire the gun. This is getting better by the second."

"Yeah I did," he said. "Only it was earlier that week. I went to a shooting range with Carl."

I sat there trying to decide if Eric was telling the truth or being like a little boy who just keeps digging himself deeper and deeper into a hole.

"Can you prove this?" I said.

"Like with what?"

"A receipt or anything?"

"No way."

"Where is this place?"

"La Cañada Flintridge."

"Maybe somebody up there remembers you being there. What was the exact date?"

He thought about it. "Friday, I think."

"Think harder."

"Yeah. Friday."

"What date?"

"Right before Carl died."

"Carl died on Friday the thirtieth. You telling me it was Friday the twenty-third? Is that what you're saying?"

"Yeah. That's right. That would have been it."

"So it wasn't earlier in the week. It was a whole week."

"Yeah. Right."

"Did you guys check in or anything? Can somebody there identify you?"

"I don't know. It was Carl's thing. He asked me to go with him."

"Look, you two are big guys. There might be somebody who'll remember that. Can you give me any details about what the guy who checked you in looked like?"

"It wasn't a guy. It was a chick."

"A woman checked you in?"

"Yeah. She had long, straight brown hair and tats on her arm, her right arm."

"Could she have seen you?"

"I don't know. I was wandering around looking at the shelves when Carl paid up."

This was good. This was promising. This was a fact that could be checked, and go in the credibility column for Eric.

72

SISTER MARY WAS with Kate outside the courthouse. I explained about the bindover for trial, and Kate leaned against Sister Mary for support. I suggested that Sister Mary drive home with Kate, and that seemed good to both of them. I walked down to the county law library on First Street to do a little research.

I was heading up the steps when my cell went off.

"Buchanan," I said.

"Zebker."

"I didn't do it."

"Hilarious. Can you come down to the station?"

"What for?"

"Some questions."

"Last time I was there you threw me in jail."

"Not this time. I want your help."

"On what?"

"A homicide."

"Whose?"

"That guy, Morgan Barstler."

"You're kidding."

"I don't kid. They found his body next to a Dumpster behind the Egyptian Theatre. He had your card in his coat."

73

ZEBKER MET ME in an interview room at Wilcox. He brought me coffee and gave me a few details about Barstler's death, then said, "You talked to Barstler when everybody thought Carl Richess committed suicide. I'd like to get a few more details from you."

"Does this mean you might have another suspect?"

"Not at all. It means I'm following up on something that needs following up on. If any exculpatory evidence comes up, it'll be filtered through Radavich."

"Some filter."

"What else can you tell me about Morgan Barstler?"

"Not much," I said. "But he did tell me Carl was involved for a while with an actor named Tim Larchmont. Who I talked to."

Zebker raised his eyebrow.

"I'm investigating this thing, too," I said.

"Go on."

"I think you should follow up with Larchmont and this Sonny Moon guy. Find out where they all were before and after the killing."

"In other words, you want me to help get your client off, after I've testified against him."

"I want the truth, just like you do," I said. "Can we agree on that?"

"With that I'll agree."

"Then what can you tell me about Barstler and how he bought it?"

"Close-range gunshot to the face."

"You have a theory?"

Zebker shrugged. "Working on it."

"You want me to work on it with you?"

He smiled, shook his head. I knew he wouldn't bite. I was, after all, repping the guy Zebker thought did it. He wasn't going to give me any more information.

"Someday, Detective, I'm going to toss you a very important piece of evidence, and I hope you'll remember how you treated me."

"I'll remember," he said.

74

IT WAS GETTING late and I was out this way, so I decided to drop in on Nick Molina. The printout B-2 had handed me gave an address in South Los Angeles, a section of the city not too far from downtown.

His house was on a tree-lined street that would have been fashionable about a hundred and five years ago. Now the sidewalks were cracked and chain-link fences guarded spare lawns.

Molina's place was one without a fence. The house was a faded blue clapboard. A Ford pickup was in the driveway. I walked to the screen door and knocked.

Movement inside the house, then someone peeped out the small square window in the door.

I thought I saw one eye narrow in the glass.

"Nick?" I said.

The door whipped open, keeping a mesh of screen between us. "What are you doing here? How'd you . . . ?"

"Can we talk?"

"You can't just come here!"

"Nick . . ."

"You don't got a right to call me Nick. What'd you do, follow me around? What gives you—"

"I just want to talk. Ten minutes." I looked over his shoulder and saw a clock on a wall next to a crucifix. Onion smell drifted out and TV light flashed.

"I told you, I got nothing," Molina said.

"You mean you won't tell me, right?"

"So what? I don't got to talk to you. They . . ." He shut his lips like a trap.

"They what?" I said. "Who's they?"

"Listen, this is it. I'm sorry what happened to Carl."

"So you don't think he killed himself."

"I didn't say nothin' about nothin'. Now don't you come here no more."

He slammed the door.

I waited a couple of seconds, then knocked again. "Nick, you've got a duty here. Anything you say to me is confidential, okay? I just want to know what happened. Nick? I know you know more. You can tell me—"

The door swung open. What peeped out this time was a revolver in the hand of Nick Molina.

"You're trespassing," he said.

"So are you," I said.

He looked confused, then mad.

I said, "You're trespassing on the sacred ground of Jesus. You have him on your wall. You have Jesus on your wall and right here in front of him you're refusing to help one of the least of these, a man in jail who should not be there. How can you do that?"

"Shut up and get off my property. I'll shoot you."

"What would Jesus say about *that?*"

He slammed the door again. Maybe he'd talk it over with his Savior. And I hoped he'd get an answer, because I needed a witness.

75

WHICH IS WHY, the next day, I drove out to La Cañada Flintridge with Sister Mary. It's a quiet little burg between the San Gabriel Mountain Range and the Angeles National Forest, about a Frisbee toss from Pasadena.

The shooting range was in the foothills, up a mountain road. We drove up a winding drive and parked in front of the office. As we did, the radio was just starting "I Will" by the Beatles. Sister Mary surprised me by saying she wanted to hear it, it was her favorite song, and would I leave the keys?

I got the distinct impression she wanted to listen to the song alone. Odd choice, I thought, for a nun. A song about romantic love. About loving someone forever, in fact. But I didn't analyze the moment. I also didn't want to listen, because the only woman that song applied to, for me, was dead. The only woman I had ever been prepared to say *I will* to. The song would be a hot stake in my gut. I didn't know if I even had another *I will* in me.

Or ever even wanted one, for all it gave you. I left the radio on for her and went into the office alone.

Inside the wood-paneled mobile was a little store full of shooting accessories. Holsters, gun cases, ammo. And a desk for check-in. Behind the desk was a man with an ample paunch and a scarlet USC Trojans T-shirt.

"Help you?" he said.

"Name's Buchanan. I'm a lawyer and—"

"That's all right, sir, we take all kinds here. No discrimination, that's my motto."

"Good motto," I said. "I'm not here to do any shooting. I'm here to ask a couple of questions."

USC Boy frowned. "If these are questions that have legal ramifications, then you should talk to our attorney."

"I just want to talk to somebody who was working here when my client came up and did some shooting with his brother. He could only remember that it was a woman, and she has tattoos on her right arm."

He paused, then shook his head. "Nobody here like that."

"You wouldn't just be playing around now, would you? I look like I went to UCLA or something?"

"Did you?"

"Yeah, but I love all mankind."

"Excuse me?"

"Yes, I belong to them, and they to me, and we can never be alien to each other, even if you like USC. So let me talk to the woman, huh?"

"What woman?"

"Friend, listen, it's only facts I'm after. Crucial facts. They affect a man's life."

"You know, I once talked to a lawyer and got my can shot off. In a manner of speaking. It was during my divorce. I tried to be honest and I got killed for it, so why don't you just pack up and—"

The door opened and Sister Mary walked in. I thought of this as just a distraction, but then the guy behind the counter said, "Welcome, Sister. This is a first."

"How do you do?" she said. "I'm Sister Mary Veritas of St. Monica's."

"Cool!" He said. "I've been up there for a retreat with some men from our church."

Church?

"Oh?" Sister Mary said. "Which one is that?"

"St. Sebastian."

"Monsignor Murphy, is he still there?"

"Yeah! You know him?"

"We've met a couple of times."

"Well, I am so happy to have you here," the guy said. "Are you here to do some shooting?"

I looked back and forth between them.

"Not today," Sister Mary said, "though I'd really like to learn sometime."

"You're very wise," USC said. "The way hate crimes are these days. It would be my great pleasure to offer you lessons, gratis, anytime you like."

"How thoughtful."

I said, "Are we almost finished here?"

USC flashed a look. "You, you can go now."

"He's with me," Sister Mary said.

"He is?"

"Hard to believe, isn't it?" she said.

"He says he's a lawyer."

"Even harder to believe, huh?"

Sister Mary and the guy shared a laugh. Then the nun said, "We're defending a man accused of murder, and it's very important to establish that he was here on a certain date, and our client said that a woman who works here with tattoos on her arm—"

"Christa," the guy said.

I just stared at him.

"Is she here?" Sister Mary said.

"Yeah," he said. "Up on number two. I'll give her a call."

76

CHRISTA DID HAVE tats, a floral arrangement with a gun motif, and hair just like Eric said she had. She was wearing a red T-shirt over a compact figure, denim cut-offs, and mid-calf black lace-up boots. She looked like she expected trouble and was ready to give it back.

She looked at Sister Mary. "What'd I do now?" she said with a forced smile. "Am I in trouble with God?"

"No trouble," I said. "My name's Buchanan and this is Sister Mary Veritas, my associate."

Christa looked at USC. He shrugged.

"It's not an ordinary pairing," I said, "but whoever thought Martin and Lewis would get together."

"Who?" Christa said.

USC said, "You don't know Martin and Lewis?"

"No, should I?"

"They don't teach these kids history anymore," USC said to me. To Christa he said, "They were big explorers back in the old days."

There was a pause in the room as education took a turn for the worse. I decided not to correct the record.

I said, "I wonder if you could take a look at this photo and tell me if you recognize this guy."

I showed her the picture of Eric that Kate gave me.

"He looks familiar," Christa said.

"He's a big guy," I said. "Six-five and wide. He would have been with his brother, same size."

"Oh yeah! I got it now. They were big all right. I remember thinking you'd need an elephant gun to take 'em down."

"Do you remember when this was?"

She looked up, as if trying to remember. "I don't know. Couple months ago, maybe."

"This would have been around the end of January. His name is Eric Richess, his brother's name was Carl."

"Was?"

"He's dead."

"Bummer. How?"

"Would you have a sign-in book or some sort of record?"

Christa put a hand on her hip. "What's this about?"

"I'm representing Eric Richess. He's on trial. And I need to confirm he and his brother were here."

"So wait a second. Your guy killed his own brother?"

I shook my head. "He's accused, that's all, and I'm looking for the truth. And you can help me."

USC said, "Let's check the records."

Christa shot him a nine-millimeter look.

USC spread his arms in a *What's wrong?* gesture.

"Will I have to testify?" Christa said.

"I'd like you to," I said.

"Cool! Will it be on TV?"

"Probably not."

"Will there be one of those guys who draws the pictures?"

"You never know."

"Close enough," she said. "Okay, Andy, let's check the records."

They did. The records were in a black binder, loose-leaf. She opened the January tab and I looked at the ledger of names with them. She found it. Carl Richess had signed in and paid for two on Friday, January 23, at eleven-twenty a.m.

It was confirmed. I almost did a dance.

I requested the page so I could make a copy, and promised to return it that same day.

Christa looked skeptical, but USC said, "I think you can count on the Sister, Christa."

"Hey," Christa said, "that sounds funny. Sister Christa. Think I'd make it as a nun?"

USC smiled. "You'd last an hour."

She shot him another nine-millimeter look, then laughed.

77

"MAYBE I WOULD like to shoot," Sister Mary said as we drove down from the hills.

"I don't know. A nun packing heat? You do enough with a ruler."

"I'm going to hurt you next time we play."

"Why should next time be any different?"

There was a print shop just off the Angeles Crest Highway. We stopped to make a copy of the sign-in page, then drove the original back to the range.

We left it with USC. Christa was out "kicking some butt," he said. I did not ask.

When we got back to St. Monica's we went to the "war room," which was a funny thing to call the little table in the library of St. Monica's. But this was where we were going to do trial prep, and lay out strategy for the trial.

I had a packet of discovery from Radavich that I spread out on the table. It included a witness list, police reports and lab reports, and a CD with digital photos of the scene taken by the SI team. Attached to one of the police reports was an itemization of the contents of Carl's apartment. I slipped this over to Sister Mary and asked her to look through it.

After an hour or so I said, "Your main job will be to watch the jury."

Sister Mary looked up from the papers in front of her. "Watch them do what?" she said.

"Everything. From the moment the panel walks in, I want you looking at them. Do it casually. Don't get caught. But notice what they're reading, what their expressions convey. Get an overall impression."

"Shouldn't *you* be watching them?"

"They don't like being studied by the lawyers. If they think a lawyer is sizing them up, they get suspicious. Even before the trial begins you've got a couple strikes against you. You blow your first impression, you can never get that back. You have to work harder just to get back to square one."

"So then how do you pick the jury?"

"You don't."

"What?"

"You unpick a jury."

"What's that mean?"

"You have no control over the names that are called to sit in the box. That's random. We can't put people in, we can only get them out, using challenges. There are challenges for cause and peremptory challenges."

"What's the difference?"

"If you can show some kind of bias, then you can challenge a juror for cause. If he's made up his mind about the case already, or has some kind of prejudice where he can't keep an open mind. That's hard to show. There are other challenges for cause, but they're rare. With peremptory challenges, you don't usually have to give a reason."

"You can just kick off whoever you want?"

"Almost. You can't systematically exclude jurors based on race, gender, sexual preference, or religion. I couldn't kick all the nuns off my jury, for example."

"And there are so many of them on juries these days."

"Then after we have a jury and start the trial, keep watching them. Watch how they react to the evidence. And especially when I'm cross-examining a witness, watch who they look at."

"What's that do?"

"It makes you the Crossometer."

She shook her head.

"That's what I call it," I said. "It's a gauge of what they're thinking. Here's how it works. If they're looking at the witness, that means they're really trying to figure out if he's telling the truth. If they're looking at me, they're wondering what I'm up to. If they're looking at our client, that means they're making up their minds he really did it."

"That works?"

"It does. And it doesn't cost a thing."

Sister Mary held my eyes for a beat, then quickly looked down at the table. "Let's talk about the inventory of Carl's apartment."

"What about it? Something on there catch your eye?"

"It's what's not on there. There's no computer. Everybody has a computer now, don't they?"

I shrugged, then remembered something. "Morgan Barstler said he and Carl were in touch by e-mail. There's no PDA or anything like that listed, is there?"

Sister Mary looked at the report. "No."

"Good catch," I said. "I'm really getting my money's worth here."

"Excuse me?"

"Lawyers can spend tens of thousands of dollars on fancy jury consultants, but that's just money down a hole. One sharp nun is all anybody needs."

She laughed. It was lilting and simple and pure. That transparency and ease made her face incredibly attractive just then. I knew that was not a good thing to be thinking. The emotion of working close in an intense situation—and there's nothing more intense than a murder trial—had to be watched.

Fortunately I could almost feel the eyes of Sister Hildegarde on me, ever watching, holding a rubber mallet.

"Enough flattery," I said. "Let's get back to work."

We worked for another hour when I got a call from Sid, B-2's computer whiz.

78

WE SNUCK HIM into the office. This was where Sister Mary handled a lot of the abbey business, being the nun computer expert. It's also where Sister Hildegarde was liable to show up at any time, unannounced.

But Sid installed the program and said it was triggered to send him an alert when it caught a whiff of our intruder.

And then we'd see.

It was all a holding pattern now. Like the way everything else in my life seemed frozen in time.

I had to get some things moving.

79

THE NEXT DAY I drove over to the Ezzo Cement Company. It was on the back end of Brazil Street in Glendale, on the east side of the 5 Freeway, across from the Griffith Park Golf Courses.

It was like a different country on this side of the 5. Brown and dusty, it could have been a set in a Mexican caper movie. Over on the green of the links, it was a golfer's paradise.

I went into the front office of the pre-engineered steel building and found a gaunt, smiling man sitting at a desk, holding a fly swatter.

"Hey hey," he said.

Hey hey? "How you doing," I said, going with the mood.

He laughed and nodded his head. Then swatted something on the desk. I assume it was a fly. But now I'm not sure.

"Do for what?" he said. Thick accent. Russian?

"Is the boss around?" I said.

The Swatter laughed and nodded. "Yea boy."

I laughed and nodded.

He swatted something else.

"So can I talk to him?" I said.

"More chesty," he said.

"Excuse me?"

He laughed and nodded.

"Maybe I'll just go find him myself," I said. I didn't know where I'd go, but anywhere but here seemed a step in the right direction.

"Sit, sit," he said. He got up and waved his swatter like a baton, presumably showing me to sit.

I laughed and nodded.

He went out a back door. A few minutes later he was back with a goateed man, tall, in a long-sleeved shirt with purple and red stripes, and jeans. About forty, younger than the Swatter.

"Help you?" he said.

"My name's Buchanan," I said. "You are?"

"Mike Ezzo." He did not offer his hand.

"I wanted to ask you about Carl Richess."

"Why?"

"I'm representing his brother."

"So?"

"Carl worked for you, right?"

"So?"

"If I could ask you some questions—"

"Carl Richess was a troublemaker," Ezzo said.

The Swatter laughed and nodded.

I said, "So that means he might have had some people mad at him. People like Nick Molina, say."

Ezzo squinted at me. "What've you been doing, snooping around?"

"Look, friend, I'm just doing my job, like you do your job. I'm not out to make any trouble for you or anybody else. I just want to know what happened."

"You are making trouble. I don't have time for this."

"Why was Carl a troublemaker?"

"Because he made trouble," Ezzo said.

"Hey hey," Swatter said.

I gave Ezzo my card and said I'd appreciate a call if he changed his mind.

"Don't hold your breath," he said.

I laughed, nodded, and left.

80

I SPENT THE rest of the day putting in calls to a couple of forensic labs. I'd need an expert or two in my pocket.

I got back to St. Monica's around four and headed straight to my home at the northeast corner. Father Bob was watering some flowers he'd planted outside his trailer.

"She got another one," he said.

I knew he meant an e-mail. This one was a full-on assault. Another graphic description, another drawing of a nun that looked like Sister Mary, and a couplet of sexual rhyme.

"She doing okay?" I said.

"She is, but Sister Hildegarde is about to bust a gasket."

"Is that a Catholic thing?"

"It does not bode well for any of us, Sister Mary especially."

I went into my own trailer. Hoping to hear from Sid about the e-mail. I microwaved some macaroni and cheese and read some of my Jake Ehrlich book. I liked the guy's attitude. I liked his approach to trial work. Stay on offense. Find the lie.

You can always find the lie, he said, especially in cross-examination.

When I looked up it was dark outside. I had dozed off. Someone was knocking on my door.

I opened it.

Kimberly Pincus stood there, lit by moonlight and holding a bottle of wine. "Busy?" she said.

81

"IT'S NOT EXACTLY the Ritz," I said. "But I call it home."

Kimberly sat at the kitchenette table and started opening the wine with the corkscrew she'd brought. "Quaint," she said.

"I've designed it in early Desi Arnaz. How did you find me?"

"Darling, this is Kimberly." She pulled the cork. "Have you got wineglasses?"

"Sure." I snagged two white foam cups from the package on an open shelf. "Don't drop them."

She poured white wine in the cups and we thudded them, then sipped.

"You like it?" she said.

"Crisp, light. Jocular without being flippant."

She laughed. "Wine snob."

"I meant you."

She shook her head, and we sipped again. Her smile was easy and warm.

"I'm glad you came by," I said.

"I'm glad you're glad. I want to ask you something."

"I'm a captive audience. There's no back door."

"I'm thinking of leaving the city attorney's office."

"So soon?"

"It's been four years," she said. "I want to open my own office."

"That's a tough go, solo," I said. "Unless you have overhead like mine." I waved my hand around the trailer.

"Who said anything about solo?" she said. "I want a partner. Somebody who is a knock-down great trial lawyer, and also tall and handsome. Know anybody like that?"

I looked into her jade lamps, and saw she was serious. "You and me, partners?"

"What I said." She put her cup on the table and folded her hands. "I've been working it out in my head. Both of us can try cases like bats out of hell—"

"Around here we say avenging angels."

"Either way, that's what we do. That's what we live for, in fact. It's one of those things you know you were born for. So we start a little boutique firm, and all we do is trial. We're not litigators. We don't sit around conference rooms and jaw. We go to court. We aren't corporate or criminal lawyers. We are trial lawyers, period. And that's why we start at seven-fifty an hour. Am I making sense?"

"Wow." I sat back and saw the whole picture unfold. A true power couple practicing law together, going to court, handling the highest profiles. Kimberly Pincus and Ty Buchanan. It would be a killer combination, that's for sure. Maybe it really was the time for my trailer days to come to an end. All parties, sacred and profane, could return to normal. Sister Hildegarde would cheer.

"You'll consider the offer?" Kimberly said.

"I'm stunned."

"Remember, things move fast in L.A. Think what we could do if both of us had a foot on the accelerator."

"I will think about it, Kimberly. After the trial. I need to stay focused. But after the trial, I will definitely think about it."

"Will you be conversational without being verbose?"

"I promise."

"Deal," she said. She lifted her cup and offered it as a toast. Before we thudded someone knocked on the door.

"I'm Mr. Popular all of a sudden," I said. I went to the door, opened it.

Sister Hildegarde said, "Can you please step outside for a moment?"

82

"You may not entertain guests, especially of the opposite sex," Sister Hildegarde said after I half-closed the door behind me.

I said, "You have a security camera or something?"

"A woman with long hair and a bottle of wine is hard to miss in a place like this."

"She's a colleague," I said.

"She's going to have to leave."

"After the wine and a few hours of making out, okay?"

In the moonlight I could see Sister Hildegarde's face get all Lon Chaney, Jr. on me.

"Kidding," I said. "I will escort the young lady off the grounds."

"See that you do," she said. "Immediately."

I went back inside. "I guess I have to—"

"I heard," she said, standing. "I can see myself out. You stay and have more wine, and dream about big-time trials. And anything else you care to dream about."

I put my arm around her waist and gave her one kiss, but one that counted. One that would last me through a trial.

83

THE NEXT MORNING I went down to the Sip. Pick fixed me up his Expresso Espresso, which he says fosters free speech. He sat at my table and lit his pipe. "Hats are the answer," he said.

"What's the question?" I said.

"Why is society hacking and wheezing in an agony of slow death? Hats! If people wore hats, we'd be much better off."

"I see," I said, not seeing.

Pick took a couple of contemplative puffs. "Listen. When was this city a calm, law abiding place to live? It was when men and women wore hats. Think about it. In the 1950s, on *Dragnet*, Joe Friday wore a fedora, am I right?"

"A little before my time."

"Trust me. Men wore fedoras, women wore ladies' hats. Crime was way down. Now, when *Dragnet* came back in the late sixties, guess what? No more hat. And I ask you, was crime up or down?"

"I'm guessing up."

"I rest my case, Counselor! And it's only gotten worse. I say, fight back! Wear a hat!"

He got up to help a customer, a woman, who sheepishly stood at the door.

I was wondering if Pick would accept a Cat-in-the-Hat hat for his comeback when my phone went off. It was Sid, the computer guy. He said he was able to trace the source of the last e-mail. It came from a computer in the Lakeview Terrace Branch of the Los Angeles Public Library. Sid even gave me the ID of the terminal used.

"I thought I was the man," I told him. "But you are the man."

"I know that," he said. "I am *the* man."

I thanked him, then called Devonshire Division and left a message for Detective Fronterotta, who had this matter on his desk.

When I got a call back ten minutes later, it was not the detective. It was an earful of very impolite language. From Nick Molina. When he paused for a breath I asked him what the matter was.

"You got me fired," he said.

"How did I do that?"

"You know. You lawyers are all just slime. Now I got to do something about it."

I waited. When he didn't continue I said, "What do you want to do about it, Nick?"

"I'll decide what I do about it, that's what. And you won't know when, you hear me? You won't know when."

"Calm yourself, Nick—"

He did by hanging up.

Wonderful. I love it when I make new friends. Now I had one that wanted to find me when I wasn't looking.

My legal acumen was having such a wonderful effect on people. I thought about a new career then. Maybe I should do something else. Being a price checker at the 99¢ store seemed like a good option. Anything but this.

Fronterotta did call back about an hour later. I gave him the information from Sid, and he thought he could do something with it. He asked me if there was anything else he could do for me right now. I thought that was nice.

"Maybe you could wear a hat," I said.

"Excuse me?"

"A friend of mine thinks crime was down in L.A. back when people wore hats. *Because* they wore hats."

"You have interesting friends," he said.

"Don't I know it."

84

THE WEEK BEFORE Eric's trial, the city showed itself hatless.

There was a shoot-out between the Grape Street Crips and two LAPD officers that ended in the death of an innocent bystander who popped his head out of the house at the wrong time.

Taggers were everywhere. It's always graffiti season. They didn't even try to hide themselves or hurry up anymore. I drove by some in commuter traffic on the 101 midmorning. Three of them. Happily doing their urination by spray paint on the sound wall.

And what was the city council doing? Passing a new city ordinance limiting the ownership of chickens.

Yes, cockfighting was on the rise, so while gunfire strafed innocent people almost daily, our brave leaders were taking on the scofflaws of the fighting-chicken set.

The mayor and chief of police were making public appearances together, flapping their lips about all they were doing to keep rogue cops in line. A better pair of actors you haven't seen since Abbott and Costello.

The rich were keeping their riches, the poor were flooding in, and the middle was moving to Arizona and Florida.

It was a great time to live and breathe in L.A.

Unless, of course, you were a chicken.

Or a trial lawyer getting ready to try a case that was as thin as the pursed lips of a New England Calvinist.

Trial is war.

It's not cricket, with tea and scones and white pants, pinkies held in the air.

It's not Canasta, Go Fish, or Twister.

Maybe it's a little bit of Balderdash, but mostly it's war.

Kimberly Pincus was right about that much. It's like Butkus, hitting the QB so hard the head separates from the body.

You don't go into a courtroom to dance or preen or show off your suits.

You go in to lay your opponent out on a slab. You obey the rules, so you don't get disbarred, but you do everything you can to prove your case and torch your opponent's. Your weapons come from the Rules of Evidence and whatever rhetorical skills you bring.

Which includes imagination and the touch of the poet.

Oh, yes.

Poetry and literature and painting are the products of the mind, putting the picture together on the page or the canvas. And so the trial lawyer paints a picture for the jury, using not just legal concepts—because the lawyer who depends upon the law alone is the lawyer who loses—but ideas turned into images.

The great trial lawyer has to make the jury see a picture, a coming together of the facts in a compelling and vivid whole. That picture has to grab them, educate them, and make them want to go to bat for your client.

Poet. Teacher. Warrior. The best trial lawyers are all three at once.

It's not a profession for the dilettante or the fearful.

Or for those who are hesitant about taking off the gloves.

If you win, you can shake the hand of your opponent and invite him out for a drink.

If you lose, you look in his eye and say, "Good job," all the while letting your look say, *I hope we have the chance to do this again, because I want another shot. I know you now. Next time, I'll take you down.*

A trial is Patton against Rommel. Magic and Bird. Ali–Frazier. To approach it any other way is to do your client ill.

85

THE MURDER TRIAL of Eric Richess began on a Monday morning in the courtroom of Judge Neil Hughes.

Sister Mary and I got an early start. We drove to the Park-and-Ride on

Canoga and took the Orange Line to North Hollywood. From there it was the Red Line downtown.

Yeah, L.A. has a subway. Don't laugh.

Now, there's nothing this town likes more than a good murder, but thankfully Eric's had flown under the media radar. There was another trial going on downtown that had all the juice—the Miracle Mile Madam, who ran an escort service for mid-Wilshire businessmen and lawyers and was threatening to name names. That sucked up all the press, and I was glad about that.

Kate met us in front of the courthouse. A retired neighbor, a nice older woman named Babs Fambry, had offered to be her driver for the trial. Kate said she was too nervous to get behind the wheel.

I kept my arm around her shoulders all the way up to the courtroom.

As soon as I walked in, the clerk motioned for me and said Judge Hughes wanted to see me in chambers.

Radavich was already there when I came in.

"Sit down," Hughes said. He was a tall, sinewy man. Sort of a Gary Cooper quality about him. He was sixty-six years old and had been on the bench longer than I'd been alive. "Mr. Radavich has a concern."

"I can't wait to hear it," I said.

"I understand you want to have a nun sitting at the counsel table with you," Radavich said.

"Not just any nun. This one's my investigator."

"Your Honor, this is a blatant attempt to attract sympathy from the jury. He wants to have a nun right next to his client during the trial. It will be a complete distraction."

The judge said, "Mr. Buchanan, is this true?"

"She is my investigator. She is integral to this case."

"But she's a nun?"

"That's still legal in the United States. And it's also a constitutional guarantee that a client has a choice of lawyer and the lawyer has a choice of investigator."

"But does she wear a habit?"

"Yes," I said.

"A full habit," Radavich said.

"It's also legal in the United States for nuns to wear habits," I said. "I don't think the Supreme Court has ruled on it, but I'd be willing to guess they'd be all in favor."

"If I thought for even one second that you were trying to pull something, Mr. Buchanan, do you know what I would do to you?"

"Judge, I guarantee that if I ever try to pull something on you I'll tell you about it afterward. Or before. Whatever works for you. But I'm not pulling anything now."

"I still ask Your Honor to find that this is prejudicial," Radavich said.

"This is a new one on me," the judge said. "But I don't know that there is any law that says a nun can't be an investigator. So what can I say? She can sit there. But Mr. Buchanan . . ."

"Yes, Your Honor?"

"If she crosses herself during your opening statement, I'm sending her out."

86

WE BEGAN UNPICKING our jury.

The process is called *voir dire,* which is French for "speak the truth," which doesn't always happen in courts of law. That's why lawyers get to question the venire, the panel of prospective jurors, and root around for fissures of trouble.

Much of the ground had been covered in a three-page juror questionnaire approved by the judge. Now Radavich and I had the chance to talk to them directly.

There were a couple of jurors I knew I had to get rid of—a retired television technician who looked and sounded like he'd convict Mother Teresa for stealing sheets, and a woman from Whittier who seemed entirely too anxious to be seated, and kept looking at Eric the way a coyote eyes an unattended chihuahua.

That's not a good look to be getting so early in the game.

Radavich, of course, started tossing off jurors, too. And the first juror he excused was one I really wanted.

Part of trial work is trusting your instincts, and a thought jumped out at me.

I leaned over and whispered to Sister Mary, and she quickly got up and left the room.

Radavich and Judge Hughes looked at me like I was some sort of sneak.

Which, of course, I am.

And on we went.

By noon, Radavich had eliminated eight jurors, and I'd knocked out ten, two for cause.

You're never fully happy with a jury. There are always one or two wild cards.

But it turns out I had a card of my own yet to play.

87

WE BROKE FOR lunch and I huddled with Sister Mary over pan-fried noodles in Little Tokyo. Sister Mary gave me a report on what I'd tasked her to do. It made me extremely happy.

Which is why I was smiling when we got back to court at two.

This time I was the one who asked for a meeting in the judge's chambers.

"I'm going to ask for a Wheeler hearing," I said. Wheeler is the Supreme Court case that says you can't systematically exclude certain groups from a jury.

Radavich practically jumped out of his suit. Which is a picture I do not want in my mind. "What a load of—"

"Now, now," I said.

"What group has he been excusing?" Judge Hughes said.

"Catholics," I said.

"That's a damn lie," Radavich said.

"I think it was three Catholics and four of the Protestant side of the fence," I said.

"I don't recall us asking for religious affiliation," the judge said.

"You didn't. I did."

Judge Hughes and Radavich just looked at me. It was Radavich's mouth that twitched.

"Explain yourself," Judge Hughes said.

"Very simply, my investigator stood in the hallway and, as each excused juror came out, she greeted them and thanked them for their service, and engaged in a bit of conversation, during which time the juror, of their own free will, revealed his or her religious affiliation. Sister Mary is quite ready to take the stand and testify to that."

The judge's chambers became as silent as a country graveyard. Radavich, I was sure, was going to have a minor stroke. Instead, he said, "And just how was I supposed to know what church they went to?"

"Are you working with a jury consultant?" I said.

"That's privileged information."

"There is no such privilege," I said. "I am prepared to prove that Mr. Radavich has systematically excluded religious people, because he is prejudiced against my investigator."

"You're trying to say that because you have a nun working for you, Mr. Radavich is trying to exclude Catholics?"

"It's worth looking into, isn't it?"

Judge Hughes said, "Tom, can you provide a justification for every one of your challenges?"

"Of course I can."

The judge sighed. "Then you better do it. I'll give you until tomorrow. And now I get to tell the jury that they won't be hearing any evidence today. You know how happy that's going to make them? You know how happy that makes me? Make it good, Tom, or I'm going to be even more upset."

The look Radavich gave me, the one framed with red cheeks, made my day. I'd sent him reeling right off the bat. It's always fun when you can do that.

88

BUT YOU PUNCH a good fighter, it sometimes wakes him up.

The next morning, Tuesday, we started with the Wheeler motion, and

Tom Radavich was the "Three C" prosecutor—cool, clear, convincing. The judge accepted his reasons for kicking off the jurors he did, and the trial began.

Radavich delivered a perfect opening statement, too.

I had to follow with my own Three C's, what I try to establish in every case: competence, credibility, and control.

So when it was my turn, I said, "Ladies and gentlemen, in criminal trials it is common for lawyers to stand before you during opening statement and tell you what the evidence will show. You just heard Mr. Radavich say that, over and over again. But as the judge told you just before opening statements began, that is only what the prosecutor *thinks* the evidence shows. I'm going to give you the other side of that argument. I am going to tell you what the evidence will *not* show.

"The evidence will not show that my client, Eric Richess, committed murder. The evidence will not show that my client is the only one who could have committed the murder in question. Indeed, there is another—"

Radavich was on his feet like a spring-loaded shotgun. "Objection. May we approach?"

"With the reporter," Judge Hughes said.

I tromped up to the bench with Radavich, knowing exactly what he was going to say. Which was: "Your Honor, Mr. Buchanan is attempting to inject an alternative theory of the shooting, but unless he can offer proof to support it, it is prejudicial and immaterial."

Judge Hughes looked at me. "Have you an offer of proof?"

"I'll get it," I said with about as much predictive power as my friend Only.

"Until you do, you will not say anything like that to the jury. And I will admonish them on this."

When I returned to the lectern, Judge Hughes said to the jury, "Ladies and gentlemen, counsel expressed that there might be another explanation for this crime, but you are to disregard that statement. All right? Disregard it. Continue, Mr. Buchanan."

I didn't hesitate. "The evidence will not show that the conclusion the prosecution wants you to draw is a conclusion that is supported by law or fact.

"I say this to you during opening statement because the highest protection in our Constitution is for citizens who are accused of crimes. As you look at Mr. Richess right now, he is innocent. That is what the Constitution says. He is innocent. The only way he can move from innocence to guilt is for the prosecution to prove its case beyond a reasonable doubt."

Radavich stood up. "Your Honor, this is a closing argument, and therefore not appropriate."

"I agree," the judge said. "Mr. Buchanan, confine yourself to a statement of what you think the evidence will show."

"A gaping hole," I said, turning back to the jury. "A great, big hole where evidence ought to be. It's not there.

"You will hear, for example, about DNA. Now, I know you have all seen David Caruso on TV, or any one of those other CSI shows, and you might be led to believe that an expert sitting in the witness chair talking about DNA evidence pretty much determines the entire case. Not so here. Because we will show you that there is another explanation for why blood was found on the gun in question. It happened when my client went shooting with his brother at a shooting range. We will have a witness from the shooting range testify to that."

I covered a few other areas, but didn't want to overstay my welcome. Most lawyers yap too much when they address the jury. But they do like a big finish.

So to end, I walked to the front of the prosecution table, which is closest to the jury box. I pointed at the table. Radavich looked like he wanted to bite my finger.

"But here is the most important thing," I said. "You see what's on the prosecutor's table? It's a giant boulder. I want you to imagine that right now. A big boulder that the law says sits there right now. That boulder is called the burden of proof. And what the prosecutor has to do, using only admissible evidence, is chip away at that boulder until it's all gone. Because any bit of it that's left is called reasonable doubt, and—"

"Objection," Radavich said.

"Sustained," the judge said. "Conclude, Mr. Buchanan."

I wagged my finger at the table once more for good measure. Then I said, "Simply put, the evidence is not there, and the prosecutor will not prove to you beyond a reasonable doubt that my client committed the murder of his brother."

I sat down. Eric seemed half calm, half tense. Exactly like me. "Sounded good," he whispered.

But was it good enough?

89

RADAVICH CALLED HIS first witness, Detective Lonnie Zebker, who was sworn.

"Good morning, Detective," Radavich said.

"Good morning."

Yes, it's always a good morning when you start a murder trial. I thought of Pick McNitt, and his rant against *Good morning.* Maybe I'd call Pick as a witness, just for entertainment.

"What is your current position?" Radavich said.

"I am a detective-two with the LAPD."

"Describe what that is, please."

Zebker looked at the jury. "There are three detective ranks in the department, three being highest. As a detective-two, in addition to conducting the investigation of crimes, I also provide supervision in the training of detective-ones."

"So you actually train detectives in proper crime scene procedure?"

"That's right."

"How long have you been a detective?"

"I've been a D-two for three years, before that a D-one for six years."

"Where are you currently assigned?"

"Hollywood Division."

"In your capacity as a detective, approximately how many homicides have you worked?"

"Oh, I'd estimate two hundred, including those I helped other detectives on in one way or another."

"Referring now to the night of January thirtieth of this year, were you notified about a homicide?"

"I was."

"At what time?"

"I was called at home a little after eleven p.m."

"And what time did you arrive at the scene?"

"Eleven-forty-five."

"Did you meet a police officer at the scene?"

"Yes, I met Officer Baron and asked him to brief me."

"Were the criminalists there?"

"SID arrived about five minutes after I did."

Radavich signaled to his assistant, who moused at his keyboard. Up popped a photo of the interior of Carl's apartment on the flat-screen monitor set up for the jury. "Showing you now People's Exhibit One, do you recognize the photograph?"

"Yes. That is a photograph of the crime scene, apartment 102."

"Did you see any signs of a struggle in apartment 102?"

"No."

"Any drawers pulled out?"

"No."

"Signs of a burglary?"

"No."

"What did you do next?"

"I entered the kitchen and saw a white male, deceased. He was seated in a chair at the kitchen table."

"Did you find a suicide note?"

"No."

"Any signs of struggle in the kitchen?"

"No."

"Which would lead you to believe what?"

I objected. "That calls for speculation, Your Honor."

"This is a veteran detective of the LAPD," Radavich said. "Surely his training and experience is more than mere speculation."

"Go ahead, Mr. Radavich," Judge Hughes said.

"You may answer the question, Detective."

"Leads me to believe he knew the killer."

"What did you do next?"

"I began to process the crime scene."

"Was the defendant present at the scene?"

"Yes, along with his mother."

"Did you question them?"

"No. The mother was distraught, and I thought it best to let the defendant take her home."

"Did you question any other potential witnesses?"

"Yes."

"You may refer to your report. Who was the first witness you interviewed?"

Zebker opened the notebook he'd brought with him to the witness chair. "That would be Ms. Alana Phong."

"And who is she?"

"She lives in apartment 104."

Radavich had another picture brought up, this one a map of the apartment building, with the apartments numbered.

"Showing you People's Two, sir, is that an accurate representation of the scene?"

"It is," Zebker said.

"Please give us the substance of what Ms. Phong told you."

"Objection," I said. "Hearsay."

"Goes to state of mind," Radavich said.

"Overruled," Judge Hughes said.

"She told me that there had been loud music playing in the apartment next to hers, when she got home sometime after nine. She let it go, she didn't complain, she put on her noise-canceling headphones. She didn't think much of it because it had happened before, and he, meaning the victim, Carl Richess, never kept it up that long. But this time he did. Eventually she started pounding on the wall. When that didn't get any response, she went outside and knocked several times on the door. Finally, she called in a complaint."

"Did Ms. Phong give you any other information?"

"Yes, she offered that the victim's brother, the defendant, had been there in the past, and that the two of them had had loud arguments."

"Objection," I said. "I doubt the woman used the term 'defendant' when talking to the detective. I move to strike."

"That's just my paraphrase," Detective Zebker said.

The judge said, "The witness will not speak when there is an objection pending."

"Sorry, Your Honor," said Zebker.

"Overruled," said the judge.

Radavich said, "Did you interview the defendant?"

"The following morning, yes."

"Where was this?"

"At his townhome in Woodland Hills."

"Did you consider him a suspect?"

"At that time, no."

"Please give us the substance of that conversation."

"I asked him to talk to me about his relationship with his brother and he seemed nervous. I told him to take his time, and then he asked me what this was all about and if he was a suspect."

"Did he offer that first? That he might be a suspect?"

"Yes. He used the word 'suspect' first. I told him he wasn't a suspect but that I wanted to know some things, such as his relationship with his brother. He said that he had a fine relationship with his brother and I asked if he had been in any arguments with him lately, and he said he would only talk with a lawyer present."

"Did you arrest him?"

"Not at that time."

"When did you arrest him?"

"When we got the blood result. His blood was found on the murder weapon—"

"Objection," I said. "Assumes facts not in evidence, and assumes this was a murder."

"Sustained," Judge Hughes said.

Radavich went right on, smooth as butter. "You did place the defendant under arrest, correct?"

"Yes."

"Did you question him again?"

"I Mirandized him and he refused to answer questions. He asked for a lawyer."

"Would that be Mr. Buchanan?"

"Yes."

Radavich had Zebker detail more of the crime scene investigation, including the collection of the forensics evidence. All according to Hoyle, as they say.

"I have no further questions at this time," Radavich said.

"Cross-examine," the judge said.

90

CROSS-EXAMINATION IS THE most abused aspect of trial work.

Most lawyers badly mishandle it. They go on fishing expeditions, like drunken businessmen angling for marlin on the weekend. Or, worse, try to act like James Woods in *Shark* to get witnesses to say things they otherwise wouldn't, through the sheer ferocity of their questioning.

That dramatic stuff hardly ever happens. You have to know exactly what you're trying to do, and it's not usually to break down the witness. Very rarely do you even attempt to do that.

Especially when it's an experienced cop on the stand.

Eager-beaver trial lawyers may attempt to show up a witness in front of the jury, but that is almost always a bad move. Unless the witness is clearly lying, or is otherwise vulnerable, what you should do is try to elicit testimony that's favorable to your cause. And if you get it, save it for closing argument.

In other words, shut up.

When lawyers try to win their case right then and there, by hammering a witness, they usually end up slamming themselves on the foot.

Only when the witness gives you a wide door should you try to drive a tank through it. And then, when you do, go for the kill.

Zebker was not the kind of witness who was going to give me any openings. He was professional, and had testified a whole bunch of times. So I gave him the friendly treatment.

"Good morning, Detective," I said from the lectern.

"Good morning."

Just a couple guys meeting over coffee.

"In your direct testimony you made a great deal of the fact that you found no signs of struggle, correct?"

"I don't know that I made a great deal out of it, I just mentioned it."

"But you did draw a conclusion from it, that you thought the victim must have known the killer, is that right?"

"Yes."

"Do you think the victim knew himself?"

"I don't understand the question."

"There would be no signs of struggle if the victim killed himself, correct?"

"We have ruled out suicide."

"That's not what I asked you, Detective. The question is, if someone commits suicide, there would not be a sign of struggle either, isn't that right?"

"That's correct."

"And, as you said, no signs of a struggle in that apartment."

"No."

I paused, letting the exchange soak into the jurors' collective mind, then said, "In your interview of the witnesses, not one of them saw anyone go into, or come out of, the victim's apartment, isn't that right?"

"That's right."

"My client is kind of a large guy, isn't he?"

"I suppose."

"Hard to miss in a crowd."

"Maybe."

"Harder to miss in an apartment complex, wouldn't you say?"

"There are ways for someone to get out without being seen, they—"

"Objection," I said. "Non-responsive. Move to strike."

"Sustained," Hughes said.

"My question," I said, "is that a large man like Eric Richess would be hard to miss in an apartment complex in the early evening hours, isn't that right?"

"It all depends. If people are inside, if someone climbs out the back window and goes down the—"

"Objection," I said again.

Radavich got up and said, "He's opened the door, Your Honor. He's asking the witness to speculate about the size of his client, and whether he could be seen at the apartment complex. Mr. Buchanan asked for an opinion, and the witness is offering it."

Hughes said, "I'm going to issue the same ruling. The witness can answer yes or no to the question. If you want to ask him clarifying questions on re-direct, Mr. Radavich, you can do that."

Two objections, two wins. The judge admonishing the witness. I decided that was a good place to leave that part of the questioning, and went to my counsel table and picked up a copy of the autopsy report.

"You are aware, are you not, of the autopsy report on Carl Richess?"

"Of course."

"You've got a copy there?"

He flipped to a page in his notebook. "Yes."

"Referring you to page two of the report, under the heading 'Gunshot Residue Kit Results.' Do you see that?"

"Yes."

"Please read to the jury the paragraph below that."

Zebker looked at the page. " 'The chemical elements barium, antimony, and lead are elements of virtually all primer mixes. Trace amounts of antimony were found on the anterior of decedent's right hand.' "

"That is referring to gunshot residue, correct?"

"Yes."

"Which the report says was found on the back of Carl Richess's hand."

"Yes."

"Consistent with suicide, correct?"

"No."

I should have stopped right there. I should have known something was coming. But the denial was so stark, so fast, I thought he could only be blowing smoke.

"You're saying that gunshot residue on the victim's hand is not consistent with suicide by gun?"

"Not when it's planted, like this was."

91

WHEN YOU GET gobsmacked in trial, you have to keep your face from showing it. I call this the Phil Ivey. One of the world's best poker players, you can never tell what he's thinking behind those cool eyes.

You use the Ivey to keep the jury from knowing the other side's drawn blood.

I was bleeding.

And I was mad.

"Your Honor, if we could have a sidebar," I said.

"Approach," the judge said. "With the reporter."

When we were all nicely gathered at the bench—Radavich, the court reporter, the judge, and Ty Buchanan—I made sure my back was to the jury so they couldn't see my face. I was afraid it might look less like Ivey and more like Sasquatch on a bad hair day.

"I wasn't given any notice of this," I said. "There is no basis for saying the residue was planted. I move for a mistrial."

"It's news to me," Radavich said.

"You expect me to believe you didn't know about this?" I said.

"Gentlemen," Judge Hughes said, "let's address the bench, shall we?"

"He sandbagged, Your Honor," I said. "There is nothing in the autopsy report or anywhere else that suggests planted evidence like this."

"What about that, Mr. Radavich?"

"I don't know anything about it," Radavich said. "Mr. Buchanan asked a question and my witness answered it. I didn't ask him about the residue. Mr. Buchanan did."

It seemed to me Radavich could hardly contain his glee.

"I am moving for a mistrial," I said.

The judge looked at the clock. "Let's send the jury out for an early lunch, and keep the witness here. We'll have a little hearing and figure out what we've got."

92

AFTER THE JURY cleared, the judge said, "All right, we are on the record. Detective Zebker is still on the stand. I'm going to let Mr. Buchanan take the witness on voir dire. Go ahead, Mr. Buchanan."

Good. The judge was allowing me to interrupt Radavich's direct examination to ask questions relating only to my motion for a mistrial. Outside the hearing of the jury, of course.

I faced Zebker. "Sir, where, in any written report, is there anything about a theory of planted evidence?"

"There isn't," Zebker said.

"Then what's the basis of your opinion?"

"I spoke with deputy medical examiner Lyle Schneuder last night. I wanted to go over the autopsy report with him one more time. He said that something had been bothering him, the pattern of the residue on the back of the victim's hand. It wasn't spotty, it was streaked. He had an aha moment, he said."

"An 'aha moment'? What exactly is an 'aha moment'?"

"You know, 'Aha.' He realized something."

"And you didn't share this 'aha moment' with the prosecutor?"

"Not yet. I didn't have the chance."

"Your Honor," I said, "this is obviously a move that was planned out by the prosecution."

The judge looked at me. "You have no proof of that, Mr. Buchanan."

"I'm having an aha moment," I said. "Which is why I am moving for a mistrial. I think somebody is lying. I'd like Mr. Radavich to take the stand."

"Excuse me?" the prosecutor said.

"I want you to swear under oath that you didn't know about this."

"Your Honor," Radavich said, "this is ridiculous."

"What have you got to hide?" I said.

"I object to that," Radavich said.

"All right, all right," the judge said. "That's enough. Everybody cool off. Be back here at two o'clock sharp. I'll make my ruling then."

93

"WHY ARE YOU trying so hard to irritate the DA?" Sister Mary asked me outside the courthouse.

"If your opponent is temperamental," I said, "seek to irritate him. Pretend to be weak, so he may grow arrogant."

"Who's that, Clarence Darrow?"

"Sun Tzu. *The Art of War*. And give your enemy no rest. Attack where he's unprepared, and appear where you are not expected."

"Sounds like super-hero talk."

"I am T Man. When you have to go to trial, call me."

"As long as you don't wear tights," she said.

"I'll wear a cape over them, so don't worry."

"I think you need some ice cream," Sister Mary said.

"That's your answer for everything," I said. There was an ice cream place on Broadway, walking distance, a block past the Times Building. We were crossing First when I said, "Maybe you need a little Sun Tzu for Sister Hildegarde."

Sister Mary didn't respond.

"It's all politics," I said. "The Catholic Church has always been political, ever since Constantine made it official."

"Can we just have ice cream?" she said.

"If your opponent is persistent, offer him ice cream. Is that it?"

"Something like that."

"Are you going to stay a nun?"

She stopped and turned on me. "Why are you asking me that? Why do you have to meddle in things? Why do you have to be so *you*?"

"I'm all I've got," I said.

She spun around like she was mad and kept walking. People on the sidewalk got out of her way, like the Red Sea parting for Moses.

Fortunately, ice cream solves everything and we were able to discuss the case. I determined not to make a big deal out of Sister Hildegarde.

For a while, at least.

94

BACK IN COURT, Judge Hughes denied my motion for a mistrial and then had the jury brought back in.

"Ladies and gentlemen," he told them, "before the break Detective Zebker made reference to an opinion, a reference to evidence being planted. You are to disregard this statement. It may play no role in your deliberations on this matter."

Whenever a judge does this, it's like telling the jury not to think of a pink elephant. Try that sometime.

"You may continue your direct examination, Mr. Radavich."

"Just one more question," Radavich said. "Detective Zebker, did you find a suicide note?"

"No," he said.

"Thank you." Radavich returned to his chair.

"Cross-examine, Mr. Buchanan," Judge Hughes said.

I asked my question as I was standing up. "Detective Zebker, you had me arrested, didn't you?"

Radavich was, of course, on his feet, shouting an objection. Hughes looked like he wanted to be in Philadelphia.

"This goes to bias and credibility," I said.

"Continue," Hughes said.

"Isn't that right?" I said. "You had me arrested?"

"No."

"I was arrested and booked into your jail, wasn't I?"

"Not by me."

"Don't you recall threatening me with arrest?"

"I recall you were interfering with an investigation."

"Did you arrest me for it?"

"No."

"Then I wasn't doing anything wrong, was I?"

"Yes."

"But you didn't arrest me, right?"

"No."

"But you told me you would."

"If you continued interfering."

"Did I get in your way physically?"

"No."

"Did I tell any witness not to talk to you?"

"I don't know."

"Ah, you don't know. How much don't you know?"

Zebker blinked. "I don't know what that question means."

"Let me help you out," I said. "You claim I interfered with your investigation, yet you can point to nothing I did. The best you can come up with is *I don't know.*"

"Objection," Radavich said.

"Sustained," said Hughes. "Just ask questions, Mr. Buchanan."

"Detective Zebker, have you ever been disciplined by the department for misconduct?"

Radavich exploded, mostly in show for the jury, I'm sure. We trundled up to the bench again. Radavich argued that the question was improper. Which led me to believe there was something in Zebker's past, but that it wasn't necessarily admissible.

Because if there was nothing Zebker could have just said no.

Hughes ruled for Radavich on this one, but I was pleased.

To the jury, he said, "The last question from Mr. Buchanan was objected to, and that objecting has been sustained. You are not to give it any credence whatsoever."

Yes, dear jury, do not think of that pink elephant anymore, I thank you.

95

"JUST A COUPLE more questions, Detective. You recall searching the victim's apartment?"

"Yes."

"And did you conduct an inventory of items you removed?"

"Of course."

I got it from my briefcase and looked at it for a moment. Then I put on my surprise face and said, "There does not appear to be a computer listed here."

Zebker frowned and flipped to the list in his notebook. "Correct."

"That's because there was no computer in the apartment, isn't that right?"

"That's right."

"In your experience, Detective, would it be difficult to send e-mail without a computer?"

"You could do it from a PDA."

"Is there a PDA listed here?"

"No."

"And none was recovered, correct?"

"Correct."

I went back to the counsel table and handed the report to Sister Mary.

"Detective," I said. "You testified on direct that you did not find a suicide note. Are you aware that, according to Di Maio's book on gunshot evidence, notes are left in only twenty-five percent of suicides?"

"I don't know one way or the other."

"Isn't it a fact that from the very beginning your investigation focused only on Eric Richess?"

"We arrested him, yes."

"Have you investigated any other leads?"

"Not after the arrest, no."

"How about before the arrest?"

"We arrested the right person."

I said, "I move to strike that answer as non-responsive, Your Honor."

"Stricken," Hughes said.

"I'll ask the question again. Did you investigate any other suspect before you arrested Eric Richess?"

"No."

"So this could be suicide, or the real killer could still be out there, right?"

Radavich objected, the judge sustained it, I paused for dramatic effect, and said, "No more questions."

And we were done for the day.

96

SISTER MARY AND I took the Red Line from downtown back to North Hollywood, discussing the case. By the time we got on the Orange Line for the ride back to Woodland Hills, I was starving. I suggested honest Mexican food at a place I knew on Sherman Way.

"Just don't get any sauce on your habit," I said.

"If you weren't an officer of the court," she said, "I'd elbow you in the gut."

"That's never stopped you before," I said.

We were almost to my car, parked on the back side of the lot, farthest from the street.

It looked, somehow, smaller.

And then I saw why.

All four of my tires were dead flat.

Because they were slashed.

"Nice," I said.

I looked around for the rarest of birds, the on-the-spot parking security guy. He (or she) was nowhere to be seen.

I circled the car, just looking, steaming. And saw on the hood a message.

A little scratchitti in the paint, probably done with a key.

It read, *Back off.*

97

"PROBLEM?" THE PARKING security guy in his cute little security car had finally seen my wave and driven over. He was about sixty and hadn't missed many meals.

"Slight," I said, and pointed to my car.

"Flat?" Security said.

"Four."

"Four? Oh yeah. Uh-huh. Four flat tires."

Man, this guy was good. "How do you suppose that happened?" I said.

"Somebody must've done it on purpose."

"You think?"

"Uh-huh."

"You have security cameras, right?"

"We got 'em over at the pickup. But your car's over here."

I slapped my sides. "Surely you have security cameras pointed at the parking lot."

He made a concerned face and whispered, "Budget."

"Then how long have you been on duty today?" I said.

"Since two. When did you get here?"

"Seven-thirty."

"Well let's see, that would be Clarissa who would've been on then, but she didn't say anything to me, so I don't guess she saw anything."

"I don't guess so," I said.

"Um . . ."

"Yes?"

"You know," he said, "you park here at your own risk. We got signs."

"Of course," I said. "And what risk is there when we've got a fleet of security vehicles keeping watch?"

"Sir, I'm very sorry. We can report this to the police."

"Report it. I've got to get four new tires before everything closes."

98

IT TOOK TWO and a half hours. There's a tire store on Canoga not far from the lot, and a tow took me and Sister Mary there. The store was closed.

So we left the car outside the razor-wired fence, near the shed marked *Friendly Fred's Tires and Treads,* and called Father Bob. He said he'd come down in the Taurus to get us.

As we waited, Sister Mary said, "Any idea who might have done this?"

"Somebody who's taken the trouble to follow me," I said.

"Or us."

"Sure, maybe it was an angry Protestant."

"Not."

"It's some bad, theatrical way to throw a little fear into me."

"Which leads again to the question, who?"

"Who is mad at me? The person who really killed Carl. Maybe somebody who works with the person who really killed Carl. Maybe somebody who was a close friend or lover of the person who killed Carl."

"Maybe it doesn't have anything to do with Carl or the murder trial."

"In which case, who is mad enough to follow me around till they had this opportunity?"

"You messed up that group called *Triunfo*," Sister Mary said. "Maybe it's a residue of one of your early cases. You also got that developer, Sam DeCosse, ticked off at you. Everywhere you go you seem to do that."

"Maybe it was Sister Hildegarde. Maybe she wants me to back out of the community."

"Now you're just being silly."

"Don't tell anyone, okay? If it gets out that I'm silly, that's the end of my rep as a trial lawyer."

"Your secret is safe." She paused. "You don't think . . ."

"What? The e-mailer?"

She nodded. Another e-mail had come in a couple of days earlier, more of the same. We had not heard back from Fronteratta yet.

"It crossed my mind," I said. "We have exactly nothing to go on. Aren't you glad you got to know me?"

"It's the highlight of my life," she said. "If you don't count the *Ice Capades*."

I nodded.

"About the e-mails," she said. "I've been thinking about one of them. The one that said I was 'not OK.'"

"With hell to pay."

"Right. What if the OK doesn't mean *okay*, but instead means Oklahoma?"

"I'll call Sid and see what he thinks."

"Cool."

I smiled. "And I want your permission to do something."

She folded her arms and waited.

I said, "If we ever catch up with this guy, I want to do a law of club and fang on him. Give me your blessing."

"I'm sorry, Mr. Buchanan. That's not my law."

"I have time to convince you."

"Don't try," she said.

I didn't. We leaned against my car until Father Bob picked us up. I had him drive us to Casa Medina on Sherman Way. There we feasted on chile rellenos and carnitas.

It was almost normal. Almost. Because normal is not a word that applies to you when you're in trial.

As we were all about to find out.

99

THE NEXT MORNING, early, Fred was indeed friendly and tired me up. I had wheels in time to get downtown.

In court, Deputy Medical Examiner Lyle Schneuder took the stand.

He was in his late thirties, maybe older. Thin, gaunt in the face, with an oblong head and severely receding hairline. Would have made a good Ichabod Crane.

Radavich walked him through his quals. He'd been with the office for four years after leaving a medical practice in the East and a brief stint in a lab in Phoenix. He was therefore still on the "way up" as far as being an expert witness.

Which was going to be my opportunity. The key to being a good expert wit is being able to hang your ego on a hook outside the courtroom door. And then be able to communicate in layman's terms so the jury can understand.

Some experts try hard to show that they know more than anybody and speak a language only they can understand. And that they have stepped down off of Mount Olympus to put us poor mortals straight.

Experts want to make a name for themselves, because they get paid to testify and can start showing up on TV when high-profile cases hit the news.

It seemed to me that Schneuder was this kind of expert.

Radavich asked, "Now, Doctor, please summarize for the jury the condition of the victim at the time of death with regard to alcohol."

"The victim had a blood alcohol content between .08 and .09 at the time of the autopsy."

"And what do you conclude about the victim's condition at time of death?"

"Calculations relating to retrograde extrapolation lead me to conclude that his blood alcohol content at the time of death was somewhere around .18."

"And .18 in layman's terms means very drunk, does it not?"

"Oh, yes. You would have been definitely out of it, to use layman's terms." Schneuder smiled at the jury, but none of them smiled back.

"Would you say, in your opinion, that in his condition he was more or less likely to be able to struggle with an intruder?"

I objected, saying this was pure speculation, and there was no foundation for rendering an opinion, as the good doctor did not know anything about Carl or his capacity to hold drink. The judge overruled me and the questioning went on.

"I would say," Schneuder opined, "that he would have been susceptible to being manipulated. Especially if he trusted whoever did the manipulation."

"Turning now to the finding of gunshot residue on the back of the victim's right hand, tell us what you found."

"We found antimony, which is an element in the primer mix of gunpowder. But there was something very strange about this."

"And what was that?"

"Rather than stippling, which is the normal pattern, this gunshot residue appeared to be wiped on the back of the hand."

"What led you to that conclusion?"

"When I looked closely at the pattern, there were streaks rather than spots, in several of the areas of the hand that I examined."

"And the victim, being dead, could not have done that to himself, correct?"

"In my experience, dead people cannot do much of anything for themselves." He smiled again at the jury. The jury looked back at him with stone faces. I was glad about this. They didn't much like him.

No doubt sensing this, Radavich sat down.

I got up.

100

"Good morning, Doctor," I said.

"Good morning, sir."

"Is alcohol a stimulant or a depressant?"

"It's a depressant, of course."

"Meaning that people who are drunk get depressed, right?"

"Not all the time."

"A good deal of the time, wouldn't you say?"

"That all depends on what you mean by a good deal of the time."

"More than half?"

"I suppose."

"Suppose?" I said. "You mean you don't have an opinion about that?"

Little flickers of annoyance skipped out of Schneuder's eyes. "I would say yes. Most of the time. But sometimes people get happy when they drink. It depends on the person."

"You would have to know about that person, his history and so forth, correct?"

"Absolutely."

"Do you know anything about the history of the victim, Carl Richess, in this case?"

"I was not provided that information."

"So your answer is no?"

"I was not provided that information. That's my answer."

"So you don't know what the effect of so much alcohol was on the victim, do you?"

"As I say, I couldn't know that."

"In fact, Carl Richess could have been severely depressed, could he not?"

"It's possible."

"Indeed, it's likely, isn't it? Based upon your agreement with me that in most cases alcohol operates as a depressant?"

"I can't say one way or the other."

Perfect. When an expert equivocates that way, he undercuts his credibility with the jury. So I shrugged at him, leaving a little nonverbal jab in the air.

"Let's talk about this *smear theory* of yours," I said. I dragged out the words so it was moistened with disdain. Whenever the jurors thought of *smear theory*, I wanted them to hear my voice. "It is your theory, isn't it?"

"Yes."

"By the way, what texts are you relying upon for the *smear theory*?"

"This is a theory I have reached on my own."

"You mean you haven't done any experiments, and published your results in a peer-reviewed journal?"

"Not yet."

"Then you have pulled the *smear theory* out of thin air?"

"Of course not. It is based on my training and experience."

"But without reliance on any text or journal, or special training, correct?"

"Of course I am familiar with Friedman and Lyle. I believe that would back me up in this."

"What edition would that be?"

"I think it's the fourth edition."

"You think or you know?"

"I would have to check. But it's the latest edition. I get it every time it is updated. It's the standard work in the field."

"May I have a moment, Your Honor?"

"Yes," Hughes said.

I went over to the counsel table and whispered to Sister Mary, "Take a walk to the County Law Library and see if they have a copy of this Friedman and Lyle book." I took out my wallet and gave her my Bar card.

It must have looked like I was giving her cash to go buy lunch.

Sister Mary got up and walked out of the courtroom. Whenever a nun walks out of a courtroom, or into one for that matter, people stop and watch.

When the doors closed, I returned to the witness.

"Dr. Schneuder, when Mr. Radavich was going over your CV with you, he mentioned that you spent two years in a private crime lab in Phoenix, is that right?"

"Correct."

"And that you left to come work for Los Angeles County?"

"Yes."

"How much did you make at the lab in Phoenix?"

"Objection," Radavich said. "Relevance."

"Give me a couple of questions, Your Honor. It goes to credibility."

"Make it fast, Mr. Buchanan," said the judge.

"How much?" I asked Schneuder.

"A little over one hundred thousand, the last year."

"What about now? What's your salary?"

"Less than that." He smiled.

"How much less?"

"I make a little over sixty thousand."

"Quite a pay cut. Did something happen back in Phoenix we need to know about?"

"I don't know what you mean."

"Did you get canned? Excuse me—fired?"

"No."

"Contract not renewed?"

"We reached a mutual agreement. I wanted to come out to Los Angeles, and work with the best."

"That was your sole motivation?"

"Of course."

"Isn't it true that the L.A. County crime labs are horribly underfunded, compared to private outfits?"

"There are some budgetary restraints."

"Which means our labs, as earnest as they are, are not the best."

"I think they're quality," Schneuder said.

I looked at the clock. "Your Honor, if we could take our lunch break a little early, I think I can finish up with this witness in another hour."

"Any objection, Mr. Radavich?" said Hughes.

"No objection."

"Then we'll come back here at two o'clock."

He admonished the jury not to talk, yadda yadda, and we were off.

101

I DECIDED TO splurge with Sister Mary again, and took her to Subway for lunch.

Over our BMTs and chips we looked at the *fifth* edition of Friedman and Lyle, *Forensic Detection,* scanning the index for anything related to smearing gunshot residue. That was a little tough, considering all the academic verbiage we had to go through.

We took turns. One looked while the other ate, then back again.

I found a section on potential compromises to residue evidence, but nothing about intentional planting or smearing.

"You going to call him on it?" Sister Mary said.

"It's tricky," I said. "Most experts know enough about the material to dodge and weave. But I may give it a whirl. The jury could be impressed with my research."

"*Your* research? Who walked to the library?"

"Okay, *our* research," I said. "Speaking of which, have you been watching the jury?"

She nodded as she took a bite of her sub. She put a finger in the air to indicate a pause, chewed. Then said, "Number seven has been taking a lot of notes."

Number seven was a retired pipe fitter from Baldwin Park.

"I think he's pulling for us," I said. "One working stiff to another."

"And, I might add, number three seems rather smitten with you."

That would be the elementary school teacher from Los Feliz. Single. Blond.

"I can't turn off my natural charm," I said. "It just seeps out."

"I'm tempted to say, try to put a cork in it. Shouldn't this be about the facts, and the truth?"

"My naïve little friend, every trial lawyer in the world wants to charm the jury. You need every advantage you can get. You need to build up even the little things. It's called the art of persuasion. You remember your Greek rhetoric, don't you?"

"I must have missed that class."

"Ethos, pathos, and logos," I said.

"Weren't they the Three Musketeers?" she said.

"Character, feeling, and reason," I said. "All three are needed for persuasion."

"I'm not persuaded."

"Just keep hanging with me, and you will be."

I smiled, but as I did she looked away. I thought there was a moment of sadness in her face then. I didn't say anything about it.

She turned back. "One more thing. I did a little Googling while I was waiting for the book. I Googled Schneuder."

"And I know how painful that can be."

She ignored me. "There wasn't a whole lot on him, but I did find something interesting. An article in one of those free weeklies, out of Phoenix. He was mentioned in a story about a local writer who wants to re-open the Robert Blake case. So I Googled the writer. His name's Troy Cameron."

"Sounds like some beefcake from the fifties. Tab Hunter. Dash Riprock."

"He seems to be a Phoenix gadfly. Always in the face of the local politicians. But he apparently has a true-crime book to his credit. Might be self-published."

"Troy Cameron, huh?"

"Can you do anything with it?"

"Maybe make our boy sweat a little," I said. "Let's try."

102

BACK IN COURT at two, I faced Schneuder. "Doctor, when we left off you had mentioned reliance on a text by Friedman and Lyle. That would be *Forensic Detection,* correct?"

"Yes."

"Fourth edition, I believe you said."

"That's right."

I went to the counsel table. Sister Mary handed me the book. I took it and placed it on the rail of the witness stand. "Showing you now a book, Dr. Schneuder. Can you read the title for us?"

"*Forensic Detection.*"

"What edition?"

He looked a little closer. "Fifth."

"That would be the most up-to-date version, would it not?"

"I believe so." His eyes flashed.

"The one you said you referred to was the fourth, wasn't it?"

"I might have been mistaken."

"Your whole testimony might be mistaken."

Radavich said, "Objection."

"Sustained. Next question, Mr. Buchanan."

"Why don't you find the section in the book that backs up the *smear theory,*" I said.

He blinked once, but I thought it was audible. *Clack.*

"That would take awhile," he said. "I mean, I'd have to research it a little."

My point was made. I took the book. "I'll withdraw the request at this time," I said. "Let me ask if you know Troy Cameron."

Schneuder's Adam's apple bobbed a couple of times. "I know him, yes."

"He's a writer of some kind, isn't he?"

"Yes."

Now was time to take a stab. "Isn't it true that you're writing a book with him?"

Schneuder said, "There's no law against that."

Defensive. This was great. "And that book is about the Robert Blake murder trial, isn't it?"

"I'd rather not say . . ."

Better still.

". . . because it's still in the writing stage."

"It might have been nice for the jury to know this before you started your testimony," I said.

Objection. Sustained.

I left it at that. In cross, you don't want to ask one question too many, giving the wit a chance to eel out of a corner. I'd caught the doc hiding a little factoid about his book-writing career, which confirmed my theory that he was a celebrity wannabe. The jurors wouldn't like that. They want experts to be objective and up front.

103

RADAVICH WANTED SOME questions on re-direct.

"Did you find any fingerprints on the gun, People's Exhibit Six?"

"We did find the victim's prints on the butt and barrel of the gun, yes."

"Was there anything strange about that?"

"Not really. But there was something strange about the print on the trigger."

"Explain that, please."

"Well, it was smudged, but we did manage to indentify it as a partial. It matched the victim's right index finger, between the first and second joints."

"In other words, you're not talking about the pad of the finger, what we normally associate with fingerprinting."

"That's right. This was the area between the first and second joints, where one would come in contact with the trigger when firing a gun."

"And what did you find strange about that?"

"It's simple. If someone places the barrel of a gun in the mouth, the trigger would be pushed with the thumb, not pulled with the finger."

"No more questions."

"Re-cross?" Judge Hughes said.

This was not good for me, and there was nothing I could say to make it good, so I said, "No further questions," and tried to look like Phil Ivey holding aces. No expression one way or the other.

Radavich put on a couple of witnesses—guys who testified about over-hearing Eric and Carl having a heated argument in a bar the night before the killing. They did not testify about the content of the argument, so my cross was only one question to each: "You do not know what this alleged argument was about, do you?"

No and no.

104

ALL IN ALL, it hadn't been a bad day in court, and I was feeling guilty about Subway.

So I insisted on taking Sister Mary to dinner at Little Luigi's, an Italian place the legal community frequents, a short drive from the courthouse. When I was with Gunther, McDonough I used to go there whenever I had a matter downtown.

So it wasn't a surprise to be greeted at the front by Luigi himself, a well-girthed, old-school Sicilian.

"Mr. Buchanan!" He pumped my hand. "Been too long."

"Hello, Luigi. I'd like you to meet a friend of mine, actually my investigator, Sister Mary Veritas."

Luigi smiled broadly. "Sister, I am so glad to have you. We need a little class around this place. All I get is the lawyers and the riffraff, and sometimes—what's the difference, eh?"

"Glad to meet you," Sister Mary said.

To me, Luigi said, "Where you been? Can't remember the last time you was here. You still with that big fancy place on the west side?"

"No, going solo."

Luigi whispered, "That because of the little trouble you were in?"

"If you call being accused of murder a little trouble, then yeah. I just thought it was time to take a look at what I was doing, and that reminds me. There's one thing I haven't done in a long time."

"And what is that, my friend?"

"Eat your veal Parmesan."

"Good to have you both. I got a booth just for you."

He took us to a booth of the color of red wine, near the back, semi-private. It was a little before five o'clock, and the place was just starting to get the after-work crowd. The bar was stuffed with coatless professionals with loosened ties and elevated voices. I recognized a couple of lawyers from Sheppard, Mullin, one of the city's powerhouse firms, sitting at the bar. They were hoisting and laughing about something.

Next to them was a bottom-feeding criminal defense lawyer named Stambler who was about seventy-five and never met a deal he didn't like. He was a grinder, doing volume pleas and never fighting it out in court. But it kept him in fine suits and single-malt Scotch. He was drinking alone.

It was like bookends of the legal profession. And somewhere in the middle was Tyler Buchanan, attorney-at-law.

"I feel like I've come to some sort of forbidden land," Sister Mary said.

"You have. This is the realm of the overinflated ego. There are no egos larger than those of lawyers and none larger among lawyers than those of trial lawyers."

"Is this a confession?"

"An admission, let's say."

"I haven't seen that in you."

"But you've only known me since I've been severely humbled by circumstances beyond my control. Slowly, I'm coming back to full-fledged self-centeredness."

"I don't know," she said. "I don't think you're going to be the same. You like to help people. I can see that at the Ultimate Sip."

"I've been trained to practice law. There's not much else I can do. I could go back to playing drums, and go on the road with Father Bob. Would you like to be our singer?"

"Only if you do 'Ave Maria' as a closer each night."

"Done. What shall we call ourselves?"

"How about Sacred and Profane?"

"I like it, but which one am I?"

"Let's think about it," she said. "We may be able to figure it out."

Luigi came back to the table with a basketed bottle of Chianti. "Compliments of the lady," he said.

"Lady?" I followed Luigi's motion across the restaurant and saw Kimberly Pincus at a table by the far wall. She was sitting with two other women. She smiled at me.

In the soft light she looked like a movie star from the 1950s. Technicolor and CinemaScope were made for Kimberly. The restaurant seemed too small.

I nodded my thanks.

"She's beautiful," Sister Mary said.

I snapped back to the present. "I don't think she has a jump shot, though."

Luigi was uncorking the bottle.

"She doesn't need a jump shot," Sister Mary said.

Luigi poured some wine in my glass and I went through the ritual of the cultured wine connoisseur. I almost swirled some out of my glass, like the untrained wine doofus. I tasted, and tried to come up with some clever adjectives. My mind shut down like a Teamster at four-thirty.

I gave Luigi the wine dork's thumbs-up. He poured and left us.

"Is she a lawyer?" Sister Mary said.

"A prosecutor. City attorney's office."

"Ah."

I raised my glass. "To the best investigator in the business."

"At least the room," Sister Mary said. We clinked and drank. And some indefinable sadness filled me. It seemed like it would only get worse if I didn't do something.

"I'll introduce you," I said.

All the eyes in the place seemed to follow my investigator and me. I was used to it by now. I didn't guess Sister Mary was.

When we got to the table Kimberly was on her feet.

"Thanks for the wine," I said.

"My pleasure, Ty."

"This is Sister Mary Veritas, my investigator."

They shook hands. Kimberly introduced us to her companions. I forget the names.

"How do you like the work?" Kimberly said to Sister Mary.

"I like it."

"Do you keep him in line?"

"I try. It takes much prayer."

They shared a laugh.

"I'm glad you two are enjoying yourselves," I said.

"We are, aren't we?" Kimberly said.

"Definitely," Sister Mary said.

Kimberly turned to me. "How's the trial going?"

"Every day in every way," I said.

"Maybe I'll try to catch your closing argument. Give me a call the night before."

I said nothing. My face got a tad warm.

"Nice meeting you, Sister," Kimberly said.

"The same," Sister Mary said.

When we got back to our table, Sister Mary said, "She likes you. I can see it in her eyes."

"What's not to like?" I said. "I've got the whole package, don't I? Charm, wit, sophistication."

"Humility, too. Maybe you and she ought to get together."

When she said that, it was almost like a request. As if she wanted it to happen for some unnamed reason. I thought about probing a little, but decided not to. We had enough to think about without getting involved in all that.

Truth was, I didn't want to think about it. If I did, it'd be like defusing a bomb. A chance to survive, but a chance to get blown up, too.

105

BUT THE VEAL Parmesan was a Luigi's masterwork, and the Chianti a perfect match.

Nothing blew up or even blew around. Until we got outside.

There was a somebody next to my car at the end of the small parking lot. Whoever it was, he was bending over, looking at it.

I touched Sister Mary's arm and pulled her back to Luigi's front door, out of sight. "Wait here," I said.

"What are you going to do?" she said.

"If I'm not back in five minutes, tell Luigi to bring every Sicilian he can out to the lot."

"Wait—"

I didn't wait. I went around the other way, circling Luigi's. There's a small passage between the restaurant and an antique store. Then you come to the retaining wall of Luigi's parking lot, which is elevated in the back.

That gave me a vantage point to watch the guy, who was still eyeing my car. The lighting was dim here and I couldn't make out much about him. Whoever he was, he was taking his time.

And he was alone.

I thought about spooking him with the alarm. But I wanted to know who it was. I was tired of not knowing.

I took off my coat and laid it on the wall. I was able to get myself up to a position where I was still unseen. A nice fat bush helped. About fifteen yards separated us.

Now what? I could charge like a Bruin linebacker. But I wasn't feeling like tackling tonight. So I waited.

The guy walked to the front of my car, the farthest point from me, and sat on the hood.

He lit a cigarette.

Maybe he was just waiting for somebody while admiring my Benz, before parking his heinie on my car. Bad manners, but nothing else.

Or maybe he was waiting for me. Or Sister Mary.

I took my keys and quietly put three of them between the fingers of my right hand, holding the rest in my fist. If I got attacked I was going to make some holes in the guy's face. Brazilian Jiu-Jitsu would have to wait.

Three people, two men and a woman, came out of Luigi's, laughing, toward a car. The guy smoking on my hood turned his head left.

That's when I made my move from the right.

I got my Wolverine fist ready.

"Evening."

He yelped. His cigarette tumbled out of his mouth. He jumped up like the hood of my car was a cattle prod.

He screamed the name of Sister Mary's savior.

It was Nick Molina. He cursed again.

"Easy," I said.

"Easy! You give me a heart attack."

"What're you doing sniffing around my Benz?"

"Waiting for you, man. Now the whole neighborhood knows."

There was no neighborhood to speak of here. The nearest houses were in the hills on the other side of the freeway.

"Everything all right?" It was Sister Mary. Behind Nick. Who yelped again.

And cursed again. Then added, "Sorry, Sister."

"How'd you know we'd be here?" I said.

"I followed you from court." He drew out another cigarette from his shirt pocket and tried to light it with a Bic. But his hands were shaking and it took a few seconds longer than it should.

"Why'd you do that?" I said.

He took a deep drag and looked up. "I'm a little nervous, okay? I don't want to be seen, okay? I don't want anybody knowing I talked to you, got it? I told you I'd come to you when I was ready, so I'm ready now, and that's it."

"All right," I said.

"Carl, maybe he's dead because of Ezzo," Nick said. "And Jamie MacArthur."

106

"TAKE IT SLOW," I said, wanting Sister Mary and I to hear exactly the same thing.

He rubbed his face. "You got any idea what kind of money is changing hands down there?"

"Where?"

"At the project."

"Tell me."

"Carl was part of it. They were all part of it. Here's the way it works. The city hires a primary contractor. When they go out and contract with the subs, there are supposed to be set limits. The city wants to control costs, so they have restrictions on what can be paid out. It's a way to keep lower-tiered subcontractors from nickel-and-diming them with markups."

"Sounds like good business practice," I said.

"Well, somebody in the know went to selected subcontractors and told them how to put in *usage* charges. It's a bookkeeping category, and with the right billing it's accepted by the controller's office."

I said, "A nice little bonus."

"Then the money takes another trip, to the Laundromat."

"But why, if it's a legit payout, at least on paper?"

"That's part of the deal. In return for getting the contract itself, and for some protection in the accounting, the sub agrees to give back a percentage of the usage charges. Guess who those funds eventually filter back to?"

"The campaign coffers of a certain councilmember."

Nick spread his hands with a gesture of *And that's how it's done.* "It's so clean, the only way to get 'em is for someone to talk. And Carl was gonna blow the whistle."

Now I felt like both Robert Redford *and* Dustin Hoffman. This was more than dynamite. This was C4, and it lined up around City Hall. "How much did Carl know?" I said.

"Just a week before he got it, we were having a beer after work. Carl had a couple of shots of tequila with his. He was drinking a lot. He was nervous. And then he said he was going to talk. Because there was somebody trying to do him dirt. That's what he said. 'Do him dirt.' "

"Did he say who this person was?"

"No, and I didn't ask. 'Cause I didn't want to get involved, which I am now because of you."

"Did Carl say anything else?"

"Said he had an accountant friend who would help him put numbers on it, and then he was going to go to the *Times*."

"Was this accountant a guy named Morgan Barstler?"

"No idea. But I told him, I told Carl, I said he shouldn't say nothing. Because there's enforcers on this thing. Every sub got a visit, sometimes more. So what happens? Next thing I know he's dead." He let out a disgusted breath. "And they think his brother did it. What a nice setup. They got this thing wired."

"You ever heard the name Turk Bacon?"

Nick shook his head. "Sounds like a name to stay away from."

"Is that it, Nick?"

"That's it. That's what I got."

And what he had was at least the start of the proof I needed to offer an alternative theory of the crime. What Judge Hughes required for me to argue it. It might not be enough to point to the actual perpetrators, but in my hands it would be enough to create a reasonable doubt.

I said, "Will you testify?"

"No way," Nick said.

"I need you to."

Sister Mary added, "Please."

Nick looked at her. She looked right back at him. Then he looked at the ground and shuffled his feet. "Sorry," he said.

He walked.

I started after him. Sister Mary caught my arm. She pointed to herself. Then went after Nick.

107

I GOT UP early the next morning and made myself coffee. Showered in the trailer shower—which was built for the guy who played Mini Me— and fired up my laptop for a look at the news.

The night before, in Luigi's parking lot, Sister Mary had managed to get Nick to at least think about testifying. She'd call him later. He made that clear. He didn't want me calling him. I couldn't blame the guy. I got him fired, now had him paranoid. All in a day's work.

I scanned the headlines in the *Times,* then popped over to LALaw-yerWatch.blogspot.com. It's an insider gossip mill that just about every city reporter and lawyer reads. It has some good stuff in it every now and then. I once got some useful info on an opposing lawyer that I used in negotiating a settlement. I can't prove it, but I think the info got my client another hundred grand.

Right out of the box, on the first entry, was this:

Who Was That Nun I Saw You With Last Night? That Was No Nun. That Was My Investigator.

You may remember Tyler Buchanan. He's the lawyer who was accused of murdering L.A. news star Channing Westerbrook (turns out he didn't do it, but he did get to see the inside of the Men's Central Jail, and lost his job at the boutique firm of Gunther, McDonough & Longyear).

I almost snorted coffee out through my nose, because curses were streaming from my mouth. No privacy anymore. None. Zip. And they couldn't even get it right. McDonough wanted me back.

Well, last night at Little Luigi's, we caught a glimpse of Buchanan with his investigator (so called), an actual nun. She's sitting right there with him in the courtroom in the Foltz Building, while Buchanan defends one Eric Richess on the charge of murdering his brother.

So who is this nun? LALawyerWatch has learned her name is Sister Mary Veritas, and she is part of St. Monica's, which is some sort of Catholic enclave in the far west corner of the San Fernando Valley.

The two looked chummy as they sipped wine and, no doubt, talked about the day in court. Ty Buchanan has done the classic "become a monk" routine after his come down. Word is he's taking cases for the "little guys." And why not? A little penance might not be a bad thing for a lawyer these days.

If I thought this was going to be ignored, overlooked, or otherwise missed by the mainstream press, I was sorely mistaken.

108

"I'M BECOMING A distraction," Sister Mary said as we drove downtown later.

"It's not a big deal," I said.

"I mean, not just to the case. At the community, too. We do not need this kind of attention."

"What does that even mean?" I said. "You can't just leave the world anymore. You have to expect you're going to catch flak. This isn't the Middle Ages."

"I didn't say it was. But there is still a need for a place of prayer and piety. Now more than ever."

"You saying you want to pull out of the case?"

"No. I made a commitment. All I'm saying is I've become a distraction, and I'm distracted myself."

She looked out the window. We were stuck in the morning commute, crawling past Vermont at about five miles an hour. A morning news chopper hovered just above us. It wasn't moving either. For some reason I thought the pilot was looking right at us.

Sister Mary, still looking out, said, "The first words of the Order of St. Benedict are, 'Listen, O child, and incline the ear of thy heart.' To hear the still, small whisper of God, in both heart and mind, is what is needed for the vocation."

"And the heart has its reasons," I said, "which reason knows nothing of."

She turned to me. "Pascal."

"I've read a little bit."

"You should read more."

"So what's your heart telling you?" I said. It suddenly seemed like the most important question in the world.

She seemed to sense the same thing. "God had a reason for me to be a nun."

"Had?"

"I mean *has*."

"Is that really what you mean?"

"I don't care to be cross-examined on the way to court," she said.

"Agreed," I said. "When are you going to call Nick?"

"Later this afternoon."

"Be sure to push that whisper-of-God thing on him. We need all the help we can get."

109

THE NEWS CREWS were camped out on Temple, waiting for us.

Sister Mary grabbed my arm as we approached. She had her head down. Reporters started shouting questions.

I waved it off, told them there was nothing to see, have a nice day. One of them almost got me in the face with his microphone and shouted, "What is the nature of your relationship?"

I just looked at this dipstick and said, "What is the nature of your intelligence?"

He blinked like he didn't understand the question. Case closed.

Security held the barking dogs at bay at the entrance, and we got inside and through the detectors. There was a clear vibe in the air, like we were suddenly the center of attention for all of Los Angeles.

When we got off the elevator, the hallway outside Hughes's courtroom was packed with court watchers. More than normal.

One of the county Safety Police guards, who keep order in the place, was waving her arms in a crowd-control gesture. It wasn't working.

Sister Mary and I waded through and got to the doors, where another guard recognized me and let us in. The gallery was packed. We were just what I didn't want to be now. A show.

110

KATE AND BABS were seated, and Kate gave me an encouraging smile.

Eric was brought in and unshackled. He touched my arm and said, "We did okay yesterday, right?"

"We did okay," I said.

"I'm worried about Mom. She looks thinner."

"I'll look out for her," I said. "Have you heard from your wife?"

"Let's not talk about that," he said.

I was fine with that.

Judge Hughes came in and called for the jury. As they filed in I felt a little like Paraguay when it plays the USA in an Olympic basketball game. Telling myself, Just hustle and try not to foul too much.

Radavich's first witness was another expert, this one on suicides. Nice specialty. He was a psych from mid-Wilshire, named Dorsini. Fiftyish, brown hair, bushy mustache. The avuncular type. Juries love that. Radavich knew who to pick.

After the qualifications, which were excellent, Radavich got into the details that did not serve my suicide theme at all.

"Dr. Dorsini, you have studied how many suicides over the years?"

"Oh, well over a thousand cases, in varying degrees. The most significant are in my case book, which is required reading in many universities and medical schools."

"How many of these suicides involved self-inflicted gunshot wounds?"

"Seventy-eight percent."

"And how many of these self-inflicted gunshot wounds were by males?"

"Ninety-one percent."

"How are most of these gunshot wounds administered?"

"Almost always through the mouth."

"As was done in this case?"

"Yes."

"In your opinion, does this case constitute a standard suicide scenario?"

"No."

"Would you explain to the jury, please, the basis of your opinion."

Dorsini turned to the jury. "The most crucial piece of evidence in a case like this comes from the hands, in the form of soot or powder. In some instances of suicide by handgun, the soot will be found not on the trigger hand, but on the off hand used to steady the muzzle. The soot would then be found on the palm of the hand, or on the radial surface of the index finger and palm, and the ulnar and palmar surface of the thumb."

"Please demonstrate for the jury what you mean by ulnar and palmar," Radavich said.

Dorsini did some pointing and explaining. Then Radavich said, "Was any such soot found on the left hand of the victim in this case?"

"No."

"What does that tell you?"

"The size and intensity of the soot pattern is a matter of how close the muzzle of the gun is to the body when it's discharged, along with things like angle of the muzzle, barrel length, caliber of weapon, and so forth. But here there was no pattern at all. That tells me someone else fired the shot."

"In this case, a gunshot to the mouth, would you expect to find soot inside the mouth?"

"Absolutely."

"And was there soot inside the mouth?"

"None."

"Outside the mouth?"

"None."

"What about the blood that was found on the gun?" Radavich asked.

Dorsini shook his head. "Deposition of high-velocity blood droplets on the back of the hand used to fire a handgun is fairly rare. Five percent. But where it is found, it is in droplets, not in streaks and patches as in this case."

The suicide theory was sinking slowly in the west, but I didn't let my face show it. Eric sat perfectly still through the whole thing.

"Does the fact that a latent print on the trigger of the gun was from the victim's index finger have significance?" Radavich asked.

"It does, but not for suicide."

"Why is that?"

"Because that is not how gunshot to the mouth would be self-administered."

"How would it be self-administered?"

"With the thumb."

Radavich took up the gun and handed it to the witness. "Would you demonstrate what you mean?"

"Certainly." Dorsini held the gun with both hands and pointed the barrel at himself. "It would look like this," he said. "This thing's not loaded, is it?"

The jury and most everybody else laughed.

"I can assure you it's not," Radavich said. "We like expert witnesses to be perfectly safe. Now, for the record, you placed the pad of your right thumb on the trigger, is that correct?"

"That's correct."

"What is your opinion about the gunshot in this case?"

"It appears to me someone wanted to make it look like suicide, but got careless with the fingerprints."

"No more questions."

I went to the lectern. "Doctor, it's not impossible to shoot yourself in the mouth, using your index finger on the trigger, is it?"

"It is not likely."

"That's not what I asked you."

"It's not impossible, no. Just highly unlikely."

"If someone is planning and deliberating about it, then using the thumb as you just demonstrated, that would be the likely method?"

"Yes."

"But if the act was not planned. Say it was done on impulse. It's reasonable that the victim might just suddenly pick up the gun, point it in his mouth, and fire, correct?"

"That can happen, yes, but as—"

"Thank you, Doctor. Oh, by the way, if a person is drunk, is he more or less likely to be deliberate?"

Dorsini scowled. "I suppose it depends on the person."

"Doctor, what is more *likely?*"

"I cannot say one way or the other."

I liked that answer. It defied common sense. And juries don't like that, especially when it comes from an expert. I decided to save this for closing argument, too. I was storing up a couple of nice nuts.

"Now, Doctor, assuming you are correct about this not being a suicide, there is nothing you can tell us about who may have shot the victim, is there?"

"Of course not."

"Anybody with a grudge against Carl Richess could have done it, isn't that right?"

"Objection," Radavich said. "Speculation, exceeds the scope of direct."

"Sustained."

No big deal. I got the question out. I had to at least plant the idea that somebody besides Eric could have killed Carl. The flower would bloom if Nick agreed to testify. If he didn't, I'd have to find another flower.

111

NEXT, RADAVICH CALLED Freeman Jenks, the tech who had testi-fied about blood at the prelim. Now he was here to talk DNA.

He did, in a concise thirty minutes of testimony. He was pretty good. Went over some of the basics of DNA sampling and matching. As he did, the jurors' eyes lit up. There it was. The CSI effect.

Even though I'd prepped the jury on this in the opening, those were still magic letters—DNA.

Especially when Jenks estimated that there was only a one-in-eleven-million chance that the sample was not a match for Eric Richess.

I felt like Jim Carrey in *Dumb and Dumber.* "So there *is* a chance!"

Instead, I was ready with something else.

"Good morning, Doctor."

"Good morning."

"You performed the DNA test on the sample provided by the prosecution, is that correct?"

"That is correct."

"Did you provide the sample to the defense so that we could also test it?"

"No, the sample was too small. It was used up in the test I performed."

"Seems a tad unfair, wouldn't you say?"

"Objection."

"Sustained."

I said, "And you used the polymerase chain reaction test, or PCR for short?"

"Yes."

"You don't know how the sample got on the gun, do you?"

"I assume it was when it was fired."

"It may have been fired several days or even weeks before, isn't that right?"

"I would say only days, because of the condition of the blood at the time I tested it. It was not degraded."

"Could it have been one week?"

"That's possible."

"So, if Eric Richess had fired the gun, say, at a firing range, and some of the webbing of his hand got caught in the slide, that would be consistent with your test results?"

"That's all speculation, but yes. Consistent."

The hard part was over, as far as I was concerned. The blood could have come from Eric on the range, and I was prepared to call Christa the tattooed range lady—which suddenly sounded like a song sung by Groucho Marx.

There was still a little more fun to be had, however.

112

"DOCTOR, ARE YOU familiar with an error known as the 'prosecutor's fallacy'?"

I didn't have to look at Radavich to know he was tense and irritable, like a businessman with a morning hangover waiting in a long line at Starbucks.

Jenks said, "I'm not sure I know what you're talking about."

"It's a term from a paper by Thompson and Schumann, titled 'Interpretation of Statistical Evidence in Criminal Trials.' Have you read that paper?"

"Not to my recollection."

"I'll give you the definition and ask if you agree." I looked at the copy in my hand and read. " 'The prosecutor's fallacy occurs when the prosecutor elicits testimony that confuses source probability with random match probability.' Do you agree with that?"

Before he could answer Radavich was objecting and asking for a sidebar.

When we got to the bench Radavich said, "I want to know the basis for this questioning."

Judge Hughes looked at me and waited.

"This is from a Ninth Circuit opinion, Your Honor," I said, handing him the copy. "I'm quoting the very language of the decision."

Hughes scanned it for a full two minutes, then said, "Frankly, I'm not sure I understand what they're saying."

"I'll be frank, too," I said. "I'm not sure I understand it, either. But that doesn't matter. I'm not the expert. Jenks is. And I'm asking him questions he, as an expert, should be able to answer."

Hughes raised his eyebrows. "He's got a point there, Mr. Radavich."

"I want to study this case before any further questioning," Radavich said.

"I'm sorry," the judge said. "I'm going to give Mr. Buchanan the benefit of his legal research. You can look at the case later and decide what you want to do."

113

I COULD HAVE kissed Judge Hughes then. A big one, right on his dome.

I settled for going back to Jenks. I had the court reporter read back my last question.

Jenks thought about it. "There is a difference, yes, between source probability and random match probability."

I read, " 'Put another way, a prosecutor errs when he presents statistical evidence to suggest that the DNA evidence indicates the likelihood of the defendant's guilt rather than the odds of the evidence having been found in a randomly selected sample.' " I looked at Jenks. "Would you agree with that?"

"Yes."

"And would you also agree with the old saying that there are lies, damned lies, and statistics?"

He chuckled. "No, I would not agree with that."

"I thought you wouldn't," I said with as much indignation as I could muster, and sat down.

Then Radavich knocked the socks off all of us. "The prosecution rests," he said.

114

"ARE YOU READY to proceed, Mr. Buchanan?" Judge Hughes said.

"I wonder if we might recess until after lunch," I said.

"Is that necessary?"

"Mr. Radavich surprised us all, Your Honor. I was sure he would take all morning." Radavich knew I thought that, too. He had sandbagged. Wanted to throw me off, like a little hip to the body as I'm driving to the hoop. He succeeded.

Hughes looked at the clock. "Then let's be back here at one-thirty. I want to get as much in as possible. Court will be in recess."

As the deputy came for Eric, he said, "What just happened?"

"The prosecutor's done. He's going with the expert testimony."

"What do we have?"

A wing and a prayer, I thought.

"Me," I said.

115

I TOLD SISTER Mary to keep trying to get Nick, and to lay as much Catholic guilt on him as possible. I don't think she appreciated that.

I had Christa Cody, the shooting range woman, on call. I phoned her and asked if she could come down now, and go on at one-thirty. She was as anxious as an *American Idol* contestant.

Which was not good. The last thing you want out of a witness is acting. During the O.J. trial, there was a prosecution witness named Kato Kaelin who used his testimony as an audition. He got about fifteen minutes out of it. And the prosecution got zip.

It was going to be one interesting afternoon. But the morning was not over.

116

I TOOK THE elevator down and crossed Spring Street to City Hall. I went through the formal front doors, usually used only for ceremony, and walked through the marble rotunda with its pillars and bronze caravel, and took an elevator to the fourth floor.

I passed a few council offices until I got to the oak door that said:

COUNCILMEMBER

JAMIE MACARTHUR

ASSISTANT PRESIDENT

PRO TEMPORE

Beneath that was the Great Seal of the City of Los Angeles. I went through the door into a reception area. An attractive African American woman looked up from her computer terminal.

"Help you?" she said.

"I'm here to see Mr. Nielsen," I said. "I'm an old friend."

She picked up a phone. "May I have your name?"

"Buchanan."

"One moment." She punched a couple of numbers, waited, then said, "A Mr. Buchanan is here to see you. He says he's an old friend."

"Not that old," I said.

She looked at me.

"Close enough for government work," I said and smiled.

She didn't smile. She told me to wait.

Which meant I got to look at another framed photograph of Councilmember Jamie MacArthur. The photo was beginning to annoy me. It cried out for a felt-tip mustache.

Regis Nielsen came out. This time missing his plastic smile.

"Mr. Buchanan," he said, "I don't really have time to talk with you."

"I bet you have time to manipulate usage charges on city contracts."

He paused, looked at the receptionist, who looked back at him. Then he motioned for me to follow him.

He led me down the corridor to his office. It had a desk, and computer, two chairs, a credenza, and a view of the federal courthouse across Temple Street.

Nielsen motioned for me to have a seat. I stayed standing. He sat behind his desk.

"I want to talk to your boss," I said.

"I don't know that that will accomplish anything," Nielsen said.

"So where is he?"

"Mr. Buchanan—"

"It's going to happen, and I suggest it is much better for you if it happens now, and not later. Because I get mad at people when they stall me. It's a real character defect. I do stuff to make their lives miserable."

Nielsen touched his lips with his two forefingers. He swiveled in his chair—right, left, right—keeping eye contact with me.

Then he said, "Have you ever seen the city from atop City Hall?"

117

NIELSEN TOOK ME to the elevators and we went up all the way, coming out to a broad staircase. At the top of the stairs was a bust of Tom Bradley, mayor of Los Angeles for twenty years, and the first African American to hold that position.

We went up another set of stairs to a reception room. There was a portable lectern with the city seal on it, and a few chairs.

Nielsen walked out the door, and we were on the outside, where there is a perimeter viewing area. The city spread out in a panorama. Walking around the catwalk gives a 360-degree view. Right now we were looking down on the Foltz Building and the old Hall of Justice across the street.

"Breathtaking, isn't it?" Nielsen said.

"A good place for a murder."

"Don't even joke about it. We had a jumper last year. They almost decided to close access. But I'm glad they didn't. I like to come up here and relax sometimes."

"And why am I here?" I said.

A voice behind me said, "To see me."

Jamie MacArthur had joined us.

118

HE WAS SHORTER than I thought he'd be. His matinee-idol head seemed better suited to a man over six feet. He had gray eyes and a full head of black hair done up in that way thick-haired politicians favor—made to look casual for around $400 a cut.

He offered his hand. "You are Tyler Buchanan?"

"That's me." His grip was firm and assumed I'd give him my vote.

He smiled and looked out at the view. "I don't get up here often enough," he said. "It's like people in New York who never go to the Empire State Building."

He was wearing a gray suit with white shirt and red tie. A gold bracelet hung on his right wrist and a Rolex on his left. At least I think it was a Rolex. He seemed a Rolex kind of guy.

"Do you love this city the way I do, Mr. Buchanan?"

"Actually, I do."

"Were you brought up here?"

"Miami. I came out here for law school."

I turned my head and realized that Nielsen was no longer there.

"You're lucky," MacArthur said. "You've had the chance to experience the city the way it really is. This is a city of immigrants. People come here because it offers hope, new beginnings. You see things with fresh eyes. I like to remind myself to have a fresh look, too. The old and the new. I look over here, and see the old Hall of Justice, and then over here, the Disney Concert Hall. Isn't it all magnificent? But my favorite is on the other side, where you can see Union Station."

"I wonder how many politicians had to leave town from there?"

He looked at me. "Is that supposed to carry some meaning?"

"I did some reading once about the old days. Political corruption. You know, Mayor Shaw. I wonder if anything's changed, or if it's just gotten more sophisticated."

He looked at his watch and said, "I'm a little pressed for time. I wanted to give you this meeting because it sounded urgent, and I know there is a tangential connection to the building project in my district."

"I'm wondering how much you know about the way contracts have been handed out. And about money changing hands that shouldn't have changed."

"Does this have anything to do with your trial?"

"I've got a client up on a murder charge, and I need to know as much as I can about the circumstances surrounding the death of his brother, who was a contractor working on the project."

"Are you honestly suggesting that someone connected with the building would have killed him, and tried to make it look like a suicide?"

"Sounds like you're up on the details."

"You're front page of the *Times*. Which I read religiously."

"Would you be willing to help out by letting my investigator look over the details of the building contracts?"

"You have to take my assurance that there is nothing that I know about, or anybody in my office knows about, that would have any bearing on this matter. I'm very sorry."

"Do you know a man named Turk Bacon?"

He hesitated. "No. Should I?"

"He sounds like a man that people should know. Maybe your able-bodied aide knows him."

MacArthur sighed. "My able-bodied aide, as you put it, is really talented, and handles my detail work. He also keeps watch over things. He has my political interests at heart, and he's very loyal. He knows all the best lawyers in town, and—"

"Almost all," I said.

"Sure. And he won't tolerate rumors, innuendos, that sort of thing. I mean, in this age of Internet crazies you simply have to cut these things off early. And Regis holds a sharp blade."

For a moment, Jamie MacArthur's face was as cold as the granite exterior of City Hall itself. Then he flashed his famous pearlies and said, "I really have to be going now, Mr. Buchanan. I'm sorry I couldn't be of more help to you. Why don't you stay up here and enjoy the view?"

119

I STAYED ONLY long enough to watch a pigeon plotz on the railing and decided it was an omen. I left before the bird could do anything to me.

I called Sister Mary and met her in the parking lot in back of the courthouse.

"He agreed," she said.

"He'll testify?"

"Tomorrow. He says it has to be tomorrow. Or he won't do it."

"Tomorrow then," I said. "Did you take any notes?"

"No. Should I have?"

"Absolutely not. Let's eat."

After lunch, and before the jury was brought in, I dutifully informed the judge and Radavich there would be an addition to my witness list. I gave them Nick's name. I said he was going to testify about the building project, and Carl's connection to it, and that I could show a possible motive for someone other than Eric Richess to kill him.

Radavich asked for a written witness statement, and I said there was none.

Radavich said that was very convenient.

I said yes, it was.

Judge Hughes said get back in court.

120

CHRISTA CODY HAD arrived on time, looking like the star of a TV show about a gun-loving woman with tattoos. She had on a white, form-fitting blouse over black pants and black stilettos.

Clearly ready for the cameras. There were none in the courtroom, but plenty outside, and I could just see her playing it up.

I spoke with her briefly in the hallway and asked her if she was relaxed, and she said she was born relaxed and was ready to kick butt on the stand.

I told her not to kick butt. I told her to calmly answer only the questions she was asked.

"You got it, boss," she said.

I did not like the way she said it. But it was time to go in.

121

CHRISTA WAS SWORN, and I began my direct examination. "You work at the Flintridge Shooting Range, is that correct?"

"Yes," she said. "Going on six years."

"Describe what your duties are there."

"Oh, a little of everything. I check people in, I police the range, I give lessons, and I slap people around if they need it."

Some laughter from the gallery. Christa smiled wide. Terrific. She was in performance mode.

Since I could not stop and wag my finger at her, or slap her myself, I stated my next question slowly. "When you say you check people in, you mean you're in the office when people come up to do some shooting?"

"That's right."

"How does that work, when someone comes in to book a time?"

"They pay for time, they sign a sheet and show a picture ID, and I tell 'em where to go. And if they hassle me, I also tell 'em where to go."

More laughter. I had to make this quick.

"How many people do you see a day, on average?"

"During the week, maybe twenty. About twice that on weekends."

"All right, taking you back to January twenty-third of this year, were you working at the range?"

"Yes, I was."

"And did two men of, shall we say, larger stature sign in?"

"Yes."

"Is one of those men in the courtroom?"

"Oh, yeah. He's right there." She pointed to Eric.

"Let the record reflect the witness has pointed to Eric Richess."

"It will so reflect," Judge Hughes said. "Continue."

"Do you know who the other man was, with Eric?"

"Yep. His name was Carl."

"How do you know that?"

"I signed him in."

I went to the table and got the copy of the sign-in sheet. "Showing you now Defense Exhibit Three for identification, can you tell me what this is?"

Christa took it and gave it a scan. "Yeah, that's one of the sign-in sheets from January twenty-third. It shows Carl Richess signed in for two people."

"And is that your handwriting?"

"Yep. Big boys, they were. A couple of trees."

Some more laughs. I thought I'd better wrap this up. "Move that Defense Exhibit Three be admitted into evidence."

"Without objection," the judge said.

122

RADAVICH STOOD. "Ms. Cody, you signed these two in, but you did not see them after that, did you?"

"Well, no. They went out to shoot."

"You don't know what they said or did on the range, do you?"

"They shot."

"Listen carefully. You did not personally witness them shooting, did you?"

"Um, no, but you don't come up there to play Donkey Kong."

She waited for a laugh, but the courtroom was silent.

Radavich pounced. "This is not a show, Ms. Cody."

I objected and the judge sustained me. But I could see some of the jurors shifting in their chairs.

"You did not," Radavich said, "with your own eyes, see the two men you have identified as the Richess brothers, actually shooting on the range, did you?"

"No," Christa said. She folded her arms.

"You don't know what happened out there on that range then, do you?"

"No, but it doesn't take a genius to—"

"Just answer the questions I put to you, Ms. Cody. I'll make them real simple. At no time after they left the office did you go to the shooting range, did you?"

"All right, no."

"They could have had a fight out there and you never would—"

"Objection," I said. "Calls for speculation."

"Sustained."

Radavich didn't care. He'd floated the words out for the jury. "And obviously you never saw the gun that was allegedly fired, correct?"

"That'd be correct, boss." Christa looked out for some feedback, but now she was just annoying.

"Well, you've been oh so helpful, Ms. Cody. No more questions."

I didn't even look at her as she walked out of the courtroom. At least we had established the brothers were at the range a week before Carl's death. And that could explain the blood on the gun.

If the jury would buy it. But they didn't look in a buying mood.

123

"CALL YOUR NEXT witness," Judge Hughes said.

I didn't have a next witness. It was 2:30 p.m.

"I wonder if we might recess until tomorrow," I said. As I spoke I saw Sister Mary looking at her cell phone. Like she had a call.

The judge didn't look pleased. But he stroked his chin and said, "Well, in view of the fact that Mr. Radavich rested early, we'll wrap up for today. But I want everyone ready to go tomorrow. Let's finish the week strong."

He admonished the jury not to talk about the case and we were through.

After the jury was out and Eric in the hands of the deputies, Sister Mary told me it looked like Nick had called.

"Call him back," I said.

As she did, I went to the rail and met Kate and Babs there. "How do you think it's going?" Kate said. She looked even more worried than usual.

"I think there are questions in the minds of some of the jurors," I said. "They're listening to both sides."

"I suppose that's all we can ask for," Kate said.

"We *can* ask. We're just getting started here. So try not to worry." I took her hands in mine, and once more I thought of my own mother's hands. It was strange, almost ghostly for a second. Like the hands were keys to a hidden memory knocking around a dark attic. I got the chills and let go.

"Are you all right, Ty?" Kate asked.

"Sure," I said. "And I want you to try and have a good dinner tonight. See to it, will you, Babs?"

"I'll try," Babs said. And then she patted my hand and said, "God bless you."

Okay. Yes. Sure. I could use it. We all could.

Kate and Babs headed for the courtroom door. Sister Mary tapped me on the shoulder and handed me her phone.

"Nick," she said.

I took the phone. "Buchanan here."

"There's a guy here from the DA's office," he said in a frantic voice. "Wants to question me. What do I do?"

"Stay calm. I can be there in half an hour."

"What if he don't want to wait that long?"

"He's got no choice. He can't force you to talk. If he wants to wait, he can. If he wants to leave, he can."

"He's standing here giving me the eye right now. Hurry up, will you?"

I hurried. But L.A. traffic didn't. There was an accident on the freeway and Sister Mary and I didn't get to Nick's for fifty-five minutes.

A little too late, it turned out.

124

NICK'S TRUCK WAS not in the driveway. There was no answer to our knocks on the front door.

"What do you suppose happened?" Sister Mary said.

"Cold feet," I said. "Maybe our boy got scared."

"Scared?"

"Maybe it wasn't a DA investigator at all."

I heard a shuffling sound and turned. An old woman was on the walkway, approaching. "Don't think you'll find anybody home," she said. Her skin was rich ebony and she wore a silky blue wig, one that a blues singer in Paris might have worn in the 1920s. She was wrapped in a pink terrycloth robe and the snouts of fuzzy slippers showed underneath, one after the other, as she moved forward, slowly.

"Do you know Mr. Molina?" I said.

"That his name?" she said. "He didn't go out much. New here. He's renting. I know the owner, he lives in Downey. I can see through my window. I live next door, and watch my stories and Oprah. But I have to get up and walk around every fifteen minutes or so, so as not to have the blood clot in my legs. Don't want to get the phlebitis, you know. Don't want to lose my legs."

She made tiny little piston motions with her arms as she walked.

"So I go to the window and I look out, just to see what's happening in the neighborhood." She reached us and stopped. Her wrinkles were deep creases in black drapes. "I kind of am the neighborhood watch, you might say. Nobody moves in or out of this neighborhood without me knowing about it. And if they try anything, I will get on the phone and call the police, yes I will."

"About Mr. Molina, did you—"

"He stays up late and he drinks beer. He even came over to my house once and said would I drink a beer with him, and I said I didn't want to. I don't like beer. I prefer bourbon."

"Have you seen him today?"

"Nothing happens in this neighborhood without me knowing about it. Now, that makes me want to know who you two are."

"I'm a lawyer," I said. "And this is Sister Mary. She is my investigator."

"My name is Mrs. April Rutherford, and this neighborhood can get pretty rough if you don't look like you belong, and Sister, I don't think you look like you belong. Nearest Catholic church is three miles. But I want you to know I went into a church once, about five years ago, and lit a candle. Does that work?"

Sister Mary said, "If it is done with the right faith. Do you belong to a church?"

"I'm a Baptist," the woman said. "But I thought I'd cover all bases that day. My son died two years ago, and his kids, my grandkids, they live with their ma in Texas. Texas! I don't get to see 'em. I'd like to see 'em again, but she never calls."

"Mrs. Rutherford," I said. "I'm starting to wonder if Nick might be inside the house, and unable to respond. Do you happen to have an emergency key or anything like that?"

"Not personally," she said. "But I know how to get in that house. I been in this neighborhood forty years, and I've seen a lot of people come and go. I've seen kids break into that house. I once went over and tried to jimmy the side window, that was oh, about ten years ago, because I thought there was a strange smell coming out and I wanted to know—"

"Can we get a window open?" I said.

"Now I don't know if I should help you anymore. I don't really know who you are, I mean if you are who you say you are. I believe the sister here is a Sister, but I don't know if you're really a lawyer. Maybe you're holding her hostage or something."

"I assure you he's not," Sister Mary said.

"Is he a religious man?" Mrs. Rutherford asked.

"I think so," Sister Mary said. "Only he doesn't know it."

"Thank you very much, Sister," I said. "Ma'am, there is a man on trial for murder, and Mr. Molina is a key witness. I just want to make sure nothing has happened to him. He could be lying inside this house, injured or something."

"Murder you say?"

"Yes."

"If you break in, you might get in some trouble."

"I'll take the chance, ma'am."

"My, oh my. You have to be small to get through that window." She looked at Sister Mary. So did I.

"Excuse me?" Sister Mary said.

125

A NUN DOES not look dignified crawling through a kitchen window. But Sister Mary Veritas did it, and didn't squawk. Just after her derrière slipped through the window, her shoes disappeared, and we heard a loud *thunk* inside.

"I'm all right," she shouted, a little anger in the tone. She opened the back door and I went in, followed by Mrs. April Rutherford.

"Nick?" I said. No answer. I did a little sweep of the place. I expected to find him. For some reason I expected to find him dead on the floor.

I didn't. The place looked lived in, man messy, but there were no signs of foul play. And no sign of Nick.

To Mrs. Rutherford I said, "Did you see anybody come here within the last hour?"

"Now, let me see." Mrs. Rutherford looked at the floor. "I was watching my story, my *General Hospital*. Do you watch the *General Hospital*?"

"I'm afraid I missed the last one."

"Now you're playing with me." She smiled.

"So you didn't see anybody come here?"

"No, I did not. Now, I watch *Judge Judy* right after the *General Hospital*. You like Judge Judy?"

"Maybe we better go outside now," I said.

We went out the kitchen door, Mrs. Rutherford insisting I'd love Judge Judy if I just gave her a chance.

Once we were on the driveway I gave Mrs. Rutherford my card. "Please give me a call if anyone comes to the house, would you do that for me?"

"You're a nice-looking young man," Mrs Rutherford said. "Have you ever thought about going on the *General Hospital*?"

Sister Mary tried to stifle a laugh.

"I may just give that a try," I said. As I did I noticed a very large man moving toward us from the sidewalk. He wore a Raiders jersey with a silver chain around his neck. The chain looked like it weighed eighteen pounds. The man weighed considerably more.

"You okay, April?" the man said.

"I'm okay, Marvin," she said.

"Any trouble?"

"No trouble, Marvin. These folks are company."

"You sure?" He gave me a middle linebacker stare.

"Now you just back yourself up," Mrs. Rutherford said. "This is a real honest-to-God lawyer and a real honest-to-God nun."

"Whatta they want?"

"That's just none of your affair, Marvin."

"Everything happens here I want to know what it is," Marvin said.

"Nice to meet you, Marvin," Sister Mary said.

"You for real?" he said.

"We think so," I said. Sister Mary gave me an elbow, just as if I was backing her into the paint.

Marvin shook his head and turned around and started to lumber away. I think the ground shook a little.

"Well now," Mrs. Rutherford said to me, "I'm glad I could help. Come back and visit if you want to."

"I'll keep that in mind," I said.

"I make a mean lemonade, with the oil from the rind," she said. "It is Wilt Chamberlain's own personal recipe, did you know he liked lemonade?"

"I did not know that," I said. I shook her hand. "Thank you, Mrs. Rutherford."

Sister Mary leaned across me, extending her hand to the woman.

But her hand never met the other woman's. I heard some sort of crack, and Sister Mary hit the ground.

126

I HEARD ANOTHER crack. And knew it was gunfire. A piece of driveway chipped near my foot.

I grabbed Mrs. Rutherford and pushed her down. She fell hard on the pavement, crying out.

Thinking the shots came from across the street, I put my body in front of the two women. Then I looked at Sister Mary. She wasn't moving.

I got my phone and punched 911. I gave dispatch the address and said, "We need immediate police and ambulance. Shots fired."

I put the phone away. Sister Mary groaned. So did Mrs. Rutherford.

"Stay still, both of you," I said. Whoever fired the shots was still out there. If we tried to get up or move, he could pop us like shooting-gallery ducks. On the other hand, I was a nice unmoving target right now.

Sister Mary groaned again.

"How bad is it?" I said.

"Have I been shot?" Sister Mary said.

"Yes. Don't move."

"Who?"

"Don't know."

"Why?"

"Don't talk. An ambulance is coming."

"Call Father Bob," she said.

And then she passed out.

127

NO MORE SHOTS were fired, but I kept the women down. Sister Mary had taken a bullet just below the left shoulder. I pressed my coat on the wound to staunch the bleeding. I had no idea what else to do, so I kept whispering to her that it would be all right. I tried to make it into a prayer.

Then I heard Marvin's voice, barking like a king. "What is goin' on?"

"Get out of here, Marvin," I said. "There's a shooter."

"Shooter? Better not mess with me." Marvin, standing a few feet from us, turned and scanned the street.

"You listen now, Marvin!" Mrs. Rutherford said.

"I'll clean him out," Marvin said. "Where is he?"

"Get down, Marvin!" I said.

"I ain't gettin' down," he said.

And he didn't. He just stood there, like he was standing guard. Maybe that's exactly what he was doing. He stayed that way until the ambulance arrived, sirens blaring.

Two paramedics took over. I asked one of them, a tall kid, where they were taking her. He said the new trauma center on South Grand. I liked the sound of *new*.

Sister Mary was still out when they put her in the back of the ambulance.

I called Father Bob and told him to meet me at the trauma center just as a black-and-white pulled up to the scene. Two patrol officers, both Hispanic, walked up the driveway fielding comments from the clutch of onlookers who had gathered.

Mrs. Rutherford got to them just before me. "A nun's been shot!" she said.

The older of the officers looked at the ambulance. "A nun?"

"Shot," I said. "I have no idea who. But from the way she fell, I'm thinking across the street at a slight angle." I pointed to a red house with green trim. "Maybe over that way."

The officer—his name plate read *Carnello*—said, "Wait here," and started across the street.

Marvin looked at the other officer and said, "It wasn't me."

"Okay," the officer said.

"He's been helpful," I said.

Two more black-and-whites joined the scene, and by now there were a whole bunch of people crowding the streets.

Officer Carnello shouted from across the street. Two of the new officers on scene went toward him, as did a bunch of the people who were watching. The crowd was shifting, the show was moving.

I looked at Mrs. Rutherford and said, "How you doing?"

"My knees hurt," she said.

"You need me to take you to a doctor?"

She shook her head. "My, no. I've had a lot worse in my time."

I nodded and then jogged over to the house across the way. One of the new officers on the scene was telling people to stay back. I asked him what was up. He told me to stay back, too. I ignored him, ran past and in through the open front door.

Three officers, including Carnello, were standing around a black male, bloodied and unconscious on the floor.

128

"Do you know this man?" Carnello said.

"No," I said. "Does he have a weapon?"

"This is a crime scene. I'm going to have to ask you step outside. I'll want a statement."

"You can have it later," I said. "I'm going to the trauma center." I gave him my card.

"If you could please wait—"

"No can do," I said.

I left, got in my car and drove to the center. I told reception who I was and that got me some information. They had Sister Mary in right now, and I was invited to wait.

I went to a waiting room stuffed with hot, anxious, impatient people. Green leatherette chairs, and a TV monitor with the drone of some talk show. I didn't hear it. Mostly I paced and looked at the walls.

Father Bob found me there around three-thirty. "Any word?" he said.

"No," I said. "She's still inside." I took him outside to the hallway so we could talk in private.

"Any idea what happened?" Father Bob asked.

"Not much," I said. "We were looking for a witness, we went to the guy's house. But after Sister Mary went through the kitchen window—"

"Excuse me?"

"Later. We were at this house, the guy wasn't there and the next thing I know somebody shoots at us and Sister Mary goes down. I'm sure the shot was meant for me."

"This is rather unbelievable."

I looked at my hands. They were balled up into fists.

Father Bob put his hand on my shoulder. "How are you doing?" he said.

"Oh, never better."

"Ty, talk to me."

"I shouldn't have used her," I said.

"We both know she wanted to do this," he said.

I shook my head. "You can't mix what you do and what I do. You can't be looking after the things of God and then run around with a crazy lawyer getting shot. I'm not good for her."

"We believe all of this is in God's hands, you know."

"Listen, Padre, we've had lots of talks about this. But you know what I think? I think your God's hands are like a little kid's at the beach. Holding sand, and it keeps seeping through. And then when it's all over, he just dusts his hands off and forgets about it."

"If I believed that, I wouldn't be a priest."

"I'm not trying to get in a fight with you. I don't know what I'm doing up there on your hill."

"I think you should go right back up there and get some rest. I'll stay here and let you know what's happening."

"No way," I said. "There's no way I'm leaving."

129

WE TALKED TO a detective before we talked to a doctor. His name was Stein, from Southwest Division. He was about forty and was built like a mannequin at Men's Warehouse. His clothes fit perfectly.

"Can you tell me what happened, please, sir?" he said as Father Bob and I sat with him in the hospital cafeteria. We all had cardboard-tasting coffees in front of us. Not many sips were taken.

I said, "We were standing outside the house, talking to the next-door neighbor, and the next thing I know Sister Mary has a bullet in her. It came from across the street—the rest you probably know."

"What were you doing there in the first place?"

"Looking for a witness. Somebody who was supposed to testify for me. He wasn't home."

"So do you think this had anything to do with that witness? I mean, like somebody didn't want him to testify?"

"He would've taken a pop at the witness, not me. Had to be a rifle."

"Maybe."

"Which would probably rule out gang activity. That's not exactly the weapon of choice."

"Why would somebody want to shoot you, Mr. Buchanan?"

"Other than the fact that I'm a lawyer?"

"Other than that."

"I don't know," I said. "A few days ago somebody slashed my tires, and scratched *Back off* in my car. Sister Mary's also been getting threatening e-mails."

"You know who sent them?"

"Somebody from Devonshire's working on that now. And that's all I've got. What about the guy they found in the house across the street?"

"He was hurt pretty bad."

"Dead?"

Stein shook his head.

"Did they bring him here?" I said.

"No doubt." He said it like he knew it was true.

"Let's go talk to him," I said.

"I don't know that I want to do that."

"Detective, I'm going to find out who did this. I will talk to this guy myself if I have to. Why don't we work together?"

"You just let me handle the investigation, Mr. Buchanan. I'll keep you informed. Here's my card. The number will forward to my cell if you need to reach me."

He handed it to me, got up, and walked away.

130

WE FINALLY GOT to talk to a doc. His name was Yang, and he was walking rapidly down the hall. We had to talk as we walked, and these ER guys walk fast.

"She got a clean wound through the left side," he said. "Missed the heart, but not by much."

"So she's going to be okay?" I said.

"I can't tell you that. There's a whole spectrum, from nerve damage to no damage."

"When will you know?"

"I can't tell you that, either."

"How long will she—"

"Can't tell." He turned to us. "Check back tomorrow." And then he was off again.

I looked at Father Bob. "A fount of information," I said.

"You try doing this job," he said. "It's Union Station with blood and guts and no schedule."

131

SISTER MARY WAS in room 103, bed C. Father Bob and I passed two other beds. The first had an old woman, unconscious. The second had a thin younger woman who was staring blankly at a TV monitor.

At the last bed, back to us, was a jumbo-sized nurse. She was so large she obscured most of Sister Mary. She turned around, looked at us, and said. "And just who are you?"

"I'm her lawyer," I said. "And this is her priest."

She gave us a scan, nodded, and walked out. And there was Sister Mary.

She was all hooked up. She looked more vulnerable than I had ever seen her. She seemed about seventeen, as if she'd been in a car accident driving home from a high school dance. Her face was bruised from the fall.

But she managed a weak smile when she saw us.

"Hi," she said, almost too soft to hear.

Father Bob moved to the bed and took her right hand. I came up and stood next to him.

"I'm sorry," she said to me. "Is this going to hurt our case?"

"Don't talk," Father Bob said.

"I want to," she said. "I've got nothing else to—" Her words ended in a wince. I felt it myself. I wished I could have shifted all her pain to me.

"Any idea who shot me?" Sister Mary said.

"We don't know," I said. "But it was probably meant for me. Sorry I was standing in the wrong place."

"I play ball with you," she said. "You're always in the wrong place."

She smiled again, the way she does when she hits the final shot in Around the World. But it faded quickly and she turned her head away.

For a long moment we were silent. I had no idea what to do. Then I saw a small pull from Sister Mary's hand, and Father Bob bent over. She whispered something to him.

He came back up and said, "Would you mind if I had a few minutes with Sister Mary alone?"

I wondered what that was all about. Last rites or something? It couldn't be that bad. I wouldn't let it be that bad. I wouldn't let . . .

There I was again, sticking myself in the middle of Catholic business. "I'll be back," I said.

132

I WENT TO the nurses' station on the emergency wing, and showed my Bar card. I said, "I'm working with Detective Stein."

Sometimes that works, sometimes it doesn't. This time it did. "The detective is in 210," she said.

When I got there I saw a cop was sitting on the chair outside the room. Only one reason for that. Protect a witness. I hung back before he saw me. I backed up into the hallway and thought about my options. I could forget the whole thing. But that wasn't likely.

Instead, I looked around, then went into a bathroom across the corridor. There was one fellow at the sink, washing his hands. I stepped over to the urinal and pretended to do my thing.

As soon as he left I grabbed a handful of paper towels, made a wad, and stuck them in a toilet. Then flushed. It stopped up nicely, so I flushed again and got the first trickles of water on the floor.

I hit it one more time and walked back to where the cop was sitting. I waited for a nurse to come by, and said, "Something's wrong in the bathroom. Somebody may be hurt."

The cop heard me and got up and followed the nurse.

I went into room 210. I found the kid in the first bed. He was not looking good. His face was like yesterday's meatloaf.

"How you doing?" I said.

He groaned.

"My name's Buchanan. I was the one who got shot at today. You have any idea who did this to you?"

He shook his head. I studied his face, the way I would a witness. But his injuries made it a much harder read. Still, I was looking for a tell. I wanted to know if he was in on the shooting in any way.

"Did you get a look at him?" I said.

He closed his eyes, but didn't indicate no.

"If you can try to help me out," I said, "maybe we can get this guy."

He looked at me through the slits that were his eyes. Like he was trying to decide if he could say anything.

"Who you?" he said.

"A lawyer. I was talking to the lady across the street from the house you were in. You live there?"

He didn't respond.

"We were trying to find a guy, and somebody took a shot at us. Didn't hit me, he hit an innocent bystander, a nun, and the shot came from your house. What about it?"

"Got hit," he said. He seemed truthful, from the gut. "Happened fast."

"Anything you can give—"

"Hey!" The cop was in the room. "Nobody talks to him. Get out."

"I may be his lawyer," I said.

The cop looked confused. I looked at the kid, and shrugged.

The cop said, "This your lawyer?"

The kid paused, then shook his head slowly.

"You have to leave," the cop said.

"You think about it," I said to the kid, and left my card on his stand.

133

I CHECKED IN on Sister Mary again. She was sleeping. Father Bob was praying by her bed. I put my hand on his shoulder. He looked up and motioned for me to sit.

I pulled up the one other chair in the room.

"She had a message for you," Father Bob said. "She wants you to go get some sleep so you can go to court tomorrow. She said she wants the blow-by-blow afterward. She said it's Showtime and you're the Lakers in 1985."

I smiled. "Boston Garden. Game six. I wish. She's lying in bed with a bullet wound and I have no idea what's going on."

"My grandmother always said, Never play leapfrog with a unicorn."

I paused. "That some sort of down-home wisdom?"

"It means don't worry about what doesn't exist. Just look at the task in front of you."

I tried to look. What I saw was a long black tunnel. Inside were people with guns and money. I thought of that Warren Zevon song. Lawyers, guns and money. Dad, get me out of this.

Father Bob put his hand on my arm. "And remember, we're your people now."

"Are you?"

"Of course."

I shook my head doubtfully. "You're my friends. Good friends. I don't know about my people."

"Explain."

I sat back in the chair. "Your religion mystifies me. It's the heart of everything you do. But it's beyond me. And here I am tearing down Sister Mary's standing with the Almighty. I have no right to do that. She's lying there with a bullet wound because of me."

"Ty, servants of God have suffered much worse."

"Martyrs, you mean? But that was for the faith. She took a hit because of a lawyer. Scrounging around looking for a witness. Isn't she supposed to be praying and looking out for the poor and all that?"

Father Bob was silent for a long moment. Then, "I consider you a friend, too, Ty. More than that. What you've done for me, for our community. It's forged bonds."

"But I'm not part of you. There's something between us that doesn't mix."

"Oh, I don't know. Jesus ate with tax collectors and even a lawyer or two."

"What *was* he thinking?"

"He was thinking of you," Father Bob said.

"I didn't get the memo," I said.

"It's written on your heart."

"Lawyers don't have hearts, haven't you heard?"

He smiled. "Augustine said God made us for Himself, and our hearts are restless until they rest in Him."

"Well, I have a feeling I'm going to stay restless, unless I find my witness." I stood. "Tell Sister Mary I'll see her tomorrow."

As I was driving away from the hospital, I got a call from Sid.

"Update time," he said.

"Go ahead."

"Earlier today the guy sent an e-mail from a computer terminal at a branch of the L.A. Public Library. Over in Sylmar. I was able to do a little hacking—just promise you won't tell anybody, okay?"

"Lips. Sealed."

"Okay, so here's what happened. You reserve a computer with a library card. Every library card has a number, and this one is fourteen digits. I was able to get to a name. The name associated with the card. Somebody named Douglas Aycock. That mean anything to you?"

"Nothing."

"Didn't think so, because he's from Oklahoma."

I tightened my grip on the steering wheel.

Sid went on. "Last time we talked you mentioned this Oklahoma theory that Sister Mary had. Pretty good theory, turns out. I checked. And I did find a guy with that name out of Oklahoma City. I found it in a newspaper account."

"And?"

"Here is the seriously strange part. This guy, Douglas Aycock, went to the same high school as your nun friend and moved to L.A. sometime after graduating. Also—"

"What?"

"That's just the strange part. I said there was a seriously strange part, and here it is. This guy has been missing for five years. They think he was kidnapped, and they presume him to be dead."

Too many thoughts were buzzing around in my mind now. I wanted to swat them. "So a dead guy comes back to cyberstalk? Then why is he using the L.A. library system with his name attached? And he'd have to have an established residency."

"You kidding? That can be faked easier than those Social Security cards they sell down at MacArthur Park. Plus, this could be somebody else using this guy's name."

"But why do that? Why take on some dead kid's name, then risk being caught by using it to get a library card and all that?"

"Like I said, he's a gamer. I think he thinks this is fun."

134

I GOT BACK to St. Monica's as it was getting dark. As I walked toward my trailer, I saw the glow of the little alcove, or whatever they call it, that has lighted candles. I went to it and did something I've never done before in my life. I took a long match, lit it by the flame of a candle, and then lit one that wasn't already going. Out loud I said, "This is for Sister Mary Veritas, who deserves to be completely okay, okay? So there you have it."

I blew out the match, wondering if *there you have it* had the same punch as *Amen.*

I walked across the grounds, over the basketball court, back to my trailer. I went inside and lay down on the bed and tried to think about the next day.

But I kept thinking about Sister Mary.

135

NEXT MORNING I went to court alone. I didn't like it. It felt like there was a big hole underneath my feet, covered by thin wood, and I could fall in at any time. I had come to depend on Sister Mary not only for her insight, but for her very presence.

Because I didn't have any witness to put on the stand, I asked the judge in chambers if we could pack it in and come back Monday.

"I don't want this jury waiting around," Judge Hughes said. "I'm sorry to hear about your assistant. But I have to think you have some evidence to present that's been in the wings."

"If I could just have the weekend," I said.

"I'm sorry, Ty. I'm not going to do that. When can I expect you to have a witness on the stand today?"

I looked at my watch, purely as a fake-out. "How about eleven?"

"How about ten-thirty?"

Radavich leaned against the door with his arms folded, saying nothing.

"I'll do what I can," I said.

"See that you do," the judge said.

136

I WENT OUTSIDE to the back of the courthouse and put in a call to my forensic guy, Dr. Harold Whitney. He knew he was possibly going to testify this week, and I told him I'd give him at least a day's notice. Now it was an hour. I left a message.

I leaned against a low wall by the parking lot and tried to figure out what to do next. Maybe I could call in the parking attendant and have him testify about parking lots in general. And I'd figure out a way to make it relevant.

In other words, I was desperate.

And wasn't expecting the tap on the shoulder I got next. I turned and looked into a familiar face. It took me a second to remember where I'd seen him. It was at Addie Qs, the bar on Sunset.

"How you doin'?" the *Sopranos* extra said.

"I'm just peachy," I said.

"There's somebody wants to talk to you."

Now this was really sounding like the show. "Who?"

"You'll be interested." He pointed to the parking lot. "He's in the black Caddy, with the tinted windows."

I looked and saw the car. It stuck out like a Secret Service agent at a kid's birthday party.

"Mr. Bacon is waiting," Sopranos said. "He's not alone."

137

INDEED HE WASN'T. Through the open passenger window I saw Turk Bacon behind the wheel. Behind him was a woman with long, silky black hair, a striking amount of which cascaded over her shoulders. She had olive skin and deep brown eyes.

"Get in, Mr. Buchanan," Bacon said.

"I'm good," I said.

Sopranos, who was behind me, opened the door. I looked at him. "Why don't you just open the trunk and be done with it?"

He didn't laugh. "Get in," he said.

"Back off, Vito," I said.

"His name is not Vito," Turk said. "It's all right, Mike. Go have a smoke."

Sopranos looked disappointed. He turned and walked away.

I waited a couple of seconds, then got in.

"I don't understand," Bacon said. "Why are you getting in?"

"Now it's my idea," I said. "So what's this about?"

The woman looked nervous. Bacon said, "This is Mr. Buchanan. He's the lawyer I told you about. You can tell him now."

She looked at Bacon, then back at me. "He was with me that night. Your client. We were at a motel in Long Beach. I have the receipt." She reached into her pocket and pulled out a folded piece of paper. I looked at it. It was a receipt for the Lavender Motel in Long Beach, with a stamp indicating 9:02 p.m. on Friday, January 30.

"You kept the receipt?" I said.

"This is a business," she said.

I almost laughed. "How long was he with you?"

"Two hours."

"Exactly?"

"Exactly. We bill by the quarter hour."

"You're just like lawyers."

Turk Bacon said, "More honest."

"That's a lot of time with one client," I said.

"It's what he wanted," she said. "It's his dime. He wanted to talk. Some clients do. They have trouble at home, whatever. It's not just about sex."

"You did have sex, right?"

"Yes."

I said, "The prosecution is going to tear into you."

"I can handle myself," she said. "I've been doing it ever since I was twelve."

I looked into her eyes. They were sincere. But I had questions.

"Why did you happen to pick this time to come forward?" I said.

She looked at Bacon, who said, "She wants to do the right thing."

That sounded about as convincing as *I didn't inhale*. "This is very convenient, you coming along like this," I said. "At just the right time. After a key witness goes missing."

"Key witness?" Bacon said.

"I'm sure you're completely in the dark."

"I don't know who you think I am," he said. "Or what magical powers I possess. But right now you have a fact before you, a proven fact. The truth, in other words."

"Why'd you hold her back, then?"

"What makes you think I held her back? She came to me."

I said, "It just smells like something's going on that you're not telling me about."

"Your sense of smell is not, so far as I can see, relevant. All you need to know, Mr. Buchanan, is that the witness who can set your client free is sitting here with you right now, and she's quite ready to testify. You want her to or not?"

Want her to? This was the bombshell, the hand grenade, the TV moment that never happens in real life. A surprise witness turning up just before the commercial break.

Which was exactly what I didn't like about it. Too scripted. But there was the receipt. There was the *fact*. And I knew I'd put her on, because not to would be legal malpractice.

I said to her, "Have you made any deals, or even talked with anyone, from a tabloid or television show, about telling your story?"

Bacon again answered for her. "I can assure you nothing like that has taken place. And if Leilana is asked anything along those lines, she can truthfully say no deals have been made."

"Leilana?"

"Leilana Salgado," Bacon said.

"What about after the trial?" I said.

Bacon shrugged.

"So that's it, huh?" I said. "Timing. You make a big splash, now that the media's covering this thing. Leilana here gets her face splashed all over. Fame. Because it doesn't matter anymore what you're famous for, right?"

"I did not make American popular culture what it is today," Bacon said. "I merely enjoy its fruits. Remember what I told you about being able to bloom in any kind of soil?"

"I'll never forget it," I said.

Bacon smiled. "So do you want us in the courtroom?"

"Not you. Just her."

Bacon shrugged.

138

I WENT UP to the lockup to talk to Eric. He was not looking well. His face was almost translucent.

"I can't take much more of this," he said.

"Listen," I said. "The escort you were with that night. Describe her to me."

"What?"

"Just do it."

"She was sort of Mexican looking. She had real long hair. I mean, how much detail do you want?"

"That's enough," I said.

"Enough for what?"

"She's here."

Eric leaned against the lockup door. "What do you mean, here?"

"She's going to testify. She's your alibi."

"Wait, wait!"

"Wait for what?"

"I don't know if I want you to."

"Eric, this is the single most important evidence we can put on. What do you mean wait?"

"Why not let me take the stand?"

"That is a bad idea, Eric. I don't think Radavich has met his burden, and now our key witness is sitting right outside the courthouse."

"What's this gonna do to Mom? And my wife?"

"Listen carefully. I don't know about you and your wife. She doesn't even bother to come to court. You have enough trouble there that this isn't going to be any major setback. And as far as your mom, what she wants is you out of here. What good is it to hang onto some sort of pride and get stuck in the slam for something you didn't do? How is that going to help your mother?"

Eric sighed, closed his eyes. He stayed that way for a long moment. Then he nodded, turned, and went to sit on the bench.

139

THE FUN PART was going to be telling the judge and the deputy district attorney exactly what I was about to do.

In chambers, fifteen minutes late, I faced an impatient Judge Hughes and an indifferent Tom Radavich. I was about to make him different.

"Are we ready to go now?" the judge said.

"I am prepared to put on a witness," I said. "This witness has just this moment become known to me. I want to put this witness on the stand today. Because the last time I noticed a witness to the prosecution, he disappeared. Oh yeah, and my investigator got shot. I don't want that happening again."

Radavich now looked interested.

I went on. "This is a key witness. This is an alibi witness. This is the woman who will testify she was with my client on the night of the murder. She has corroborating evidence. I will tell you right now it is a motel receipt, and I will make sure that Mr. Radavich has a copy. I'm sure they will want to spend the next night and day checking out her story. But I want her on the stand before something happens to her, like a DA investigator showing up on her doorstep and then she disappears, like Keyser Soze."

"What are you talking about, Mr. Buchanan?" Judge Hughes said. "Who is Keyser Soze?"

"*The Usual Suspects.* Poof. He's gone. Like my witness, Nick Molina, who was talking to somebody Mr. Radavich sent around."

"What is this about?" the judge said to Radavich.

"We sent an investigator to question Mr. Molina, yes," Radavich said. "Mr. Molina was not responsive. He said he would not talk without his lawyer present. Our investigator left, and that was that."

"So where is this Mr. Molina?" the judge said.

"Poof," I said.

"You mean you don't have contact with him?"

"No, but I know how to get in his house and get shot at. You just show up."

Judge Hughes looked at the ceiling. "I don't want to delay this trial any more. I'm going to let Mr. Buchanan put on his wintess."

Radavich said, "We object, of course. This is the second surprise witness Mr. Buchanan has suddenly tossed our way. I don't know how many more Mr. Buchanan is going to buy before he finally gets—"

"Now, now," the judge said. "Let's think about this a moment. We all know that discovery these days tends to favor the prosecution."

Radavich's cheeks started to pinken.

"Oh, don't bother to deny it, Tom. You spring this stuff all the time. I'm going to let this one happen. When I first started trying cases, you had to be able to think on your feet and deal with surprises. A little of that won't hurt you. So we're going to go out there and I'm going to allow Mr. Buchanan to put his witness on the stand and we're going to see what happens. And I'll give you a chance to recall the witness later, if you find anything out."

Before I could look too smug, the judge said to me, "And this better be a credible, reliable, truthful witness. Because if I find out that you are manufacturing anything, or allowing frivolous testimony, I'm going to be, you know, very upset. And then you know what will happen to your career?"

I shook my head.

"Poof," Judge Hughes said.

140

AND SO I called Leilana Salgado to the stand. She looked ready.

"Ms. Salgado," I said, "please tell the jury what you do for a living."

"I'm an escort."

"Do you work for an escort service?"

"Yes."

"That means that clients will go through the service, and arrange for a price to spend time with you, is that right?"

"Yes."

"That includes sexual favors as well?"

"No, that is not part of the service. If it happens, it is considered optional with each one of us."

I had to be up front with the jury. "Some people would call you a hooker or a prostitute, isn't that correct?"

"I've been called a lot of things."

"In fact," I said, "by testifying here today, you are putting yourself in legal jeopardy, aren't you?"

"Yes."

The foundation was set. It's powerful evidence of credibility when what you say in court could hurt you. The jury was ready to listen.

"On January thirty of this year, were your services retained by the defendant, Eric Richess?"

"Yes."

"Please tell the jury when and where you arranged to meet."

Like a seasoned pro, Leilana turned toward the jury. "He wanted to meet me in Long Beach, so I gave him a price for the time. He wanted me to select a location. Our escort service has a database of acceptable places. I chose one and had him meet me there."

So far, so good. She sounded certain and credible and somewhat humble. No chip on the shoulder. The jury would like that. Some of them, anyway.

"What time did he meet you?" I said.

"Approximately eight-thirty."

"How can you be sure?"

"Because we went to a bar and had a drink, and got back to the motel around nine o'clock. That's when I paid for the room."

"You paid for the room?"

"Yes."

"Is that a common practice?"

"Sometimes, if the client wishes to remain anonymous."

I went to the counsel table and got the receipt Leilana had given me. "Showing you now what has been marked Defense Exhibit Four for identification, can you tell me what that is?" I put it on the rail of the witness box.

She picked it up, looked at it, put it down. "It's the motel receipt."

"What time does it say on the receipt?"

"9:02 p.m."

"Did you secure a room?"

"Yes."

"Without going into any detail, how long were you with Mr. Richess?"

"I was with him until eleven p.m."

"How can you be sure?"

"That's the time he paid for. He paid me for two hours. Then he left."

"And what did you do after he left?"

"I watched TV. I watched the *Tonight Show.* I like Jay Leno."

A little laughter broke out in the courtroom. Most of the jury laughed, too. They were warming to her. There is something about witnesses completely open about what they do that juries appreciate. A witness who tries to hide things is the one you don't trust.

"After the Jay Leno show, what did you do?"

"I checked out and went home."

"Ms. Salgado, is there any doubt whatsoever in your mind that you were with the defendant, Eric Richess, from approximately eight-thirty p.m. to a little after eleven p.m. on the night of January thirty?"

"No doubt whatsoever."

"Why didn't you agree to testify earlier?"

"I was scared. When you do what I do, you don't exactly want to be spreading the news in court."

"And why have you decided to come forward?"

She looked at Eric. There was warmth in her eyes. "He was nice. He was one of the nicer men I've been with. I just couldn't let him be convicted of something he didn't do."

I paused. "Ms. Salgado. Have you contacted, or been contacted by, any tabloid newspaper, book publisher, Internet site, or any other media outlet whatsoever, in connection with your testimony here today?"

"No, I have not."

"Have you received any money, or the promise of any money, for your testimony?"

"No."

"Thank you." I turned to Radavich. "Your witness."

141

TOM RADAVICH WASTED no time. He stood up, buttoned his suit coat and, without notes, tore into the witness.

"You're a hooker, is that what you said?" he said.

Leilana's eyes darkened. "I said I am an escort. I don't walk the streets."

"You have sex for money, don't you?"

"Sex is optional."

"Please, madam, you don't expect anyone in this courtroom to believe in a legal fiction, do you?"

I objected. "I object to the use of the term *madam*. It's argumentative and Mr. Radavich is just using loaded language for the jury."

Judge Hughes looked at me. "I've allowed your witness to take the stand, Mr. Buchanan. I'm going to allow the prosecutor wide latitude in his cross-examination. You may continue, Mr. Radavich."

"Thank you, Your Honor. You have sex with the men you escort, don't you, madam?"

"Sometimes."

"Always."

"Not always."

"And that's because, for one reason or another, you call off the whole deal, isn't it?"

"That sometimes happens."

"Meaning you don't get paid for your time."

"Sometimes."

"Let me put it this way. Every time you get paid to escort someone, you have sex with him, isn't that right?"

"No. Sometimes the client opts not to."

"Oh, that must happen all the time, right? I mean, that's why men use these escort services, just so they can enjoy some intellectual conversation."

"Objection," I said.

"Sustained."

"Let me rephrase the question," Radavich said. "You are, to use an old English word, a whore."

"Objection!"

The judge looked at Radavich. "Sustained."

Radavich didn't miss a beat. "How many men have you had sexual relations with in the last year?"

"I object," I said. "A witness's sexual history is inadmissible."

Judge Hughes shook his head. "This falls under 782 of the Evidence Code, and she is not a complaining witness. This goes to credibility. The witness has testified about her services, and Mr. Radavich may cross-examine her on it. Overruled. Answer the question, Ms. Salgado."

"I don't know," she said.

"Too many to count?" Radavich said.

Leilana flipped her hair back. "I don't count."

"How about more than ten? Is it more than ten?"

"I suppose."

"We don't want any supposing here, madam."

Radavich was going to back her up into a dark, dank corner. And there was nothing I could do. The judge was going to allow everything short of Radavich slapping her around. I could keep objecting, but the jury gets annoyed with that, once they know the judge is not going to sustain you. I'd have to wait for an objection I could win.

"Mr. Buchanan asked if you have received any offers regarding your story. You denied that, and denied seeking any offers, is that right?"

"That's right."

"Of course nothing can stop you from shopping this around after you're finished, right?"

"I don't know. I'm not interested."

"Are you telling us today that you will not sell your story, in any form whatsoever?"

"Yes."

"And do you, madam, expect anyone here to believe you?"

She flashed anger. "I don't care what anybody believes."

"Exactly," Radavich said. "I have no further questions."

142

ON RE-DIRECT, I had to rehab my witness but fast. I didn't know if I could do it.

Then it turned out my wit did it for me.

"Ms. Salgado," I said, "the prosecutor was pretty rough on you just now."

"It's all right," she said quietly.

"When Mr. Radavich called you a whore, how did that make you feel?"

She looked at Tom Radavich, then back at me. Her breathing got labored. Then tears pooled in her eyes. She fought them back. She opened her mouth to speak, and couldn't.

"Do we need to take a short break?" Judge Hughes said.

Leilana shook her head. "I'm sorry. No. I can answer."

The clerk brought her a box of tissues. Leilana took one and touched her eyes. Then she said, "He didn't say anything I haven't heard before. Since I was twelve, that's what I've been told I was. By my father, then my stepfather, then my brothers. You get to believe it after a while. And you hang on to anything that'll keep you from killing yourself. Like this."

"This?" I said.

"This trial. To tell the truth. To help somebody. Because that's what you're supposed to do. That's all."

And then she was in tears again.

For a moment the courtroom was silent. Then I said, "No more questions."

The judge said, "Anything further of this witness, Mr. Radavich?"

"No, Your Honor."

"Ms. Salgado, you are excused," Hughes said. "But you are subject to recall if the prosecution so wishes. Do you understand that?"

Leilana nodded. She left the witness box and crossed the courtroom, head down, moving quickly. As she did, Hughes said, "You may call your next witness, Mr. Buchanan."

I paused until Leilana was out the courtroom doors.

And had a sudden inspiration, the kind trial lawyers learn to trust. I decided not to put on my forensics guy. You can overtry a case, the way the prosecutors in O.J. did. I didn't want the jury to think of the science any more than they already had. The whole thing was going to be about the alibi.

I turned to the judge and said, "The defense rests."

143

NOW RADAVICH WAS the one thrown off his game. It was 11:54 when I wrapped it up, and the judge wanted to know if Radavich would present anything on rebuttal. Radavich moaned and whined and said he would need the weekend and the judge gave it to him.

After talking to Kate, and assuring her that things went about as well as they could, I told her to try to get some rest. She asked about Sister Mary and I told her I would see her in a little while.

"Tell her God is being merciful to me," Kate said. "I feel, for the first time, that I might possibly get my son back. The one son I have left." And then she cried, and I held her.

144

SISTER MARY WAS still hooked up and in bed, but at least was able to read a book. She waved me over as soon as I showed my face.

"Feeling better?" I said.

"Never mind that. How'd it go in court today?"

"You shouldn't be thinking about that. You should be—"

"Come on, give. I've been dying to know."

"You remember that alibi witness Eric wouldn't talk about?"

"The woman?"

"She showed."

Sister Mary slapped the open book down on her knees. "And I wasn't there."

"She's credible," I said. "At least the jury is going to think so. I'm pretty sure. It's the best we can hope for. All the other evidence we have can be given an alternative explanation. But if the jury believes Eric was with this woman at the time of the murder, it's over. He walks."

Sister Mary put her head back and looked at the ceiling.

"What's wrong?" I said.

"I didn't expect to miss it so much. Being in court."

"You can always go into law. UCLA offers a nun discount."

She looked away, toward the window.

"Does the name Douglas Aycock mean anything to you?" I said.

She snapped back to me. "How do you know that name?"

"Sid gave it to me. He got it by tracing one of the e-mails through the library system."

Sister Mary's eyes got that faraway look. When she spoke, it was in the low tones of recounted memory. "I went to high school with him. Dated him a couple of times. And then later, after high school, I heard he died. How—"

"Missing, actually, according to the reports."

"But we all figured he was dead."

"He wasn't a serious boyfriend?"

"He took me to a dance, a couple of movies. He wanted it to go further, but I didn't."

"Why was that?"

"We didn't have the same interests. He was totally into the game world. He had this circle of friends and I found them a little weird. Role playing all the time. It started to cross over . . ." She looked at me with an astonished gaze. "He's alive and sending me e-mails?"

"That's all I know."

She thought about it all for a moment, then lifted her book. It was *Conjectures of a Guilty Bystander* by Thomas Merton. "I was just reading something," she said. "About that time in Louisville, remember? When Merton felt connected to all those people?"

"Yeah."

"He says here that he suddenly saw the secret beauty of their hearts." She paused. "I had a very discomforting thought about that. For a moment, I didn't know if I agreed with him. That he was seeing things through rose-colored glasses. And I didn't like feeling that. And now this . . ."

"You've just been shot. Naturally you're not going to see all this beauty in people's hearts."

She placed the book on the table next to the bed. She looked a little lost.

I said, "How about I run my closing argument by you?"

"Walk it by," she said. "That's about my speed right now."

145

AFTER TWENTY MINUTES I could tell Sister Mary was tired or in pain, or both. So I went back to the kid's room. There was no cop there this time, so I wondered if he was even in there. But he was, and I guessed Stein had talked to him and pulled the guard cop off.

I said, "So, how you doing today?"

He was a little more aware, and had a little more attitude. "Man, you back?"

"I take it the police talked to you."

"I got nothing more to say."

"You do to me."

"Why?"

"Guy who did this to you is still out there. Ever think he might want another shot at you?"

"You think you gonna help me? You want something, you just mad."

"You're just stupid. You got no idea what's going on. No idea how big this could be."

"Man, who are you?"

"Ty Buchanan, and I can help you. What's your name?"

"Daryl."

"Why don't you tell me how you got beat up?"

"Got jumped is all."

"How many?"

"Just one, I think."

"You get a look at the guy?"

Daryl shook his head. "He was on my back, all over me. Then I was out."

"All right," I said. "Let's take it a step at a time. Where were—"

"I don't want to take no steps or nothin'," Daryl said. "I just want to get out of here."

"You got anybody to come get you?"

He shook his head. Sadly, it seemed.

"Where you at, Daryl?"

"Why'm I talkin' to you, man?"

"Maybe I can get you out of here," I said. "Get you looked at by a private doc."

"Why?"

"Because I need to know what happened. Now, make me your lawyer. What you say I keep to myself, always. Got it?"

He closed his eyes. Winced. "How much I got to pay you?"

"Nothing. You pay me nothing."

"I got a record. I don't need no trouble. I smoked me a blunt before I got jumped. They gonna get me for that?"

"Daryl, my job is to keep trouble away for my clients."

He thought about it a second. "Plus I wasn't even s'posed to be there."

"At the house?"

"My mama owns it. Rents it. She won't rent it to me. She don't like me. She lives with her boyfriend in Monrovia. I got a key and take stuff."

"You rob your mother's house?"

"So?"

"Who lives there?"

"Nobody. I seen they ain't nobody there, like from a week ago. Skipped out. Cleaned out. So I go to clean out what's left, you know?"

"And smoke a little weed?"

"That's it. I go in, find some stuff in the kitchen. I fire up, take a nap. Life's good."

"Only you left the door open, right?"

"Back door, yeah. I didn't think nobody was gonna come in. There's this kinda road in back, against a fence. Nobody usually uses it."

"So you're taking a nap, then what?"

"Then bam, back of the head. I get pulled to the floor, facedown. Bam again. That's it."

"That's the last thing you remember?"

"Yeah."

"Nothing else?"

Daryl closed his eyes again. "Smell," he said.

"Smell?"

He was concentrating. "Kinda sweet."

Sweet. That tipped over a jar in my brain. "Think you could ID the smell if you smelled it again?"

"Like what, you know who it was?"

"Just a theory. You think you could ID it?"

"I don't know, man. Maybe. Hey . . ."

"Yeah?"

"I look as bad as I feel?"

"You look rough hewn," I said.

"What's that mean?"

"Like you can take it and dish it out."

The bare hint of smile pushed on his face. "That ain't bad."

"Think you can dress yourself, tough guy?"

146

I EXPLAINED TO the desk that I was now the young man's lawyer, and that we were leaving. We had to do a little song and dance, then Daryl signed a waiver and out we walked into the fading sunshine.

We got to my car and I angled for the freeway. "What's your favorite food?" I said.

"My favorite, or what I can eat?"

"Your favorite."

"I had me this steak once, I don't even know what it was, but it was like all melt in your mouth. But I don't think I can chew nothin'."

"Can you suck through a straw?"

"Yeah, I guess."

There's a place on Alvarado that makes old-fashioned chocolate milk shakes. Family business since 1948. Started by one Frank Lonegger a few years after he came back from the war. One shop. None of that franchise surrender. The grandson runs it now.

Daryl actually seemed excited when the shake with the whipped cream and cherry was put in front of him.

"When's the last time you had one of these?" I said.

"I ain't never had one of these."

"No way."

He shook his head. "Not like this."

"Dig in," I said.

He did.

I called my doctor friend, George Mazzetti, a guy I used to use a lot back in my Gunther, McDonough days.

"How's the celebrity lawyer?" he asked.

"Don't believe everything you read," I said. "I'd like to ask you a favor and count on your professional discretion. A guy I'd like you to look at, who for certain reasons doesn't want to be in the hospital. Would you mind, and then send me the bill?"

"For you? Of course. You almost doubled my practice with that one accident case your firm handled. The school bus on Western."

"I remember it well. Thanks. Can I bring him over?"

"Bring him."

I drove Daryl to the office, which was in a two-story professional building on Los Feliz. I shot a little breeze with George. Then I said, "Give him a good look over and call me when you're finished."

"Where you going?" George said.

"Yeah," Daryl said. "Where?"

"A little tourist shopping," I said. "I'll be back."

147

I DROVE DOWN Hollywood Boulevard. As I crossed Western I became aware of the song playing on the radio. It was right in the middle of Eric Marienthal's rendition of the Beatles' tune "I Will."

Nobody blows a smoother sax than L.A. boy Marienthal, if you like smooth, and right now I did. I remembered Sister Mary listening to the Beatles' version at the shooting range.

I liked Marienthal's treatment, but was glad the words weren't there. The forever words. The words that would have cut me.

So I just drove and listened to the music. And realized I was wishing that Sister Mary was in the car with me and we had no trial happening. That we were just cruising around town, listening to jazz. Then I pushed the thought right out. I had to not think that way anymore.

Because this would have to be the last case I worked with Sister Mary. She liked it too much, and I liked her liking it. If there was a God I didn't want to be responsible for tearing a soul away from him.

I turned the music off and cursed and hit the steering wheel a few times.

Finally I parked about a block and a half from where I had first seen Sonny Moon. I walked down until I could see him and his disciples passing out literature. A guy playing guitar. Knuckle Face wasn't there, as far as I could see.

In hiding maybe. He was my number-one suspect and I had to find a way to prove it.

I popped into a novelty store and bought myself four Indiana Jones hats, paying the typical tourist freight. I put a hat on, then my sunglasses, and rolled up my sleeves. Then I went out to hang out on the boulevard of dreams. I would fit right in.

I waited around about half an hour, watching the moonies across the street harass passersby. Pretty boring show.

Batman walked by me, on his way to the Kodak to pose for pics with the tourists. "Nice hat," he said.

"Nice mask," I said.

I got a call from my doctor friend. "He'll be all right," he said. "But he's going to be in a lot of pain for a week. I can prescribe something for the pain, and I suggest he not hit things with his face for a while."

"Good advice," I said. "I follow it myself."

"Where do I send the bill?"

"I'll tell you when I come in."

"And when will that be?"

"Give me another hour or so. Tell Daryl to sit in the lobby and read a magazine."

"I think I've got the latest AARP mag."

"He'll love it."

148

ABOUT TWENTY MINUTES after the call a blue Lincoln pulled up to the curb across the way and parked in a loading zone. The big guy, Knuckle Face, got out. He high-fived a couple people and sat down next to the guy with the guitar.

I went to the corner and crossed the street. I pulled the Indy hat low over my eyes, slouched a little, and, holding the other hats under one arm, ambled toward the quasi-religious gathering.

A girl with a fistful of flyers got to me first, handed me one. The title was *The End of the World and the Dirty Little Secret Your Goverment Won't Talk About.*

Goverment was spelled that way.

She said, "Would you like to take our survey?"

"No thanks," I said, with a gravelly *Sling Blade* voice. "I want some Gover Mints."

"Huh?"

"Want a hat?"

"Um, no, but they're pretty cool."

I touched the brim of my hat, the way the old cowboys used to do when meeting a lady on the street, and continued on. Since I already had my flyer, nobody paid me much attention.

I stopped next to the guy with a guitar and Mr. Knuckle Face. I held out one of the fedoras and said, "Anybody want to buy a hat?" Then I quickly shoved one onto Knuckles' head.

"Looks good," I said.

Knuckles ripped it off his head and threw it at me and told me to get out of his face. I never wanted to do anything more in my life. I took the hat, turned, and slouched on, memorizing the license plate of Knuckles' car.

When I got to the corner of Hollywood and Highland I saw two boys, twins, with their mother. They were eight or nine, and pointing across the street at the El Capitan Theatre. The latest Disney spectacular was about to suck them in.

"They are a couple of fine-looking Harrison Fords," I said. "Would they like to have two hats? Free?"

The mother said, "Oh, no thank you."

One of the tykes said, "What's a hairy man Ford, Mommy?"

"Great question," I said, holding out the fedoras.

The mother looked at the kids. She looked at me. I smiled. She grabbed the kids by the hands and hurried across the street.

You just can't trust a man in a hat anymore, I guess. I made a mental note to tell Pick McNitt about this. His hat theory was taking a beating.

I crossed the street. On the other side was a homeless guy talking to no one in particular. He was saying, "Try to get a date if you don't have money. Try to get a date if they say you're a sex offender."

He didn't have anything on his head. So I handed him the hats, except the one with Knuckle smell on it. He took the hats. Maybe it would help him find a date.

I hoped not.

149

I TOOK KNUCKLES' hat back to the doctor's office.

Daryl was glad to see me. "Man, I'm bored! Where you been?"

"Trying to figure out who beat you up. Smell this." I held the hat up.

Daryl pulled his head back. "You crazy?"

"Just do it."

He looked at me, eyes narrowing, then grabbed the hat. He gave it a tentative nose. His eyes widened. "Man, I think that's it. Where'd you get it?"

"You got a place to stay?" I said.

He took in a long breath. "Yeah, sure, a fancy hotel."

"You on the street?"

"I was gonna sleep at the house tonight."

"Not a good idea. I'll get you a room."

"With TV?"

"Oh yeah. I'll make sure you got a TV."

I did. At the Hollywood Motel 6. I prepaid for a week's stay. Daryl thought it was heaven. He looked like he needed heaven. I gave him twenty bucks and wrote the room phone number down in the margin of a jaunty *Welcome to Motel 6* card.

"I'll check back," I said.

"Where you goin'?"

"To get some religion," I said.

150

I DROVE BACK to Hollywood and had to park on Las Palmas, near the church at the end of the street. I walked back to the boulevard and hung out between the Scientology building and the Believe It or Not Museum.

I kept wondering if I believed what I was doing, or not.

Mostly not.

In the same place across the street was Sonny Moon and his hangers-on. Minus Knuckles. Minus the Lincoln. Great. Now I had to make like a real live PI and be bored waiting around for somebody who could be long gone. We had a couple hours of daylight left. This was not my idea of a good time.

My idea of a good time was nailing the scumbag who shot Sister Mary. And I wasn't too particular about how I'd do it. Various options kept auditioning in my mind. I was leaning toward the ones with the most pain.

A half hour went by. Then a full. I ducked into the Mickey D's next to the Guinness World Records Museum and used the oval office, snagged a Filet-O-Fish, went back to my post.

Still no sign of Knuckles.

As I was munching, an old man with Fred Mertz pants and two days' growth of beard came up to me and said, "Wyatt Earp died here."

His eyes were watery and grasping. Like he needed to talk to somebody. Like he was chiefly known for being ignored.

• I wasn't going anywhere, so I said, "Is that right?"

"Advised the movie business, he did. And one of the Dalton Gang died here, too. Emmett Dalton. He moved to Los Angeles in the 1920s, after serving fifteen years in prison for attempting to rob a Kansas bank. Guess what he did here?"

"Tell me."

"Became a real estate agent."

"So he followed the money."

"Darn tootin'," the old man said.

I looked across the street and saw Knuckles walking past Frederick's of Hollywood. It wasn't hard to spot the ape in front of a window of skimpy lace. He had come from the Las Palmas side, so I had to figure he'd parked his car on the same street.

Now was my shot.

"Where you from, son?" the old man said.

"Been nice talking to you," I said, turning.

"Wait," he called out. "John Wayne's real name was Marion!"

I gave the man a wave, then crossed the boulevard. I started looking for the Lincoln. I walked past the Las Palmas Hotel, not seeing the car. I got to the corner and that's where I spotted it, parked on Yucca, in front of the community center, with its gaudy orange, red, and turquoise buildings. Four hours' free parking here. A good spot for a guy wanting to save some quarters.

I thought it fitting that he'd parked right in front of the sign on the fence that read *Dog defecation must be removed immediately by owner under penalty of law.*

The spot where the car was parked was perfect for me. I could go back and watch the little group pass out their pamphlets. That would be exciting. Then whenever Knuckles decided to leave, I'd have time to get my car, get across the street, and tail him.

It did turn out to be one great snooze-fest. When the highlight of your day is seeing SpongeBob in front of the Kodak Theatre, and Captain Jack Sparrow walking up and down the sidewalk hawking maps to stars' homes, you know you've pretty much reached the abyss.

No wonder people were looking for a new way of life. No wonder Sonny Moon over there could get people to take his stuff and give him money in return.

151

AFTER AN HOUR more of hanging out with Sonny Moon, Knuckles finally headed back toward Las Palmas. I went for my car and got across the boulevard in time to see him pulling away from the community center. His Lincoln wouldn't be hard to follow, as long as I didn't get caught at a light.

I didn't get caught.

And didn't have far to follow.

It was a duplex on Beachwood, with a straight-on view of the Hollywood sign. A sago palm in front, twin cypresses on the sides. Well kept.

Friendly. Like I wasn't.

Knuckles turned into the driveway and went all the way back. I parked on the side street, got the tire iron from my trunk, and walked up the same drive.

I knocked on the oak door in the back unit. I held the tire iron behind my right leg.

Knuckles opened up.

"Where's the rifle?" I said.

He just looked at me.

"You have any felonies you want to tell me about?"

He started to slam the door, but I was ready. I kicked it flush with my right foot. It flew open and Knuckles stumbled back a few steps.

He recovered and the look in his eye told me he wanted to pounce. I held up the tire iron and said, "Hold it, Sparky."

He held, then asked me, in very uncivil language, what I was doing.

"Get on your knees," I said.

Knuckles didn't move.

"This thing makes dents," I said. "I will dent you. Get on your knees."

"What are you gonna do?"

"Now!" I brought the iron down on a little table by the door. It smashed in half.

Knuckles, gape mouthed, just looked at me. I gave him a Jack Black stare-down. Crazy eyes.

He lowered himself to his knees. The place had a hardwood floor. Good.

"Now lace your hands behind your head," I said.

"You can't just come in here. This is my house."

"You own it?"

"Come on, man. What do you want?"

"A confession."

He said nothing, but didn't look confused.

"I'm going to search the place," I said. "And to do that, I have to incapacitate you. Or you can just tell me where it is now, and we'll be done."

"You're whacked out, dude. The cops are gonna love this."

"What, you're going to turn me in? There is no criminal conduct here. You opened the door, I came in, we talked."

"You have a tire iron!"

"Do I? And you can prove this how?"

"You can't just come into a guy's house. You can't do this."

"And for what I'm about to do, my role as an officer of the court and champion of justice is to inform you that after I'm through searching your house and your car, and you, if need be, you have the right to sue me. You can take me to court. Maybe a judge or jury will look at you favorably and say, this man deserves some compensation. Of course, you may have to do it from a jail cell, but people are very flexible and open these days."

"Am I supposed to just sit here while you go through my house?"

"I'm going to need you to lie flat on the floor while I tie you up. Got any duct tape around?"

"What is it you're after?"

"You know what it is, Sparky. You think you can shoot a nun and walk away. But you tell me who put you up to it, maybe I can help you stay out of the joint. You don't want to go back to the joint, do you?"

"What are you talking about nuns?"

"How much hard time you do?"

"Come on."

"The kid can ID you, the one you beat up. He can ID the stink in your hair. What is that junk anyway?"

"What ID?"

"You're making this hard on yourself."

He told me to perform an anatomically impossible act.

I gave him a love tap on the back of his thigh.

He shrieked. For a tough guy he sure made noise. Then he puffed a few times and said, "Someday I'm gonna find you."

"After your kneecaps are replaced?"

He said nothing. I was tempted to do it. But I could almost see Father Bob shaking his head at me. And Sister Mary, waving her Thomas Merton book. I wanted to argue with them, but I heard a scuffing sound behind me.

I whipped around. Sonny Moon and his hair filled the doorway.

We froze for half a second. Which is when Knuckles made his move. He was quicker than I anticipated, and got me around my knees and pulled.

I slammed forward, still holding the tire iron.

Sonny moved fast, too. I saw his legs coming my way. I managed to whip the claw-end of the iron out, and caught his ankle.

Sonny screamed and the sound went through me like electricity from a generator. I realized again that part of me was truly capable of killing someone. I could do it and sort it all out later. The law of club and fang. It energized me.

Blood spotted the floor around Sonny's leg as I tried to twist out of Knuckles' grip. But he started reeling me in, like a marlin. He grabbed a fistful of my pants and I slid backward on the slick floor.

Then he gave me a fist to the kidneys. It scored. Emergency lights exploded in my head.

I struck with the iron and hit my own leg.

The pain was a numbing fire, in both my leg and my back. I had to start getting some hits in or I'd be chopped up.

Literally, because I saw Sonny now had a knife in his hand.

Some religion.

Desperation mixed with pain and I went wild.

I gave the iron a backward slam and heard the sickly sound of a head smash. Knuckles' grip loosened. At the same time, blindly, I shot the iron around about two inches from the floor. It found leg.

Sonny went down, screaming louder, but he went down on me, and his blade got me in the left buttock. It was a deep wound, soft and almost painless at first, but I knew I would not be sitting for a long time.

What saved me from worse was having a tire iron perfectly positioned between Sonny's legs. The pain I inflicted on him then was a whole lot worse than what I had.

He shrieked so loud I thought he was miked. I pushed him off me, and rolled. The knife was still in my cheek. Fresh pain shot through my backside and up my spine. With my left hand I got hold of the knife and felt the wetness of blood. With my right I gave Sonny an iron shot to the head. He was out. Maybe even finished, sent to whatever god he thought he worshipped, or to some hell reserved for bad hair.

I stood up, my left leg getting numb, but with two moonies on the ground. Sonny groaned. I was almost sorry to hear that.

I limped to a lamp in the open living room and ripped it out of the wall. I used Sonny's own bloody knife to cut the cord. I tied Knuckles' hands behind him. He barely moved, moaning.

I went to the TV and cut that cord, and came back and tied up Sonny Moon.

The toaster in the kitchen gave me one last length of wire. I tied Sonny's left leg to Knuckles' right.

And then I made a search of the house.

A rifle was in plain view in Knuckles' room. Leaning in the corner. If it *was* the rifle, the guy was not too concerned about being found out. Maybe Sonny Moon told him he was invincible, or invisible, or could eat planets or something.

Just for good measure, I looked through the closet and found a couple of handguns, in cases. Knuckles had the look of an ex-felon. If that were true, this would be enough to put him away for a good while.

I came out to the front and found the happy couple in the same spot. Knuckles looked the most aware. Poor Sonny's eyelids were fluttering.

"You're in some hot water, my friend," I said. "Ex-felon with guns. Not good. Why don't you tell me who sent you. Was it Sonny Moon here?"

Knuckles said, "You're dead, man."

I stepped outside, keeping the door open so I could watch them. I called Detective Stein. He picked up. I gave him the address and the particulars. "I just solved a case for you," I said. "Bring some Mountain Dew or champagne."

I went back in, to the hall bathroom, and took care of my bloody cheek with a damp towel.

I wouldn't be winning any beauty contests with my backside. I'd have to get it looked at. And forever I'd be marked with a scar. I guess if you had to pick a spot for a scar.

Knuckles kept screaming about me being a dead man. So I took another towel, ripped off a strip, and gagged him. Then I went outside again to wait.

152

A BLACK-AND-WHITE PULLED in about seven minutes later. Two officers, male, one old, one new.

The old one said, "You the guy who called the Southwest detective?"

"Stein," I said.

"He's on his way. What's going on?"

"Two inside," I said. "Attacked me with a knife. Weapons in plain view. I think we have an ex-felon in possession here."

The new one was looking through the front door. "He's got 'em tied up."

"How'd you do that?" the old one said.

"I'll explain when Stein gets here," I said. "You might want to order up an ambulance. The rooster is going to need medical attention."

"Rooster?"

"Have a look. And don't let them talk to each other."

Stein arrived about thirty minutes later. Still no ambulance, but Sonny was now on a sofa in the house, covered with a blanket. Knuckles was screaming from the kitchen, where the new cop was holding him.

Stein had a partner named Santos. Santos started talking to the older patrol officer while I talked to Stein.

"First thing," I said, "make sure you question these two separately so they can't cook up a story."

Stein said, "And what's *your* story?"

"You'll find a rifle and some handguns in the bedroom," I said. "The rifle will turn out to be the one that shot Sister Mary. The screamer, he's got to be the ex-felon."

"You searched the house?"

"I did."

"How?"

I was still holding the towel on my wound. I showed Stein the blood. "The one on the sofa is a street guru—he knifed me. I came here to question the other one, who I followed here. The kid who got beat up, Daryl, he said—"

"Where is he?"

"Motel 6. He ID'd the smell of this guy's hair. He thinks this guy is the one who bopped him. So I followed him here, and knocked on the door. He didn't want to let me in at first, but I convinced him."

"How?"

"Let him tell you."

Stein scowled.

"And so," I said, "if you know your Fourth Amendment jurisprudence, the amendment does not apply to private citizens, so long as they are not working in concert with law enforcement. That's why I didn't contact you first. I didn't want some tricky lawyer, somebody like me, arguing for exclusion of the weapons because I was acting as your agent. So now I'm giving you the observation, and I suggest you get a warrant before going in. Then we've covered all the angles."

"You've done some thinking about this," Stein said. "You realize, of course, you could be facing a big fat lawsuit from one or both of these guys."

"Be still my heart," I said.

Stein smiled.

153

I FAVORED MY good cheek as I drove to St. Monica's. When I got there, I told Father Bob what happened and he laughed.

"Very sympathetic," I said.

He put me facedown in his trailer and started dressing my wound. It was the most humiliating experience of my life.

"Humility," Father Bob said. "It's a good thing."

"Can we talk about something else? Can we talk about Sister Mary?"

"By all means. You want stitches?"

"No," I said. "Just tape me shut. Just don't tape the wrong crack, okay?"

"I think I'm capable," he said. "Sister Mary is doing fine physically."

"Okay, what's that mean?"

"That's as far as I can go."

"Come on, tell me what's wrong with her."

"I was talking about your buttock. I'm through. That's as far as I can go with it. You can get up now."

I did. "What's wrong with Sister Mary?"

Father Bob sighed and sat at his little table. He offered me a chair but, under the circumstances, I preferred to stand.

"I suppose it would be easier if you heard it from me," Father Bob said. "Sister Hildegarde is going to officially sanction Sister Mary, for being a recalcitrant. She is stating her opinion in a letter, which will go to the archdiocese, that she has strong doubts about Sister Mary's fitness to continue as a nun."

My face got hot.

Father Bob put his hand on my arm. "Let us handle it from here. I'll be speaking for Sister Mary."

"I have a few words to say, too."

"Don't. You'll only make it worse."

"I don't get you people."

"Most people don't get us. Leave it there."

I started to say something but he gripped my arm harder. "Leave it there," he said again. "Sister Mary and I believe that God works all things for the good of those who follow him."

"Which is another way of saying when people shaft you, it's a good thing. No worries. God's plan. And the Hildegardes of this world take over, a little at a time."

"Ty, you're upset—"

"A couple hours ago I had a knife in my cupcake. Yeah, I'm upset. And now your commandant is putting the screws to the best nun in the whole place. It makes me sick."

"May I suggest you cool off?"

It took me the rest of the weekend to do that.

154

ON SUNDAY MORNING I called Daryl and made sure he was all right. He was. Basically watching TV and ducking out to McDonald's, trying to stretch my twenty bucks. I told him I'd get him more.

He said I was the man. So maybe I really was.

I called Sister Mary and we talked for about twenty minutes or so. Neither one of us mentioned the Sister Hildegarde thing. But it seemed to be hanging between us just the same.

155

ON MONDAY MORNING I limped into court. The clerk and bailiff asked if I was all right, and I told them I'd had an unfortunate accident and wouldn't be sitting down much.

The bailiff said Preparation H was actually very good for this sort of thing. I think he was serious. I thanked him and said, "Let us never speak of this again."

I went back to chambers and met with Radavich and Hughes. "Tom's not putting on rebuttal evidence," Hughes said. "We'll go right into closing arguments."

"Fine," I said. "And can you explain to the jury that, due to a slight injury, I may have to stand for most of the proceedings?"

"Injury?" Judge Hughes said.

"I'd rather not go into it right at the moment, if you don't mind."

He shook his head. "You have a very dangerous way of practicing law, it seems."

"My problems are all behind me now," I said.

I went back in to a packed courtroom. The deputies brought Eric in. He looked tired. Or in complete denial.

Kate was in her usual spot. She was chewing on a scarf.

Me, I was chewing on the insides of my cheeks. There's nothing like the anticipation of a closing argument. If you've done your job, you'll be okay once you start talking. It's the lead anticipation that juices you. You try not to show it, but the other lawyer knows what you're feeling, because he's feeling it, too.

Eric leaned over and whispered, "You nervous?"

"Me? Why should I be nervous?"

"Because they're going to convict me. They hate me. There's no way we can win this thing."

"You've calmed me down now just fine, Eric. Don't say anything else."

156

JUDGE HUGHES ENTERED and called for the jury. The courtroom got real quiet. This is the high point, the closing arguments. Last chance at the sale. What lawyers call the law of recency, meaning jurors tend to remember most the last thing you say to them.

You need a boffo exit.

In a criminal case the prosecutor gets to argue first, since he has the burden of proof. Then comes the defense, and then the prosecutor gets one last bite at the apple, in a rebuttal argument.

Radavich was great. Workmanlike, dispassionate. Laid out his case in logical order, covering all the evidence, and leaving Leilana Salgado until last. Then he got out the long knives.

He said, "And then the defense comes up with its only possible card, an alibi witness, but a complete surprise. Conveniently waiting for maximum impact. You didn't hear about this witness in Mr. Buchanan's opening statement, did you? No, it was only at the last second, with all the evidence pointing at guilt, that this woman is produced."

Radavich paused. I couldn't see his face because he was at the podium and his back was to me. But if you can read the back of a guy's head, his spelled out total contempt.

"What kind of a witness? A prostitute. A call girl. Yet one who desperately wanted you to think of her as something else. Some noble woman of great purpose. Yet she lives a life making up illusions for others, and she wants you to believe an illusion now."

The way he said it didn't sound hateful. He wasn't spitting the words. But the impression was unmistakable.

When he sat down, the courtroom was dead silent.

Except for the sound of Kate Richess issuing a single, pathetic sob.

Judge Hughes said, "You may begin, Mr. Buchanan."

I stood up and buttoned my coat, and started the way I usually do, with "Ladies and gentlemen . . ."

157

. . . THANK YOU FOR your attention during the course of this trial. Sometimes trials are complicated. You have hours and days and weeks of expert testimony and exhibits and recollections from the witness stand. And you have to try to piece all that together as you go back to the jury room and deliberate. But this case is not complicated. The prosecution tried to make it seem that way, by introducing experts and going through all sorts of scientific rigmarole to try to make a case where there was no case. To try to prove that something happened that nobody witnessed. And on the flimsiest of evidence they try to convince you, beyond a reasonable doubt, that Eric Richess killed his own brother.

The judge is going to give you the law to apply to the facts. He will instruct you on the rules. And he will tell you that the fact that a criminal charge has been filed against Eric Richess is not, I repeat, not evidence that the charge is true. And you must not be biased against the defendant just because he's been arrested, charged, and brought into this courtroom for trial.

Must not. That's the law.

A defendant in a criminal case is always presumed to be innocent. This means the prosecution must prove any defendant guilty beyond a reasonable doubt. You've all heard that phrase. But what does it mean?

The judge will tell you what it means, and what the judge says you have to abide by. Proof beyond a reasonable doubt means proof that leaves you with an abiding conviction that the charge is true.

Not just a conviction, or certainty, that the charge is true. But an *abiding* conviction. I looked up *abide* in the dictionary, just to make sure. And that's what it means. To make sure. Something that will endure.

You can't wake up a week after your verdict and think, You know, I still have this part of me that doesn't believe he's guilty. If you have part of you that thinks that, you don't have an abiding conviction.

The judge will tell you that unless the evidence proves Mr. Richess guilty beyond a reasonable doubt, he is entitled to an acquittal, and you must— must—find him not guilty.

Do you remember that boulder I told you about? The one that sits on the prosecutor's desk? The one called the burden of proof? The prosecutor has failed to remove that boulder. It's not enough for him to chip away at it. He has to obliterate it, get the whole thing off. But he hasn't, and there's a simple reason why. You can take all of the evidence that was presented, all the speculation about the science, and you can put that aside and ask yourself only one question. Do I believe Leilana Salgado?

That's it.

Remember all that DNA testimony? You can forget it. The prosecutor never established when Eric's small blood trace actually got on the gun. We presented a witness, Christa Cody, who established that it could have been days before Carl's death. In any event, we don't have the burden of proving anything. Despite all the expert testimony, Mr. Radavich offered no proof that the blood got on the gun when the fatal shot was fired.

But even though we don't have to prove anything, we have. We have proved that Eric Richess could not have fired that shot, because he was in Long Beach at the time.

You twelve jurors, the law says, are the sole judges of the facts in this case. And you are the sole judges of the credibility of witnesses. And, therefore, you all sat here and looked Leilana Salgado in the face as she testified, and in your hearts you know this woman was telling the truth. That's all you have to decide, that if you believe in your heart she was telling the absolute truth, backed up by printed evidence, that this case is over. And it should be over.

There is nothing worse in our system of justice than that an innocent man should be convicted of a crime he did not commit. That's why the system is set up the way it is, that's why the system gives the prosecution such a large burden of proof.

And that's why the system does not trust any one person to decide the facts. No, in its wisdom the system entrusts all twelve of you to get together and to agree.

And the law makes each one of you a sovereign. That means that if you believe that Leilana Salgado was telling the truth, and eleven other jurors don't believe, you are entitled to resist them, and to hold on to your belief as you see it in fact. If you don't, then you are violating your oath as a juror.

Ladies and gentlemen, I leave this decision to you, with full confidence in your ability to do what is right. Answer that one question, and your decision will be the right one.

158

KATE LOOKED SO weary I thought she might faint. Criminal trials are hard on everyone, especially family. And most especially mothers. Their maternal desire to protect and comfort is locked up in a cold room, guarded by bailiffs and court personnel. Each day they suffer a little, uncertainty weighing down their delicate balance.

So I insisted on bringing over a Chinese dinner, back at her house. She'd dropped about thirty pounds, it looked like. And for most women that would be a godsend. But for a former Roller Derby queen, it looked unhealthy.

I went from court to the hospital and gave Sister Mary the blow by blow. She was like a trucker with the sports page, wanting the whole story. Maybe I even did her some good. She was starting to look stronger, and said she'd be out in a couple of days.

When she said *out,* it sounded almost like it had a double meaning. But I left it at that.

159

THAT NIGHT I went to Kate's with a bag of take-out from Yang Chow. Incomparable slippery shrimp and hot-to-trot Hunan beef. Kate made tea, and we sat at the dining room table. I was able to sit as long as I did a little leaning.

"I guess waiting is the hardest part, isn't it?" Kate said.

"It's pretty grueling, for sure," I said.

"Could you tell anything? From their faces, I mean?"

"You never really know," I said. "You can feel one thing from the jurors, and get completely blown away when they come back in. Jurors you were sure were on your side are not, and those you thought hated your guts end up loving you. It's one of the reasons trial lawyers like to have a good, strong belt at the end of the day."

She took a sip of tea. "And how was Sister Mary today?"

"Wanting out of the hospital, that's for sure."

"I'll go see her tomorrow. Take her some flowers."

It was the way she said it that got to me. Without pretense. Just an expression of someone whose desire to help others is woven through them in rich threads of decency. And I felt then how much I wanted her to get her surviving son back. That this would be the decent thing I could do for her.

And I felt something else. The fear that I might fail her in this. It was a large, black, gaping fear, too. Not the usual, garden-variety, waiting-for-the-jury kind of anxiety.

"Tell me about your mother, Ty," Kate said.

I looked down from her eyes. When I did, I saw Kate's hands around her tea cup. As if to warm them.

Hands. My mother's hands . . .

"You would have liked her," I said. "I think you would have been friends."

She smiled. "That's nice. What was she like?"

I swallowed hard. "She was there. That's the thing I remember most. My dad was a cop and had to be out a lot. My mom was always around when I needed her. Like when I was thirteen and stole some M&M's. Well, more than some. One of the big bags. Stuffed in my pants. I had the whole thing worked out. Crime of the century."

"Sounds like it."

"Mom found them in my room, asked me where I got them. I was going to say I got them from the store, with my own money, but my face wouldn't cooperate. I couldn't lie to her. My dad was dead and I knew what that had done to her, to both of us really. I just couldn't lie. So I didn't say anything, and she knew."

I had not told this story to anyone, ever. Now the memory came flooding back. "She made me go to the store manager. Tell him exactly what I'd done and tell him I was sorry and pay for the candy. She stood there and

I did. I thought I was going to juvi. Mom let me think that. The manager said nothing like this had happened to him before, but that his mom would have made him do the same thing. And then he offered me a job."

"You're kidding."

"I bagged groceries all summer. And Mom made sure I was never late. She did what she could to keep me in line without my dad around. Until I was fifteen."

"What happened?"

"That's when she died. A virus, just took her over. Antibiotics did nothing. Some swamp thing. Like a horror movie."

"I'm so sorry."

"Thing was, I thought there was a time there, when she was in the hospital, all tubed up, that if I tried hard enough I could get her out of there. But I couldn't think what to do, and it was almost like I got paralyzed. Right there in her room. I wanted to will her better because . . ."

We were silent for a long moment. I could hear my own breathing. It sounded like a guy on life support. I wanted to clam up. Couldn't.

"I wasn't exactly a model son around then," I said. "I wanted her to live so I could make up for it. So I could make her proud of me. In the hospital, she reached out her hand to me." I saw it now, clearly, as if a fog had suddenly blown away. "She reached for me and I was afraid. I took her hand, but I was afraid. Like I was the reason she was there. And I was the only one who could pull her back. But she didn't come back. That night she died. . . ."

That was it. I couldn't go on. I put my face in my hands and tried not to lose it. I was aware of movement, and then Kate was at my chair. Her arms went around me, pulled me close, as if I were her own child.

160

I COULDN'T SLEEP that night. The adrenaline during a closing argument is like liquid electricity, running through pipes of flesh, leaving every nerve with the feeling it's on fire.

The next morning, I shot hoop for a while, alone, testing my sore patoot.

It was nothing compared to what had happened to Sister Mary. I hoped her wound wouldn't hold her back, from ball or anything else she wanted to do.

In fact, I hoped I wasn't holding her back from what she wanted to do.

At two in the afternoon I was sitting—tenderly—at the Ultimate Sip, reading the *Daily News,* when I got a call from Hughes's clerk. The jury was ready with a verdict.

I didn't like that it was so soon.

I made my own calls. To Kate, then the hospital. But Sister Mary, they said, had been discharged. I called her cell and got voice mail. I called Father Bob. Told him what was up, and where was Sister Mary? He said he'd make sure she got the message.

But not in time, apparently. Because it was just me and Eric at the counsel table when the jury came back in.

I watched their faces. Several made eye contact with me. A good sign. If they're sending your client away, they usually don't look at you.

But I've been fooled before.

161

THE CLERK, MS. Mavis Elliott, read the verdict in her official-sounding monotone. "We, the jury in the above-titled action, find the defendant, Eric Mark Richess, not guilty of the crime of murder."

Kate cried out behind me. Eric turned to me and gave me a giant bear hug.

And I was transported to another dimension. Not the *Twilight Zone* variety, but the trial lawyers' magic carpet ride above the clouds. There is no feeling like a verdict in your favor, and no higher high than *not guilty* if you're a criminal defense lawyer.

Radavich was not ready to give in. He requested that the judge poll the jury, and Hughes did exactly that. He asked each individual juror if *not guilty* was their true verdict, both in the jury room and now, sitting in court.

Each one answered, "Yes."

And that was that.

Eric turned and embraced his mother at the rail.

Kate had her son back. That's the thing that mattered. Watching her hold her son was like watching a drowning woman grab onto the rescue boat.

It was as perfect a day as a lawyer could have.

It's the crash after the high that you have to watch out for, especially when it comes at you like a fifteen-foot wave.

162

RADAVICH LEFT THE courtroom without saying a word to me.

Outside, Kate told me she wanted to have me and Sister Mary over to the house, so we could all celebrate together. She promised to make her secret-family-recipe cheesecake. I told her that sounded fine.

Some reporters wanted a statement from me, and news about Sister Mary. I wasn't ready to give either. I went around to my car and sat in it for a few minutes. The sky was clear. City Hall loomed.

Which reminded me there was another thing looming, a question—so who killed Carl?

I knew Kate would be asking me that later. I didn't know what answer to give. I wondered if any of us would ever know.

I called Sister Mary, got voice mail. "We won," I said after the beep. "And tonight we're going to Kate's house. Can you make it?"

I didn't get any call back.

Five minutes later my phone vibrated. It was a text message. I brought it up.

Congratulations. I must take you to dinner. K.P.

You must, I thought. You must.

163

AT ST. MONICA'S, I collared Father Bob, an appropriate thing to do with a priest. "What's up with Sister Mary? She got out of the hospital—where is she?"

"Come into my humble abode," Father Bob said. We were outside his trailer, the orange hotplate of the sun dropping behind the hills.

"Let's talk right here," I said. "I'm not sitting down for a while."

"All right," he said. "Maybe it is better this way. Sister Mary has left St. Monica's."

It sounded like the report of a death. "Meaning?"

"She is going to reassess her calling, in a time of prayer, away from . . ." His voice trailed.

"Me?"

"From everything," he said.

"Where is she?"

"She's fine."

"That's not what I asked."

"Ty, it's best that you just leave this alone for now. Let things simmer down."

"She leaves? Just like that? Says nothing to me?"

"She asked me to tell you. It's best this way."

"I want to know where she is," I said.

"It's best that you don't know," Father Bob said. "And please don't call her."

"Padre, do not treat me like some pimple-faced teenager, okay? Do not."

"Just give her this time."

I said nothing.

"And please remember," Father Bob said, "that you always have our love and support and friendship."

"Fantastic." I looked at the basketball court. They could tear it up now. Put in outhouses if they wanted to. Or a statue of Saint Hildegarde. In fact I was ready to start tearing it up myself.

164

AND I WAS still feeling that way when I got to Kate's house. Father Bob was there before me. Kate had a spread laid out, cold cuts and bread and soft drinks on ice. And a big cheesecake. With a piece missing.

"Eric was here," Kate said, "but had to go." She tried to smile, but it was an effort. She added, "His wife. He needs to work things out with her."

"She didn't come with him?" I said.

"Fayette is, well, high-strung sometimes," Kate said. "But that doesn't mean we all can't celebrate. My son is home. Like in the Bible story, right, Father?"

Father Bob nodded. "The Prodigal Son. He was lost and is now found."

We sat around and ate sandwiches, but this felt more like a funeral than a celebration. Kate was hurting but tried not to show it.

I was steaming. Eric should have had his ungrateful heinie right here. But for Kate's sake, I made conversation. That seemed to help her a little. And the cheesecake was, in fact, delicious.

Around nine o'clock Kate asked what her legal obligations were concerning Carl's debts and papers and effects. She was getting his mail forwarded to her and had a stack of bills. I told her to give them to me and I'd arrange for all the notification. I told her I'd handle the estate. Carl had died intestate, so she would be entitled to the assets under the laws of succession. But creditors could take a bite out of the assets.

She was glad to hand it all over to me. She said she wanted to pay for the work. I told her to make me two cheesecakes. One for me, and one I'd take to Father Bob.

Deal, she said.

I made conversation for an hour or so longer. Then I said I should get going. Father Bob stayed. I took off for the townhouse in Warner Center. I had a few things I wanted to say to my client.

165

HE WASN'T HOME. Neither was his wife.

At least they didn't answer the buzzer.

I sat in my car across from the townhouse. No lights on in the window. I decided to wait.

While I did, I went through some of Carl's mail, separated the bills from the junk. He had bills and dunning letters from the cable company, the DWP, the gas company, and three notices from Capital One Visa. I opened the Visa bills and looked at the last one with any charges, from mid-January to mid-February.

The last purchase Carl made was on the night he was killed. He bought something at BevMo, the big wine and liquor store. I remembered one of the tenants mentioning she saw Carl walking into the apartment building with a BevMo bag. No doubt with the tequila that he had in him when he died.

I stayed out there another hour and a half without anybody coming home. I gave up and went back to St. Monica's.

That night I dreamed I was in Dodger Stadium, alone, at night. The lights were out and I was wandering the seats, looking for someone to shine a light and get me to the exit. Nobody came.

166

THE NEXT MORNING, early, I called Zebker from my trailer.

"You want me to congratulate you or something?" he said.

"I don't want you to start the day on a sour note," I said. "So skip it. But you do have a killer to catch."

"We had the killer."

"I have a credit card bill here that says Carl bought something at BevMo a few hours before he died. Somebody saw Carl going into his building with a BevMo bag. I didn't see that listed on your inventory. What happened to the bag?"

Pause. "Maybe he dumped it before he went into his apartment."

"How likely is that? You bring your shopping bags in, you unpack, you toss the bag in the trash. And what else was in that bag?"

"What does it matter?"

"I thought you'd be curious, that's all. You know me. Willing to help, right? I'm not ready to pack this case in."

"Good luck," he said.

"If you find something out, I'd appreciate a call."

"I can't promise you that."

"Detective, I know all about your culture of silence, not sharing case information with the common shlub. But I am not a common shlub. I am, in fact, a remarkable shlub. I sacrificed my left butt cheek to catch a potential killer. And I've been very open with you. Now you can, in your discretion, give me any information you choose to. I'm asking you to so choose."

"What does the judge say? I'll take it under advisement." Then he disconnected.

I looked out at the empty basketball court for a while, then got ready for the day. I had someone to see.

167

BOTH ERIC AND Fayette looked hungover. They were in bathrobes, but Eric let me in and offered me coffee.

"Sorry about last night," Eric said. "I needed to spend some time with my wife, you understand."

I tried to. I sat with them around a kitchen table. Fayette looked like she didn't want me anywhere near the place.

"I can't thank you enough," Eric said. "What you did in there was amazing."

"We caught a break," I said.

"Some break," Fayette said.

Eric looked at her, then back at me. "It all worked out for the best."

I took a sip of coffee, trying to figure out how I felt about Eric Richess. Finally, I said, "I'm very fond of your mother, and I don't want to see her hurt. I think she needed you last night more than you two needed each other."

"That's really none of your business," Fayette said.

Eric patted her arm, to mollify her. She jerked away. Now I felt totally out of place.

Eric said, "I hear you, Ty. Don't worry about it."

"But I am worried about it, Eric. I'm worried about it a lot. And I tend to get very cranky when I get worried."

"That sounds like some sort of threat," Fayette said.

Lady, you haven't heard me come within twenty yards of a threat, but just tempt me. Go ahead.

Eric said, "Ty, you are above and beyond. I'll do the right thing by my mom."

Which reminded me, I had a right thing to do, too.

I got out of the Richess love nest and drove down to the Motel 6 and gathered up Daryl. He wanted to stay and watch more TV, but I told him he was ready to re-enter society as a productive citizen.

He didn't know if he wanted to.

I did not give him a choice, even though he still had some facial healing to do. "But you don't scrub pots with your face," I told him.

"Say what?"

"Say, get in the car."

I drove him to St. Monica's homeless shelter and went to the front desk, where Sister Barbara ran things. They had one room available. I said Daryl would do especially well in the kitchen, starting with the pots and pans.

"Oh, man!" Daryl said.

"And you are grateful to the Sisters, aren't you, Daryl?"

He opened his mouth but I glared it shut for him. "Yeah," he said. "Sure. Happy to do it."

I nodded my approval.

Outside, my old pal Only, the medical marijuana maven, was waiting for me at my car.

"Dude!" he said.

"Dawg," I said.

"Guess what? I'm starting my own business!"

"Whoa. Does Wall Street know about this?"

"They will, man."

"What's this new venture called?"

"Psy Chic," he said. Pronouncing it *sheek*. "Get it? It's psychic services for the upscale crowd."

"My congratulations," I said. "I think you have found the perfect niche market right here in L.A."

"Maybe you could help me incorporate," he said.

"Definitely. You're going to need the protection of the corporate veil."

"Thanks, man. And I want you to be the first."

"That's okay—"

He grabbed my left wrist and closed his eyes. "Quiet, please. Just make your mind a blank." Only put his left hand up in the air, like an antenna. "You are going to do something very, very important."

I waited.

"And soon," Only said.

He opened his eyes and let go of my wrist, and smiled.

"You'll make a bundle," I said.

168

I DROVE TO the Sip and found, as usual, Pick McNitt in a snit.

"When did saving money become an idiot thing to do?" he said. "Putting money in the bank, every paycheck, that's what my dad did, how he raised his family. So what dipstick decided this was stupid, and convinced us to gamble, to become a nation of consumers instead of savers? To drown ourselves in debt to let the good times roll? Who was it? Who?"

I declined to guess and went to the back to read the paper. I hadn't gotten too far in when my cell buzzed.

It was Zebker. "Courtesy call," he said.

"Am I going to be happy about it?" I said.

"Remains to be seen. I just talked to Detective Stein. He gave *me* a courtesy call. Are you sitting down?"

"Unfortunately, yes," I said.

"Then here it is. The rifle you found in that guy's house is not the one used to shoot the nun."

I waited for a punch line. And waited.

"You still there?" Zebker said.

"I'm picking my jaw up off the floor, I'll just be a second."

"Yeah. The guy, his name's Gruber, is an ex-felon. You were right about that. But the other guy's clean. He's back on the street."

"Oh, that is good news. Anything else?"

Zebker said, "And I thought you'd like to know we traced the receipt at BevMo. Carl used his card to buy two bottles of Jose Cuervo Black Medallion, a liter of Pepsi, and a bag of pretzels. We found the tequila bottles, one empty and one half full, and pretzels in the apartment. We didn't find a liter bottle or the bag."

"Why are you telling me this?"

"Look, there's things I don't like about this file. But we can't arrest your guy again, and if he didn't do it, somebody else did, and maybe you can help me find out who."

"How?"

"Just think about it, will you?" he said.

"You're not mad at me?"

"You did your job. Fine. No hard feelings."

"Thanks."

"Maybe I'll bump into you at a Dodger game sometime. We can talk about it over a Dodger Dog."

"Yeah, right, and—" I stopped myself.

"You there?" Zebker said.

"The inventory list. You have it there in front of you?"

"Just a second." Pause. "Yeah, right here."

"Is there a Dodger hat on it?"

Another pause. Then, "No. Why?"

For a few seconds I couldn't speak. Then I said plenty.

169

AT SEVEN O'CLOCK that evening, I went to see my client once more.

Fayette was not happy to see me.

I walked right in and said, "I need to talk to Eric. Alone."

"Hey, you can't just—"

"Tell him I'm here," I said. I went to their balcony door, opened it, and went outside to look at Warner Center Park.

"Now listen," Fayette said, "we have plans—"

"What's going on?" Eric said, coming into the living room. He saw me at the balcony door. "What's up, Ty?"

Fayette said, "He wants to talk to you alone."

"Fine," Eric said.

"What's this about?" Fayette asked.

"Eric can tell you later," I said. "If he wants to."

"What does that mean?" she said.

"It means I want to talk to Eric alone."

Husband and wife looked at each other for a moment. Eric said, "Honey, why don't you run out and do an errand or something?"

She seemed to pick up a message from him, because she didn't say a word. She grabbed her purse from a table with a whiff of annoyance, and went out the door.

I was still standing between balcony and room. I could hear a TV going next door. Some show about the entertainment biz, I think it was.

Eric turned to me. "Sorry, Ty, she's a little uptight. We're still working on things."

"I bet you are."

"What can I do for you?"

"Confess," I said.

He smiled and said, "What?"

"Confess. Or do I have to beat it out of you?"

For a long moment Eric looked at me, trying no doubt to find out if I was serious. I let dead serious spill out of my eyeballs.

Finally he said, "What do you think you know?"

"Where's Carl's Dodger hat?" I said. "The one you wore to BevMo when you bought the Cuervo and Pepsi?"

No answer, which was answer enough. Now was the time to hit him with a theory I'd worked out with Zebker.

"With the hat pulled down, you could pass for Carl. If you moved fast and didn't talk to anybody. My guess is you went to see Carl and somehow got his Visa and lucky hat. Maybe you offered to go to BevMo for him.

Maybe he was already buzzed, but you went out for the stuff at BevMo, borrowing his car. You came back, got him good and liquored up, which wouldn't have been hard. I didn't know until now that with a little prep an empty plastic liter bottle makes a good sound suppressor. Was Carl passed out when you shot him? Maybe leaning back with his mouth open? But no soot in the mouth, right? You blasted him, then used the plastic bag to transfer gunshot residue. How'm I doing?"

Eric issued a long breath, never taking his eyes off me. "You're my lawyer. Whatever I say you can't repeat, and I can't be tried again, because of double jeopardy, right?"

"You watch a lot of TV, don't you?"

"Am I right?"

"You're right. You can't be tried again for Carl's murder, and whatever you say to me about it is privileged. That doesn't mean I have to like it, or you, or suppress my desire to turn your face into a Picasso."

"Look, Ty, listen, please." Eric rubbed his hands together, as if he'd dipped them in holy water and was rinsing away his sins. "It's this way. Carl *wanted* to die, okay? I hope you can at least understand that. He was unhappy and hated his life. But he didn't have the guts to kill himself. I did it for him."

"That's what he told you he wanted, was it?"

"Yes."

"You lie," I said. "You wanted Carl dead because he was going to blow the whistle on the subcontractor scam running up to Jamie MacArthur's office."

Eric looked at me a moment, wheels turning somewhere in his lying head, then shrugged.

"The call girl," I said. "Is she even a call girl? She was so good, a good little liar. Is she an actress or something?"

"I think real. I mean, I never met her. Bacon set it up."

"Set it up?" A couple of thoughts bumped in my mind. "Bacon did all this to get you off."

No response.

"Bacon was the heavy hitter for MacArthur, or Nielsen, or whoever on the contract scam. And you, you were in on it. A bagman maybe. And Carl was going to talk. You took his computer, didn't you? Why? Did he have it all on there?"

Eric said nothing.

"Did Bacon pay you to get rid of Carl? And then promise to get you off if you blew the suicide thing and managed to get yourself caught?"

"Ty, please."

"And your lovely wife," I said. "She was in on this too, wasn't she? That's why you're not out on your ear. Was she with you the night you shot Carl? Waiting out back to drive you away?"

"Now Ty, you got to understand," Eric said. "Carl's better off. He was going to do himself sooner or later, I guarantee you. And yeah, Turk Bacon is not a man you want to mess with, Ty. I'm telling you for your own good."

"You threatening me?"

Eric didn't hesitate. "Yeah. I don't want to, but Ty, come on."

"And I sat there like a rube and got you acquitted."

"It's the system. You're not at fault for that."

"Sure, I did my job in that system, didn't I? I get to pretend I was only upholding the Constitution, that the system worked. But this time it didn't, and I can't stand to look at your ugly, lying face another minute."

"Now, look—"

"You don't deserve a mother like Kate."

"You're not gonna tell her anything, are you?"

"It would destroy her," I said. "But she will find out. Someday you, or the De Medici you're married to, will say something or give out a vibe. And when that happens, I'll come to see you again."

"And do what?"

"Lay a little retribution on you."

Eric snorted. "You can't do anything to me."

"It might be better if you moved out of town."

"What?"

"Make some excuse. Go get a job in Texas. Write to your mother on a regular basis. But I want you out of here."

Eric shook his head. "You should go now. Thanks for the help. I really mean it."

I stepped up to his face. "I'm serious."

"Back off," he said. "Or I'll make sure you don't try any more cases—know what I mean?"

"Oh, and as your lawyer I should warn you to be careful about what you say, because conspiracy is a crime. Did you know that, Eric?"

He blinked a couple of times.

"You and Turk Bacon and the lovely Mrs. Richess. You've said some incriminating things here."

"And you can't say a word."

"Not as it relates to Carl's murder, maybe. But you should know there's a clause in the canons of ethics, that a lawyer may disclose client information if he believes it's necessary to prevent death or serious bodily harm. And pal, I believe you just threatened me with serious bodily harm."

"Yeah, I did," he said. "But it's your word against mine, brother."

"Not exactly," I said. "Look over at the park."

He frowned, then took a step to the open door. I turned with him. Zebker was on the sidewalk across the street, and next to him was Fayette, cuffed and being held by a uniformed officer.

I said, "What if I told you that cop down there has heard every word we've said here?"

Eric's eyes filled with flame. He grabbed my throat with his left hand. It was huge. His fingers were like sections of steel pipe. I couldn't breathe.

With his right hand he ripped my shirt. Looking for a wire. Which I didn't have.

I shot the base of my right hand up under his chin.

His head snapped back, good and hard. His grip loosened and I knocked his arms away.

Now fire was in me and the room seemed to go dark. All I saw was this filth in front of me, a ton of it. I wanted it destroyed.

Eric threw a left. It caught the right side of my head and felt like a looter's brick.

I gave him a foot to the knee. Heard something crack. He cried out and bent forward. He charged and hit me like a tackling dummy.

We both went down.

Eric wrapped his arms around me and gave me the old-fashioned bear hug. I got my right forearm against his chin and pressed.

That's how we stayed for about ten seconds. Then his grip started to weaken.

I wanted to go all the way. I wanted to take his head off. Do a Butkus on him.

So when his hands finally let go I slammed my fist into his right ear. He howled. I grabbed the hair on the back of his head and gave his face a quick slam to the floor.

I was going to play New York jackhammer with his nose when I heard the door crash open, and felt somebody pulling me off Eric Richess.

170

AN LAPD BLUE took Eric into custody.

I sat in the Richess living room, catching my breath, with Zebker standing in front of me. My body felt like a card table, folded.

"Just take your time," Zebker said.

"Did you get it?" I said.

Zebker held up B-2's iHear, the earbuds dangling. "Didn't work," he said.

"*What?*"

"All I got was somebody watching *Entertainment Tonight.* Did you know George Clooney likes women?"

I sat up. "That's just great, Detective."

"But I got something better. I told his wife I could hear him confessing, and implicating her. She started screaming that he was the one, and she'd spill if we'd make her a deal."

"Find out if he threatened her," I said. "It's pretty sure he did. But you'll need that to get around the spousal privilege. Then she can talk."

He nodded.

"You can use me, too," I said. "I will testify against this dirt bag on the assault."

"It's fun being on our side for a change, isn't it?"

"A barrel of laughs," I said.

"You need to be looked at," Zebker said. "Let me take you—"

"No," I said. "I have something I have to do."

"You sure?"

"I'm sure."

171

KATE KNEW THERE was something wrong the moment she opened the door. For one thing it was late. For another I looked like a half-deflated basketball.

She took me in and sat me down. "What on earth happened?"

How could I even begin to tell her? How could I hope to spare her any more grief? I couldn't. It was not a matter of being the wire that held her up. I'd have to be the net that caught her when she fell.

"Kate," I said, "there's someone I'd like you to meet. Her name is Fran. She lost her daughter, the woman I was going to marry. In fact, she lives not too far away."

"I'd like that, Ty. Does she need to talk to someone?"

"I think maybe you both do," I said.

"It's true. I don't think you ever really get over losing a child. You have a scar and you learn to live with it. There's a verse in the Bible about how God comforts us in our sorrows, so we can comfort others. So yes, Ty, I'd like to meet her."

She had no idea what was coming next, but she must have seen something in my eyes. Because her face changed. "What is it, Ty? Is it about Eric?"

I searched for the right words.

"What's happened?" she said. "Where is he?"

"Kate, Eric and Fayette are in custody."

"But why? Did they have a fight? Did he hit her? Did she hit him?"

"Nothing like that," I said. "Let me say this quickly . . ." I still couldn't get started. I could not become the hammer that smashed her last hopes. But I knew I would be before the night was over.

She studied my face and a look of resignation came to her own. "Oh no," she said. "He did it, didn't he? He really did kill Carl."

I said nothing, but nodded slowly.

She stood and put her hand on her chest.

"Kate, I'm so sorry. I wish—"

"No. I think I knew it could be true, deep down. I just didn't want to admit it. I just . . ."

I got up, went to her, held her. For a long time. Then we sat and talked until she said she'd like to go to bed. I offered to sleep on the couch, in case she needed me around. She said she'd be all right.

I kissed her cheek and said good night. I went out and got in my car and drove. Just drove. Around the city. Wondering where Sister Mary was and if I'd ever see her again. Wondering if I should go spit on somebody's grave, somebody who died preaching that the law is a fine and noble thing, and lawyers purveyors of justice and all things good. I drove the streets past hustlers and gangbangers and kids who were in between. Past old men and drunk men and about ten different ethnicities, people sitting on bus benches or walking fast, before their fears or doubts or somebody with a knife caught up to them.

I just drove, my own fears and doubts sitting in the backseat, playing tag team. Playing for keeps.

172

I CAME TO in a parking lot in Hermosa Beach.

I'd pulled in late the night before and fell asleep in my car. I was stiff all over, sore underneath, and my mouth tasted like old salami. I uprighted my seat and looked at myself in the rearview. Scary.

Which didn't concern me. I didn't have anyplace I needed to be, or wanted to be, or cared about being. Who cared what I looked like? Who cared if I went down to the beach and walked up and down, people avoiding looking at me for fear I'd ask them for spare change. Or some kid could point and say, "What's wrong with that man, Mama?"

And I'd bend over to the little tyke and say, "People in this life use you, sonny. And they leave without saying good-bye and don't tell you where they're going. So don't invest in anybody, junior. Make a lot of money and hoard it and tell the world what it can do with itself. How's that? Oh yeah, and you got any spare change?"

I fired up the car and found a Denny's on the way back to the freeway. I went to their bathroom and freshened up, as they say, and came out feeling like three bucks. I ordered up a French Toast Slam and downed four cups of coffee, and started to feel like five bucks.

And then I got mad.

I headed up the 405 then took the 10 west. I got off at Lincoln and drove to the Blumberg Building. I got there at 8:57.

The security guard recognized me, though he did a triple take. And was tentative in announcing me. But then he got the word and buzzed me in.

I took the elevator to the top floor, and B-2 was waiting for me as the doors opened. His eyebrows went up.

"You don't look too good," he said.

"Really?" I said. "I feel like five bucks."

He put his arm around me and started walking me toward his office. "So what's the trouble?"

We sat and I told him everything that happened. Including laying the hurt on Knuckles and Sonny Moon, and coming up empty on the rifle. Including getting a guilty man off. Including the failure of the iHear.

That did not please B-2. He opened his phone, hit a key, said, "My office," and clicked off.

Thirty seconds later, Sid the computer whiz came through the door. When he saw me he said, "Hey, man!"

"Hey nothing," B-2 said. "The iHear has a problem."

"We already know that," Sid said.

"What are we doing to fix it?"

"All will be well, sir," Sid said. "I have it on schedule for today."

"Don't worry about it," I said. "You are still the man."

"You found that gamer yet?"

"It's in the hands of the LAPD," I said. "Do you make any devices that inflict slow, painful death?"

"That's on the agenda," Sid said.

"Get back to work," B-2 said.

173

I STAYED IN the office for another forty-five minutes. B-2 told me some stories about his early failures, as if that might prop me up. I appreciated the effort, but I was still hovering at the five-buck level when I got up to go. It was just after 10 a.m.

As I was heading for the elevator, Sid ran up to me with a look of excitement. He was holding his Palm device, which is more advanced than anything on the open market.

"Dude, your boy just sent another e-mail to the nun," he said.

"You're kidding."

"I don't kid about my work, I just create magic." He held up his PDA and showed me a map. "He's at the branch library at Exposition Park, even as we speak. Station 15. If he takes the full hour they usually give, you might even be able to catch him."

The elevator doors opened. Sid hit a key and handed me his PDA. "It's got the GPS now. Just listen to the voice. Go get him."

The voice gave me a straight shot east on the 10, south on Western. The branch was located right there at Martin Luther King, Jr. Park.

I still had that Indiana Jones hat in my trunk. I put it on, and some shades, so I would look like any other eccentric trying to hide his identity.

Nobody noticed me.

I snatched a book off the new release shelf, a Robert Crais as it turned out, and kept looking at it as I walked by the computer stations.

It was 10:37. And there was a skinny guy sitting at number 15, intent on the screen.

He could have been eighteen or thirty. He was one of those types with fair skin and baby features. Hair long and ignored. Earbuds plugging both ears.

I circled behind him.

He was playing a game.

Could it be him?

I found a chair by the CDs where I could keep an eye on him. I opened the Crais book and made with the fake reading.

At 10:52 the guy stood up from the station. He flipped some hair out of his eyes and started getting funky with whatever was coming out of his earbuds. It was not pretty. It was a bad case of white man's overbite, the bane of every inept nerd who thinks two wires running up to his head plug into cool.

I nearly laughed. At myself. This couldn't be the guy. Not this Bizarro world hipster.

And yet, what better profile to hide behind if you wanted to send anonymous e-mails threatening a nun?

He bopped right out the door.

174

I CAUGHT UP to him as he was about to get in his car. An old, dirty Chevy Malibu. I wasn't thinking more than one move ahead. My move now was to bluff him into a facial tell.

I took off my hat and sunglasses and tapped him on the shoulder.

He spun around like he'd heard a gunshot.

Appropriate.

Up close, he looked closer to twenty than thirty.

He took out one of his earbuds.

"Hi," I said.

His close-set brown eyes did a little side-to-side move. Like he was trying to recognize me.

"What?" he said.

"Harassed any nuns lately?" I said.

He swallowed. "What?"

"I know about the e-mails."

"Um, I think you think I'm somebody else."

"I know who you are."

His eyes widened with urban paranoia. "Hey, I don't know what you're talking about, but just leave me alone."

"But you don't leave other people alone, do you?" I said.

He kept his eyes on me as he fished out his keys. Then he turned toward the door of the Malibu. I stepped in front of him and leaned on the door.

His face broke out in full-on fright. He ran toward the library screaming, "Help!"

I started after him.

"Help!" he shouted again. And then a car leaving the lot almost hit
him. It screeched to a stop and the driver leaned on an angry horn.

It came so close Earbuds slapped his hand on the hood, then ran right
up to the library doors. "Help!"

The car, a black LaSabre, stayed put a second. The driver was looking at the backside of Earbuds and maybe saying something through the
passenger window.

I started after Earbuds myself.

Then stopped. I saw the front plates on the LeSabre.

Oklahoma plates.

My mind kicked on its alarm system.

The driver turned his head and looked directly at me. He had black
hair in a bowl cut, with straight-edged forelocks. Glasses with black rims.
Pudgy. Drew Carey's less successful brother.

And the worst poker face in the world. His eyes got owl-big behind
his lenses, his mouth opened, and then he burned rubber out of the
lot.

175

MOVIE CAR CHASES are ridiculous, of course. And not half as dangerous as the real thing done by complete amateurs.

But one thing this one did was confirm I had the right guy. How many
Oklahomans at a branch library flee in fear when they see me?

Sister Mary had advanced the theory that her tormenter was from her
home state. I believed it now.

I caught up to the LeSabre at Jefferson. He started ignoring the lights.

So did I.

At Adams he almost hit a woman in a crosswalk.

So did I.

He sped right through the red.

So did I. And saw, as we passed the Met Medical Center on the left, a cop car about to turn right out of the lot.

I gave the black-and-white a huge honk and waved at him to follow.

Then scorched over the double yellow lines for good measure.

The cop car made a beautiful U, its lightbar flashing.

The LeSabre hopped onto the freeway, heading east.

So did I.

So did the cops, starting with the siren now.

I stayed with the LaSabre and called 911. I told dispatch I was chasing a possible felon who had almost killed a woman and was now heading east on the 10. I gave her the make of the car and the Oklahoma plate number and answered a few more questions and clicked off.

Traffic was semi-heavy. Oklahoma was trying to weave in and out and get an advantage. Dork. Nobody drives like L.A. drivers. We do this every day. He wasn't pulling away from me, and never would.

The cop car, on the other hand, was getting pretty impatient.

It was now a double high-speed chase. The kind that shows up on the news, live.

Good. The more the merrier.

176

OKLAHOMA TOOK THE Harbor Freeway south, back toward Exposition Park and USC. In effect, he'd done a horseshoe.

Traffic was lighter here and he stepped on the gas.

So did I.

So did the cops. I kept wondering when the rest of the cavalry would get here.

The answer was Slauson. Another black-and-white got on and joined the festivities.

At Manchester, we got the attention of a Chippie on a motorcycle.

We convoyed to El Segundo Avenue, where Oklahoma decided to hit the street again.

Bad choice.

He went east, and just past Avalon ran right into road work and a jam.

In front of us, on the left, was, of all places, Magic Johnson Park.

Which is where Oklahoma headed, right over the curb. I followed. He was Larry Bird on a fast break. I was Magic running him down.

The cops were the referees, blowing their whistles.

And then it got deadly.

177

OKLAHOMA FISHTAILED ON the grass between two California oaks. The LeSabre was now facing me, two cop cars and a California Highway Patrol officer.

For a long moment nobody seemed to breathe.

Then, calmly, Oklahoma got out of his car and walked around to the trunk.

Out of one of the cop cars' speakers came a warning to stop immediately and get facedown on the ground.

What happened next you probably saw, like half the nation did later that night. It was caught by a Mr. Frank Jones of Watts on cell-phone video.

That's how I viewed it, anyway, because the moment I saw Oklahoma step out with what looked like an AK-47 in his hands, I dove to the floor of my car. My face did, that is. My poor, abused keister stayed seat high.

But I could hear the gunfire. The pinging of rounds into my car, and over it.

What Mr. Jones's vid later showed, fuzzy though it was, was a fattish man in glasses and bad hair blasting the living tax dollars out of two police cars.

And wounding one highway patrol officer.

And walking steadily forward, firing from what turned out to be a 100-round drum magazine. Doing so with a confidence that belied his looks.

Then the return fire starts, with me right in the middle.

The video shows Oklahoma getting peppered with an AR-15 and shaking for two seconds, like an abridged version of Sonny Corleone at the toll gate.

Then crumbling to the ground.

Suicide by cop, they later said. But not to me. They screamed at me and got me out of my car at gunpoint, then smashed me into the ground, cuffed me, and screamed at me some more.

Not that I cared. My butt was safe. I had no fresh holes in me. I could wait this one out.

Face on the ground, I could see a man behind an oak tree, peeking out, holding a cell phone and shouting "Day-uhm!"

178

THEY HELD ME for six hours at South Bureau, questioned me up and down. I told them to get in touch with Detectives Fronterotta and Stein and Zebker.

Finally, they let me go. But not before telling me I'd be on the hook for emergency services and maybe even reckless driving. I didn't care about the money, or the citation. I felt horrible about the CHP officer. When they said he was in stable condition I felt better than I had all day.

I was now up to seven bucks.

I counted my blessings.

179

ON THE TUESDAY following the shoot-out, I got the info that the shooter's name was Milton Markley. Last known address, Oklahoma City. A computer programmer.

And until his death living in a rented house in a remote part of Canyon Country.

In said house, in the crawl space, cops found an arsenal that included an illegally modified Heckler & Koch HK 41, two Glock semi-automatic pistols, 400 bottleneck rifle cartridges, 900 rounds of nine-millimeter ammunition, two improvised explosive devices, and one Kevlar vest.

In the trunk of his LeSabre they found a Mauser hunting rifle with scope, and several rounds of ammo. Ballistics confirmed this to be the rifle that shot Sister Mary.

Reconstructing Markley's computer use, a detective found him to be an expert user of several violent games, including the latest version of *Grand Theft Auto*.

Nice.

They also found a skin cream he was using for a rash running down his neck. It had a strong, semi-sweet smell. Stein wanted me to know that. Maybe he thought it would make me feel a little better about my methods of investigation. Though he did tell me not to go door to door with any more tire irons.

They also found a computer file containing links to and clips from every Internet mention of the trial of Eric Richess.

In the kitchen, laid out on the table, was a map of L.A., with markings in red of locations for St. Monica's, the downtown courthouse, Nick Molina's neighborhood, and several places in the Valley I knew well.

The guy had been following me.

"Almost like he was making it a big game," Detective Stein told me two days later at the station. He'd debriefed Sid about his gamer theory, and now had something else to add—that Markley killed Douglas Aycock and took his name with him. To assume the role. At least, that's what he wanted to talk to Sister Mary Veritas about when she arrived.

Only she was no longer using the Latin. Or the Sister.

She was now simply Mary Landis, from Oklahoma City. She wasn't wearing her habit, of course. A hoodie and jeans. It was the first time we'd seen each other since she left St. Monica's.

"I did know him," she told Stein in the interview room. "In high school. He was a year behind me. He was one of this group of gamers led by Doug Aycock. Doug was the charismatic one. Milton was more of a follower. I was on the basketball team and he was the manager and scorekeeper. He seemed nice enough. Then he gave me a ride home one night after a game but instead of taking me home to Deer Creek he took me out toward Tinker Air Force Base, and we ended up off the highway on a dark, dirt road. He told me he loved me. He tried to kiss me and then tried to do more than that, and I ended up slugging him in the face a couple of times and he cried like a baby. Then I jumped out of the car and ran back to the road, and jogged all the way home. And he was suspended because my dad went down to the school and made sure they knew."

"And you never saw Markley after that?" Stein said.

"Never," she said. "This is all so bizarre."

"But not as uncommon as you may think," Stein said. "Obsessives are on the rise for some reason. National stats on it, it's just about everywhere. They often carry around a slight for years before it fully festers and bursts."

She thought about that for a moment. "Maybe when he heard I was a nun?"

"Might have snapped him," Stein said. "How do you think he heard?"

Mary looked at me.

"Publicity from previous cases," I said. "It's what happens when you work with celebrity lawyers."

180

MARY WAS STILL shaking her head outside the station. I filled her in on everything else, just as I'd gotten it from Detective Lonnie Zebker.

"It seems Eric and Fayette are falling all over themselves to make deals, and trying to implicate each other," I said. "Isn't marriage a wonderful thing?"

"I still can't believe he did it. He was such a cool liar."

"He's singing now. Trying to drag Turk Bacon down and Jamie MacArthur with him. Claims Bacon's guy, remember the Mafioso-looking guy from Addie Qs? Claims that guy killed Morgan Barstler. A real web. Well, good luck to Eric. The politicians have levels of protection we mere mortals don't."

"So who vandalized your car?" she said.

"I don't know. Maybe the Oklahoma Kid, part of his game. Maybe Bacon had it done to keep me believing Eric was innocent. Leave the impression the real guy was out there. Or maybe it's just a sign that I need a new car. Especially now that the engine block has bullet holes."

"In your lovely Benz?"

"I'm in a lovely Buick now. Rental."

"Whatever happened to Nick Molina?" she said.

"He skipped town, as far as we know. I'm sure he got scared of the whole thing coming down on him and took off. Right before we got to him."

She winced. "Why did Milton choose that time and place?"

"We'll probably never know," I said. "I think it juiced him. It was a real street scene, a game. You have to move fast, make quick choices. He may even have scoped out the place before, thinking we'd be back. And I wonder if he was shooting at me, and not you."

"Why would anybody shoot at a lawyer?"

She smiled then and it seemed so real and natural, but at the same time kind of sad.

"So how's the shoulder doing?" I said.

"It's sore, but it works," she said.

"Does it affect your hook shot?"

"I haven't tested it yet."

"Well, I can't imagine Sister Mary Veritas without her full range of motion."

"Just Mary," she said.

"Uh-huh. So where have you been?"

"A place in Eagle Rock. A crisis-pregnancy house."

"Oh yeah? When's the bundle of joy due?"

"Funny, Buchanan."

"You still driving that old Taurus?"

"I took the bus."

"The *bus?* Come on, I'll give you a lift."

181

AS I DROVE her back to the Valley I said, "So is this permanent? This new—what do you call it—non-nunship?"

"Close enough," she said. "I am to continue to reflect, but I think I realize this is not to be my vocation. That happens sometimes. It's for the good of all concerned."

"So what will you do?"

She paused. "I think I'll go back home for a while. My mom and dad want me to. I can sort of regroup."

"That's probably a good idea," I said. "Then you can come back to L.A. and set up shop as an investigator. I'll be your first client."

She didn't answer. But her silence said that wasn't going to happen. It would be a clean break.

We both knew that.

When I pulled up in front of the yellow, two-story house in Eagle Rock, I said, "I want to say good-bye to you before you go. Maybe take you to Subway."

"I don't need such extravagance," she said as she got out of the car.

"And I'll want you to send me a postcard from time to time," I added. "From Oklahoma City itself. Make sure there's a tractor in it."

"Just work on your jump shot," she said. "You need one."

She turned quickly and headed up the walkway.

182

THE NEXT COUPLE of days were as empty as a congressman's promise. I sort of sleepwalked through them, coming to life only on the afternoon I introduced Kate Richess to Fran Dwyer and Kylie.

They hit it off immediately. Kate and Fran were very much alike. They had copious amounts of caring that had to pour out. I played some Frisbee with Kylie in the backyard as the two women watched and talked on the patio.

And thought maybe a house and a yard and a child and a wife were good things to have. Now. Time to move on.

I moved on. At six-thirty that evening I met Kimberly Pincus at Morton's on Figueroa, downtown. Best steaks in the city.

And the company wasn't something to shake a gavel at, either. Kimberly was as dazzling as ever, and making a good argument.

Not verbally. But in every other way, she was calling me off my mountain and back into the real world. It was time. Time to allow myself to get together with someone again.

When you put it down on paper, Kimberly Pincus was the one. She had everything. Looks, intelligence, drive.

Yeah, it was time. I even had a Grey Goose martini in honor of her. We toasted and clinked glasses.

"This," she said, "is a good thing."

"The martinis?"

"You and me, stupid."

We got caught up on our lives. Kimberly was mowing them down in court. She said she had not lost a motion or trial since my seat-belt victory. "You inspired me," she said. "Now I'm dying for another shot at you." She took the pick with her olive on it and placed it between her teeth for a moment. Then it disappeared into her mouth.

"Maybe I'll pick up Jamie MacArthur as a client," I said, "and you can help the poor dumb prosecutor who gets assigned to the case."

Earlier in the week, MacArthur had held a press conference denying any knowledge of accounting schemes. Eric Richess had squawked from the jail, pointing the finger at the councilman. MacArthur, looking tanned and confident, said he was working with the controller's office and was ready to clean house. It sounded to me like he was getting ready to throw Regis Nielsen under the bus. It was going to be fun and games throughout the summer. Just the kind of show L.A. eats up during the dog days.

Over our steaks Kimberly and I talked about trial work and juries, cops and robbers, liars and truth tellers. We traded good-natured jabs and laughed at absurdities. Like the time she had a DUI trial and the young, nervous defense lawyer opened his cross-examination of Kimberly's test expert with, "Are you truly qualified to give a urine sample?"

In short, we had a good time, and I needed that. I needed it to wash out the stench of Eric Richess.

We ended up back at her place, and sipped wine and watched the city from her window. The lights mesmerized. Not just the brights of Disney Hall, but also the pinpricks in hills, in Angeleno Heights and across the border of Hollywood, and the river of headlights and taillights ebbing and flowing on the freeway.

"What do you think?" she said. "Can we own this town or what?"

"Shall we just rule it from here?"

She smiled. "Sure. Maybe we can put in a moat, keep out the common folk."

"You're starting to sound like Marie Antoinette," I said.

"Am I?"

"Just thought I'd give you a heads-up."

Kimberly winced, put down her wineglass, and kissed me.

"Stay," she whispered.

I knew if I did, it'd be one of those things that changes your life forever. Kimberly Pincus was not a one-night stand. She was a forever changer.

Forever . . .

I took a half step back and tried to jumble some thoughts together.

"What's wrong?" Kimberly said.

"I have to do something," I said.

"Here, I hope."

"I have to see something."

"When?"

"Now."

"Not again," she said. "You can't be doing this again."

"Can I call you later?"

"What is it with you?"

"A good question, Kimberly. That's what I have to find out."

She looked at the ceiling. "Is this going to be a journey of self-discovery or some other retro thing?"

"Maybe."

"There are some aging hippies in Topanga Canyon who can help."

I touched her arm. "I had a great time tonight."

"Oh, wow. I haven't heard that one since high school. No, come to think of it, I was the one who said it." She laughed.

"I believe you," I said.

"You're going to regret this. You're going to look back and realize what a mistake you made."

"You may be right."

"I don't win cases by being wrong."

I kissed her cheek. "See you in court, then."

"I look forward to it," she said.

183

WHAT I HAD to see was in Eagle Rock.

I got there at eleven the next morning, after a trip to the Apple store. Mary Landis had the room in the very back corner of the house. She let me in, but kept the door open.

Her room was spare. Nothing on the walls but a crucifix and a calendar.

"Where are my manners?" Mary said. "Can I get you something to drink? Some water? Or . . . some water?"

"I think I'll have water," I said. "Do you have a Sparkletts 'ninety-three?"

"I'll check the cellar," she said.

There was a small white refrigerator by the window. She pulled out a bottle of water and tossed it to me. She opened one for herself.

I held my bottle out in the gesture of a toast. She laughed and tapped her bottle on mine, then we drank.

I hoped she couldn't see that the bottle was shaking in my hand.

"What's in the box?" she said.

"A little present." I handed it to her.

She opened it and took out the iPod and dock that I'd purchased.

"You're kidding me," she said.

"It's the least I can do for the best investigator I ever had."

She looked like she wanted to speak, but the words were sticking in her throat.

I gently took the dock and iPod from her. "Let's try it out," I said.

I went to an outlet and plugged it in. I set it on the carpet because there was no table nearby. I got on my knees and stuck in the iPod, which I'd specially prepped at the store. I turned it on.

"I have some of my own selections on here," I said. "I hope you like 'em."

I looked her way. She was at the other wall, her right arm across her body, holding her left arm. As if to relieve some pain from her shoulder wound. Or some other kind of pain.

I found the song I wanted. The soft, smooth Eric Marienthal version of Mary's favorite Beatles song.

I stood.

Mary was looking at the floor. There's about ten seconds of intro before the tune gets recognizable. Mary's face was expectant, waiting to hear what the song was.

She may have heard my pulse. In my ears it sounded like a Salvation Army drum. But this was the only way I could figure this thing out. I didn't know what words to use. I thought if I used the wrong ones, it would be like touching a soap bubble.

I didn't want the bubble to pop. But it wasn't my call. It had to be hers, all the way. Which is why I was silent. Which is why I cooked up this crazy plan. I guess I put my own faith in this: I've spent a lot of years studying faces. Jurors. Witnesses. Judges. Prosecutors. But this was going to be the most important judgment of my life.

Then Marienthal's sax started in on the first line of the tune. Recognizable. Mary's eyes widened, and she snapped her head up to look at me.

The song was what connected us, across the small room, which now seemed the size of a football field.

But I could see something. I could see tears forming in her eyes.

I went to her. Mary didn't move. I put my hand out and waited. It seemed to hang there for an hour, but that was okay with me. I wanted her to think about it.

The second verse started in. Just before I lowered my hand Mary reached out and took it. Now mine was steady and hers was trembling. She squeezed my hand as if she were falling from a cliff and I was the one who'd caught her.

I pulled her to me.

She let go of my hand and wrapped both arms around me. She put her head on my chest. I felt her warm breath through my shirt. The music enveloped us and we didn't move for a long moment.

And I realized then that all fear was gone. For just that moment, at least, it wasn't inside me in any form. Or doubts. Or questions.

For just that moment I was whole.

I slid my head down so my lips were next to her ear. She inclined her head a little, listening.

And then I said, "I will."